Joss Wood loves books, coffee and traveling – especially to the wild places of Southern Africa and, well, anywhere. She's a wife and a mom to two young adults. She's also bossed around by two cats and a dog the size of a small cow. After a career in local economic development and business, Joss writes full-time from her home in KwaZulu-Natal, South Africa.

https://josswoodbooks.com

facebook.com/josswoodbooks
instagram.com/josswoodbooks
tiktok.com/@josswoodbooks

Also by Joss Wood

Confessions of a Christmasholic
One Bed

RIDING HIGH

JOSS WOOD

One More Chapter
a division of HarperCollins*Publishers* Ltd
1 London Bridge Street
London SE1 9GF
www.harpercollins.co.uk
HarperCollins*Publishers*
Macken House, 39/40 Mayor Street Upper,
Dublin 1, D01 C9W8

This paperback edition 2025

1

First published in Great Britain in ebook format
by HarperCollins*Publishers* 2025
Copyright © Joss Wood 2025
Joss Wood asserts the moral right to be identified
as the author of this work

A catalogue record of this book is available from the British Library
ISBN: 978-0-00-876951-2

This novel is entirely a work of fiction. The names, characters and incidents portrayed in it are the work of the author's imagination. Any resemblance to actual persons, living or dead, events or localities is entirely coincidental.
Printed and bound in the UK using 100% Renewable Electricity
by CPI Group (UK) Ltd
All rights reserved. No part of this publication may be reproduced, stored in a retrieval system, or transmitted, in any form or by any means, electronic, mechanical, photocopying, recording or otherwise, without the prior permission of the publishers.
Without limiting the exclusive rights of any author, contributor or the publisher of this publication, any unauthorised use of this publication to train generative artificial intelligence (AI) technologies is expressly prohibited. HarperCollins also exercise their rights under Article 4(3) of the Digital Single Market Directive 2019/790 and expressly reserve this publication from the text and data mining exception.

Chapter One

Elmsleigh House was about an hour south of London and, importantly for polo aficionados (something Eden Ennis wasn't), midway between the two best polo clubs in the country, Cowdray and Beaufort. Elmsleigh, apparently, didn't host any of the top-tier polo matches but, in Eden Ennis's exceedingly amateur opinion, it should. Because, man, it was beautiful. The polo field, surrounded by oak trees, looked like an AI-generated photograph. Or one straight out of a glossy society magazine.

Eden took in the Georgian manor house, elegant and refined, sitting behind the polo field. It wasn't excessively big, but with its old, honeyed stone walls and thick, possessive ivy creeping up and over a good portion of the façade, it was still impressive. To the right of the house, and on a slight rise, was a long block of stables, a more recent addition built in the same stone and style of the house. In the fields beyond the house and stables, gleaming thoroughbreds munched on what she presumed was premium-quality grass. This was a billionaire's country estate, where his exceptional polo team was headquartered and trained, a place where his elite friends came to stay and play.

Eden rocked on her heels, enjoying the hot sun on her bare shoulders. It was a perfect English spring day, one they hadn't experienced for a while, warm and rich and, she presumed, perfect for a game of polo. She pulled in a deep breath, unused to the combination of horses, freshly cut grass, leather, and more than a whiff of money. *It wasn't just a polo field – it was a whole damn vibe.*

Although this event was advertised as a friendly Saturday afternoon practice match between two teams as a warm-up to the upcoming polo season, everything about the setting and the sport suggested luxury, a sense of timelessness imbued with a dash of fuck-it attitude only the very rich could pull off.

Turning her attention back to the field, Eden watched as two teams of riders – eight in all – on magnificent horses trotted onto the pitch. Six of the eight riders were men, and all wore white pants tucked into black, knee-high riding boots. One team wore navy shirts, the other white with red patches. Every one of the riders looked as comfortable on their horse as Eden did on her couch watching K-dramas.

An elbow connected with her arm. 'Here we go.'

An older man, dressed in ancient green, faded cords tucked in gumboots, and a stylish linen shirt, stood to her right. The low brim of a battered cap and sunglasses covered his tanned, stubbled face.

'Are you a virgin?'

She blinked. *What?* The man half-snorted, half-chuckled,

his eyes not leaving the field. 'A polo virgin? Have you watched a game before?'

That would be a solid no. Also, since it had been years since she last had sex – four? five? – it was possible she was a born-again virgin too. 'Can you tell?' she asked wryly.

He rubbed his hands together, his attention on the field. 'It will only be a friendly polo match and, because they are getting the horses back into training after a long break, it'll be a bit slow. You won't see the speed, but you'll still see the skill involved. These are some of the best riders in the country.'

They certainly looked fit and muscled. She couldn't see their faces, but with bodies like that ... who cared? Her eyes settled on a man in the centre, attracted by his barely contained ferocity. Unlike the others, he sat perfectly still in the saddle, his hands loose on the reins of his equally calm horse. He appeared taller and bigger than everyone else, and ... mmm, *harder*. More focused, six feet plus of power and intensity.

A whip on the edge of cracking...

'Who's number three?' she asked, lifting a hand to shade her eyes. She hadn't been able to find her sunglasses when she left her flat this morning, and now she was regretting not taking the time to track them down. The sun was making her eyes water. She sneezed and received a 'bless you' from her new companion.

'Number three is Jed Harris, a nine handicap.'

'Is that good?'

'Ten is the highest, and there are only fourteen players in the world who have a ten handicap. Right, here we go.'

Eden jumped at the smack of the mallet against the ball,

and her mouth dropped as horses flew down the field, looking like they possessed invisible wings, their muscles rippling under glossy coats. She lifted her hand to her mouth, entranced by the spectacle of eight horses and riders chasing what looked to be a too-small ball. The riders were all focus and finesse, and, yeah, exceptionally talented. You had to be when you were balancing on a speeding horse while swinging a stick. Every move they made was smooth, considered and totally, utterly *badass*.

Eden watched Number Three, Jed something, sprinting toward the goal – this was slow? seriously? – the ball rolling next to his horse's hooves. She winced when a rider from the opposing team thundered toward him at a right angle. Shit, they were both going too fast; they were going to collide! Number Three braked and spun his horse around in a pirouette, the manoeuvre so quick it raised a collective wheeze, and then a cheer, from the crowd.

'It's so fast,' Eden stuttered, unable to pull her eyes from the action. Or, to be honest, off Number Three. He was *magnetic*.

'They are currently in slow motion,' her new friend told her. 'In professional matches, the average speed of the ponies is sixty miles per hour. It's called chess at speed. Each player thinks three steps ahead while trying to dodge attacks from their rivals.'

Number Three managed to outwit his opponent and galloped down the field, the crowd cheering him on. With an easy, elegant thwack, the ball sailed through the goalposts, and the crowd erupted. Eden jumped up and down, holding on to her new friend's arm. She wasn't a sporty girl, didn't know a damn thing about polo, had never met a horse before, but this was wild and magical.

And unexpectedly exhilarating.

Then she spoiled the moment by sneezing and sneezing again. She took the old, but clean cotton handkerchief her new friend offered her and winced. 'I'd have to post it back to you.'

He shrugged and patted the area of his jacket above his heart. 'I have another, and I have dozens at home. Allergies?'

'I have no idea,' she replied, after thanking him. She placed the handkerchief under her eyes to soak up the moisture, and then blew her nose. 'Maybe it's the fresh air, I'm used to car fumes and smog.'

'There's nothing like a day out in the country to clear your lungs,' he said.

'Nothing like it,' Eden nodded. She couldn't remember when last, if ever, she'd visited any place this rural. When she travelled, she headed to European cities, Copenhagen, Berlin, Prague, Dublin – she understood them and knew how they worked. The country, with its woods and fields, narrow roads and high hedgerows? Not so much. Or at all.

Eden turned her attention back to the match, quickly realising danger was a polo player's constant companion. One wrong move, one mistimed swing, and the rider could find themselves on their arse on the ground or have a limb smacked by a mallet. Yet, she somehow understood, on a visceral level, that danger, for both the players and the spectators watching, was what made the sport addictive. Each ride toward the goal was a heart-pounding race, every quick turn, an opportunity for a daring steal, and every shot, a way to swing the game in your team's favour. It was thrilling. And utterly delicious.

If this was the players taking it easy, then a proper match would be a fantastic spectacle.

A whistle blew and a few beats later the horses slowed to a walk, and the riders relaxed. Eden raised her eyebrows and spread out her hands, hugely disappointed. 'That's it? It's over so soon?'

The man looked at his expensive watch. 'They only play for seven minutes, but a normal match is played at double the speed.'

Thank God for her new friend, else she would be floundering to understand the game. Eden watched as grooms led new horses onto the field. A young man walked to sexy Number Three and guided the new horse, the colour of heavy caramel, to stand next to his horse, both facing forward. Without fuss, and with a great deal of skill, he hopped from one horse to another, and without looking, slid his boots into the stirrups. 'Why are they all changing horses?' Eden asked.

'Ponies, we call them ponies,' her companion replied. 'It's for their welfare. Polo is a demanding sport, played at high speed, and they don't want to overwork their animals.' He sent her a sweet smile and waved at someone in the crowd. 'I must go, there's my girl.'

Eden watched him weave his way through the clumps of spectators to stop by a middle-aged woman dressed in jeans, a tight t-shirt and wellington boots, a jaunty straw hat perched on her grey curls. A tall, slim blonde wearing a short white mini dress and wedges, thick straight hair pulled back into a ponytail, stood next to her. She was exceptionally pretty, and Eden suspected he was proud of his stunning daughter…

Eden's eyes widened when he reached up to place an open-mouth kiss on the younger woman's mouth and slid a possessive arm around her oh-so-tiny waist.

Right. Serve her right for making snap judgements.

Eden watched the next chukkas and resisted the urge to rub her itchy, watery eyes. After the fourth, and more changing of horses, the riders left the field. Around her, people streamed from their deck chairs and left their picnic blankets to swarm the field. Laughing and chatting, they started to stomp down divots in the bright green grass.

Eden made her way down the bank, the hem of her sundress fluttering around her knees. Instead of heels, she wore very sensible trainers, and she'd slathered her skin with sunscreen. But stupidly she'd forgotten to bring a hat. She fought a never-ending battle with freckles in the summer, and she could feel them popping out on her chest, shoulders, nose and cheeks.

And what on earth was wrong with her eyes? Why were they watering?

Walking away from the field, Eden turned to look at the country house behind her, taking in the many rectangular, precise windows along the ridiculously large façade of the three-storey house. The early nineteenth-century house was owned by Troyden Castle, mega-billionaire, polo aficionado, bon vivant and…

Apparently, her uncle on her father's side.

At least that was what her genealogical DNA test had revealed six years ago.

Eden rocked on her heels as a five-year-old boy ran into

her, and with a brief 'sorry' he was off again. His father chased after him, the slight breeze lifting his shirt. A pregnant woman carrying a toddler trundled after them, and she caught Eden's eye. Her smile was tired but good-natured. 'Have kids, they said. It'll be fun, they said.'

Eden wished her luck.

'I'm going to bloody need it,' she muttered, but laid a hand on her bump, and Eden caught the affection in her eyes. She looked like she was exactly where she wanted to be.

Had her mum ever looked at her like that? No, she never recalled seeing that easy affection on her mum's face. Frustration and resentment, sure, sometimes what she thought was flat-out dislike.

God knew her mother had never been the warm-and-fuzzy type. As an emergency foster carer, she'd been hailed as a saint, a selfless crusader for vulnerable kids. And she'd believed the hype and took immense pride in her good works, her sacrifices and her hand-to-mouth life.

To her mum, Eden hadn't needed saving. Eden was just there – silent, steady, waiting.

Their house was never hers, not really. It had been too full, too loud, too temporary. A revolving door of faces, names and stories, all so much more important than hers. Up until earlier this year, she'd dreamed – foolishly and desperately – that one day, just once, she'd be chosen. That her mother would look at her and see her. That she'd be her mum.

It never happened.

She'd always been the afterthought, the one who stayed while everyone else came and went. The one who didn't need attention, or love, or to be put first. The daughter who could be discarded. Her mum dropping out of her life annihilated any hope of a mother-daughter relationship. She couldn't avoid the hard truth any longer: she wasn't her mum's first choice. And never would be.

Eden hauled in a deep breath, then another and shoved the memories away into her mental junk cupboard. One day it would fly open and projectile vomit a stream of unresolved emotional gunk, but it wouldn't happen today. Hopefully not tomorrow, or anytime soon, either.

Suddenly thirsty, she headed toward a refreshment tent, wishing she could dodge the crowds. She sighed at the long line of people waiting to be served. G&Ts and beers were popular options, but she needed to rehydrate. Eden joined the queue, her attention caught by a blunt, deep-as-night Phryne Fisher bob. *Crap...*

Eden immediately looked for Vincent. Yep, there he was, on the other side of the tent, talking to a woman in a blue dress. *Shit.*

Tara and Vincent were the remoras of the charity fundraising world, attaching themselves to the bellies of the wealthy, socialising and cajoling their way to receive mammoth donations for their foundation supporting a range of charities. This was a minor, pre-season match, and she'd thought it would be a waste of their time because there wouldn't be a 'hoard of high-net-worths' in attendance. But she'd forgotten that Troyden Castle was their favourite whale.

Stupid. So stupid.

Not wanting her ex-bosses to see her – *keep your mouth shut about the investigation, Miss Ennis* – and wanting a conversation even less, Eden hurried out of the tent and away from the crowd. She hadn't seen the Bancrofts since abruptly resigning from their foundation six weeks ago, but they were still blowing up her phone with text messages begging her to come back. Tara and Vincent took turns phoning her, calls she didn't answer. And she'd yet to respond to their why-are-you-ignoring-us emails. She still, dammit, missed them. On one hand, she wanted to kill them; on the other, she would do anything to go back six months, a year. To *unknow*.

To not light the fuse that would, sometime soon, blow up their world.

She, Troyden Castle and the Bancrofts were a messy, knotty skein of human wool. Six years ago, after taking a DNA test, she'd discovered that Troyden Castle, the popular billionaire, was her paternal uncle. Most people would've rejoiced at the connection, but Eden was wary. Most people had disappointed her, especially anyone related by blood, and she was pretty certain Troyden Castle would do the same. After all, it was a truth universally acknowledged that a multi-divorced man in possession of a good fortune must be an arsehole. But she couldn't let go of the nagging thought that she needed to take another look at him, to dig deeper. A quick internet search had informed her he was the Bancroft Foundation's biggest benefactor, so she'd approached Tara and Vincent, offering to work as their unpaid intern for three months, hoping that she'd gather some information on her 'uncle' to help her decide whether he was someone she wanted to meet or avoid.

Months passed, her responsibilities increased, and soon she was employed as their right-hand person. She'd loved her job, happy to stay in the background at the foundation, unseen but useful. Time rolled on, but she kept delaying the decision to acknowledge her connection to Troyden. Busy at work, it had been enough to collect scraps she could from the Bancrofts, gathering intel that Troyden, despite his reputation, was a nice guy, sweet and generous.

His only bad habit seemed to be his inability to stay married – five ex-wives were a lot! – and being a magnet for gold-diggers.

Year after year, she put off the decision to meet him. The DNA site would've told him that he had a close family member, but she chose to keep her details private until she was certain whether she wanted to meet him or not. Until recently it had been enough to know he was *there*. If she kept him at a distance, he couldn't disappoint her.

But the last few months had been an emotional watershed – with her mum permanently exiting her life and the Bancrofts' criminality forcing her into making hard decisions she never expected to make.

As her life continued to flip inside out, her curiosity about Troyden Castle, her only blood relative, increased. He was connected to the Bancrofts, was their donor, and despite being ordered not to by the police, a part of her wanted to warn him of the Bancrofts' behaviour. Because that's what families did, right?

But she needed to decide whether they were family first. *Arrgh!* Complicated.

You're overthinking this, Eden. She hadn't come to Elmsleigh today to meet him, but thought that being on his property might help clarify her thinking about whether she wanted to walk through life with or without family…

Eden saw a path and veered left, grateful for the huge branches of the oak trees providing respite from the hot summer sun. She lifted her dress off her hot chest and flipped through her mental dossier on Troyden.

Elmsleigh House was the property – he had several – where he spent the bulk of his time. He'd been married numerous times but had no biological children of his own. However, various stepchildren lived on the grounds. The house had a billiards room, two libraries, more than a dozen living rooms ranging from huge to cosy, and God knew how many bedrooms.

From her position behind the trunk of a wide oak, looking down into the walled courtyard behind the house, Eden watched an SUV swing in and park close to what she thought might be the kitchen door. A lithe woman of Indian descent, dressed in ragged denim shorts and a man's oversized, knotted, button-down shirt, jumped out of the car. She lifted a little boy out of the car. A girl, older, jumped down and the kids ran into the house. The woman bundled her long, thick dark hair up onto her head, and tied it into a messy bun. Eden sighed at her effortless elegance, her long, slim legs and cut-glass cheekbones. Even from a distance, she was gorgeous.

Another path skated off to her right. She couldn't go back to the polo match, not when Tara and Vince were there, but she might be able to walk around the house and leave via a circuitous route. At the end of the path was the stable block, which, she figured, would be deserted. She just needed a cool place to sit and think.

Even if she was ready to meet Troyden, this wasn't the right time or place to approach her uncle. They needed privacy for what would be, she was sure, a difficult conversation.

How would it even go? 'Hi, my name is Eden Ennis. A DNA test says you are my uncle on my father's side. I'm not sure I want a relationship and don't need to be part of a family, but I would like any information on my father. Any idea about where he is and why he took off when my mum told him she was pregnant with me? Is he even alive?'

Eden sneezed and wiped her streaming nose, her heart hammering as she approached the impressive stable block.

She'd spent her life watching foster kids come and go, knowing that given the choice, her mum would choose them over her. The fear bubbled up at the thought of making a new, blood-related, connection. What if Troyden looked at her and saw nothing? What if she was just, once again, simply there?

What if her existence didn't matter to him, just like she never mattered to her mother? Her thoughts tumbled over each other, becoming bigger and bolder, veering off in another direction. Another what-if slammed into her… What if, after meeting, he thought she wanted something from him? She didn't, but with her life crumbling how could she not look like an opportunist, showing up just when her world was about to detonate?

He'd look at her and see an outsider, might consider her an irritation or a problem to solve, a charity case. But if he went to the opposite extreme and welcomed her into his world … what if she started to believe she had a place in his life and then he eventually decided, like her mum, she wasn't worth his time and effort, wasn't worth keeping?

Would she simply pass through his life like sand through his open fingers?

The safe option would be to walk away and do nothing. She'd rocked one boat recently and was still wiping water out of her eyes. Maybe it was better to deal with that storm before sailing headfirst into another.

Leaving his teammates in the branded Castle Kings players' tent during the break, Jed Harris grabbed a bottle of water and headed over to where Troyden lounged in a deckchair, thankfully alone. He needed to head to the stables to check on his favourite pony – she'd favoured her left forelock earlier – but he could take a few minutes to talk to his stepdad first. Today was a demo match, held between two neighbouring clubs, as practice for the upcoming, maybe his last, season.

He rubbed the back of his neck, irritated. Thoughts about retiring from the game, maybe coaching or making furniture full-time kept ambushing him. He needed to think about the future at some point... Where was he going? What was his next goal? Where did he want to be in five years?

Adulting. Fucking bullshit.

But today the sun was shining, it was good to be back in the saddle playing polo without any pressure. Unlike the intense, professional matches, today he could miss a few chukkas, allowing a junior player to get some game experience.

He dropped into the empty chair and stretched out his

long legs. Chugging his water, he looked across the field to where he'd earlier spotted Troyden talking to a slim woman. He'd first noticed her hair, and the way the sun bounced off it, turning it a stunning shade of rose gold. She'd been dressed in a simple navy polka dot dress showing off long, shapely legs ending in trendy trainers. From his saddle, he'd clocked her heart-shaped face, wide mouth, and thought he could see the freckles on her nose and cheeks. Maybe she was a natural redhead...

He loved redheads.

'Who were you talking to earlier?' he asked Troyden, keeping his question casual.

'I talk to a lot of people, so you're going to have to be more specific.'

'Strawberry blonde, blue dress, no hat.' Long neck, small waist and curvy hips. And, yeah, great boobs.

'Didn't catch her name. Polo newbie, didn't know what was going on. Had to help her understand,' Troyden laconically replied. 'Pretty girl.'

Jed scanned the field, didn't see her and silently cursed. He was surprised by his keen disappointment and his level of interest. He didn't normally react so strongly to women. He was a veteran of the polo circuit and had been chased by 7-Ups – women who only dated players with a handicap of seven and up – on every continent and found most women unoriginal. He was a jaded bastard with high standards and a low boredom threshold.

Still something about the strawberry blonde called to him... But she was gone, and he wouldn't see her again. Pity.

Troyden adjusted the brim of his cap and folded his

arms, sinking lower into the chair. Jed knew Troyden would wait for him to raise the subject of the Duke's death last night. He'd been found by his wife in the kennels, sitting up against the wall, hand on his heart, a massive cigar between his fingers, and reputedly, a *'what the fuck'* look on his face. They said he'd suffered a massive heart attack, which was a surprise to Jed.

He hadn't realised the Duke had a heart.

'You heard, then?' Jed asked, his eyes on his scuffed boots.

'How do you feel about it?'

'It couldn't have happened to a nicer arsehole,' he stated. He'd hated the Duke in life, and he wasn't about to do a one-eighty and hypocritically change his views because he was dead.

'It wasn't like it was my father who died,' he continued, answering Troyden's earlier question. Though, technically, it was.

No, the man next to him was his father, not that waste of space dickhead who'd donated his sperm. Troyden became a permanent part of his life after he married his mum – she was wife number three – and moved them into Elmsleigh. He and his mum divorced twenty-five years ago when he was ten, but he and Troyden remained close. When his mum died, Elmsleigh became his permanent home and Troyden his guardian. Two more wives came and went before Jed's eighteenth birthday, but all of Troyden's stepchildren stuck close.

Within a few months of living at Elmsleigh, Jed realised Troyden, a man who had a rep for being a corporate bastard, was an absolute pushover, stunningly generous, and that it was stupidly easy to take advantage of him. Troyden's inability to say no to any of his ex-wives, girlfriends, stepchildren and friends, gave Jed a way to repay his stepfather for his generosity, and Jed made a point of never asking for anything from his super-wealthy stepfather.

And when he thought Troyden's nearest and dearest were pushing the envelope of his generosity, he stepped in and shut them down. Even as a kid, he was fiercely protective of the man who gave him a home. Helped by Diana, Troyden's no-nonsense housekeeper who took no shit, Jed's protective streak had rubbed off on his stepsiblings, and they frequently banded together to protect the man who'd been, was, the father he didn't have to be.

Jed's bullshit radar remained finely tuned.

Talking of BS artists... 'Where's Sugar Baby?' he asked.

'I wish you and your siblings would learn her name,' Troyden muttered.

They did know her name – this one was called Lana – but they liked giving their father shit about his terrible taste in women.

'Bring home someone worthy of us learning her name and we will,' Jed retorted. Lana was the last in a long line of beautiful but vapid, money-hungry women who wanted to be the next Mrs Castle. She wasn't doing badly: in the six weeks since she'd arrived on Troyden's radar she'd scored a trip to the South of France, a Birkin bag and a diamond tennis bracelet.

'She went to lie down. She has a headache,' Troyden explained, then archly continued, 'I think she might be The One.'

Jed rolled his eyes. Troyden had said the same thing about at least three women in the past five years. How the hell the man amassed a fortune in retail, dealing with the sharks and backstabbers of corporate UK and America, while being a sucker for anyone with big eyes and a great line of charming crap, God only knew.

And *The One*? Such bullshit.

Jed didn't believe in love, not much and not for him anyway. It always came, he believed, with an expiration date.

His mum's words to him, shortly before marrying Troyden, still played in his head. *Do not make him regret taking us in. If you want to stay, you have to prove your worth.* And if he didn't? That's when, he was convinced, the people who said they loved him would walk away.

'I asked how you were,' Troyden reminded him, keeping his voice low.

Damn, back to the Duke, his least favourite subject. 'I'm fine, I'm just pissed Junior gets to inherit,' Jed replied.

Troyden frowned. 'But you've never wanted to inherit Bythesea Hall or the Duke's money. Or even be associated with him.'

Jed pushed his thumb and index finger into his eyes. When it came to Lysander, the Duke of Bythesea (pronounced bithsee), or the Fucking Duke, his emotions always got twisted up. The FD had an affair with his mother, his groom, when she was eighteen and he newly married. As in, just-back-from-his-honeymoon married. Around the same time his wife announced she was pregnant with the next generation of Bythesea arsehats, his bio-father made the first payment to ensure his mum's silence about their affair and her pregnancy.

Every year, until the time Jed had turned eighteen, the Duke had paid a yearly stipend, first to his mum, then to Troyden, to keep their connection from being exposed. Troyden handed his hush money to his money guy – his first stepson, Alistair – and thanks to Al's nerdy love affair with numbers, Jed owned a ridiculously healthy portfolio of stocks, shares and crypto. He'd also inherit a share of Troyden's assets one day, which scared him a little. What the fuck was he supposed to do with so much money? He was just a part-time polo player, part-time furniture maker. Full-time grump.

He did his best to add value. He wasn't just any polo player, he was the captain of his country's team, and he made sure Troyden's team were regulars on podiums all over the world. He was the shield protecting Troyden from gold-diggers, con artists and anyone wanting to take advantage of his too-soft heart. The rock for his stepsibs, the one they could always rely on. There was no space for a woman, his plate was full, his capacity maxed out.

'Jedson?'

He jerked and remembered Troyden's question. 'No, I don't give a shit about the estate or the *by-the-sea* title, for fuck's sake.' He saw Troyden narrow his eyes at his swearing and winced. Troyden hated profanity – he called it unoriginal – but he was also pragmatic. He knew there wasn't much he could do to keep adult stepkids from occasionally swearing. Or, in Jed's case, swearing often.

'I object to Henry inheriting,' Jed muttered, his skin

feeling too tight for his body. 'Because he's the biggest knob I know.'

'You've always hated him.'

He didn't hate the Baby Duke because he was Lysander's son and heir, when he, the Duke's oldest son by a few months, wasn't. No, he hated Junior because he was acknowledged and accepted. His birth had been celebrated, not reviled. From the moment he arrived in the world, Henry had been encouraged to stand in the sunlight of his heritage, while Jed had been relegated to the darkest corner of the dungeon.

Interestingly and, frankly, conveniently, Henry hated him too. He didn't know if Henry knew he was his half-brother – he doubted it – or if they had a personality clash, but his animosity ran as deep as Jed's.

After a run-in as kids, one that involved knuckles and blood, they'd ended up at the same boys' boarding school, in the same form. Henry'd been loud-mouthed and obnoxious, and Jed, born with no fucks to give, routinely called him on his BS. They both joined the school's boxing team – a mutual excuse to beat the shit out of each other. After a particularly nasty bout – an off-the-books, no rules, mock cage fight – he broke Junior's nose and bruised his ribs. Henry's right hook to Jed's temple gave him a minor concussion.

They'd both been immediately expelled – *we don't condone violence, no matter the circumstances!* – but then the Duke and Troyden had hauled out their chequebooks, made massive donations to the school, and they were both reinstated.

Thankfully their paths hadn't crossed much since they'd

left school, with Henry going to uni and Jed straight into professional polo.

'I believe life shouldn't reward wankers.'

Troyden simply smiled and changed the subject. 'I saw the table Sally posted to your website last night,' he said, pride in his eyes. 'Damn good job, son.'

Jed shrugged. The table, made from a piece of driftwood he'd found on an extremely southern New Zealand beach and had shipped home, was one of his favourite pieces. The price tag Sally decided on made his eyes water. But, as she told him, it was a J. Barkly piece – Barkly was a name he sucked from the air – and collectors were prepared to pay huge money for his furniture. They were, he'd been informed, works of art. He didn't see it and it didn't make any sense to him; he just found a piece of wood, saw a shape within it, and got to work with his power tools in the silence of his workshop.

'Are you ever going to stop imitating Banksy and reveal to the world you are J. Barkly?' Troyden demanded. Troyden thought he should take the praise and the credit, but Jed didn't give a shit about what other people thought. He was just a guy who loved horses, played excellent polo and made furniture.

All he wanted to do was look after his family. Keep pushing back that expiry date.

The Duke's death wouldn't change a damn thing.

He'd make sure of it.

Chapter Two

Eden slipped through the half-open arched doors of the long stable block, grateful for the cool space and the drop in temperature. Her skin tingled, the little pricks of pain suggesting she'd had too much sun. She needed to put more sunscreen on her bare shoulders and arms. Damn, why did she forget her hat and her sunglasses? At least she'd pulled her hair back from her face into a complicated French plait.

Her eyes itched as she passed a tack room filled with saddles, bridles and a hundred other things she couldn't identify. A city girl through and through, she'd had no contact with horses, ever, and this was the first time she'd been in a stable. Despite being what the older gent would call a 'stable virgin', she could tell it was grand. Each stall had piles of fresh straw, a big water trough and a horse blanket hanging off the door. She rubbed it between her finger and thumb – it was softer than she expected – and traced the name and estate's oak leaf logo embroidered on the fabric. This blanket belonged to Jabba. Jabba wasn't currently in his stall; none of the horses were.

Then she heard a soft whinny and the stamping of a hoof from the far end of the stable. Okay, at least one animal was in residence. Eden ambled deeper into the building, and as her streaming eyes adjusted to the shadows, she saw a tall man standing in a stall, his forehead resting against the snout of a fawn-coloured horse.

Number Three...

'Hello, beautiful,' he crooned. A shiver travelled down Eden's spine, and the hair on her arms lifted. His was the ultimate bedroom voice, low and velvety with the slightest hint of a rasp. 'I missed you out there today. Nobody gets me like you.'

He lifted his head, and Eden took in his strong profile, stubborn chin and ever so slightly hooked nose. His dark hair, almost black, was damp with sweat, and his white and red shirt stuck to his broad back. White jodhpurs covered strong thighs and were tucked into knee-high riding boots. He was tall, an inch or two above six feet. How did that little horse hold such a big man?

God, he was gorgeous. With his stubble and strong arms, he radiated masculinity and raw power. Eden glanced around and thought about bolting; she didn't like how he made her feel...

Unsteady, hiccupy, a little breathless.

A lot breathless. Eden put a hand on her chest, tried to suck in some air and found she was pulling in less than usual. Really, she was reacting like a fifteen-year-old meeting her celebrity crush. Pathetic. She needed to start dating again if this was how she was going to react whenever she saw a sexy man.

Turning to go, she made a scuffling sound, and Big and Sexy looked up, a frown pulling his black, thick eyebrows together. 'Hey, what are you doing here? This is private property.'

She winced. 'Oh. I'm sorry. I was looking for a cool place to sit for a while.' Her eyes were furiously itchy and was her lip swelling? She lifted her foot to scratch the back of her leg. What was wrong with her? Wanting to appear normal, or as normal as she could when she felt like ants were burrowing under her skin, she nodded at the horse. Was that jealousy she saw on its pretty face? Yeah, yeah, if her one-on-one time with this man was interrupted, she'd be irritated too. 'What's her name?'

'Her proper name is Rey Skywalker,' he answered. 'Her owner is a huge Star Wars fan, and all his horses have a name from the franchise.'

'Judging by the way you were talking to her, I thought she was your horse.'

Man, why did she sound like a breathless sex kitten?

'I just ride them.' His big hand stroked the animal's glossy neck. 'Rey is one of my favourites and I think she's injured her forelock.'

'Ah,' Eden replied, wiping her eyes, with the now damp handkerchief. 'She's very pretty.'

'Do you want to stroke her?'

She did, because when next would she meet a horse? Rey gave her a do-it-and-die look. Eden scratched the inside of her wrist. 'She looks pretty big,' she said, forcing herself to move closer. She inhaled the unique combination of horse and man, cologne and straw. He shouldn't smell so good, but he did, like sunshine on steroids.

'She's tall,' he replied. 'Stands at fifteen hands.'

Eden tentatively lifted her hand and placed it on the horse's neck. Rey gave her the side-eye – yeah, yeah, she'd prefer Number Three's hands on her too! Not wanting to be cowed by the horse's snotty attitude, she stroked the animal with her open palm. 'I thought ponies were smaller than horses.'

'The word pony is a reference to their agility, rather than their size,' he said, his deep voice rumbling over her. Rey snorted and tossed her pretty head. That she resented Eden's presence was pretty damn obvious.

'I'm Jed Harris.'

Eden left her hand on the horse's neck and looked up. And up. 'I saw you playing earlier, right?' He'd whipped his horse into impossibly tight angles, leaned halfway down its back and thundered across the field at warp speed. Even she could tell he was the best player on the field.

'Did you enjoy your first polo match?'

Eden winced. 'That obvious, huh?'

'Yeah.' He leaned a big shoulder into the wall next to the stall and crossed one black boot over the other. 'What's your name?'

'Eden Ennis.' Eden wanted to lean down and scratch the back of her leg but knew she would give him a great view of her boring, sports-bra-covered boobs. Why was she *so* itchy? Everywhere?

She looked down the long stable block. The open doors framed Elmsleigh House, looking oh-so-grand with its thick stone walls and rows and rows of narrow windows. 'It's quite a house,' she stated. That was like saying that Notre Dame was quite a church. And that he was quite a man.

Okay, do stop being ridiculous, Eden! Anyone would think she hadn't come across a good-looking man before. And she had, of course, she had. But not one who was so tall, so fit, so effortlessly masculine. With his dark hair, thick stubble and long, lean muscles, he was quite the package. What would his lips feel like under hers? Was he as good a kisser and a lover as he was a rider?

His gaze dropped to her mouth and lingered. Desire rushed through her, pooling low in her belly. Right, hadn't felt that for a while. He moved a fraction closer, his hand coming to rest next to hers on Rey's neck, and the heated, silent suggestion of a kiss hovered between them. Who would make the first move? Him? Her? And in that quiet stable, it felt like the universe was holding its breath, waiting for one of them to move closer.

Attttttttchoooooo!

Eden whirled around and slapped her hands to her face, embarrassed by the force of her sneeze. Damn, had she lost a lung in the process? She wiped her nose with the now grubby handkerchief and discreetly lifted the hem of her skirt to wipe her streaming eyes.

Embarrassed, she changed the subject. 'You ride for the Elmsleigh Team, right?'

'The Castle Kings.'

'And the team is, like the estate, owned by Troyden Castle?'

His eyebrows pulled together, and Eden sensed he'd

taken a few mental steps backwards. 'Why are you asking?' he demanded, his tone frosty.

There was now a whole polo field between them. Man, she was super talented at alienating hot men. Oh, well, she wasn't going to see him again and now she had nothing to lose. 'What's Troyden Castle like?'

She might as well ask, because, while the Bancrofts thought he walked on air, this guy worked for him and would have a more realistic view of her uncle.

His expression darkened and his mouth tightened. He placed himself between her and his horse, and she immediately noted his protective gesture. God, she wasn't going to hurt his precious pony!

'I don't appreciate the question and you're trespassing,' he stated flatly. 'Leave now and I won't have to toss you out on your pretty arse.'

Jeez! She'd just asked a question.

'Sorry, I was just curious…' Eden stated, her voice now thin and a little high. The ants were morphing into caterpillars and every inch of her skin felt hot. She desperately wanted to rake her fingernails over her body. Looking down, she watched welts appear on her arms. *Shit*. The same thing was happening on her legs. She instinctively knew that scratching would make it ten times worse.

She needed… God, she didn't know what she needed…

She needed to go home, have a shower, and take this as Life's warning that contacting Troyden Castle was a very bad idea. Did she need to be part of a family? She'd been on her own for more than a decade, since she was eighteen, and she'd managed. Families were overrated, right? They were full of drama and dysfunction, and she'd had enough of both to last her a few lifetimes.

Eden gripped the stable door and closed her eyes, conscious of her jelly-like legs and her hot-everywhere body.

Jed frowned at her, his expression now serious. 'You're looking quite red,' he stated. 'Are you overheating?'

She didn't know. She didn't think so; she'd been fine outside. Before she could answer, he whirled around and walked away from her. From swollen eyes, she watched him walk over to a fridge in the corner of the stable and remove two water bottles. In the sunlight streaming in through the cracked door, his hair was dark brown, not black, curling over the collar of his shirt. His name, Harris, was printed across his back, and a streak of dirt ran across his truly excellent butt.

He shoved one bottle under his muscled arm, cracked the other bottle's lid and passed it to her. His eyes caught the light. They were true amber, a warm coppery hue she'd never seen before, enhanced by stubby, thick eyelashes. They were the perfect complement to his olive skin. He looked like... Damn, who did he look like? Right, a Caucasian version of the hero in one of her favourite K-dramas, *Crash Landing on You*. Stoic, implacable, unreadable ... distant.

The cold bottle of water slipped from her grip. Trying to catch it, she smacked it instead, dousing her face and chest with water. Actually, that felt rather nice.

Eden ran her hand down her face and tried to wipe the water away, but her eyes kept streaming. And her top lip was growing fatter by the second.

'I think I am…' she replied, reaching out to steady herself by gripping his strong forearm. She didn't feel well. Something was badly wrong…

'Here, wipe your face,' he shoved a rough fabric into her hands. 'It's clean, I promise.'

Eden didn't know what else to do, so she ran the horse blanket over her face. She hauled in some air, but as she breathed out, her chest tightened and contracted. There was no dismissing her symptoms now. This was bad.

'Help,' she wheezed before her knees buckled.

She was pretty sure that the sexy polo player had had more than a few women fall at his feet – looking like that, how could he not? – but none, she was certain, because they were about to slide into anaphylactic shock.

'Hey, my name is Mick. I'm a GP, and you're having an allergic reaction.'

Eden's eyes fluttered open and she stared into the rich green eyes of a Priyanka Chopra lookalike. It was the woman from earlier, and she looked older than she'd first thought, in her early thirties perhaps.

Patting the ground next to her, Eden realised she was sitting on a shady patch of grass just outside the stable, protected from the sun by the thick foliage of an old oak tree. Two EMTs in yellow vests stood behind her, their expressions concerned. Right, she must look a fright. Glancing down at her red-welt-covered legs and arms she winced. Then forced herself to look back at Mick. 'My face?'

'It's everywhere. Face, torso, limbs, back.'

Shit. A red face to go with her pale red hair, fabulous. The only good thing is that the guy from earlier – Number Three, Jed, the Big and Sexy polo player – wasn't looming over her anymore.

'I rifled through your purse to get your name, and to see if you had any meds in it. By the way, I've given you an antihistamine injection, quite a strong one, and it should kick in soon,' Mick told her. 'And you and I need to talk about your obsession with Hyun Bin.'

Eden blinked, off guard. 'What?'

Mick held her phone to her face, it opened and up popped the face of the gorgeous K-drama star. Oh, God, how would she explain this? Few people understood her obsession with K-dramas, and no one but her looked at her phone. '*Um…*'

'I mean Hyun Bin is super sexy, but Daniel Henney as al'Lan Mandragoran is my guy-at-night fantasy. Also, Hyun Bin is married.'

Sadly.

Mick recognised K-drama stars and watched her favourite fantasy series? Would she marry her?

'We'll talk hot guys and about how incredible *When the Phone Rings* was—'

Oh, man! 'The twists, the turns!'

'—later,' Mick continued, her expression now serious. 'Can you tell me what happened?'

Eden nodded, her mind slowly clicking into gear. 'My eyes started watering as soon as I got here. It got worse the longer I stayed in the stable. The hives erupted after I patted the horse.'

Mick held her wrist before looking up at the hovering

EMTs. 'Her throat isn't closing, and her pulse is normal. You guys can go back to the field.' When they moved off, Mick shifted back, wrapping her arms around her bent legs.

Eden couldn't help it and reached under the hem of her dress to scratch her thigh, but Mick grabbed her hand before she could make contact. 'Scratching will make it worse, just breathe through it, okay?'

Easier said than done.

She recalled the world turning wavy and remembered it going black. She rubbed the back of her head, wincing at the ridge of a welt forming there. 'I don't feel like I hit my head.'

'You didn't, Jed caught you before you hit the deck,' Mick told her. 'He called me, and I came up from the big house. You should start to feel better soon.'

'I feel like a walking nerve end,' Eden muttered. 'And so embarrassed.'

'No need,' Mick replied, her brisk manner a complete contrast to her grubby shirt and ragged denim shorts. 'So, I'm pretty sure you are allergic to horses.'

'I am?'

'You haven't felt like this before around horses?'

Eden winced. 'I've never met a horse before or been in a stable.' She sighed at Mick's raised eyebrows. 'I'm a city girl, and horse-riding lessons weren't in the budget. Or even on the radar.'

'Ah.' Mick's eyes darted over Eden's face. 'You're still pale and your eyelids are drooping.'

Eden nodded. They felt concrete heavy. 'I'm so tired.'

'That's a side effect of the antihistamine,' Mick said,

standing up dusting off her shorts. 'How did you get to Elmsleigh? Did you drive?'

'Yeah.'

'Well, you're not going to be able to drive anytime soon, because you're basically drunk on meds. Can you call someone to drive you home?'

Eden looked at her hands and then shook her head. She had friends, but no one close enough to drive ninety minutes to pick up her sorry self. And her mum, well, she wasn't available, in any way, anymore. Even if she was, she'd say that Eden was an adult now, and it wasn't her job to pull her out of tight spots.

Eden thought that she knew what it was like to feel lonely, but at this moment, far from home and feeling woozy, the depth of her isolation was a mental slap. Just sometimes, not often, the acute, almost physical ache for a connection was debilitating. She closed her eyes and blinked away her tears. Feeling unknown, invisible and disconnected *sucked*.

'Right,' Mick briskly stated, 'Let's go with Plan B.'

'What's Plan B?' Eden asked, taking the hand Mick held out and allowing her to help her to her feet. She liked Mick and wondered what it would be like to have her as a friend. At the Bancroft Foundation, she'd had co-workers but she'd kept her distance. Probably a good thing now. At some point, when the police finished their investigation, they'd probably lose their jobs because of her.

No! *Crap*. Why did she keep blaming herself? She wasn't the one who misappropriated funds for expensive cars, luxurious trips and to pay for renovations on their house, who stole money meant for various charities, including

Hope Harbour, her favourite: a house for kids, run by four single mums, who supplied emergency protective care to vulnerable children.

She'd lived with children like that; she'd witnessed their pain and seen them trembling in fear. The women who took them in, who made them feel safe, deserved, at the very least, financial support. That was why she'd originally brought Hope Harbour, by then on its knees, to Vince and Tara's notice and persuaded them to ask their rich patrons to save the house from being disbanded. When she discovered the embezzlement, Eden had selfishly prayed that Vince and Tara had kept their sticky fingers off their funds.

But no, if anything, they stole a higher percentage from Hope Harbour than they did from other charities. After she'd tallied up the total amount – more than thirty thousand pounds over two years – and stopped crying, she'd gone to the police.

Eden pulled her scattered thoughts back to a still-serious Mick.

'You're going to feel a little weird'—*roger that*—'and you're going to feel sleepy for a while. And that means you need a place to sleep. I would take you back to my place, but I have two kids under the age of six. Mm, Justin is away and Jed is playing polo.'

Mick wrapped her arm around Eden's waist and steered her toward the big house. 'You also need to be away from horses, and anyone who has had contact with horses. So that means staying in the big house.'

Eden pointed to the house in front of them. 'There?'

'There,' Mick firmly stated. 'Troyden is a sweetheart and

won't mind you sleeping in one of the guest rooms until you feel better.'

Eden shook her head. 'I don't think... I can't...' She wasn't ready to step into his world, not like this, not looking like a zombie with a contagious disease, and so sleepy she could barely form sentences.

'Eden, all you need to do right now is to walk to the house and up one flight of stairs,' Mick told her, in what Eden recognised as a 'Scary Mummy, don't test me' voice. It had been her mum's default setting.

She didn't want to. Walk, that is. Sleep she could do, right here and right now.

Eden felt a warm, big hand on her back and turned too fast, her feet half left the ground as her body went one way and her balance the other. She caught a glimpse of a wide chest covered in a white shirt, and a strong tanned neck, before being swept off her feet by a solid arm under her legs and another around her back.

'I'll carry her back to the house, Mick.' His voice, deep and delicious, rumbled through her, and Eden, exhausted, rested her cheek against his pec as every muscle in her body lengthened and stretched. Maybe it was the medication, maybe it was him, but she instantly relaxed. Was this what safety felt like?

She liked it. She shouldn't, but she did.

'Dammit, Jed, you can't!' Mick half-yelled.

Jed's grip tightened. 'Why not?'

'You are covered in horse dander and hair,' Mick retorted.

Jed put her down and told her to stand. Off balance, she locked her knees and watched him whip off his shirt and shove it into the back of his jodhpurs. Eden watched, mouth open, as he strode over to the hose attached to the outside tap, and doused his head with water, then his chest, and back of his neck. His muscles bunched and rippled as he stroked water off his body with a broad hand, and droplets flew as he shook his head.

She felt off balance and woozy, tired but wired. And so turned on that she expected her panties to burst into flames at any moment. Hot, hot, hot … or was that from the allergic reaction? A bit of both?

Jed returned and scooped her up, cradling her against his now cool, damp, bare, wide-as-Australia chest. 'Whatever I have left on me isn't going to make a difference, Mick,' he snapped. He looked down, and their eyes connected. The fuzzy edges of sleep and the narcotic efforts of the antihistamine distorted his image, but he was still ridiculously, stupendously sexy.

'Put her down, and I'll walk her up,' Mick sounded annoyed, but from very far away.

'She's woozy, and besides, we need you down at the field,' Jed said. 'Kit fell off and has dislocated his shoulder again. You need to go shove it back in.'

Mick dropped an F-bomb. 'That's the third time in two years. That man is a lunatic.'

'You go attend to him; I'll take her up to the house,' he said and tightened his grip as he started to walk, his stride steady and sure. Eden curled up in his arms, put both her hands between her cheek and his chest and allowed sleep to claim her.

She'd deal with whatever madness life had handed her later.

Riding High

'Jungkook!'

'Jin!'

'Seriously? Jungkook for the win.'

'RM is amazing, too.'

Later that afternoon, after a long sleep, Eden couldn't believe that she was sitting cross-legged in the middle of what she was sure was a seventeenth-century bed, discussing K-pop with Mick. They'd been chatting about being fully fledged members of ARMY and the band's performances for the last twenty minutes while Eden drank two cups of tea and scoffed four scones topped high with home-made strawberry jam and yellow clotted cream.

She was still covered in hives, but she felt a lot better than when Jed had deposited her on this bed several hours ago. Mick had also jabbed her with another antihistamine dose ten minutes ago, so she was expecting to feel sleepy again soon.

Mick sighed. 'They are so incredibly talented. But sometimes I think of the sacrifices they made to get to where they are today and how difficult it must be to live a vaguely normal life.'

Eden nodded. She had no concept of what it would feel like to be that visible, to live your life in a fishbowl.

Frankly, she couldn't think of anything worse. Just going to the police, being questioned by them, had been bad enough – terrible, actually – and she couldn't imagine having reporters and fans in your face all the time.

While her uncle wasn't K-pop, BTS famous, he was well known, and his liaisons with much younger women often made the online, and print, gossip columns. From what she'd seen, he didn't seem to mind the attention.

Eden placed her teacup on the tray. 'Are you sure Mr Castle doesn't mind me staying here?' she asked, once again looking for reassurance.

'He loves having people to stay. Did I tell you that this room is called the Tatooine Suite? There are five other empty guest rooms on this floor. Alderaan is opposite, with the Yavin, Hoth and Dagobah further down the long passage. Troyden's obsession with Stars Wars knows no bounds.'

So she wasn't putting anyone out. Good to know. 'And you live on the grounds?'

Mick nodded. 'With my demon spawn. Gemma is six, Liam is four.'

Should she ask? Would she be overstepping the mark? 'Where's their dad?' she asked. 'You don't have to tell me if you don't want to.'

'Why wouldn't I want to?' Mick asked, reaching across the bed to snag the last scone, popping it into her mouth and closing her eyes. 'Yum. Xavier is an Argentinian polo player, one of a handful of ten-handicap players in the world.'

Eden blinked, trying to keep up. 'That's good, right?'

'Very. He's not a bad father; he's affectionate when he remembers they exist. Xavier is'—she hesitated—'loud and brash and sucks the marrow out of life. He's made to keep moving through life at speed, and children slow him down. Naturally, I blame the kids' wild streak on him.' Mick wrinkled her nose. 'Though, to be fair, I used to be that way too.'

She was so open, so very honest, and in her company, Eden felt herself relaxing. She'd never met anyone who made her feel so quickly accepted and more at ease than Mick. Is this what it felt like to have a friend? It was a silly thought, because she'd be leaving Elmsleigh House in the morning and she wasn't sure she'd ever return. Eden slid down the bed, tucked a pillow behind her head and yawned.

'How long have you been living on the estate?' Eden asked, feeling satiated. And sleepy.

'I moved in shortly after Liam was born,' Mick said, stretching like a cat. 'Alistair had been living here for a few years already and I moved in with him—'

'Who?'

Mick rolled onto her stomach and placed her pointed chin in the palm of her hand. 'Alistair, one of my three stepbrothers.'

'You have *three* stepbrothers?'

Mick grinned. 'Growing up with them was why I mistakenly thought I could handle Xavier.'

Eden loved hearing stories about other people's families. 'How did you come to have three stepbrothers?'

Oh, she knew that Troyden had been married and divorced, that he had stepchildren, but Eden suspected Mick's version of the story would be a lot more interesting, and vivid, than what the press reported.

This felt like a girly heart-to-heart, a combination of a sleepover and gossip-sesh. And she was here for it. Because it might, realistically, be her first and last.

'Okay, so Troyden is very bad at keeping wives, but he excels at keeping his stepkids around. Alistair is his oldest step and he occupies the first cottage. He's crazy about Justin, his saint-like husband, gym and boring spreadsheets, for the love of God.'

'Spreadsheets are incredible,' Eden protested, because she was partial to a good spreadsheet.

'What's wrong with a Post-it?' Mick waved a hand in the air and lifted her nose. 'If you defend Al and his love of spreadsheets, we can't possibly be friends.'

Seriously? Oh, wait, the smile lifting Mick's lips suggested she was teasing. Right. 'Tell me about your other siblings,' she murmured.

'Anyway, Al and Justin, first cottage, no kids. I have the second cottage and share it with the demon spawn. Kael uses the next cottage along when he's at home. He's a war correspondent and photographer, very intense, seldom around, and the youngest of my sibs. I miss him.' Mick pulled out her phone and scrolled through her photos, stopping on an image of a dusty, stubbled blonde staring into the camera. Eden noticed the streak of soot across his cheekbone, and his intense, flinty green eyes. He was hot, in a touch-me-and-get-singed way.

Although they weren't related, something about him – his sheer masculinity, his no-bullshit stare, his wide shoulders – reminded her of Number Three.

'I worry about him and am terrified we're going to get a call saying that he's been kidnapped by Somalian pirates, or by those scary dudes in Indonesia.'

He looked like he could handle himself. Eden passed Mick her phone, her eyes feeling like they were weighted down with concrete blocks. 'And Number Three?'

'Jed's cottage is at the end of the row and is attached to his equally big workshop.'

A workshop for what? Eden yawned and pushed her cheek deeper into the softly scented pillow. She was so tired, she'd just close her eyes for a minute…

Jed knocked and poked his head around the door. Mick stood between him and the bed, but he could read his sister's face and didn't pick up any worry in the green eyes he knew so well. She held up a hand, halting his progress into the room.

'Have you showered?' Mick demanded, in her bossy doctor voice. She placed her hands on her lower back and arched her spine. Dressed for a day spent with her kids, Mick did not look like the shit-hot doctor he knew her to be. She looked like what she was, a tired single mum trying to cope with two kids under the age of six and a busy job. He nodded.

'Washed your hair?'

Jeez, Mick never took this much interest in his hygiene. 'Yes, Mum,' he muttered, pushing his hand through his wet hair.

'Okay, then you can come in.'

Jed walked to the bed, looked down at the sleeping woman, and his heart bounced off his chest. He could see the tiny veins in the thin skin hiding her blue-green eyes and took in the length of her thick eyelashes. Her strawberry blonde hair was half in and half out of a complicated plait, and the freckles on her nose and cheekbones were flecks of cinnamon on her pale skin. Her lips looked a little bloodless.

'How is she?' he asked Mick, placing his hands on the bed next to her calves, unable to look away from the woman who'd collapsed at his feet and scared the shit out of him.

'She's okay. She had an allergic reaction, but she didn't go into anaphylactic shock.' Mick patted his arm. 'I didn't need to use adrenalin and that's a good thing.'

Why did he care? And why, for the love of God, did his voice sound like it was trembling? God, he hoped Mick didn't hear it; she'd never let him live it down. 'Should she have gone to A&E?'

Mick shook her head. 'They probably would've just sent her home with instructions to ride it out.'

'But she fainted.'

'Her blood pressure probably dropped. Her throat didn't close, and her airways were clear. I gave her an antihistamine injection – you know I keep them on hand for Gemma – and I've been monitoring her flare-up.'

Gemma, his goddaughter, was fatally allergic to bees and everyone in Mick's life knew what to do if she collided with one. Jed winced as he took in the welts on her arms and chest. 'Shit. They look damn itchy.'

Mick nodded. 'She's definitely allergic to horses. That's why I asked whether you'd showered and washed your hair.'

'Come on, I'm not a horse,' he protested.

'A horse's arse, maybe.' Okay, he'd walked straight into that one.

'So she'll react like this whenever she comes into contact with someone who's into horses?'

Mick wrinkled her nose. 'I wouldn't expect her to have such a bad reaction by just being around people who have horse dander on their clothes. She was in the stables; she stroked Rey; she wiped her face with a horse blanket. She got a megadose.'

Jed stood up and pushed his hands through his hair. '*Shit.*'

If he'd had any ideas of making a move on her, her allergy to horses blew that notion straight out of the water. He sometimes spent the best part of the day either on or around horses and was *always* covered in horse dander.

Jed resisted the urge to push a long tendril of rose-coloured hair off Eden's cheek and behind her ear. Not wanting to do anything stupid, he folded his arms and tucked his hands under his armpits. He was a guy who knew how to keep his distance, fully in control of his body and actions, so why did he want to put himself between her and the world? He had enough people in his life he was responsible for, enough people to protect, why would he want to add one more?

He stared at her, annoyed by his fast heart rate and prickling skin. She was so gorgeous, in a woodland sprite, *Midsummer's Night's Dream*, type of way. But he wouldn't allow his out-of-the-norm fascination to blunt his cynicism.

He'd seen it all before. He just needed to find out what her story was, what she was up to? Why was she interested in his stepfather? Was she really allergic to horses or did she take something to make her break out in hives? Okay, drastic, but it wouldn't be the first time a woman did something extreme to catch the attention of an older, exceedingly rich man. Rubbing his forehead, Jed felt exhausted. Jesus, keeping an eye out on Troyden, a silver fox with more money than common sense, was an exhausting job.

Mick picked up her backpack, no black doctor's bag for her, and slung it over her shoulder. 'The meds have knocked her out, and her urticaria has settled down. We can leave her to sleep.'

He nodded, as always amused when Mick went into doctor mode. She stood on her tiptoes and kissed his cheek. 'I'll see you in the morning,' she told him. 'Wish me luck, Gem's decided that she wants dreadlocks, and Liam thinks bathing will rub his skin away.'

He smiled, remembering how revolting Mick had been when he'd met her as children. She often blamed Xavier for their kids being out of control, but Mick frequently forgot there were years when they were all convinced she was one breath away from turning feral.

Turning his attention back to Eden, Jed's throat tightened. She looked much younger than earlier, more vulnerable. He picked up a long, loose curl to see if her hair was as soft as it looked. It was. He rubbed the strands between his fingers and frowned. As pretty as Eden was, something about her felt off. Very off.

What brought her to Elmsleigh?

It sure as hell wasn't an interest in polo.

On the plus side, he'd pushed all thoughts about the Duke dying to the back of his mind.

Chapter Three

> I hope you slept well and are hive-free. There's a spare toothbrush in the bathroom, feel free to use the toiletries. Breakfast in the salon, down the stairs, turn left, and follow the noise. M.

> PS. ARMY forever!

Eden picked up her bag, wishing she could take that huge double bed with her. It was the nicest mattress she'd ever slept on and would marry it if she could. Before opening the bedroom door, she looked down at her hand, then inspected her arm and was relieved to see she was rash-free. Still anxious, she lifted the hem of her dress to check her thighs. She looked normal: pale, but normal.

Rubbing her temple with the tips of her fingers, Eden was conscious of her still heavy limbs and the headache pulsing behind her eyes.

Note to self: avoid horses at all costs. Apart from being

carried by Number Three and chatting with Mick, yesterday hadn't been a fun experience.

Eden walked down the passage, idly taking in the stern faces of the portraits on the walls. Everyone looked so bloody miserable, like they were chronically constipated. When she caught her reflection in the mirror above a hall table and checked her face, she was relieved to see no swelling, rash or watery eyes. No make-up either, apart from a swipe of gloss from the tube she always carried in her purse, and while her dress was creased, trainers a little dirty, she looked okay-ish. Tired but presentable.

Checking Mick's note in her hand, Eden needed to decide whether to accept the invite to breakfast or not. This was her uncle's house and there was an excellent chance he'd sit down to breakfast in the dining room of the house he owned. Did she want to open the 'we-share-DNA' door?

Did she want to meet him? Sort of.

What did she want from him? No idea.

Was she ready to tell him who she was? Not sure.

Was it right to sit down at his table under false pretences? Definitely not.

Eden sat on the top stair and tipped her head back to look up at the glass oculus a long way above her head. The last couple of months had been eventful to say the least; it felt like she was living life from behind the wheel of a high-performance sports car she didn't know how to drive. While her mum had been distant this past decade (situation, sadly, normal), she'd never considered she'd permanently drop out of her life. When her mum had made her big announcement, it'd shocked and rocked Eden's world.

It had been a mini-death. It was so damn final, so ... irrevocable.

Shaking her head she tried to focus on the issue at hand, meeting Troyden Castle, and whether she wanted to meet him or melt away. If she walked away from Elmsleigh House without explanation, that was it. She'd never get any information about her dad and his family. She would be eternally family-less.

Having a proper family, being part of one, was a childhood dream she'd carried into adulthood. A partner, kids of her own ... that was the Disney-version. But, since she rarely dated and when she did, it always led to disappoint, she knew she had to make her expectations about having a family more realistic and settle for less. Much less.

Someone to send her a Christmas card, to call on her birthday. An occasional lunch. Having a connection to someone who shared her DNA.

At this point Troyden Castle was her only hope of a family. But could she trust their tenuous DNA connection? Could she trust *him*?

Should she delay her explanations and lie? Or rather, not tell the whole truth? If she told Troyden one truth, that she worked as an event coordinator (true-ish) but kept her connection to the Bancrofts a secret, she could, at least initially, avoid being judged for what she did and not for who she was. Keeping her professional life private was also a way of giving herself space to simply be. She could keep her options open as she navigated the complexities of her new, Mum-free reality and its accompanying emotions – sadness, grief and resentment.

But she needed to decide. Right here and right now.

Honestly, being a sensible adult every day seemed a bit excessive.

Jed half-expected her to slip down the stairs and hightail it out of the house, but there she was, pushing open the door to the dining room, unsure whether to enter. Before he could push back his chair, Diana, Troyden's long-term housekeeper, stood up and walked over to her.

'Eden, come on in.' Diana's tone was, as always, kind but brusque. 'You didn't eat much last night, so I'm sure you're starving.'

Eden's eyes bounced from Diana to the table, her eyes lingering on Troyden, before smiling at Mick. Then their eyes connected, and he felt electricity skim his skin. For some ridiculous reason, he couldn't pull his eyes off her lovely – hive-free – face and sea-green eyes. Her face was make-up free and she'd pulled her wavy hair into a loose knot at the back of her neck. Her dress was crumpled, her trainers grubby, but she looked … *right*. It was the only world he could think of.

She looked as right as Lana, sitting next to Troyden, didn't.

'I'm Diana, Troyden's housekeeper.' Diana steered her into the room. Her eyes widened as she took in the long dining table, carved chairs and scary-looking portraits on the wall.

Mick jumped up, rushed over to Eden and placed a hand on her arm. 'Don't take another step.' Her eyes flicked from Jed to Troyden, then to their oldest stepsib, Alistair, and his husband, Justin. 'Who's been to the stables this morning or out on an early morning ride?' Mick demanded.

Jed had spent hours on various horses yesterday and slept late, before showering and ambling up to the big house for breakfast. He shook his head, as did Alistair and Justin. Diana hated horses and stayed away from the stables, so Mick ignored her. 'Troyden?' she asked again, hands on her hips.

Embarrassment passed over Eden's face and she shifted from foot to foot. Jed watched her lock eyes on Troyden's stubbled face, as if she was trying to commit his face to memory, to look inside his brain. Jed remembered her out-of-the-blue question from yesterday…

Why was she here and what did she want?

'Hello, welcome to Elmsleigh House. I'm Troyden Castle, the owner,' Troyden said, standing up and laying his serviette beside his plate. 'I am so sorry you had such a horrid time.'

Eden managed a smile of light surprise. 'You're the man I spoke to yesterday, the one who gave me some pointers on polo.' She had an interesting voice, a little deeper than normal, with a slight rasp, as if she'd swallowed some smoke. It was sexy. *She* was sexy.

Dammit.

Mick snapped her fingers impatiently. 'Troyden, stables? Yes or no?'

He pulled his faded blue eyes off Eden's to look at Mick. 'You know I always go down to the stables before breakfast, Michaela.'

Mick pointed to the chair furthest away from Troyden.

'Sit there, Eden, so that the dander on him has less chance of reaching you.' She placed her hands on her hips. 'Anyone else?' she demanded.

Jed saw Eden's embarrassment. 'Chill, Mick, nobody has Ebola,' he told her and waved at the empty seat opposite him. 'Sit down, Eden. Mick is being dramatic.'

'I'm a doctor. I am never dramatic,' Mick shot back. 'Eden is allergic to horses, and until we find out how allergic, and how much exposure she can tolerate, I will protect her from another allergic reaction.' She frowned at Eden. 'Did you take the antihistamine pill this morning?'

Eden nodded.

'You should be fine,' Mick said, sliding back into her seat. 'But keep your distance from Troyden.'

Interestingly Jed noticed a flicker of disappointment cross Eden's far too expressive face. Why?

Diana slid a full breakfast plate in front of Eden, and her eyes widened at the mountain of food.

'Meet Alistair and Justin.' Troyden said, before pointing at Mick's kids. 'And those are my monsters, my grandkids, Gemma and Liam.'

Liam pushed out his bottom lip. 'I'm not a monster, Troypops.'

Troyden smiled at him, then laid a fatherly hand on Jed's shoulder. 'Jed is another stepson, and Michaela is my stepdaughter, but I consider them my children.'

Jed didn't explain that they'd already met, that he'd held her in his arms. She'd been asleep, but... *Shit*. Why was he remembering how she smelled of sunshine and sweet lemons, how he loved the dense freckles on her nose and cheekbones, how he'd noticed the lighter ones dusting the rest of her face and chest? How he'd wished he could taste her plump lips, lift her dress up and over her head in the stables... He squirmed in his chair, conscious of the semi behind the buttons of his fly. *No.* She'd been asleep, covered in welts; she'd been hot and drug-hazy ... but all he could think about was getting her naked.

Troyden didn't bother to introduce Lana, the only other person at the table, who was absorbed in pushing mushrooms around her plate. Jed quietly snorted, so much for being The One. Troyden was being exceptionally polite, but his failure to introduce Lana meant either they'd had a massive fight or that she was on her way out. Jed prayed for the latter.

Unsurprisingly, Lana didn't notice Troyden's subtle insult.

Introductions done, everyone looked at Eden and she squirmed in her chair. 'Thank you for allowing me to spend the night, Mr Castle, I appreciate it.'

Troyden reached for the coffee carafe. When Lana lifted hers to be refilled, Troyden's mouth tightened, but he poured her coffee before topping off his. Yep, there was trouble in paradise.

Jed, who'd finished a second helping of breakfast, pushed his chair back and rested his ankle on his knee. He watched Eden as she picked up the heavy silver cutlery and prodded the black pudding with her fork, her brow furrowing. Cute.

She looked up at Mick, but Mick was refereeing an argument between the kids and wasn't paying attention. Alistair and Justin were talking to Troyden about a holiday in Spain, and Diana was reading the newspaper. Lana was still staring at her mushrooms.

'It's black pudding,' Jed told her.

She winced slightly. 'I figured.'

'Have you tried it before?' he asked. Black pudding was an acquired taste, not one he'd ever mastered, but Troyden and his sibs loved it. It was a staple on the Elmsleigh Sunday morning breakfast menu.

'Um, no.' She prodded it again. 'Also, I'm *supposed* to be a vegetarian.'

His eyebrows lifted at her statement. Supposed to be? Surely you either were one or you weren't?

Eden placed a bite of bacon and egg onto a small chunk of black pudding. She popped it into her mouth, chewed, tipped her head to the side, and chewed some more. He guessed being a vegetarian was a fluid concept rather than a life choice.

'It's good,' she told him, going back in for another bite.

Liam rested his elbows on the table and peered around his sister to look at Eden. 'You know that's made from blood and hearts and yucky stuff, right?'

His nephew and niece took vicarious, and possibly psychotic pleasure, in trying to scare the adults around them. Or, at the very least, getting a reaction from them. Jed waited for Eden to blanch, turn white, and look around for the nearest bathroom, but she simply carried on eating. 'It tastes pretty good for blood. No wonder vampires like it,' Eden mused.

It was a perfect response and one that took the wind from their sails. Mick sent her an approving look. 'So why are you *supposed* to be a vegetarian?' she asked, reaching for a slice of toast.

This was one of the rare occasions where Jed was grateful for his sister's nosiness, as he too wanted to hear her answer. Eden dabbed the corners of her mouth with her linen napkin and accepted Diana's offer of a cup of coffee. 'My mum was a staunch vegan, and so was I until I left for uni. At uni, I rebelled and became a vegetarian. When I graduated, I became a pescatarian. I've only recently started eating meat.'

'How long ago did your mum pass away?' Mick asked gently.

Eden looked down at her plate and closed her eyes, those long eyelashes resting on her cheek. 'She's not dead. She's just ... gone,' she quietly replied. What did *gone* mean? Was she missing? Hiking in India? Suffering from dementia?

'I take it she was a pushy vegan and didn't believe you were entitled to make your own food choices?' Mick pried.

'Something like that.'

Mick nodded. Man, Mick was good at this shit. He'd simply thought that Eden'd grown up and discovered new foods, as young people discovered shagging and tequila shots at uni. But Mick went straight to the heart of the matter. No wonder she was the most popular doctor at the village practice.

'I keep expecting her to pop up and shout at me for eating bacon,' Eden admitted. She picked up a piece and popped it into her mouth. 'But I love it. It's the food of the gods.'

Well, not for some religions, but he got her point, it was delicious.

Jed sipped his coffee, pulling his eyes off Eden to look out of the tall, open French doors leading out onto the terrace. Below them, a wild meadow rolled down to the pond, half surrounded by a small group of trees. It was another glorious spring day, and throughout the grounds, he saw new buds on branches, daffodils and crocuses pushing their way up through the soil. Because Troyden wasn't a fan of hard landscaping, the house would, come summer, be surrounded by out-of-control wildflowers and the season would start, forcing him to leave his quiet life as a furniture maker to embrace the glitz of being one of the country's best polo players. Troyden paid him a shit load to captain his team every year, and he loved the sport. He just hated the attention.

'Are you going to the Duke's funeral, Troyden?' Justin asked. Jed turned his head to see Troyden's grimace.

'I know you didn't like the man, but you've been neighbours for forty years,' Justin pushed. While Alistair was the family's money guy, it was Justin who handled Troyden's PR – the little of it there was. He was also Troyden's PA and right hand. 'Everyone knows you didn't care for the man, but you don't need to rub their faces in it.'

Troyden sighed and looked up at the ornate ceiling, painted with horny-looking cherubs. 'I suppose I should.'

'It's on Wednesday morning at eleven,' Justin said. He turned to look at Jed, who shook his head.

'Do not even suggest it,' he growled.

His sibs didn't know he was the Duke's illegitimate son, and he knew they were curious about the origins of his hatred. He felt bad for not telling them, but his mum always insisted on keeping his father's identity secret.

Jed tapped his finger on the rim of his empty coffee cup. 'Even if I wanted to go, and I don't, I'm leaving shortly. I'm doing a training camp for the junior national team. I'll only be back next Sunday or Monday.'

He looked at Eden, wishing there was a way to get her number, to see her again. But what was the point? She was city; he was country. She was allergic to horses, and his life, for at least half the year, revolved around him spending most of the day in the saddle. He didn't do anything but one-night stands and brief flings, and while she might be up for that, hot-footing it into London for a hook-up with her seemed … off. He'd done it before, too often to count, but lately, dinner and clubbing followed by sex wasn't as much fun as it used to be. It was also a little exhausting. Was he jaded? Getting old? More than likely.

'Can't you go in my place?' Troyden asked Justin. Justin often stood in for Troyden and was his official representative. Justin was calm and polite, urbane and debonair, whereas he, Al and Mick were … *not*. Al could only talk about numbers; Mick was busy and impatient and had her hands full being a single mum and a full-time GP. He wasn't a guy who could charm and bullshit; he far preferred to spend time in his workshop, in the saddle or stable than exchanging small talk. Troyden often complained that his stepchildren were socially inept, possibly even savage, and he wasn't wrong.

'What time are you leaving, Jed?' Mick asked, holding out her mug in expectation.

He obliged and then looked at his watch. 'Shortly. Kit is on his way.'

Mick frowned. 'Tell him to watch that shoulder, to take it easy.'

'Have you met Kit?' he asked, shaking his head. His best friend and teammate had one speed and no one could keep up with him. Even Jed had long since given up trying.

Talking of leaving, he really should get his arse off this chair and head down to his cottage where he'd arranged to meet Kit. He was packed and ready to go, but damn, he was reluctant. Eden was the magnet keeping him stuck to his seat.

He was being ridiculous: women came, and women went. She wasn't anything special, and when he was away from Elmsleigh, busy with coaching, immersed in polo, he'd soon forget about her.

Troyden drained his coffee and pushed back his chair. His stepdad looked down at Lana and jerked his head. 'Diana, can you arrange a taxi to take Ms Bertolli back to the city?'

Lana, brown eyes flashing, flung her serviette onto the table and stumbled to her feet. Jed glanced under the table and saw that she was balancing on three-inch, scalpel-blade-sharp heels. Who wore heels on a Sunday morning? 'Fuck you, Troyden.'

Troyden looked from her to the children and then to Mick. 'I would ask her to apologise for swearing in front of the children, but I doubt that would happen,' he calmly stated.

'That's alright, Troypops,' Liam said. 'Jed said that word

when he dropped a piece of wood on his foot last week. But *he* said it a few times and hopped around for a while.'

Jed scowled at his nephew. 'Snitch,' he muttered, as Lana weaved her way to the door. When she was out of earshot, he turned to his stepdad. 'What happened?'

Troyden shrugged. 'I found the five hundred pounds I was missing tucked into her bra.'

Jed winced. Where did his stepfather find these creatures? GoldiggersRUs?

'Can you please do some background checks on the next one before you move her into your life?' Mick asked, looking a little desperate.

'What about dating someone a little ... older?' Justin suggested.

'Yeah, you should date someone really old, like she should be at least thirty,' Gemma earnestly told her grandfather, her expression serious.

Jed winced, as did Alistair and Justin, who were closer to fifty than his thirty-five. Mick, whose thirty-third birthday was just a few weeks away, frowned at her daughter. 'This is an adult conversation, Gemma,' she told her. Her daughter merely rolled her eyes.

Jed looked over at Eden; her expression held a fair amount of incredulity. She had to think this was a madhouse, and to be fair, it often was. Though today was a relatively quiet Sunday morning: most of the polo team was often in residence, and the guest rooms were usually filled with Troyden's friends. As a result, the sixteen-seater table was crammed and deafening. Troyden resumed his seat and linked his hands behind his head, turning his attention to

Eden. 'Well, that was embarrassing,' he deadpanned, shooting her a grin.

'But not as embarrassing as my mum hassling my friends' mums to join Lighthouse at every match and every damn parent-teacher meeting,' Mick retorted with a smile.

'I forgot about that,' Troyden murmured. 'She's done with them, right?'

'I think so… But it's Mum, how can I be sure of anything?'

'At least you didn't catch your mum snogging *your* boyfriend when you were sixteen.' Al countered.

Jed winced. *Ouch.*

'Your mother was the first of my complicated, slightly weird, wives, Alistair,' Troyden agreed. 'I've been married five times, and this lot have put a moratorium on me marrying again.'

'Is your mum a little mad or is she normal?' Mick asked Eden, before taking a huge bite of marmalade toast.

Clearing her throat Eden dropped her eyes to her plate. Her shoulders came up to her ears, the tips of which he noticed flushed pink.

'Uh … well, um…'

Jed watched her chest rise with each deep intake of air. 'Well, ten or so years ago, and out of the blue, my mum joined a convent as an aspirant nun. A couple of months ago, she renounced her previous life and everything in it, including me, to enter into a formal marriage with God.' Eden's voice turned husky, and Jed knew it hurt more than her breezy attitude suggested. 'She's in a cloister now and has taken a vow of silence. I'll never see her again.'

So her mum was alive, but also, sort of, dead. Holy shit. That was a lot. After a long silence, Mick tossed her serviette on the table, lifted her eyebrows and pulled up a smile. 'Okay, you win because who can compete with having a nun for a mum?'

The flash of sadness and deep vulnerability in Eden's eyes made him want to lean across the table and gather her to him, placing his body, his strength, both mental and physical, between her and the world. He suddenly wanted to see the world through her eyes, dive into all that blue, and swim through her psyche. She was mysterious and intriguing, a vortex he couldn't fight.

Jed shook his head, disconcerted by his off-the-rails imagination. Where the hell did all that come from? She was a woman, one of many he randomly encountered, nothing special. *Get a grip, for God's sake!* He didn't have a romantic bone in his body, so what was he thinking? Swimming through her psyche, a vortex he couldn't fight? He was losing his mind…

His thoughts were ridiculous and unproductive, illogical and idiotic. The reality was simple: he was leaving shortly to do what he did best, and that was to play and coach polo. She would leave the estate, return to London and he'd never see her again.

Every muscle in his body tightened and his head spun at the thought. That felt wrong. Like he was in the wrong saddle or trying to sand a piece of wood against the grain.

His watch beeped and he grimaced at the message on the screen.

> Waiting. Where u?

Right, time to get his head in the game, to get back to normal. For the next six months, his time would be taken up with polo, coaching, practising and playing. He'd look at some ponies Troyden might consider adding to his string. He'd try not to think about the FD's death.

He pushed back his chair and stood up. It was time to walk away and get on with his life. Eden was a blip on his radar, one of the first women in a long time who'd captured his interest, but they were just two random people who'd collided. He'd never see her again.

He met her eyes. 'Good to meet you, Eden,' he said, hoping none of his family heard the slight hitch in his voice. He needed to get his shit together. He briefly gripped Troyden's shoulder, dropped a kiss on Mick's head and ruffled Liam and Gemma's hair.

'Be good, okay?' he said, giving them his version of the stink eye. It didn't impress them much, not that he expected it to.

Without looking at Eden again, and ignoring the disappointment sliding through him, he walked out of the dining room and back into real life.

Chapter Four

She was doing this.
Was she doing this?

Blurting out a request for a quick, private word with Troyden felt like she'd subconsciously decided, whether her brain was on board or not. Maybe she'd been convinced by the warmth the family exuded at breakfast, the teasing and laughter, the way they interrupted and finished each other's sentences without a second thought. Maybe it was the easy affection between Troyden and his stepchildren, the way love simply existed between them.

But whatever it was, she'd sat there, quietly watching, and listening. *Longing.* The warmth, closeness and easy affection on display were what she'd dreamed of having with her mum. All impossible now.

Maybe she was reaching for Troyden because she envied the family he'd built, because she ached to belong to something that solid, that real. Maybe the thought of walking through the world alone, untethered, was too much to bear. Maybe, at the heart of it, it was just loneliness.

Did it matter?

Whatever the reason, she was doing this.

Eden followed Troyden into his study – aubergine-coloured walls, expensive landscapes, dark, heavy wooden desk, leather chairs and green enamel reading lamps – and perched on the edge of a slipper leather chair. She folded her hands and clasped them between her legs, her knee bouncing.

Maybe she should just thank him for his hospitality and walk away.

Panic crawled up her throat and settled on her tonsils. She didn't think she could do this; she no longer *wanted* to do this. She wasn't brave enough to open this Pandora's box. On the verge of standing, she flashed back to being in Jed's arms, secure and protected, safe.

She closed her eyes and took herself back there, to when she'd felt like nothing could touch her, that a force field surrounded her. Peace, or something close to it, settled her jumpy nerves.

'You look just like him, like Thom.'

Eden jerked, her eyes skittering to Troyden's, half-sitting on the edge of his wide, dark, antique desk. His head was cocked to the side, and the corners of his mouth lifted, just a little. He pushed up, walked over to the credenza and lifted a silver-framed photograph of two young men sitting on a wall. One was Troyden, while the other man sported a masculine version of her face.

'I thought you looked familiar when we met yesterday,

but I didn't put it together until I walked in here and saw the photograph of Thom and me.'

Eden took the frame and stared down into the face of the man who was her father, her heart missing a beat. 'Was that his name? Thom?'

'Thom Castle, two years younger than me, as mad as a box of frogs.'

Eden swallowed. Did he mean mad as insane, or mad as in eccentric? She had so many questions and didn't know which one to ask first. 'We do look alike,' she admitted, her voice shaky. 'But I'm surprised you made the connection so quickly.'

Troyden took the wingback chair opposite her. 'Well, it wasn't that big a leap,' he told her, his voice soft. 'The website did inform me I had a close biological match, most likely a niece. But because your settings were private, I couldn't contact you; I had to wait until you made a move, and I didn't know if you would…' Troyden trailed off. 'You have the same eyes, the same colouring, the same number of freckles.'

Eden lifted a hand to her face, conscious that she hadn't any make-up with her to hide the majority of her dots. 'He was also a redhead?'

Troyden nodded.

She frowned, taking in his olive complexion and dark eyes. 'You aren't.'

'We were half-brothers. I took after our mum, and Thom was the spitting image of his dad.'

Eden nodded and looked down at the expensive Bukhari carpet beneath her trainers, taking in its cream and hunter-green swirls. She felt embarrassed and jumpy.

'I'm sorry about gatecrashing your house, and your breakfast. I really didn't know I was allergic to horses. It wasn't a ploy or anything.'

'You could've set up a meeting or sent me an email, but you chose to come here. Why?'

There was no judgement in his voice, so she opted for honesty. 'I wasn't sure if I wanted to meet you. I thought that if I came to the polo match, if I saw you, then maybe I would know whether I wanted to or not.'

'Why wouldn't you want to meet me?' Troyden asked, gently. 'I'm not so scary, surely?'

She could lie, but she'd already decided to keep her personal life and her connection to the Bancrofts from him, so she needed to be as honest as she possibly could. 'I wasn't sure if I was strong enough to risk you rejecting me.' *Okay, maybe that was a bit too honest, Ennis.*

'And you've experienced quite a bit of that,' he stated.

How was she supposed to respond to that? 'Yes, all my life' sounded overly dramatic. But wasn't it the truth? Her dad had left before she was born, and her mum had avoided any emotional connection with her by treating her like just another foster kid needing ongoing care. Then she left for a goddamned convent... Uh, could a convent be damned by God? Probably not.

Now she was married to the Church, and it was a possessive bastard.

No, she wouldn't bore Troyden with her shitty childhood, but she could ask him about the man who gave her half of her DNA. 'Can you tell me about my father?'

Troyden steepled his fingers and banged the tips against his lower lip. 'What do you know?'

'Nothing.'

'Right.' Troyden crossed one leg over the other and lightly clasped his hands around his knee. 'Well, Thom was a decade younger than me, so we weren't that close. He was … wild.'

'You said that before,' Eden frowned. 'What do you mean?'

He twisted his lips. 'He did whatever he wanted to do. He was all about himself, all the time.'

Eden bit the inside of his lip. 'So he's dead?'

Troyden nodded. 'Yes, I'm sorry. He died in a car accident thirty-odd years ago.'

'So, while my mum was pregnant with me or shortly after I was born.'

Troyden tapped the arm of his chair with his index finger. 'I can find the exact date,' he assured her. 'I have his death certificate somewhere.'

'How old was he when he died?' Eden asked.

'Thirty … -four or -five?'

Eden's eyebrows shot up. 'My mum was eighteen when she fell pregnant, nineteen when she had me.'

Troyden winced. 'Yeah, he was nearly double her age. He was also…' he hesitated.

Eden knew what he was about to say. 'Married?' Did she have any half-siblings? Finding an uncle was enough of a shock. 'Did they have children?' she demanded.

Troyden shook his head, and Eden experienced both relief and disappointment, an odd combination. 'No, they didn't. They had a tumultuous relationship, mainly because Thom couldn't be faithful. I didn't have much to do with him after I left home, Eden, but I heard about his exploits from our mum.'

Eden grimaced. Her father sounded like he caused a lot of drama for everyone in his life. 'Do you know anything about my mum, how they met?'

Troyden lifted one shoulder. 'I don't. But I got a call from him a week or so before he died. He said that he'd got someone pregnant and that she wanted to get married. I reminded him he was already married, and suggested an…' His words rolled to a stop, and he looked away. He pulled in a deep breath and carried on, his cheeks pink. 'I suggested an abortion, but he said that he'd tried to convince her, that she was religious and wouldn't consider one.'

It felt like they were discussing someone else, someone wholly unconnected to her.

'A week later he rolled his car and died on impact.' Troyden gripped the bridge of his nose and closed his eyes. 'It was a bad time for me. There was so much death to deal with. My first marriage was on the rocks and my business was taking off. I was juggling quite a few balls.'

She got it: her pregnant mum was low down on his list of priorities. 'Did my mum ever make contact with your family?' she asked, feeling incredibly tired.

Regret passed through Troyden's eyes. 'She didn't, not as far as I know.'

Eden stared out of the tall window. It was a bucolic English scene, perfect for a tourist brochure extolling the virtues of the English countryside in the spring, but all she could see was her mum, eighteen, pregnant, and scared. Being religious, sleeping with Thom would've been a big deal for her. She wouldn't have done it unless she genuinely believed he was the man she was going to marry. But why didn't she choose to give her up for adoption? Why did she keep her?

'It's a lot to take in, isn't it?' Troyden said, his tone kind.

She met his eyes and nodded. 'There are so many unknowns, and no one to give me the answers.'

He rubbed the back of his neck. 'I can tell you about my parents, about what your father was like growing up, about where we came from, how we lived—'

'Have you always been rich?' she interrupted.

He laughed. 'God, *no*. We were solidly middle class. Before he died, my father was a telephone technician, and my mum a nurse. My stepfather was a truck driver. Thom never bothered to study, but I managed to work my way through uni. I was always the driven one, wanting more. My parents never understood why I couldn't be satisfied with the life they'd created.'

Eden looked around the room, taking in the bronze sculptures, the expensive furniture and the impressive paintings on the wall. 'You did alright for yourself.'

'I did better than alright. But, unfortunately, none of them got to see my success.'

'Oh?'

'My real dad died when I was a kid, and my stepdad when I was twenty-two. My mum was in the car with your father when he crashed. They were both killed instantly.'

Eden lifted her hands to her mouth, shocked. 'Oh … *shit*. I'm so sorry. You lost your entire family in one hit.'

'Losing my mum was tough. I wish I could say the same for Thom, but I barely knew him. When he called me just before he died, I hadn't spoken to him in five or more years.'

She'd lost her family too, in a different way. But loss is loss, and how could it be judged and measured? It hit people at different times, in different ways. She pushed her hands through her hair and released a long sigh.

She'd come here to find out about her father, but it didn't seem like Troyden could tell her much about him. She knew a little more than she did before, and she'd have to be content with that. Rubbing her hands on her thighs, she creased the fabric of her dress even further.

'If you could give me copies of his birth certificate and jot down who my grandparents were, where they were born, and whether there are any medical issues I should be aware of, I'd be grateful.' She had taken enough of his time, and there wasn't much more he could tell her. And he had to be wishing she'd be on her way.

'I'll give you my email address and maybe you could email me scanned copies?' she suggested.

Eden was surprised by Troyden's frown. 'That's it?' he asked. 'You're just going to walk out?'

She looked at the closed door, then at him. 'I'm not sure what you mean?' she said, hesitant.

'I put my DNA on that website, hoping to find blood relations, Eden, to connect with what little family there was left. I put it there hoping to connect with *you*.'

He had children. Grandchildren. A whole, sprawling family. Was he really looking to add her to the mix? 'I've always felt incredibly guilty for not doing more for your mum and you. DNA testing became my only hope of finding you.'

But… *What?* 'But why would you…' She heard the raised voice of Mick yelling at her kids not to run, telling them to mind a vase, and winced when she heard glass shattering.

Troyden gripped the bridge of his nose. 'I swear to God, if those monsters have broken the Ming, I will lose my shit.'

The door opened, and Mick popped her head through the gap. 'Relax, it was the awful glass ornament Gemma won for you at the village tombola last spring,' she told him, before slamming the door shut again, rattling the windows.

'One day, hopefully before I die, Mick will shut and not slam a door,' Troyden murmured, his eyes returning to her face. 'I'm very glad to meet you, Eden. And I would very much like to welcome you into the family.'

Eden violently shook her head. She wasn't anywhere near that point. In fact, she was in a state of information overload, her mental CPU on the verge of frying. She needed time to process everything she'd heard.

She couldn't forget he was a close friend of the Bancrofts; Troyden was by far the biggest donor to their foundation, and she was the reason they were under investigation.

'I'm not sure I want to do that,' she told Troyden, mentally wincing at his obvious disappointment.

He nodded. 'It's a lot to take in and I won't pressure you.'

He paused and then continued, 'Why don't you spend some time with us, with me? Come down for weekends, for the occasional midweek supper. I'll get my driver to fetch you and take you back if necessary. We can eat earlier so that you get home at a decent time.' Jesus, a chauffeur, that would be new. 'Would that suit or does your job require you to work late? What *do* you do, by the way?'

Ah, crap. The question she didn't want to answer. 'Actually, I'm between projects at the moment.' That wasn't a lie: she *was* between projects, and she had no boss to answer to. 'I'm taking the summer off, actually.'

A smile curved Troyden's lips. 'Oh, *excellent*. Then why don't you relocate here, to Elmsleigh, for the summer? We can get to know each other, and at the end of the summer, you can decide whether you want to stick around.'

A part of her wanted to. She wanted to spend time with this kind and gentle, maybe even sweet, man. But what if he wasn't? What if she came to stay, not for the summer – that was too drastic a step – and he changed his mind? What if he wanted her around now, but got tired of her hanging around and rejected her? What if she came to care for him and he decided that she wasn't good enough to be acknowledged, to be a permanent part of his family? What if she was found lacking?

And God, he was so wealthy, beyond anything she'd experienced before. His house was filled with priceless objects – Ming vases, for God's sake! – and exquisitely decorated. His shirt, while it looked old, was designer; he wore a fancy watch, and she knew, after an ill-fated Google search, that the designer trainers on his feet cost more than her monthly rent!

Her entire flat could fit into this study! Well, nearly.

There were a million reasons why she didn't belong in his world – most of them in his bank account – but she blurted out the first one that came to mind. 'I'm allergic to horses, and you love them.' As if to punctuate her statement, she released a huge sneeze, and her eyes filled with water.

'Oh, dear, that's a deal-breaker.'

Disappointment pinned her heart to her ribcage. Right, okay. Eden reached for her bag and looped it over her shoulder, about to stand up and leave. She wouldn't cry in front of him. She refused to show that much emotion.

'Okay, sorry to have wasted your time.'

Surprise jumped into his eyes and settled on his face. He followed her to her feet and stepped forward, stopping her by laying a hand on her arm. 'Eden, hold on. Did you think I was being serious?'

Of course, she did. It made sense, after all. He was horse mad – his whole family seemed to be – and her being allergic to horses was a good reason not to have her around. Why would he want the hassle of worrying about her?

'Good grief, Eden, you're going to have to learn to recognise sarcasm and dry humour if you're going to survive in this family,' he muttered. He pushed his hand through his hair, his lips thinning. 'Of course, you being allergic to horses isn't a problem. I was just being facetious.'

'So my allergy isn't a problem?' she clarified, confusion making her head pound.

'No, of course not. You'll avoid the stables and horses, and if you want to see an allergy specialist, I'll pay for it. In the meantime, we'll all just shower when we come in from the stables, so you don't have to be exposed to more dander than necessary.'

How easy he made it sound! 'You'd do that for me?'

'It's not that big an ask, Eden,' Troyden told her, squeezing her arm before letting his hand drop.

'Now, my dear, I think you need to be on your way.' Before she could respond, he lifted his hand. 'I'm not kicking you out, but I think you need a little time to think about what I said. If you want to have nothing more to do with me, I'll be disappointed but I'll understand. If you want us to meet over lunch in London, we can do that too. Spend a few weeks here, every weekend, or move in for the summer, whatever works for you.'

Eden appreciated him understanding that she felt overwhelmed, that she needed time and space. 'Thank you. I'll let you know. I can message you through the DNA site.'

Troyden picked up a simple white card from a silver card holder on his desk and handed it over. On it, plainly printed, was his mobile phone number and email address. She took it and sent him an uncertain look. 'Shall I give you a missed call, so you can have my number on your phone?'

'Yes, please,' Troyden calmly replied. A few seconds later, his phone buzzed. 'That's me,' she stated. *Lame*. She was out of processing power, and he was right: she needed time and space. To not only decide what she wanted from Troyden, but also figure out – if she did decide to embark on a relationship with her uncle – how she was going to handle her red-hot, skin-blistering attraction to his stepson.

Arrgh! Why did her life always have to be so bloody messy?

Troyden walked over to her, dropped a quick kiss on her cheek and squeezed her hand. 'Don't look so worried, Eden. Our meeting is a good thing. Trust me on this.'

She tried to nod, conscious that she hadn't told him

everything. The secrets she was keeping – her career, and her connection to the Bancrofts, their investigation – hovered in the air for a split second before she shoved them down again. Troyden didn't need to know, not right now. If and when she decided on whether to have a relationship with him or not, she'd broach the subject.

Until then there was no point in adding fuel to an already raging fire.

Chapter Five

It took Eden five days to make her way back to Elmsleigh House. She'd spent a hefty amount of time thinking about Troyden's offer to get to know him and his family, veering between deciding to go and then questioning her decision. Yes, she was worried about how she'd contribute to the Castle clan, how to go about creating new ties, and whether she'd bond with her uncle, who might, ultimately, end up rejecting her.

But she also, sod it, *desperately* wanted to see Jed again. It was humiliating to admit, even to herself, that she lay awake at night in her shoebox flat thinking about him. She'd even taken to spending an unhealthy amount of time plugging his name into search engines to pull up photos of him.

She'd just, just, managed to stop herself from printing an image of him off the 'net.

Despite exchanging numerous text messages with Mick – that had started with Mick checking on her and swiftly moved on to them bonding over K-culture discussions, their mutual love of junk food and having crazy mothers – she knew that staying in London, keeping her distance and her head down, was the smart option, the safe option. Eventually, when she'd just about managed to push her searing attraction to Jed aside, she finally admitted it: she wanted to get to know her uncle better.

Not because he was a billionaire, or because he lived in a fantastic house on a fantastic estate, but because she saw humour in his eyes and kindness in his smile. His stepkids clearly adored him; it said a lot about him that they were all still in his life when their mothers had moved on. And she knew that neither Mick, Alistair or Jed were there because they were mooching off him or using him to further their careers. Over the last few days she'd done her research: Alistair had a kick-ass double degree from LSE and had held a high-pressure job as an investment banker before switching over to work as Troyden's finance guy. She was pretty sure he could get a job anywhere.

Mick was a GP, and if the local messaging boards were anything to go by, the clear favourite in the village. And Jed was one of the best polo players in the country. Any professional team in the world, from Argentina to Hong Kong, would pay him great money to play for them. He was also the face of quite a few horse- and polo-related products, and likely earned decent money from those sponsorships.

No, they stayed because they loved Troyden. And that told her he was, on some level, a good guy. Why wouldn't she want to get to know an uncle who was by all accounts a decent man and the only family she had left in the world?

However, it was really important not to make this more than it was. If they got along, she would, maybe, be invited to family Sunday lunches, to birthday parties and to spend Christmas with them. That would be enough. It was far more than she had now.

She'd already planned to backpack this summer, she wanted to explore Croatia, so she wouldn't spend too much time at Elmsleigh. She didn't want to take advantage of Troyden's hospitality, and decided that she'd initially stay for ten days and reevaluate afterwards. She'd see how Troyden and his family reacted to having her around. If there were any signs of her being unwelcome, she'd return to London and book her flights. She wasn't going to stay where she wasn't wanted.

Arriving in the village of Bythesea late yesterday evening, she'd skirted the village and quickly covered the final two miles to Elmsleigh House. Mick, excited to have her back, tagged along when Troyden gave her a tour of the manor house, and she was offered the same suite she'd occupied earlier. Then she'd enjoyed an early dinner with Troyden, Diana, Mick and her kids, eating at the huge wooden table in the kitchen. The dining room, apparently, was only used on Sundays, for either family breakfasts or lunches. The rest of the time, depending on who was around, Diana told her, they ate in the kitchen.

Diana, forthright and no-nonsense, scared her a little.

During the meal, as if knowing that she needed time to settle in, nobody peppered her with questions about her life, work and job. Soon after they'd finished eating, Diana excused herself to watch reruns of the Great British Bake Off, and Mick hauled her sleepy kids off to bed. Troyden said he had some business to take care of in the study and gently suggested she could either watch TV in the snug, turn in early or take a walk.

Eden, feeling overwhelmed, opted to go upstairs and wallow in the enormous slipper bath in her en suite for a while. She'd tried to read, but the combination of a fantastic beef wellington, a few glasses of red wine and a hearty helping of chocolate mousse, home-made from dark cocoa, had sent her into a food coma. At a little after nine, she climbed into the huge bed and passed out.

It was now just gone half six in the morning and she knew she wouldn't be able to get back to sleep. After pulling the heavy curtains apart, she opened the window and rested her forearms on the sill, sucking in the aromas of jasmine and honeysuckle, freshly mowed grass and the faint smell of manure. The sound of a rumbling tractor buzzed in the distance and the sun pierced a bright blue sky. She sneezed twice, a reminder to take her daily antihistamine pill. If that didn't help her allergy to horses, she might have to see a specialist, something she wasn't keen to do.

The OTC medications would work, she was sure of it. That and staying away from horses and stables, of course. And hot guys who hung around horses and stables.

Pulling on a pair of leggings and a shirt, she tied her trainers and pulled her unbrushed hair through the gap at the back of her cap. She splashed water on her face and brushed her teeth, thinking she'd take a run through the grounds. She wasn't great at running, but if last night was a preview of the meals Diana served, she needed to exercise or she'd be blue-whale plump in a month.

The house felt like it was still dozing when she skipped down the stairs, and Troyden's motley pack of dogs, all rescues and a mixture of breeds, barely deigned to raise their heads as she tiptoed past their beds in the kitchen. She slipped out of the kitchen door, shut it behind her and lifted her arms, feeling the muscles in her back warm as she stretched. She did a couple of lacklustre lunges, before setting off on a slow jog.

Her body immediately started protesting and Eden forced one foot in front of the other, jogging down a path that ran along a high wall.

She heard low voices coming from the other side of the wall, and stopped when she recognised Mick's voice and a deep male rumble that ignited fireworks on her skin. Jed. She ran a little further ahead to an open door leading to the walled garden.

'You need to tighten your core, Mick,' Jed said, his words now distinguishable.

'I am tightening my sodding core,' Mick muttered, sounding huffy.

'If you did, you could hold that pose for longer,' Jed countered.

'Why are you always picking on me?'

Fascinated, Eden peeked through the door, her eyes widening as she took in the four squares of perfectly manicured grass within the walls and the luscious fruit and vegetable beds lining three walls of the garden. Three people, including her uncle and Diana, were using the wall as a brace to perform a forearm headstand, their toes pointed to the sky. Two men, a young girl and Mick stood on mats across the lawn, their arms and legs extended, trying to hold what she thought might be – from her on-off forays into yoga – a warrior two pose. Mick dropped her outstretched leg and arms and sunk onto her mat, her face pink, hair stuck to her face. She didn't look like she was having any fun.

Eden didn't blame her; yoga was *hard*.

The group evidently had various skill levels, from impressive, Troyden and Diana and Justin, to competent, like the two muscled guys and the blond teenager with good balance. And then there was Mick, who looked like she'd rather be lancing a boil on someone's bum.

But Eden's eyes were drawn to Jed, barefoot and dressed in a pair of sweatpants elasticised at the ankles and hanging low on his sculpted hips. He was bare-chested and his back muscles rippled as he elegantly and expertly flipped into a handstand. Eden sucked in a hard breath as those muscles bunched and lengthened. With all the control of a world-class gymnast, he held himself steady and slowly, so slowly, bent his left leg and extended his right over his head. Eden never expected an alpha polo player to be able to do yoga poses with such ease, but her jaw dropped open when he bent his right leg and lifted his head toward his toes. Then his left leg mirrored his right, his toes just a few inches from his messy air, as he contorted his body into a circle.

'What do you call that?' Mick demanded, sounding cross.

'Scorpion pose,' Jed replied. 'And shh, you're not supposed to talk, jabber jaws. Yoga is supposed to be meditative.'

'Solving the Middle East crisis would be easier than

getting Mick to shut up,' one of the men said, as he lowered his leg and shifted to place his forehead against his knees.

'Funny, Kit,' Mick muttered. She sighed, looked around the walled garden and caught sight of Eden. With an excited whoop, she jumped to her feet and ran over to her.

'Eden!'

Eden kept her eyes on Mick, while training her peripheral vision on Jed, who'd started to wobble. Instead of unfurling slowly from his complicated pose – show-off! – he flung his leg back, misjudged where he was and kicked the edge of a hip-high blue and green flower pot. It toppled sideways and hit the hard tiles on which it stood. The pot cracked and soil spilt out onto the tiles, and the ornamental topiary bush lost its lollypop head. It was a horticultural blood bath.

Whoomph! Eden sucked in some air as Mick collided with her in an over-exuberant hug that rocked her from side to side. Uh, they'd seen each other last night! Eden patted her shoulder – when was she going to let go? Over her shoulder, Eden watched Jed climb to his feet, scowling down at the broken pot. Troyden and Diana placed their feet on the floor in perfect synchronicity, and everyone but Mick looked at the shattered pot.

'Fuck,' Jed muttered, pushing back his hair. 'Shit, shit, shit.'

'That was only a hand-fired, hand-thrown pot from one of the foremost Japanese potters in the world, son,' Troyden said, his tone mild.

'Never mind the pot, it took the gardener five years to get the topiary into that exact shape,' Diana stated, hands on her hips. 'I'd practise extreme avoidance for the next year, Jed.'

Eden looked around for the scary gardener, expecting to see a grizzled old man with a pitchfork. Mick nudged her with her elbow. 'Jo is our gardener, and this walled garden is her pride and joy. She lobbied for three years to get Troyden to buy those pots, and she will be furious to see one in pieces. She might also ban us from doing yoga here now, after it took Troyden weeks to persuade her that we wouldn't do any damage.'

'But doesn't she work for Troyden?' she asked, puzzled by the employer/employee dynamic.

'None of the staff work for Troyden,' Mick said, her eyes laughing, putting air quotes around the word work. 'Jo is one of the best gardeners in the UK and Troyden gives her a free hand, as well as a cottage on the estate, a huge salary and all the time off she needs to consult on heritage gardens around the UK. Troyden doesn't like formal gardens, so she doesn't even have that much to do, hence her dedication to this walled garden. Troyden poached Diana off a billionaire; she studied at Le Cordon Bleu in Paris and worked as a sous chef at three Michelin-star restaurants. They allow him the privilege of paying them.'

'I heard that!' Diana told her.

'I know!' Mick said gaily. 'Jed, look! Eden's back.'

Jed's amber eyes slammed into hers. 'Yeah, I got that, Michaela. Your screech of welcome caused me to lose my balance.'

'Bullshit!' Mick shot back. 'If you can keep your balance on a thousand-pound horse going fifty miles an hour while the crowds roar, my shouting wouldn't cause you to tip over. No, I think it's—'

'Shut up, Mick,' Jed growled, cutting her off. His eyes glittered and the tips of his ears reddened. Eden lifted her eyebrows. Was Jed *embarrassed*? Because he'd broken the pot, or because her presence caused him to falter? Hell, she wasn't feeling too steady on her feet either. And, dear God, she wished he'd put a shirt on! Any moment now, she might start drooling, and that was never attractive.

Mick grabbed her arm and pulled her toward the broken flowerpot. Damn, it did look expensive.

Jed finally pulled his eyes off her and looked at his stepfather. 'I'll buy you another one,' he said, rubbing the back of his neck and not sounding at all convinced. 'If I can afford it, and if I can find one.'

'You can't and you won't,' Diana crisply told him, jamming her finger into his bicep. His big, tanned and gorgeous bicep. The bicep she wanted to sink her teeth into. Oh, boy, hot panties. Eden looked down at her trainers, wishing for a breeze to cool her suddenly red cheeks.

'Best emigrate now to some place where Jo can't find you,' Diana added.

Eden reached the edge of the group, Mick's hand still on her arm. Judging by his flinty stare, Jed didn't share Mick's enthusiasm at her reappearance. And why did she have to make it sound like she was relocating to the area? Nothing could be further from the truth. It was a trial, for a week or so. She'd even, when she called to accept Troyden's invitation, asked him not to reveal that she was his niece so she could make a clean getaway if she needed to. Although disappointed, Troyden had agreed.

'I'm just visiting for a little while, Mick,' Eden explained, not wanting Jed to think that she was moving in permanently. 'Maybe ten days, or two weeks.'

Jed's eyes narrowed, and he looked at his stepfather, obviously surprised. Troyden seemed to hear his unspoken question. 'I haven't had a moment to tell you, Alistair and Justin, Jed, but Eden is here as my guest.'

Jed's eyes met hers and every muscle and micro-muscle in his body tightened. 'You met him ten days ago and you're already moving into the house,' he drawled. Oh, his words weren't offensive, but his tone was. What was his probl—

Oh. Did he think she had the hots for Troyden? Oh, come on!

Shit, he *did*.

She wanted to reassure him that she wanted nothing more than to get to know her uncle – she certainly wasn't looking for his money – and winced at how that might sound without adding some context. Then she remembered that Elmsleigh wasn't his and that Troyden had invited her to stay. And if Yummy Yogi didn't like it then he could just downward dog lump it.

'Oh, stop being a tosser, Jed,' Mick cheerfully retorted. 'Ignore him, Eden, he's a grump if his yoga gets interrupted. And it's his fault he ended up on his arse, because he's a show-off.'

'I did not end up on my arse; I was startled when a banshee yelled in my ear,' Jed grumbled.

Mick waved his words away. 'Eden, meet Kit and Mateo, they are polo players on the Castle Kings team, along with Grumpy Guts here.'

Grumpy Guts had a glorious six-pack Eden was trying not to look at. Swallowing, she held out her hand for the men to shake, taking in their easy looks and rangy bodies. Kit was tall, blond and Australian, while Mateo was from Argentina, all dark hair and dark eyes with a dimple that flashed when he smiled. They were classically, undeniably attractive. But when they shook hands, she didn't feel a spark of attraction. What she did do was sneeze. And sneeze again.

Mick pulled her behind her and scowled at the polo players. 'Did you swing past the stables before you got here?' she asked.

Kit and Mateo exchanged WTF looks and shrugged. 'Since we're polo players and we have a fondness for the ponies we ride, that's our normal routine,' Kit told her, folding his arms and narrowing his eyes. 'I didn't realise we had to get permission from you, princess.'

'That's Dr Princess to you,' Mick snapped back, hands on her hips. 'And Eden is allergic to horses, that's why I asked—'

'Demanded. In a snotty tone,' Kit countered.

Jed gripped the bridge of his nose. 'Enough, for the love of Christ,' he snapped. 'Can you two stop griping at each other for one second?'

Mick raised dark eyebrows and her shoulders. 'No.'

'Probably not,' Kit added at the same time.

Jed muttered a 'for fuck's sake' under his breath.

Troyden, shaking his head, stepped in. 'Eden, meet Daisy, she's our head groom—'

'No, don't shake her hand!' Mick slapped her

outstretched hand away. 'You've got to keep your distance from anyone who has been in contact with horses.'

Right, she didn't seem to be able to remember that. But surely shaking hands couldn't affect her that badly? Then she sneezed and sneezed again. Mick threw her hands up in the air. 'I'm researching how to desensitise you,' she told Eden.

'Um … why?'

'Because you are my patient and my friend! And I look after both.'

Wow, okay. Judging by Mick's ferocious expression, she apparently had a friend, whether she wanted one or not. And it felt good.

'Well, I haven't been anywhere near a horse,' Justin stated. 'I met you the other day at breakfast, but you won't remember me. I'm Justin, married to Alistair, Troyden's eldest.'

Eden smiled, liking his thin, intellectual face and the hint of mischief she saw in his eyes. 'I remember. Hi, again.'

Jed who seemed to, finally, remember he was shirtless, walked over to a mat in the middle of the others and scooped up a black t-shirt. He pulled it over his head.

Sadness.

But his actions allowed Eden to take in her first full breath since she poked her head into the garden. Breathing was rather nice. It was ridiculous that two-day-old stubble on a masculine jaw, cat's eyes, and a muscular torso could affect her speech, vision, breathing and make her synapses misfire. Maybe she was allergic to him, rather than horses.

Mick threaded her arm through hers and Eden had to

stop herself from flinching in surprise. She wasn't used to physical affection and wondered if it would be rude to pull away. Unsure, she simply stood there, as stiff as a rake.

'Guess there's no point in carrying on with yoga now,' Jed said, bending down to pick up his mat.

Mick jerked Jed's towel from his loose grip, then wiped her face while he rolled his eyes. 'Why do you have to do that? You're a smart woman, so why can't you remember to bring a towel?'

Mick shrugged, unrepentant. 'Because it's far more fun to annoy you by using yours,' she retorted tossing it back to him. She bunched her mat under her arm, and Eden took it from her and rolled it up.

Troyden patted his face with his towel. Diana simply lifted her t-shirt, flashed her ample stomach and wiped the sheen of sweat from her forehead with its hem. 'I made cinnamon rolls last night,' she announced. 'If anyone wants coffee and rolls, come up in fifteen minutes.' She pointed at Kit and Mateo. 'You too, and shower before you come up.'

'Working around her horse allergies is going to be a pain in the arse,' Jed muttered, loud enough for her to hear.

His words were the equivalent of a knife grazing her stomach. It shouldn't sting, but it did. 'Jed,' Troyden said, his warning unmistakable.

'We're a horsey family, Troyden. It's what we *do*,' Jed countered.

'Well, for as long as Eden is here, or until she gets a handle on her allergies, we are going to be horse people who wash before entering the main house,' Troyden told him. 'I don't think that's a lot to ask, is it, Jedson?'

Eden noticed Jed's quick grimace at the use of his full name, then he met his stepfather's eyes. 'If that's what you want,' he said, shrugging.

'That's what I want,' Troyden replied, his tone mild.

Jed shoved his feet into flip-flops. No one, she realised, carried phones, and she wondered who'd banned them from morning yoga. Probably Jed, control freak.

The group started to disperse, but Eden lingered on, wanting to explore more of this extraordinary space, filled with abundant flower beds and regimented rows of vegetables.

She'd tried to grow herbs in pots in her flat, but they always died, as did the indoor plants she'd bought and babied. She was a plant's kiss of death and was in awe of anyone who could plant and maintain such a riotous space.

'I'm going to look around,' she asked Diana. 'Is that ok?'

The housekeeper nodded. 'Just don't pick anything, or else Jo will lose it,' she told her. 'See you back home in fifteen.' She looked, momentarily, horrified. 'You're not allergic to gluten or carbs or anything like that, are you?'

No, carbs were her spirit animal, as she told Diana, not bothering to remind her that she'd eaten two helpings of her beef wellington last night. 'I eat everything,' she assured her. She came from a house where money had been tight, so her mum hadn't let anyone be picky about food.

'Excellent. My cinnamon rolls are yum,' Diana assured Eden, and she didn't doubt her statement for a second. But she would have to go for a long run later.

She noticed Jed look at her, shake his head and drop to his haunches to make a pile of broken pot shards. Eden twisted her lips and scowled at his back. She wanted to grab him by his cotton t-shirt, stand up on her tiptoes and yell that she wasn't a gold-digger, that she just wanted to get to know her uncle, the only family she had. That she wasn't a threat to any inheritance he might receive down the line.

That he could trust her...

Except he couldn't. Her shoulders slumped. She was, after all, the one keeping secrets. She hadn't told Troyden what she did for a living, or that she was involved in a situation that might blow up in her face when the truth came out. Even if she wanted to tell Troyden the Bancrofts were in legal peril, she couldn't. The police had made it clear that if she leaked anything about the investigation, even that there was an investigation, she'd be charged with obstruction of justice.

When Mr Shit met Mr Fan, and given the circles the Bancrofts moved in, there was a good chance their arrest would make headlines. She'd get caught up in it too. And, although she'd deleted her social media accounts, taken her profile off the Bancroft Foundation's website and tried to erase every trace of herself from the internet, it wouldn't matter.

She'd still be outed as the whistle-blower. Would the Castle clan let her explain? Would they understand why she had to go to the police? And how would it affect her standing within the family? Badly, she was sure.

Because the adage was true: last in, first out.

Suddenly everyone was gone, leaving her alone with Jed, who was bent over, resting his forehead on his knees, his eyes closed.

Was he praying for patience? It seemed highly likely.

He lifted his head, straightened, and his eyes slammed

into hers, and Eden took half a step back. His hard stare pinned her feet to the ground, cynicism drifted through his eyes, and suspicion settled on his face. Jed wasn't a guy you wanted to get on the wrong side of.

And somehow she'd done exactly that.

Chapter Six

It wasn't even half-seven yet and Jed had already had a crappy day.

He'd destroyed a pot that he probably wouldn't be able to replace, and even if he found one, he *probably* wouldn't be able to afford it.

He might've also pulled a muscle in his back when he inelegantly fumbled his exit from the Scorpion pose, something he'd only recently mastered. And he'd scraped the side of his foot on a shard of the broken pot when he stood. And before all that, he'd spent another hour cyber-stalking – no other word for it – Eden Ennis.

It worried the hell out of him that a woman in her late twenties had no social media footprint. It made him wonder what she was hiding, who she was and, most of all, why she was at Elmsleigh House. He didn't trust her. He didn't trust anyone new who made a concerted effort to get close to Troyden.

But worst of all Eden unsettled him. Even looking at her

made him feel itchy and restless; he was just too damn aware of her. And that was a problem. Because no matter how much he wanted her, protecting Troyden came first.

And nothing – especially not a woman with secrets in her eyes – was going to get in the way of that. After checking on the ponies, making sure that the grooms were doing their job – they may be the best in the business but the ponies were valuable so he felt justified checking in – Jed walked back up to the house, wondering how many times he'd made this walk before. A thousand? Five thousand? Ten? He could do it in his sleep, backwards, and blind drunk.

He might live in, and love, his cottage, but Elmsleigh House was home. With its big beds and huge wardrobes, pantries and attics, it had been the best place to grow up. He and his sibs had enjoyed their version of bowling in the long gallery, playing hide and seek, and those hot summer nights when he, Kael and Mick would drop a rope made from bedsheets out of his window to run off to the stables for a midnight bareback ride, followed by a swim in the pond.

He'd lost his virginity in the first stall in the stable on the right, had his first blow job in the tack room. He'd recovered from chicken pox, pneumonia, a broken leg, a broken elbow and a dislocated shoulder in the library and media room, fussed over by Diana.

He'd bonded with his stepsiblings over the kitchen table, as they'd watched Troyden's bizarre search for love and the woman of his dreams. Troyden's love life was a real-life version of a soapie. Two more wives followed his mum out the door, and after divorce number five, Troyden stopped proposing. Thank God.

When it came to love, Troyden could be idealistic and a little naïve. It was a terrible combination and one that allowed predatory women to take advantage of him. Now he had to add Eden to the list.

He could see why she'd caught Troyden's eye. She had an air of vulnerability, an attractive, innate grace. With her reddish-gold hair and changeable eyes, she wasn't blow-your-head-off stunning, but she was someone you looked at twice, and then a few more times. With copper-coloured freckles on her nose and cheeks, the deep dent in her lower lip, and those thick dark eyelashes, hers was a face that a man could look into for a very long time and still find interesting…

Despite spending the last week running through a list of 'what ifs' – what if he'd got her number, what if he'd taken her to dinner, what if she wasn't allergic to horses – Jed had to remember she was just another pretty package queuing up to become the next Mrs Castle.

God, he was so tired of doing this, of giving warnings and playing the bad cop. But he was the family protector, and he wouldn't stop now. He couldn't. It was what he did.

Jed turned the corner of the house and saw movement in the back entertainment area overlooking the stables. Eden sat on the edge of a wooden Adirondack chair, her hands between her thighs, looking young, lost and a little desolate. His heart flung itself against his ribcage. He didn't want to do this, not today and definitely not with her.

He leaned back against the stone wall, warmed by the

morning sun, and took a moment to take her in. The sunlight picked up the hints of copper in her hair, and he finally understood the allusion to old pennies. Lycra leggings clung to her slim legs, and her once expensive trainer had a tiny hole in the left big toe. Her t-shirt fell over her gorgeous breasts and round hips. But her shoulders were hunched, and he couldn't stop thinking she looked ready to bolt.

Just rip the plaster off, Harris. Make it quick, make it as painless as possible.

'Having second thoughts about hooking up with an older guy?' he asked, noticing his tone was more wary than scary.

Her head shot up and her eyes slammed into his. 'What?'

'He's wealthy, very fit and looks twenty years younger than he is. But you should know that he falls asleep while watching the news, has to take Viagra, and loathes clubs and big parties. He's a Star Wars and Second World War history buff and will bore you rigid with deep-dive descriptions of the campaigns in Africa and descriptions of Tatooine. He's crazy about horses and you are allergic to them—'

As if to highlight his point, she sneezed. He sighed. 'You're going to be sneezing a lot more if you hang around him, because trying to keep Troyden away from the stables is like trying to keep a meth addict off the pipe. You'd better up those antihistamines, sweetheart.'

'What are you talking about?' she asked, sitting up, a scowl pulling her eyebrows together.

'I'm talking about you. And Troyden.' He linked hands.

'Together.' He folded his arms across his chest. He was getting too old for this shit.

He nailed her with a hard look. 'Let me tell you how this is going to go: you and Troyden will hook up, and, in a week or two, you'll tell him your bank card isn't working, or that your ex scammed you out of your savings. You'll bat your eyes, maybe cry a little, and he'll offer to help you out of your jam. The week after that, you'll be in London and you'll suggest a walk down Bond Street. When you walk past Gucci or Jimmy Choo, you'll stop to admire a pair of shoes in the window and you'll tell him it's your longest dream to own a pair of shoes like that, or a bag, or a bracelet. He'll buy it for you.'

Those copper-tinged eyebrows lifted and her eyes turned bluer. 'Generous of him.'

He sighed. That was the problem. 'Very. But you'll push for too much, too quickly, and he'll dig in his heels. Or you won't dig at all, and he'll be suspicious. Either way, he'll be bored of you in six to eight weeks, maybe in two to three months.'

'Wow, you're cynical,' she breathed.

The hand on her heart was a nice touch but he wasn't fooled. 'Sweetheart, I've seen this scenario play out a few times. I'm telling you; he's not worth your time or energy.'

'Your concern for me is touching,' she muttered, her sarcasm as sharp as a scalpel blade. The look she gave him made his balls shrivel up, just a little.

'Mm, I've never owned a pair of Jimmy Choo shoes or a Gucci bag, or any diamonds, at all. So if I play my cards right, I can get him to pay for them?'

Her lack of self-respect was a sharp, acid-tipped knife.

Why did he feel more disappointed than usual? He'd spent thirty minutes, even less, with her. Nothing about her made sense. He gripped the bridge of his nose, pushing down hard. He needed to get this done and leave. 'Just know that if you steal from him, we will press charges. And don't bother trying to sell any pictures of the house or Troyden, he has an arrangement with the tabloids that he will buy the photos for double what they offer you. It's a waste of your time.'

She tipped her head to the side. 'Good to know,' she murmured. 'I'm learning so much this morning.'

Despite the yoga session, the headache he'd woken up with had yet to dissipate, and he needed a handful of paracetamols. He'd delivered the warning speech, what she did now was up to her. And Troyden, he supposed. But God, he hoped she was a flash in the pan rather than a long-term fascination. He couldn't cope with seeing her across the breakfast table, fresh from his stepfather's bed. *Ugh*, was that bile on his tongue?

Eden stood and handed him a flat smile. She held her index finger in the air. 'Would you give me one moment? I'll be back in a minute...' She looked behind her and scrunched up her nose, a completely adorable gesture. No, *fuck*, nothing about this, or her, was adorable. 'It might take a few more minutes because the house is big. But stay right here, okay?'

He frowned at her, sensing heat behind her too-chirpy tone. Something was off, but he couldn't put his finger on it. Before he could tell her to stop wasting his time, to assure her that she had nothing to say that he wanted to hear, she slipped through the French doors into the summer sunroom. He lost sight of her when she walked into the hallway.

He glanced at his watch. He had stuff to do, for God's sake. After breakfast, he planned to put a new pony through its paces. Then he was joining Kit, Mateo and the rest of the team in the state-of-the-art gym in the basement of Elmsleigh House for their trainer to assess their fitness. Later this afternoon, they'd do stick and ball training.

The season was fast approaching, and he fully intended his team to be the top-ranked British polo team. It was up to him to make that happen because anything less was unacceptable.

A bumble bee buzzed over his hand and the smell of the wild roses in the bed below drifted past his nose. He inhaled deeply. Summer was just around the corner and soon he'd be immersed in the fast-paced game. Polo meant sore muscles and injuries, suntanned skin, and charging across fields on an ultra-responsive pony that enjoyed the game as much as he did. God, he loved it. But he didn't know how much longer he could compete at this level. At thirty-five, he was getting on, and his muscles ached more than they used to.

The thought of life without polo used to scare the shit out of him, but not so much now, not anymore. He'd played for his country for years, had made a ton of money off the sport and had lifted trophies all across the globe. No, retirement didn't bother him anymore, especially if he could spend more time in his workshop, with the odd trip to buy horses for Troyden, or coaching the newbies and playing the odd match for fun.

Maybe this season, or maybe the next, would be his last...

He heard the sound of footsteps, looked into the pretty, feminine sunroom, and watched Troyden and Eden move toward him, a cinnamon bun in Troyden's hand. Over her head, his eyes met Jed's and he saw the 'what's this about?' question on his face. Jed simply raised one shoulder and Troyden continued to eat his pastry.

When Troyden stepped outside, Eden slapped her fists on her hips and lifted her slightly pointy, utterly stubborn chin. 'Please tell this cretin why I am here, Troyden,' she asked with excruciating politeness and a heap of 'fuck you'.

Where was she going with this?

Troyden swallowed his last bite, dusted his hands and slid his hands into the pockets of his linen trousers. 'Are you sure about that?' he asked Eden, frowning. 'When I invited you to move in, you said you didn't want anyone to know.'

She sent him a hot glare. 'Oh, that was because I never imagined I would be mistaken for a gold-digger,' she said, her voice tight.

'Ah, damn. I didn't think about that.' Troyden glanced at him and Jed caught the amusement in his eyes. Oh, Troyden was enjoying himself immensely. Jed loved him, but he could, on occasion, be an arsehole.

'Just tell him, Troyden,' Eden stated, annoyed.

'Eden is my niece, my brother's daughter.'

What?

'I uploaded my DNA onto a genealogical website that connects long-lost family members,' Troyden explained. 'Eden was my only hit.'

Jed rubbed his jaw, struggling to make sense of his words. Eden wasn't Troyden's lover or girlfriend?

No, this had to be bullshit. His deeply cynical outlook reasserted itself and he decided this was too good to be true. 'And I presume you've done additional tests to make sure she is who she says she is?' he demanded, unconvinced by Troyden's blithe explanation. 'Surely you're not just going to take the website's word for it, *her* word for it?'

'Hey!' Eden protested.

'It's a reputable site,' Troyden calmly replied. 'But because I'm not a total idiot, I did ask for additional testing. An independent lab confirmed we are related.' Troyden touched Eden's shoulder. 'But I didn't need the tests. As soon as I saw her, I knew: she looks just like my younger brother.'

Jed recalled the photograph of the Castle brothers in Troyden's study. If he looked past their different eyes and colouring, he could see the subtle resemblance between Eden and Troyden. It was in their smile, the way they both lifted their chin when pissed. He closed his eyes and dropped his head. Right ... *fuck*.

Troyden had a niece? A blood relative? And he couldn't help feeling hurt – juvenile, but still – that Troyden had been looking for more family. Weren't he, Mick, Kael and Alistair enough? Was blood really that important? It hadn't been to the Duke...

'So, I'll take that apology now.'

Jed blinked at the steel-hard voice and opened his eyes to see Eden tapping her foot. He wasn't the type of guy who took orders, so he simply looked at her. It was galling to admit that, in her position, he'd demand an apology too. But that didn't mean one would easily roll off his tongue.

'You accused me of being a gold-digger.' Her words held all the outrage of a Victorian maiden who'd been asked to join a threesome. In his defence, there was precedent and he hadn't conjured the possibility out of the ether.

He jerked his head in Troyden's direction. 'He keeps bringing them home. I try to scare them away. Some run; some stay.'

Eden looked at Troyden. 'Is that true?' she demanded.

He shrugged, not fazed. 'I'm afraid so. I'm an eternal optimist, and I'm looking for love.'

'Maybe start looking for love with someone a little more your age, for a change, and you might have some luck.'

Troyden simply grinned. 'I only seem to meet younger-than-me women.'

'No, they approach you and your ego likes them fawning over you,' Jed snapped.

Eden looked outraged. 'Don't talk to him like that! He deserves some respect from you.'

Oh, he respected the hell out of Troyden, and loved him as much as his stunted and battered heart could, but Jed and his other sibs saw Troyden clearly. And they weren't the type of family that pulled their punches. They called it straight, every single time. Eden would have to get used to that if she wanted to find a place for herself within their ranks.

But Jed had no intention of letting her claim any ground. Ever. At all. Partly because he was stupidly attracted to her; partly because he was smart enough to know that just because she was Troyden's niece didn't mean she wasn't standing here looking for a payout, or a way to leverage the situation to her advantage, lay her hands on her uncle's cash, and write herself into the will.

Outrage in the face of being pegged as a gold-digger was a clever move, but that didn't mean she wasn't still trying to scam Troyden. Instead of using the girlfriend card, she could now use the '*I'm your only blood family, please spoil me*' card. Knowing Troyden, he'd crumble like a wave-doused sandcastle.

God, he was a suspicious bastard. But that didn't mean he was wrong.

'I couldn't find you on social media.'

She jerked, just enough to deepen his suspicions.

'Is that a crime?'

Her reply was quiet and calm, but he sensed her irritation. 'You're elusive,' he pushed, wanting to see her crack. 'Who are you really? What are you hiding?'

'Why do you care? And who appointed you as Elmsleigh's interrogator?'

Most women would be sounding pissed right now, a bit screechy. But Eden simply held his hard stare, refusing to back down. He was taller, bigger, fiercer, but she didn't seem intimidated. And hell, he liked that about her.

Dammit.

As long as she kept standing in front of him, looking mutinous, he'd push for more. 'Where do you live? Do you have other family? What do you do for work?'

Eden looked at Troyden who simply shook his head. 'Jed is mule-stubborn and as persistent as hell,' he said, his deep sigh lifting his shoulders. 'I'd tell him to stop hassling you but he's not going to listen to me. Just ignore him.'

'I would if he'd get out of my face,' Eden muttered. She bunched her fists and placed them on her hips. 'Do you want me to send you a copy of my CV?'

He didn't hesitate. 'Yes, I would.'

'I was being sarcastic, you berk!' Finally, a tiny crack, a hitch in her voice.

'I'm not.'

'I'm not sending you my CV!' Eden half-shouted. 'I didn't even give it to Troyden.'

Why not? Jed's narrowed eyes flickered to Troyden, who was dusting sugar off his shirt. 'For the record, I think that's a mistake.'

'For the record, noted,' Troyden replied.

Eden snapped her fingers and Jed returned his attention to her. Impatience flickered in her eyes.

'I'm still waiting.' For what? When he lifted his eyebrows, she waved her finger between his chest and hers. 'My apology.'

Not happening. 'Then you're going to be standing here for a while, *sweetheart*.'

Anger flashed in her eyes, and they turned an icy blue. 'I am not, and never will be, your sweetheart!'

Her words slashed through him, and Jed swallowed, conscious of the regret crashing over his head. Why did he feel disappointed at her rejoinder? Why did her words cut through layers of cynicism and distrust to slice into his soul? He didn't allow a woman's compliments to turn his head, and on the rare occasion he pissed someone off – usually because he couldn't or wouldn't commit to anything longer than a one-night stand – he ignored the bitchy comments and complaints.

But Eden's words, a trite phrase said in anger, slashed and burned.

Luckily, he was saved from responding by the sound of a deep-throated engine in the distance. He turned and lifted his hand to block off the glare of the sun, not recognising the matt-black, top-of-the-range Range Rover powering its way up the long drive. He looked at Troyden. 'Expecting someone?'

Troyden shook his head. 'No. I don't recognise the car. Do you?'

Jed pushed his hands into the back pockets of his jeans, watching as the car disappeared from view, heading for the front of the house. The engine cut, probably in front of the double staircase leading up to the imposing front door. The visitor was a stranger. Friends used the kitchen door to access the house.

They heard the distant peal of the old doorbell. Diana would open the door and question the visitor. In five minutes, she'd have the reason for his unannounced visit, his life history and possibly his bank account details. Diana's grandmother was French, in the Resistance, and had passed her not-impressed-by-anything-or-anyone attitude on to her granddaughter.

The last person he expected to follow Di into the sunroom and onto the deck was Henry, the Baby Duke. His half-brother.

His mouth went dry, and a red mist appeared in front of his eyes.

'What the fuck does he want?' he demanded, keeping his eyes on Diana.

Diana shrugged, not in the least intimidated by his muted roar.

'He said he wanted to see you, that it was important. He wouldn't leave until you spoke,' Diana replied, her words laced with asperity. '*He* is also your neighbour, the new Duke of Bythesea, and his father died recently.'

Shit. Shit. Fuck. Shit.

Jed pushed a hand through his hair and looked at Eden, her eyes filled with curiosity. As were Di's. They were both wondering why he was making a big deal out of a neighbour's visit, and why he was acting like a jerk. And that was precisely why Henry had rocked up at Elmsleigh and not at his cottage. At his cottage, he would've told him to fuck off and slammed the door in his face.

He glanced at Troyden, who sent him a sympathetic look. But then lifted his head in a gesture suggesting he find out what his unacknowledged half-brother wanted. As Troyden always said, knowledge was power.

But…

Fuck.

He'd failed at finding anything on Eden, had his yoga session interrupted, broken a one-of-a-kind pot, sparred with Eden, then was caught off guard because Eden was Troyden's niece and not his lover. Now his half-brother was here wanting to speak to him for some unimaginable reason. His day was already a shitstorm and he'd yet to eat breakfast. But, as his mother once told him, when you were walking through hell, your only choice was to keep walking. Or running. Standing still and allowing the flames to consume you was never a reasonable option.

Eden surprised him by stepping forward and holding

her hand out to Henry. 'Hi, I'm Eden Ennis, a friend of the family.'

So she still wanted to keep her and Troyden's connection a secret.

Henry's appreciative eyes slid over Eden, and he held on to her hand for a few seconds too long. He was a guy and Jed knew Henry found Eden as attractive as he did. Closing his eyes, Jed imagined his fist connecting with Henry's aristocratic nose.

Seeing him on his arse would make his day. Year.

'Henry Raynott.' Huh, he'd expected him to add his title and that he owned half of Gloucestershire, but Henry did neither. He and Eden exchanged a flirty smile, and Jed ground his teeth so hard he was sure he tasted enamel. He bunched his fists, fighting the urge to stand in front of Eden, to be the barrier Henry had to break through to get to her.

There were a couple of things Jed knew for sure: his biological father was a prick, the earth was round, and Henry was *not* going to get Eden.

'It's nice to meet you, Eden. How long are you staying in Bythesea?'

The dude had a freakin' village named after his family, for the love of God. How ridiculous was that? Jed ignored the rogue thought that, had the Duke acknowledged him, he would be part of that fucked-up family. Thank God he wasn't.

Eden smiled at Henry, and Jed was in imminent danger of cracking a tooth. 'I'm not sure.'

'Well, maybe we could go for a drink or a cup of coffee? I could show you around,' Henry offered. Jed looked at Troyden, who lifted his eyebrows. He was hitting on

Troyden's guest on Troyden's property. He had to admit the guy had balls. Balls he wanted to ram up his throat, but still…

Right, he was done. As Eden opened her mouth to respond, he stepped in front of her, met Henry's eyes and scowled at him. 'Let's walk.'

Henry nodded and sidestepped him to smile at Eden. Prick. 'I'm sure I'll see you soon, Eden.'

Not if he could help it. 'If you want to talk to me, you'd better get moving,' Jed called over his shoulder, stalking away. Henry's footsteps behind him assured him he was following, and Jed released the air he was holding. He'd walk him back to his fancy-arse car so that Henry could get back into his vehicle and leave. There was nothing to say. Never would be.

He'd had no contact with their father, and he could live without having any interactions with the Baby Duke. Blood wasn't, as far as he was concerned, thicker than water.

Eden watched Jed walk away, his broad back and shoulders stiff with tension. Man, he could rock a pair of Levi's. The way the denim highlighted his spectacular arse should be declared dangerous. But great looks and shitty attitude aside, beneath the tough guy exterior, he was flustered. His face was also a few shades lighter than it had been earlier.

Under the anger, he'd looked blindsided and a little scared. So, who was the *GQ* model who'd managed to rattle the normally unflappable Jed? Dressed in navy chinos and an untucked, white shirt with the sleeves rolled up, and wearing trendy trainers without socks, Henry looked ready for brunch at a bistro in Notting Hill.

But she was more curious about Jed's reaction to him than about the man himself.

Why did a man who'd just called her a gold-digger, who implied that she was using Troyden, intrigue her? Eden rubbed the back of her neck as she watched the two men disappear around the side of the house.

While she didn't like the assumptions he'd made and the conclusions Jed had reached about her, she *did* like the fact that he was loyal and protective of those he loved. She'd experienced so little of that in her life, and even though he'd insulted her, family loyalty was a deeply attractive trait.

What would it feel like to have a man like that, hard and strong, mentally and physically, to choose you? To have him standing in your corner, prepared to put himself between you and a threat?

Sighing, she turned to face Troyden. 'Who's the Henry Cavill lookalike?'

'That's another Henry, the new Duke of Bythesea. His estate is to the west, and his father died about ten days ago.'

'I recall a discussion about his funeral at breakfast.'

Troyden rocked on his heels. 'I attended the church service; Jed did not.'

A note of exasperation in his voice caught her attention. 'Was he expected to?'

Troyden's eyes skittered off her face. 'I believe that funeral services are deeply personal events. If you want to go, you go. If not, don't. The occasion is for the living, not the dead.'

It was an answer, but it had nothing to do with what she'd asked. It didn't matter what Jed did or didn't do; it was none of her business. What *was* her business was how people saw her and Troyden's relationship. Her hands landed on her hips again. 'I cannot believe that he thought we were lovers, and that I was after your money!'

Troyden pulled a face.

Eden narrowed her eyes. 'This is the part where you tell me he erroneously misjudged the situation.'

Troyden sat down on the arm of the nearest chair and stretched out his legs. In the sunlight, his hair was more grey than blond, and the deep grooves bracketing his mouth and the fine lines radiating from his eyes looked deeper than before. 'To be fair, I've been dating much younger women for a while now. Quite a few of them like the fact that I am rich more than they liked me.'

Ah. Eden dragged the toe of her trainer along the edge of a slate tile. 'You know what Einstein said, right?'

'Remind me?'

'The definition of stupid is doing the same thing over and over and expecting a different result.' She closed her eyes as she turned and stretched her arms into the air, enjoying the warm sun on her arms and back. 'Maybe you *should* start looking for companionship somewhere else.'

Troyden's faded blue eyes met hers, amused. 'My kids have been telling me that for years, but it's yet to sink in.' His expression turned serious. 'I'm sorry for what he said.'

'I don't care what he thinks,' she said, ending her sharp statement with a huff.

'No, of course, you don't, that's why you stomped into

the kitchen and dragged me out here, steam coming out of your ears.'

Ack. She couldn't argue the point. 'I dislike being labelled a gold-digger,' she told him in a cold voice.

'Naturally. A few women I dated had the same reaction, and two dumped me because Jed had "*the chat*" with them.'

'The one where he tells them the best they can hope for is a Gucci bag, Jimmy Choo shoes or a diamond tennis bracelet?'

'Ah, you got it too.' Troyden pulled a face. 'I've asked him not to interfere, but Jed is a protector. He says that if a woman is scared off by him, then she's not worth keeping anyway.'

Eden reluctantly admitted Jed had a point. She hoped that if she was into a guy and believed in him, nothing anyone else said or did would make her leave him. Not that she had any experience in sticking and staying – she was too much of an emotional coward to date, never mind forge a relationship with a man.

'You seem to have very good relationships with your stepkids,' she commented.

'I was a terrible husband to their mums – I tend to get bored too easily – but I was a damn good stepfather.'

'Did you bribe them with horses and overseas holidays? The latest iPhones and Xboxes?'

Troyden tipped his head to the side. 'Actually, I never spoiled them with money. I married Alistair's mother before I made any. Both Jed and Mick initially approved of me marrying their mothers because, well, because, manipulative cretins that they both were, they thought I'd buy their approval with worthless crap. I refused to do that.'

'Then how did you win them over?' Eden asked, intrigued.

'I was retired by the time I married Jed's mum, and I gave them what they most needed, time and attention. I taught Jed to ride and helped him with his homework. We did science experiments in the shed together. I attended every parents' meeting, picked him up and dropped him from and to boarding school every weekend. I drove, because being in a car with a kid, someplace where they can't run away, gave us a chance to talk.' He shrugged, a small smile on his face. 'It seemed to work, and after his mum died, he asked whether he could come live with me.

'I did the same for Mick, then Kael,' he continued, seemingly caught up in his memories. Right, she remembered there was another brother out there somewhere. 'Somehow, I managed to keep being their dad after I divorced their mums.'

She liked Troyden more than she expected to, and hearing about his life was fascinating. 'Why did you marry their mothers?'

Troyden linked his hands around his knee. 'Ah, probably because I had to chase them harder than I did all the others. They made me work for their affection.'

'And after you got it, you didn't value it anymore?'

'You're not wrong,' Troyden winced. 'They fell in love, and I fell out of it.' He stared off into the distance. 'I'm not proud of my actions, Eden; I don't want you thinking that. I played with their affections, and that was wrong. But I love love— No, that's wrong, I love *falling* in love. When the heady feeling dissipates, I find myself looking around for the next high.'

He was so very honest, and she appreciated his openness. Her mum was a closed vault, and she was never allowed to peek inside her mind and had no idea how it worked. She was so private that Eden hadn't understood how important religion was to her until she'd joined a convent as a novice nun. Her switch from the secular to the sacred a few months after Eden had turned eighteen upended her life. Up until then, her life had been a second-hand, but still complete, puzzle, a little ragged, a little faded, but the picture was clear. Her mum joining the convent flipped the table, scattering pieces in every direction. Lin taking a vow of silence was the equivalent of taking those puzzle pieces, dousing them with petrol and setting them alight.

'I'm a terrible partner, but I'm a reasonably good dad.' Troyden commented. 'I'm grateful to all my wives for the gift of their children.'

Eden rubbed her fingertips across her forehead. 'Your family is pretty complicated.'

'Are you still deciding whether you want to be a part of it?' Troyden gently asked. 'Because taking me on means taking *them* on, I'm afraid.'

She couldn't help her little wince. 'I don't have any experience of families, Troyden.'

'So? I didn't have any experience with kids, but I married four women who had them,' he countered.

She tipped her head. 'Were the kids an added incentive?'

Troyden's eyebrows shot up, and his surprise made her wonder if he'd ever been asked that question before.

'I've never thought about it that way before,' he replied, slowly parsing his words. 'I was never interested in babies, so maybe marrying women with kids was my way to be some kind of father. I don't know. I'm going to have to think about that some more.'

Eden played with the hem of her t-shirt and lifted her eyes, taking in the ivy-covered walls above her and the edges of the tiled roof. Elmsleigh House was different from anything she'd experienced before, and this family was so very different from hers, if she and her mum even qualified as a family.

There was love here, tinged with frustration, protectiveness and a small measure of crazy. Did she want to be part of it, or would she feel more comfortable going back to her independent, emotionally insulated life? It was safer and easy to navigate, and her actions wouldn't affect anyone else. But it was, she admitted, lonely. Isolating.

'You need to decide whether you are going to tell the rest of the family that you are my niece or not, Eden.'

Her gaze landed back on Troyden's face. 'I assumed Jed would tell them the minute he got a chance.'

'That's not who Jed is. It's your story; he won't tell it for you.'

Ah, okay. 'Do you want me to?' she asked.

'I don't like keeping secrets from them,' Troyden admitted. 'We've always had an open and honest relationship. And that's why they feel they can butt into my love life.'

After a beat, he added, 'But ultimately, the decision is yours.'

She nodded and thanked him, surprised by how

tempted she was to walk into the kitchen and make the announcement. But she wasn't an impulsive person. She needed to give it more thought, and work out the consequences. 'I'm going to think about it,' she told him.

Troyden surprised her when he stood up, placed a hand on her shoulder and kissed her temple. 'You do that, Eden. Whatever you decide, I'm very glad you're here.'

Eden felt the lump grow in her throat, the prickle of tears, the heat in her skin. It was both weird and wonderful to feel wanted, to be welcomed. To feel like your presence was necessary and needed. It was strange and lovely...

And so very, very confusing.

Chapter Seven

They reached Henry's car and Jed scowled. *Why the hell was he here?*

Henry smirked. 'I heard Troyden had a pretty guest and I wanted to see for myself.'

Jed clenched his fists. Bythesea ran on gossip, but Eden had only arrived last night. Even for professionals, it was too soon for the village grapevine to swing into action. No, Eden wasn't why Henry was here.

'Who is she? And is she single?' Henry pushed. 'Are you interested?'

Jed's jaw tightened. 'Would it stop you?'

Henry laughed. 'Of course not. It'd just make it more fun.' This was classic Henry: poking, pushing, needling like he had since they were kids.

Now, after a fifteen-year break, he was picking up right where he'd left off.

Arsehole.

But an observant one. He'd clocked Jed's reaction to

Eden and noticed the way Jed had bristled when Henry's gaze had lingered on her legs, her chest, her face.

Jed shoved his clenched fists into the back pockets of his jeans. *You're not ten or sixteen. You can't punch him.* But damn, he wanted to. Mostly because he didn't feel as indifferent as he wanted to be. A part of him, tiny but annoying, kept looking for similarities, a connection. And he hated that. His family, the one he'd worked so hard to be a part of, was solid. It was also complete. There wasn't any room for half-brothers or new people – Eden included – making waves.

Henry rocked back on his heels, arms crossed. His expression shifted, unreadable. 'You didn't come to the funeral,' he commented, his tone bland.

Henry had noticed his absence. Why? 'Why would I?'

'He was your father.'

'Bullshit. The Duke and I had no relationship. Eighteen cheques a year didn't make him a father.'

'Fair point.' Henry exhaled. 'Yeah, he was a bastard. A deeply unlikeable man.'

Well … *shit*. Those weren't words he'd ever expected the Baby Duke to utter. 'I still don't know why you're here.'

Henry hesitated. 'I've moved back to Bythesea Hall.'

Marvellous. 'So?'

'I'll be around. At the pub, in the village.' He hesitated a beat. 'I thought we could have a beer sometime, maybe get to know each other.'

Jed blinked as the words settled and burned. 'Where the hell did that come from?'

'I've thought about it for a long time.' Henry ran a hand through his hair. 'I considered approaching you a couple of years ago, but the Duke would've lost his shit. Now that he's dead, what does it matter?'

Oh, so now it was convenient? Now he wanted to play at being brothers?

Jed's eyes narrowed to slits. 'Let's recap, dickhead. I punched you when we were ten because you were a smug little knob. You ran crying to Daddy. The rest of the summer, and the summers after that, you and your posh friends made my life hell. Three years later, you showed up at my not-that-fancy boarding school instead of Eton. You spent the next few years undermining me at every turn. And now you think we're going to grab a pint and bond?'

Henry winced. 'Look, I admit I was a shit—'

'Damn right.' Jed cut him off. 'To be clear, I have a family. Two brothers, a sister, and a father. I don't need an entitled arse like you in my life.'

To his credit, though Jed loathed to give him any, Henry didn't flinch. He just nodded, his face unreadable.

Jed turned to leave, then stopped. 'And if you so much as hint that I'm the Duke's son to anybody, I'll kick your balls so far up your body you'll taste them.'

Now that was a solid exit line.

The *fuck* he was going to let Henry into his life.

Thinking back to that conversation earlier, Jed pushed down on his stirrups, lifted his butt out of the saddle and swung his mallet at the ball. There was nothing more satisfying than the thwack of a stick connecting. It scooted across the empty field, and Padmé, one of his less experienced beasts – and one of the most excitable – tensed, and he leaned forward to pat her neck. After a long time away from the polo field, he needed to get all the horses, his players and himself, back into the rhythm of the game.

The practice match had been a good start but they all needed more work. Standing in his saddle, Jed turned to look over the rest of the huge field and saw Mateo and Kit, and their fourth member, Kimba, putting their horses through the same routine. Thwack, chase, tap chase, all practising back swings, near side swings, tail shots and offside swings.

He turned back to make a series of taps with the ball, half-standing in the saddle. He was fighting to keep Padmé at a steady canter, as she was keen to storm across the field like her tail was on fire.

Jed missed the ball, cursed a blue streak and turned Padmé to canter back in position. He never missed and was annoyed by the small slip-up.

And because his teammates were bastards, they noticed. 'We saw that,' Kit yelled. Jed raised his middle finger, put his back to them and took his frustration out on the ball, sending it rolling to the far end of the field.

Jed sighed, thinking that he'd run out of energy to chase it. But because he was a professional, he kicked his heels into Padmé's side and galloped down the field, turning his head to look at the stables. He saw the flash of red-gold hair, and long legs emerging from a pair of ragged denim shorts. *Eden.*

Troyden's *niece*.

He slumped in his seat and allowed Padmé to slow down, slowly transitioning from a canter to a trot, then to a walk. He was sweaty, horsey, pissed off and exhausted. He pushed his helmet back and wiped the sweat from his forehead with the back of his wrist.

How the hell was he supposed to work with all these distractions? Henry, Eden, what else was life going to throw at him today?

He'd never expected Henry to stroll into his life and suggest whatever the hell he'd suggested, just like he'd never expected to see Eden again. He especially hadn't anticipated his reaction to Eden would be more intense than before, and that every time he laid eyes on her his heart would become a loud bass drum in his ears, his blood would turn warm in his veins, his IQ would drop and his skin would prickle.

The last rational part of him suggested that he owed her an apology for assuming she was Troyden's newest girlfriend. But because he was pissed off, tired, feeling emotionally battered and nowhere near able to be bloody rational about anything, he pushed the annoying thought away.

He watched her hips sway as she walked, the way her hair went from gold to red to rust, deepening as the sun's rays hit it. He slumped in the saddle knowing that he needed to get a handle on his attraction. He rarely, if ever, gave a woman this much mental energy. Yes, she was gorgeous, and yes, he wanted to take her to bed but...

But something about her niggled at him – he was damn sure she was hiding something.

The way she dropped into Troyden's life, and his, was suspicious. Not five-alarm fire suspicious, but enough to make him feel uneasy. And her not wanting to give him her CV? Red flag.

Realistically, everyone had something to hide; nobody showed the world all their cards. He certainly didn't. So why was he having such a hard time accepting she had secrets, facets of her personality he wasn't privy to? And why was he so incredibly … what was the word…? Fascinated? Aware? A little obsessed?

He didn't recognise himself. And he sure as hell didn't like it.

A week and a bit later, after breakfast, Eden walked out of the kitchen into the courtyard to find Troyden in the centre of his pack of unruly mutts, having his face licked by various canines of mixed parentage. He looked up at her and grinned.

'I'm taking them on a long walk, do you want to join me?'

She'd joined Troyden for a walk the day before yesterday and her body still ached from the three-hour 'stroll'. Admittedly, it had been lovely to spend concentrated time with her uncle, delving into the history on her father's side. Luckily, because she'd spent most of the three hours panting because of the fast pace he set, she'd waved any personal questions away or gave one-word answers.

Troyden, because he was a true gent, didn't push her to talk about herself.

'I'm going to pass, thanks,' she told him, smiling when a

grey and brown lurcher mix pushed his long snout into her hand. She stroked his wiry head. 'But I'll walk with you as far as the polo fields, if that's okay.'

Troyden lightly touched her shoulder. 'Spending time with you is always okay, Eden.'

Troyden seemed genuinely happy to have her here, living at Elmsleigh. Since she arrived, they'd fallen into an easy companionship, sharing meals and opinions, comfortable in their occasional silences. For the first time, she felt truly at home. Over the last week or so, she'd explored the area with Troyden, accompanied him to London twice, and spent a few mornings curled up in the window seat of his study while he worked.

Troyden had Alistair – huge and not much of a conversationalist – and lovely Justin over to dinner one night, and a few days later, Mick and her kids had joined them. While she'd seen him in the distance, she hadn't run into Jed.

That was fine with Eden. She was here to get to know her uncle, not be distracted by a sexy, incredibly annoying polo player. But it was time for her to go travelling, to move on.

She fell into step with Troyden, the dogs scattering. 'You looked suddenly sombre,' Troyden commented, adjusting the cap on his head. Today he wore chino shorts, expensive hiking boots and a Jimi Hendrix t-shirt.

It was time to have an uncomfortable conversation. 'I've had a lovely time here, but—'

Troyden stopped abruptly to stare at her. 'You're not leaving?' he asked, horrified.

She winced. 'I think I should,' she replied. 'You need to

get back to your life.' She managed a small smile. 'You also need to start socialising again, looking for the next Ms Wrong.'

Troyden pulled a face. 'I'm not going to lie, but my life has been remarkably peaceful lately without one.' He narrowed his eyes at her. 'Do not tell my kids that!'

Eden grinned. 'I won't.' She wrinkled her nose, wondering how to tell him that she was moving on before she got too comfortable, before this felt too much like home. If she settled in here, if she came to rely on Troyden, on the friendship she was building with Mick, and was made to leave – the Bancroft saga was a sword hanging over her head – she'd set herself up to be emotionally eviscerated. She needed to protect herself by distancing herself from Elmsleigh House and its residents.

'My ten days are up, and I was planning to explore Croatia,' she said. Her enthusiasm to do that was not overflowing. 'I'm thinking about… I'm leaving tomorrow.' That sounded convincing. Not.

Troyden briefly squeezed her shoulder. 'Do whatever you want to do, Eden. You're always welcome here, I hope you know that.'

Troyden, somehow, knew what to say to make her feel most at ease, so Eden nodded her thanks, and uncharacteristically for her, slipped her hand through the crook of his elbow as they walked to the practice field.

Elmsleigh would always be here… That was a lovely thought. But after the Bancroft scandal broke, after Troyden and the clan discovered that she was the one who blew up their friends' lives, would she be welcomed back? She doubted it.

No, it was better that she left. Her two weeks here was a step out of time, a lovely sojourn away from her normal, too-solitary life. But it wasn't real, and it definitely wasn't sustainable.

Troyden veered off and Eden jammed her hands in the back pockets of her jeans, enjoying the sun on her bare shoulders. She should've put sunblock on and knew she would curse her new freckles in the morning. But she didn't care enough to turn back and make the trek back up to her second-floor suite.

'Eden!'

While Troyden walked in the opposite direction, Eden watched Mick emerge from a small wood, behind which she knew were the cottages where Troyden's stepchildren lived. She smiled as she took in Mick's kids; Liam was dressed in gum boots, swim shorts and had a cape hanging from his neck. He also wore dark, wraparound sunglasses. Gemma, wearing shorts and a t-shirt, carefully cradled a tiny marmalade-coloured kitten to her chest.

They reached her and Eden immediately bent to scratch the too-cute kitten behind its tiny ears. 'Oh, he's gorgeous, Gemma. Or is it a she?'

'We have no idea,' Mick cheerfully replied.

'Aren't you a doctor?' Eden asked, amused. Mick, once again, wore ripped denim cut-offs, another oversized men's shirt knotted at her waist, and her feet shoved into battered leather flip-flops.

'I'm a human doctor and can tell the difference between a penis and a vulva. Kitten bits are a bit more complicated,' Mick explained, taking a sip from her travel cup. 'To be fair, I could work it out but it's low on my list of things to do.'

Mick was busy, so Eden understood why it would be. Eden looked at her travel cup, and sighed. 'I wish I'd thought to bring a cup of coffee on my walk,' Eden said, sending it a wistful look.

'Coffee?' Mick hooted. 'I'm a single mum, it's past five and it's wine time. Chardonnay, darling.'

Okay, then.

They started to walk down the road to the paddocks, with Liam running ahead pretending he was a superhero and Gemma carrying her precious cargo. 'Actually,' Mick said, sliding her arm through Eden's, 'I'm so glad I ran into you. I was going to come up to the house later to check on you, but thought I'd let the kids run off some energy. It's been a week for them. And me.'

Eden knew there had been an outbreak of a stomach flu, and that both kids had been sick for twenty-four hours. Mick had been run off her feet dealing with her kids and the sick villagers. Mick lifted her mug to her mouth and then offered it to Eden. 'Have a slug, you look like you need it.'

Eden lifted the mug to her mouth and then hesitated. 'Any chance of me catching the stomach bug?'

'Doubt it,' Mick replied. 'We were all sick a couple of days ago. Viruses are pansy-ass weaklings; they generally die off quite quickly.'

She was the doctor, so Eden took a healthy glug of the wine, enjoying the way it slid over her tongue and down her throat. 'How's your allergy?' Mick asked.

Eden shrugged. 'It seems to be okay. I think the daily antihistamine is working. I haven't been to the stables, but I've been going down to the practice field to see how I do in the open air around horses.'

And yeah, she also wanted to see Jed. He was a cynical jerk, but she could still admire the very sexy package that made up the man. There was nothing wrong with a little window shopping. She had no intention of trying him on for size or taking him home.

Eden heard her phone buzz, pulled it out and looked at the message. It was from Troyden.

> Eden, love, am heading back to the house, I think I've picked up that stomach virus that's going around. Do you mind an evening on your own?

Mick, who had no concept of privacy, peered at her phone. 'Dammit!'

She pulled her phone out of her back pocket and phoned her dad. Eden listened to her side of the conversation: Troyden didn't have a fever, he didn't think, but was nauseous and had stomach cramps, and felt very, very tired. After telling him that she'd check on him in a little while, Mick disconnected the call and wrinkled her nose.

'He'll be fine in twenty-four hours,' she said. 'Listen, it's Di's night off so come for supper. We're having lasagna, super relaxed, super informal.'

'I don't want to intrude…'

Oh, she so did, because she didn't want to spend her last night at Elmsleigh on her own. Weird, because being alone was something she excelled at.

'It's lasagna, Eden, not a business meeting.'

'Okay, that sounds lovely. Can I bring something?'

'Maybe a bottle of red?' Mick suggested. 'And for God's sake, don't buy one, nick one from the wine cellar. The cheap, supposed-to-be-drunk bottles are on the left. Troyden's precious bottles, supposed to be kept until he is ten minutes from dead, are on the right.'

Right. No, left, the cheap bottles were on the left. 'Are you sure he wouldn't mind?' Eden asked.

'He'd be annoyed if you didn't,' Mick told her, sounding cheerful. 'Come up at about six, the second to last cottage on the left.'

Wait, wasn't her cottage the second on the left? Isn't that what she said the first night they met? 'I thought your cottage—'

'Gem, you're holding your kitten too tightly,' Mick interrupted her. 'She looks a little hot and bothered.'

Since the kitten was fast asleep, neither she nor Gemma knew what Mick was going on about.

'Mum, chill,' Gemma retorted as they approached the long field where four riders, including Jed, all dressed in jodhpurs, knee pads and a variety of shirts, cantered up and down the field, swinging their mallets and hitting a ball. She followed Mick to the pole fence and watched as she elegantly climbed to sit on the top rail. How she did it one-handed, Eden didn't know. Eden followed her up, far less gracefully, and took the kitten Gemma handed to her. It was still asleep, and she stroked its nose with one finger.

'He seems to like you.'

The deep, growly voice created fireworks on her skin, and Eden looked up to see Jed sitting on a cocoa-coloured pony, his big hands holding the reins lightly. Beneath his helmet, his hair was damp with sweat and light stubble covered his cheeks and jaw. His honey-coloured eyes glowed between sooty eyelashes and against his tanned face. He smelled of horses and hay and sunshine...

Eden released a sneeze that started in her toes and rocketed up out of her body. Another one chased it, and she sneezed again, louder than before.

The kitten raised its head, gave her a filthy look for being disturbed and dug its tiny, but sharp claws into her skin. *Ouch.*

'Antihistamines not working then?' Jed asked, his deep voice rolling over her. She narrowed her eyes at his smug tone.

'Maybe I'm not allergic to horses; maybe I'm allergic to you,' she shot back, blinking her watering eyes.

'I've never had that effect on a woman before,' Jed replied.

'I'm sure that's what the first man who passed on syphilis said as well.' Eden took the crumpled tissue Mick offered her and, with the fleeting hope it was clean, wiped her nose. She waved her hand at Jed and his pretty horse, who seemed to be doing the salsa. 'Can you please back up a bit?'

Jed and the horse pulled back a yard or two and Eden drew in a deep breath. She looked down at her arms, didn't see any spots and realised that her eyes weren't watery. The pills were working. Damn that she was allergic to horses, as she would like nothing more than to stroke that velvety head, to rest her forehead against that dark, rich neck.

The pony's or Jed's? Either would be good.

God, what was wrong with her? Why was she thinking of Jed as someone she'd like to get to know up close and very personal? He had a smart mouth and was as annoying as a persistent mosquito, but he had the body of an athlete, muscular and graceful.

She was just reacting as any normal woman would when a good-looking specimen crossed her path. Females of every species wanted to give their offspring good, strong genes so it made sense that pretty boys – *men*! – turned heads.

It was nature, and impossible to fight.

But she could look and keep her hands firmly in check. Window shop but not walk into the store. Look, but not touch. *Okay, you've made your point, Eden. Enough now. And do start acting like the grown woman you profess yourself to be.*

'You still haven't apologised,' Eden told him, scowling at him. She might not have seen him for a while, but his accusation that she was a gold-digger still rankled.

'I'm sorry you were upset by that remark.'

That seemed too easy. She suspected that life, and women, were a little too easy for this man and he needed to work a little harder. Wait, hold on, that wasn't an actual apology. He wasn't sorry for what he said, but for how she felt.

'I thought I trained you better than that, Jedson,' Mick said, scooting up closer to Eden in a show of support. During a drinking session at the pub a few nights back, Eden had told Mick exactly who she was, and that Jed thought she was gold-digger. 'That was a half-arsed apology. Do better.'

Jed's eyes didn't leave her face. 'Stay out of this, Michaela.'

Mick hauled in a deep breath and Eden knew she was on the verge of blasting her brother. While she appreciated her support, she didn't want to be the reason Mick and Jed fought. 'It's okay, Mick,' she murmured, briefly squeezing her arm.

Mick huffed her displeasure. 'God, you're annoying. Not you, Eden. Jed.'

'Stay out of it, Mick,' Jed repeated, his words full of steel. Before she, or his sister, could reply, Jed nodded at the kitten. 'Cute. Where did you find him?' he asked.

Mick scowled at him. 'Don't BS me, Ugly. You know that Gem found it in a cardboard box on the doorstep this morning because you put it there!'

Jed lounged in his saddle, looking thoroughly at ease, like he'd spent his whole life in it. Which, in fairness, he probably had. 'I went to the village and heard it mewling. It was stuck between two bins and had lost its mum.'

After checking to see that the kids weren't watching, he pulled his thumb across his throat, silently telling them the mommy cat was dead.

'You should've asked me if the kids are ready for a kitten, whether *I'm* ready for a kitten. I'm a single mum working in a bloody busy practice, Jed, and I barely have time for all the shit I need to do, never mind adding a pet to look after.'

'Then you shouldn't have joined the organising committee for the charity polo match,' Jed replied, sounding unsympathetic.

'You volunteered me, you berk!' Mick yelled. She lifted her mug, and Eden knew she was thinking of throwing her wine-filled cup at his head.

He dug his heels into the pony's side and backed two steps away. 'Not that I think you would be able to hit me if you let fly,' he said, confirming her suspicions. 'But you might hit Padmé and that would piss me off.'

'I'd never hurt an animal!' Mick shouted. 'God, you're such an annoying shit!'

'Mum, do you want to go sit on the naughty step?' Liam demanded, lifting his chin and looking like a wizened old man. 'You're not allowed to yell, and you're not allowed to swear!'

'You owe us at least five pounds,' Gemma added, reaching up to take her kitten from Eden. She immediately felt the loss as the kitten settled into Gemma's neck. Eden knew the kids would start a world war if Mick tried to relocate the kitten.

Mick seemed to come to the same conclusion and sent Jed a look hot enough to burn through steel. 'I will get you back for this, you bastard!'

'That's six pounds.'

Jed smiled at his sister, his mouth curving up at the corners and showing a hint of a dimple deep in his left cheek. His smile was a punch to the stomach, a kick to the head. On seeing it, Eden felt wobbly and off balance, like the world had shifted off its axis, knocked off course. And with the disorientation came heat, lovely and liquid, sliding through her veins, burning a path to her womb and to her long-neglected lady parts.

This was attraction, deep and dangerous. She finally understood how men could be lured off the rocks by the siren call of mermaids, because, damn, when Jed Harris smiled like that, she'd follow him anywhere. And hoped that there was a bed on the way. Lots of beds.

Or walls.

Desks.

Hell, any flat surface would do.

'See you later, guys' Jed said, his big hand stroking Padmé's strong neck. Eden could not believe she was jealous of a horse. A horse that would make her sneeze and erupt in spots.

And because this was her crazy life, she released a series of explosive sneezes. When she stopped, seven or eight embarrassing seconds later, she raised her watering eyes to look at Jed. Damn, he was still there.

'I'll see you around, Sneezy.'

Great, now she had a nickname. She was vastly, ridiculously, stupidly, insanely attracted to a man who thought of her as one of Snow White's dwarves.

Excellent.

'It's a good thing I'm leaving tomorrow,' she muttered, watching him trot away.

'*What?*'

Oh, crap, she didn't mean to say that out loud. Right, now she needed to explain to Mick that her time at Elmsleigh House had come to an end. She'd tell her Croatia was calling, that she'd made plans and needed to stick to them.

She wouldn't tell her she was so, so tempted to stay and that given the smallest excuse, just might.

Jed checked on the lasagna he'd made earlier, from scratch – it was bubbling and looked and smelled great – and reached for the glass of wine standing next to the stove. He took a long sip. He enjoyed cooking, but he'd done enough so he had Mick making a green salad. Justin was spreading homemade garlic butter onto the inside slices of a ciabatta and Alistair, the unsociable bastard, was on his phone, checking something.

'Al, phones away at my dinner table, mate,' he said. Alistair, as he always did, ignored him. He could push the point, but Al would, in a minute, maybe two, pick up his phone again and immerse himself in whatever had captured his attention on the screen. His older brother was not social, and Justin had had to drag him to dinner tonight. But it was part of their deal: they'd stop nagging him to spend time with them if Al joined his siblings for dinner once a week.

Knowing it was a losing battle, Jed decided to leave him alone until they ate, then Justin would confiscate his phone. He hoped.

Kit and Mick were bickering – if there was a world championship for squabbling, those two would win it – and Justin and Mateo were discussing, of all things, the size of a pumpkin at last year's village fete. Jesus. Jed felt like he'd been rocketed to his life forty years from now, minus the Zimmer frames and the occasional signs of forgetfulness.

He slugged back more wine, leaned against the counter and crossed his long legs at the ankles. God, he loved evenings like this, even when the people closest to him acted like they were a hundred and ten. Nothing said family like a good meal around a dinner table, good wine, or hands wrapped around beer bottles.

He'd made quite a few pieces of furniture for his house – his huge bed, his glass and driftwood coffee table, the chairs on the deck – but the eight-seater square table in his overly large kitchen was his favourite. With a square table, no one felt left out, and everyone could contribute to the conversation. Everyone who sat at it wanted one just like it. He had bigger and more interesting pieces to make, but it was nice to know that if he ever ran short of cash – unlikely – he could make square tables and matching chairs. The money earned from them would keep him in red wine and good food.

Mick's head shot up at the sound of a shout coming from next door, and she cocked her head. Everyone looked at her, but she shook her head, completely calm.

'Don't you want to go check whether they are okay?' Kit asked.

'That's a frustrated scream, not an "I'm dying" scream,' Mick said with complete certainty. Mick always hired a babysitter, normally Daisy, their favourite groom, to look after the kids for their weekly sibs supper. She needed some time out, and to be able to swear without Gemma keeping score on how much she owed the family coffers. Jed was quite convinced Mick could pay off the national debt with what she owed in swearing fines.

'When Daisy starts yelling, that's when I run. And I told her that I'm not to be disturbed for anything less than a six-foot Swedish masseur or arterial bleeding.'

Jed smiled, enjoying his sister. He'd lucked out on keeping her when Troyden's marriage to Usha had fallen apart. They bickered like all siblings did, but he had her back, and she had his. Family. It was everything.

His only niggle, a small annoying thorn, was his guilt that Eden was sitting in the big house alone tonight because

Troyden was communing with the God of Porcelain. She wouldn't even have Diana for company because it was Zumba night at the village hall. The world could explode but Di would still rock up at the hall, addicted to her weekly dose of shaking her hips and twerking. He should've invited Eden to join them, but these dinners were his way to relax and Sneezy made him feel anything but chill.

Jed, remembering the way the sunlight had shot streaks of copper into her hair and lightened her beautiful eyes, shifted on his feet. Around her, he had to fight the urge to cover her mouth with his and take, and take, and take. He could see her naked, could easily imagine the freckles peppering her shoulders and chest, and her untouched-by-the-sun, creamy white skin. His nose still held the scent of her shampoo from when he'd carried her up to the house. He was in his thirties, but was reacting like a schoolboy hanging around his first crush. And damn, just thinking about her started a party in his pants, so he turned his back to the room to look into his eye-level oven. The lasagna looked as good as it did before, but if he was more flushed than he was before, he could blame it on the oven's heat.

He needed to get a grip. Or several grips. Immediately.

Or he needed to make a move on the bloody woman, talk her into bed and get her out of his fucking system so that he could go back to normal. Whatever normal was.

Jed gripped the bridge of his nose and closed his eyes. He had a polo team to whip into shape and a championship to win. He needed Eden like he needed a shot of ketamine injected straight into his heart. He didn't have time for this shit. He had even less inclination for complications, and

Eden was a complication on steroids. He didn't have time for a relationship, nor the energy to put in the required effort to make someone need him. Hell, he barely had time to keep Troyden in check. Though, to be fair, Troyden seemed to be taking a break from dating, or whatever it was called when a billionaire met a babe. Al had Justin; he struggled to keep track of Kael – his youngest brother wasn't great at keeping in touch – and he kept a close eye on Mick and her kids.

For some reason, he couldn't look at Eden and see one night of fun. He couldn't imagine easily letting her go … and that was why he had to keep his distance. She was a huge red flag, a massive complication. The sooner she left Elmsleigh, the better.

A rap on his front door made him lift his head and he frowned. It wasn't Daisy; she would've walked straight in the back door.

Mick dropped her knife and sent him a brilliant smile. He narrowed his eyes at her. What the hell was she up to now? 'Oh, by the way, I invited Eden to supper. There's always plenty and I hated the idea of her spending another night in the big house alone.'

His bloody sister. Seriously, one of these days he was going to…

Do something. What, he had no idea. But something. Bad.

Or, at the very least, uncomfortable.

Chapter Eight

Eden expected one of Mick's kids to answer the glossy back door, but when it swung open, Jed stood in the hallway, his dark hair mussed and stubble three days overdue a scrape.

He looked, dammit, yummy. Icy margarita on a steamy summer's day yummy...

A button-down shirt, sleeves rolled up his tanned forearms, skimmed his wide chest, and faded-from-wear Levi's hugged his narrow hips. He wore no shoes and, God, even his feet, wide and big, were sexy. Feet had never turned her on before – she didn't think she'd paid much attention to them before – but his...

Yeah, hot.

She was losing her mind. This man was the sexual equivalent of a fair's pendulum ride, rocking her from one axis point to another at warp speed. She'd come to Elmsleigh to connect with Troyden, not to add a layer of crazy to her life. But all she could do was look at him, take in his rugged face and bold eyes, and wish his arms were around her, that his mouth was on hers.

Later she would remember the front door slamming behind Jed, but wouldn't know who moved first, him or her, but one moment she was on her feet, the next she was off them, her aching breasts flattened against a hard, hot chest, the door behind her. She tasted wine on his lips and need on the tongue that swept into her open mouth. Her hands lifted and locked around his neck as colours consumed her. Her head spun and she lost her breath, literally, but who cared about something as inconsequential as breathing when Jed was kissing her? One hand cradled her cheek, the other lay across her lower back, pulling her against his hard-as-hell and bigger-than-she-imagined cock, and she wanted more. She wanted everything and anything he could give her.

The need to suck in some air became important so she pulled her mouth off his, hauled in a breath and caught the wild look in those dark amber eyes. He hesitated, searching her face. Knowing he was asking for her permission to continue, she nodded. But he didn't move so she tunnelled her fingers into his hair and yanked his head down so she could take what she needed.

Jed caught up and took control, feeding her an intense kiss, twice as addictive. He lifted her off her feet and he held her easily, taking her weight. In a move that felt both completely natural and intensely foreign – she'd never been consumed by a kiss like this before – she wound her legs around his lower back, crossed her ankles, one heel digging into him. Her beaded flip-flops dropped to the paving stones with a barely noticed clatter.

Jed continued to kiss her with single-minded intensity. His tongue wound around hers, pulling back to nibble her lips, and to drop a long, open-mouth kiss on her jaw. He pulled back an inch, giving himself just enough space to slide his hand between them, and he covered her breast with his big hand, his thumb swiping her already hard nipple into a stronger peak. His erection pushed against her mound, the heat and strength of him burning through the barrier of her lightweight summer dress, thin cotton panties and his jeans.

Their heat could power Siberia during a winter blizzard.

He returned to her mouth and lifted his other hand to hold the back of her head, lifting it to change the angle to kiss her deeper and harder. The weight of him kept her pinned in place against his front door, and his other hand dropped from her breast to skim up her thigh, to cup the edge of her exposed left cheek, his fingers sliding under the barrier of her panties to edge close to the juncture of her thighs. She squirmed, trying to move closer to his creeping fingers, needing him to finger her, wanting his finger inside her.

Wanting every inch of him, in the most biblical way possible…

'Fuck, you're so hot and so wet,' he muttered against her mouth.

'Touch me,' she whispered. 'I need you to.'

'Eden…'

His finger skimmed over her lips, flirted with her entrance and found her clit, and she arched her back, releasing a combination of a squeal and a hum as heat and power rolled through her, a staircase of need and light and sensation. Just a few more steps and she'd reach nirvana…

Then she started falling, but not because she was experiencing a happy ending. The door behind her back opened, someone shouted, 'HOLY SHIT!' and she felt the world spin. And then she was falling, with Jed underneath her. Her knee hit the stone hallway and her chest bounced off Jed's and her forehead connected with his nose. Droplets of blood arced through the air… Was it his or hers? A hot spike of pain ricocheted through her. And damn, yet again, she couldn't catch her breath. Not because she was overcome with lust and flying on the wings of passion, but because she'd had all the air knocked out of her when her chest slammed into his. Jesus and all his cherubs, the countryside was determined to kill her.

Splayed across Jed's wide chest, conscious of the cool evening air on her butt and the back of her legs, she couldn't find the energy to pull down her dress. She needed air to move, and she couldn't find any yet.

'Fuck, I think my nose is broken,' Jed muttered from somewhere beneath her. 'And which one of you nosy bastards opened the door?'

Mick's face appeared in front of hers, wavy and indistinct. 'Eden, are you okay?' she asked, sounding like she was at the end of the Channel Tunnel.

Eden opened her mouth, tried to talk, couldn't find air and shook her head. She knew she shouldn't panic, she wasn't dying, but damn, it felt like it.

'You're winded, sweetie, just relax and air will flow into your lungs,' Mick crooned, stroking her hair off her forehead.

Eden looked up. Behind Mick was Justin, and Kit and Mateo. Despite having no oxygen going to her brain, she noticed their eyes flickering to her butt. Justin looked concerned, and then Alistair, his skin and eyes as dark as night and his expression ferocious, walked into the hallway. He looked down at them, shook his head and, as if seeing a tangle of limbs on the hallway floor was a common occurrence, pulled his phone from his pocket and started to scroll.

'Do you think you can stand up, Eden?' Mick asked, finally pulling her skirt down. Awesome to not be flashing everyone.

Eden nodded and tried to move her legs. Unfortunately, due to her disorientation, her inability to tell which way was up, and the do-me-now hormones still coursing around her body, she lifted her knee straight into Jed's crotch. He released a screech that set off car alarms in London and stripped paint from walls.

Dear God, quite an overreaction from a man who had, as Troyden had told her, broken his collarbone twice, once on each side, dislocated his shoulder and broken an ankle. It was just her little knee in his crotch; it couldn't be *that* sore!

Jed's fingers, bloody from his nose bleed, left his face and cupped his balls, and he curled up into a foetal position. Eden took the hand Mick held out and climbed to her feet. When she caught the sympathy on the men's faces, even Alistair's, she winced. So maybe having a knee in your balls was agony…

She looked down at Jed, who was chanting a series of creative curses, at great volume and fluency. If she wasn't so embarrassed, she'd be fascinated and impressed. He'd yet, as far she could tell, to repeat himself.

Beyond uncomfortable, she looked around, her eyes widening. Mick's place was surprisingly tidy and quite masculine for a doctor with two wild kids. There were no toys, kids' books, homework, empty glasses or uneaten plates of food anywhere. This space looked adult and spare, filled with light and gorgeous furniture. The hallway ran into a lounge filled with leather couches, at the back of which was a kitchen and a stunning table. She wanted one just like it and instantly knew she could never afford it. There were no crayon pictures on the stainless-steel fridge and no marks from messy hands on its glinting surface.

This wasn't Mick's house.

And the huge artwork of polo ponies in motion, abstract but stunning, on the hall wall, suggested she was in Jed's house. The man she'd dry-humped against his front door before they even exchanged a hello.

Alistair looked up from his phone, jammed it into his suit pocket and walked over to Jed. He put his hands under his armpits and with one swift lift, had Jed on his feet. His head dropped down and blood droplets landed on his tiled floor.

'Shit, Alistair, you could've warned me,' Jed muttered, lifting his shirt to wipe the blood away from his nose. Eden swallowed at the trail of hair that arrowed down over his flat, ridged stomach into the low band of his Levis.

Still hot. Still embarrassed.

Alistair placed his enormous hand in the middle of Jed's back and pushed him in the direction of the kitchen.

'Stop being a wuss. I'm hungry and I think the lasagna is burning.'

Jed winced when Mick pushed a kitchen towel filled with ice against his snout. Shit. *Ow*. That hurt.

'Do you want an ice pack for your balls?' Mick asked, not letting up the pressure.

He narrowed his eyes at his sister, as he pulled the makeshift ice pack from her grip. She was enjoying his pain a bit too much. 'No, I do *not*.'

'I can get you one,' Mick insisted, her eyes dancing.

He grabbed her wrist and waited until he looked at her. Their eyes met, and when she swallowed and nodded, he knew that she'd received his silent message to can the teasing. Not only was it tiresome, but Eden's face was telephone-box red.

He put the ice pack on his empty plate, and released a frustrated sigh. He'd broken his nose before and knew it was dinged, not fractured, so he doubted he'd have a black eye in the morning. But, and pity he couldn't check, he *knew* he'd have blue-tinged balls. His tailbone was aching from being the first point of contact with the floor, but at least Eden had, mostly, landed on him, and not the other way around. If he hadn't turned as soon as he felt the door opening, thank God for his quick reflexes, his bulk would've flattened her.

Mick took her seat, dished up some lasagna and tucked in. Jed looked at the half-empty tray of food and hoped there would be some for him to eat later. But knowing his brother, and the rest of the savages, there probably wouldn't be. Eden had yet to serve herself, but she'd slammed down a whisky and was now making her way through a huge glass of red wine.

As if feeling his eyes on hers, she lifted her head, and in those colours of the sea, he saw remorse and a metric ton of embarrassment. These were his people, and he was used to feeling an arse around them – they made it their mission to keep his feet on the ground – but they were strangers to Eden. And anyone with a brain could work out exactly how they came to be on the floor.

'I don't understand why you both fell,' Alistair said, looking up from his second, possibly third, helping.

Okay, occasionally things needed to be explained to people with super big brains and no emotional intelligence. But hopefully, nobody would. He didn't want to cause Eden more embarrassment.

Justin patted his big arm and shook his head. 'Don't worry about it, baby. It was just an accident.'

How had his oaf of a brother landed such a nice guy? Honestly, if he blew that way, he'd be half in love with Justin himself.

Mick looked up from shovelling food into her mouth. Her helpings were at least as big as his.

'Yeah, Jed, how did you and Eden come to be on the floor?' she asked, her tongue firmly in her cheek. Jed picked up an ice cube and flung it at her. Because he had excellent aim, it landed wedged in her cleavage. 'You bastard,' she muttered, digging her fingers into her bra to pull out the rapidly melting ice cube. She flung it at his head, and it bounced off his cheek. Her aim was getting better.

'The only way that could've happened is if you and she—'

'Al—' Jed wearily interrupted Alistair.

'—if you and Eden were leaning against the door together...'

Jed watched, fascinated, as Al added two and two and reached four. His eyes widened and his skin lightened with the faintest hint of pink. His big, broody brother was a bit of a prude. 'Oh...' he muttered.

Justin clasped his hand and squeezed. 'There you go, big guy,' he said, grinning.

Eden, now beetroot red, started to stand. Before Jed could follow her to her feet, Mick was out of her seat. Her gentle hand on Eden's shoulder pushed her pretty butt, the one he'd squeezed, back into the chair. 'Eden, drink your wine, eat some food. Jed might be an arse, but he's an arse who can cook. Eat something. You'll feel better for it, I promise.'

When Mick used her I'm-a-doctor voice, people tended to listen and Eden was no exception. Justin, being quick on the uptake, reached for her empty plate, dished up some lasagna and added the last piece of garlic bread. He slid it in front of her, and Eden grabbed a fork. She tentatively lifted a small bite to her lips, ate and then went in for a bigger forkful. Yeah, Jed was sure of a couple of things: he was a good polo player, a better craftsman, and he could cook a damn fine lasagna.

And that he was desperate to take Eden to bed and to finish what they'd started. Unfortunately, he didn't think his balls could handle it tonight. *Fuck.*

'It's good,' Eden said, sounding surprised.

'I know.'

'Arse,' Mick muttered, just loud enough for him to hear. She leaned sideways to flick his ear. Ignoring his protest, she topped up Eden's glass, then her own, and leaned back in her chair. 'Right, now that the excitement is over, can we have a normal meal?' she asked.

'I've been hanging around you guys for five years now, and I've yet to find normal,' Kit stated, lifting his beer bottle in a mock toast.

Justin placed his hand on Al's and shook his head when he reached for his phone. 'No, baby, you still need to be sociable.'

Al sighed, frowned and tipped his head back to look at the ceiling. Jed, from experience, knew they had about fifteen minutes before he excused himself and went back to his home office and lost himself in the markets and his spreadsheets.

Trying to ignore his aching nose, and balls, Jed sipped at his whisky. He pulled the lasagna dish toward him and, deciding there was no point in dirtying another plate, ate directly from the serving dish. And Eden was right, it was good. He looked at Mick. 'How are the plans coming along for the charity polo match?' he asked.

Mick tapped her finger against the bowl of her wine glass and wrinkled her nose. 'We still need a main sponsor,' she told him. 'And we need to find a charity to be the recipient of any money we raise.'

Eden's fork stopped halfway to her mouth. 'I'm sorry … what?'

She looked genuinely confused. Jed started to explain, but Mick beat him to it. In between bites, she explained how a casual discussion they'd had about hosting a polo match to raise funds for charity a few months ago had led to an organising committee being set up by the village 'do-gooders' and Mick – she shot a dirty look at Jed when she got to this point – being elected its chairperson.

'You're raising money for charity, but you don't have a cause in mind?' Eden asked, obviously confused. 'That doesn't make sense.'

'If we don't find a charity we can all agree on, we'll just donate the money to the Bancroft Foundation and ask them to distribute it,' Jed explained. 'The Bancroft Foundation is—'

Eden's face tightened. 'I know who they are and what they do.'

'Troyden has said that he'll sponsor the day if we need him too,' Mick said. 'I have to say, it's pretty handy having a billionaire hanging around.'

Al lifted his attention off the phone he'd snuck out of his pocket. 'Not going to happen. We've spent the budget for charity contributions this quarter and I'm not releasing any more money.'

Mick pouted. 'Oh, don't be annoying, Al. It's for a good cause.'

Al's expression turned stubborn. 'Do you have any idea how many people ask Troyden for money, how many people expect him to bail them out when they hit a sponsorship snag? It's a full-time job for Justin to handle the emails, and then Troyden is besieged by personal calls as well. That couple, your mum's old friend, Jed—'

Al was terrible at names. 'Tara and Vincent Bancroft, Al,' he supplied, weary. He wanted to go to bed. Preferably with

Eden. Who now looked ghost-pale instead of fire-red. He'd never met anyone who could change colour as fast.

'Yeah, *them*. They're always asking for last-minute sponsorship.'

Yeah, his godmother and Vincent could be pushy, but you had to be when you ran one of the most successful foundations in the country. But they made a difference in many people's lives, so he thought their persistence was an asset, not a fault.

Because he couldn't keep his eyes off Eden's gorgeous face, he saw an indecipherable emotion jump into her eyes. Tipping his head to the side, he watching as she pushed her food around on her plate. She hadn't eaten more than a couple of forkfuls.

'Are you okay?' he asked, his voice gruff.

'Fine,' she snapped, as prickly as a cactus. 'Why wouldn't I be?'

Because my bloody sister invited you to dinner at my house instead of hers, because we didn't say a word before we started devouring each other? Because we ended up on the bloody floor looking like randy teenagers? 'You hit your knee pretty hard,' he said, trying his best to sound bland.

She lowered her hand to rub her knee. 'It's okay.'

But she wasn't. And he knew that not all of her unease was due to their runaway wildfire attraction. What was her story? He wanted to know.

'Alistair, stop being a frugal prat,' Mick snapped at Al, pulling Jed's attention off Eden. 'I'm Troyden's daughter, and this is a worthy cause!'

'You don't have a cause yet, Mick, and they are all worthy causes,' Alistair replied, sounding bored.

'And Troyden wouldn't stay a billionaire if we didn't stick to a *budget*.'

Jed thought he was overegging it, but Al was pedantic about Troyden's finances. He also understood, because Troyden could be too generous and tended to fling his credit card around like it was confetti, Al needed to keep a close eye on Troyden's money.

'You are so annoying,' Mick told Alistair, tossing her head.

Al, because he was Al, ignored her. He never wasted energy on drama.

Jed rubbed his forehead, desperate to take his rather battered body into a hot shower and then into bed. He wanted Eden in it as well, but there was more chance of him being beamed up by aliens. Their kiss took her by surprise, but he knew that she was now weighing all the pros and cons, and the chances of seeing her naked tonight were slipping away.

As he reached for the whisky bottle for another hit, thinking he might as well get slammed, his phone beeped with a message from an unknown number.

> This is Henry. Our last conversation was unproductive and I would like to revisit.

Jed tipped his head back and looked at the ceiling. Henry bugging him was the last thing he needed. And their conversation had been unproductive because Henry wanted something he couldn't give him, a place in his life.

C'mon, did he really think that one meeting could change the habit of a lifetime? The Duke refused to acknowledge him, so he'd thrown up barriers and created as much emotional distance between himself and his biological family as he could.

Henry had made it easy for Jed to hate him as an individual, as he'd gone out of his way to make his life hell at school. Was he supposed to forget all that because Henry had grown up and supposedly reformed?

Fuck that. And him.

Jed pushed his thumb and index finger into his eye sockets. His head, nose and balls ached, and so did his heart, just a little. But he didn't have the time or energy to deal with Henry.

He was perfectly fine with the status quo.

Mick leaned over and looked at his phone, her eyebrows rising. One day, maybe, he would be entitled to some privacy. But with Mick around, he wasn't holding his breath. 'He's still hassling you?'

To be fair, one visit and one text message couldn't be called hassling, but it was still annoying that Henry hadn't taken his first no as his final answer. He lifted one shoulder and turned his phone over in a silent rebuke. Not that Mick noticed. 'I've heard that he's moved back into the Hall and is taking an active role in the management of the estate,' Mick said. 'He's been at the Goat a lot lately too.'

Jed liked the village local, the Fainting Goat, and it pissed him off that he'd have to see Henry's not-ugly mug in it when he went down for a pint. 'He's playing at being the Duke. Give it a week or two; he'll get bored soon enough and go back to London.'

'Wow, you really don't like him,' Mick said, her eyebrows rising.

'Whatever gave you that idea?' Jed sourly replied.

He was tired of talking about Henry, and it was time everyone went home. If he couldn't have Eden under him, on top of him, on her knees – okay, cool down – he wanted to pop a couple of ibuprofen with another shot of whisky and climb into bed.

But Mick, because she was Mick, someone who took any opportunity to extend her kid-free evening, stood up, walked over to his fridge and pulled out a jug of home-made chocolate sauce. *Damn*. He loved Mick's home-made chocolate sauce – hazelnuts, double cream, a few bars of melted chocolate – and she knew he always kept vanilla ice cream in his freezer. She pulled out the tub, plonked both on the table and went back for bowls and spoons. *Mi kitchen, su kitchen.*

When she was seated again, Jed reached for the ice cream, dished himself up a decent helping, and poured chocolate sauce over the top. His friends and family could fight for the rest…

Eden sent a longing look at the ice cream. Jed stopped eating, yanked the tub of ice cream away from Al and dropped a couple of scoops into a bowl before his brother and friends annihilated what was left. He dashed a decent glug of sauce over the top – she looked like she needed the sugar – and pushed it in Eden's direction. Her eyes lit up as she picked up a spoon, spooning the dessert into her mouth and closing her eyes in appreciation. Her skin flushed and she released a breathy sigh. God, if this was the way she reacted to ice cream, how would she look with her skin flushed by an orgasm?

Jed squirmed in his chair, his pants now tight.

'Oh, that's the best thing I've tasted, ever,' she said, digging in for more.

'Good, right?' Mick confirmed. 'It's my mum's recipe, the best thing she can make.'

'Her samosas are good, too,' Al added.

'You're right; she makes great potato samosas,' Mick agreed, before taking charge of the conversation again. 'But we were talking about the charity polo match and how Eden could help.'

'What? No, we weren't,' Eden protested.

'Now you're just making stuff up,' Jed said, pointing his spoon at his sister.

Mick stuck her tongue out at him.

'Okay,' she conceded, 'I think you should help organise the charity polo match, Eden.' Eden's eyes widened and her spoon stopped halfway to her mouth.

'Why would I want to do that?' she asked, politely, resting her spoon back in her bowl and sitting back. 'Besides, you know that I'm leaving tomorrow.'

What? The fuck she was…

'We need your help because everyone on the committee has a full-time job and can't give it the attention it deserves. You have time; you said you are off for the summer. And it's been scientifically proven that doing good helps improve your mental health.'

Annoyance flashed across Eden's face. 'Are you questioning my mental health?'

Mick simply smiled at her. 'We live in a crazy world, Eden; everyone's mental health is taking a battering.'

Eden didn't break eye contact with Mick. Jed liked how

she held her own with his pushy sister. 'That's why I'm taking a couple of months to explore Croatia.'

'But you'll be doing it alone, and where's the fun in that? Stay here instead, and fill those empty hours by doing something that could make a difference in someone's life. Croatia will be there next time.'

Danger ahead, because Mick was using her charm-birds-out-of-trees voice.

'It's a couple of phone calls, some spreadsheets, a little advertising, attending some meetings,' Mick said, sounding breezy. Another warning sign. When Mick sounded breezy, she was leading you straight into a fucking tornado. 'And you've just met us, met *me*. It's been such fun having you around, and I love spending time with you. Do you realise a few nights ago we went to bed at three because we were talking so much?'

Huh. Jed hadn't realised they were spending so much time together. Mick was extroverted, but with the kids, her job and, well, probably the family, she didn't have many close friends. 'I don't want to lose you yet, Eden.'

And then she added, 'And neither does Troyden.' He didn't know Eden's history, but he'd watched how Eden acted around Troyden and it was obvious that she adored Troyden.

Eden bit down on her bottom lip and he knew Mick's statements resonated with her. She liked that she was liked. Then again, who didn't?

'I've had some experience working with charity events, Mick. I know what it involves and it's *not* relaxing.'

She had? Interesting. And what was it she did for work

anyhow? Why didn't anyone seem to know and why did he care?

Mick pushed out her bottom lip and, swear to God, batted her eyelashes. She was shameless. 'But we'll do it together, E! Can I call you E? Eden is such a mouthful!' *Jesus, Mick.* 'Don't you want to help me?'

If he was a better man, he'd tell Eden she was being played. He met Justin's amused eyes and knew he was thinking the same thing. 'Troyden is devastated she's leaving,' Justin murmured, just loud enough for Jed to hear. 'He doesn't want her to go.'

Shit.

'And while she's been here, he hasn't shown any interest in finding a new Sugar Baby. Bet you that as soon as she leaves, he'll look for a new one to push the loneliness away.'

He stared at Justin, a lightbulb flickering on in his mind, then burning strongly. He was so right about Troyden. His stepfather always said that he was looking for love, and maybe he was, but maybe he was looking for a way to banish loneliness. Come to think of it, Troyden only started sugar-hopping after Kael left home, when all his chicks were out of the nest and living their own lives.

Why had he not realised this before? And yes, if it meant keeping Troyden out of the clutches of money-hungry GD's, he was in favour of Eden staying.

You keep telling yourself that's the only reason you want her to stay. Maybe you'll start to believe it in a decade or so.

Mick clapped her hands together. 'Thank you for agreeing to help, Eden, that's awesome!'

'Wait ... what?' Eden whipped her head around the table. 'I didn't say yes! When did I agree to anything?'

Mick sent her a self-satisfied smile. 'You didn't say no, either.'

Eden muttered a curse, picked up her spoon and started to shovel ice cream into her mouth. She glared at Mick and muttered something intelligible. Jed understood exactly where she was coming from…

And that made him think of her coming again. He scooted closer to the table, grateful it hid his semi. And damn, it *hurt*. They'd moved off the subject of him and Eden falling through the door in a tight clinch and he didn't want to revisit it.

Then Mick, his best friend, sister and bane of his existence, smart enough to back down when she had the upper hand – Eden might not have said yes, but she didn't say no, either! – put her chin in the palm of her hand and waved her spoon between him and Eden. 'I feel like we moved on too soon from why you two landed on the floor earlier. So, are you two seeing each other or what?'

Mick's laughter-filled eyes told him how much fun she was having annoying him, deeply thrilled that she got to do this for the rest of his life. Jed dropped his head and banged his forehead on the table. He might as well add to his throbbing nose and aching balls.

Chapter Nine

'Sod it.'

From the window seat in Troyden's study, her legs tucked up under her, Eden looked over to Alistair sitting behind the large oak desk, glaring at the computer. He released another curse, his shoulders hunched and lips pursed. Across the room Troyden and Justin sat on the leather couch, looking at a shared document on a laptop.

A few days had passed since her and Jed's confusing, can't-stop-thinking-about-that kiss, why-hasn't-he-followed-up encounter, and Eden had yet to book her ticket to Croatia. Somehow, while eating Mick's devil chocolate sauce, she'd caved, succumbing to Mick's blatant emotional manipulation by agreeing to attend the first meeting of the charity polo match organising committee. She wasn't going to commit to more than that.

It would be, Mick airily informed her, sometime soon.

In the meantime she'd taken to exploring Bythesea village, and enjoyed the way it embraced its agricultural, horsey and artistic residents. The upmarket coffee shop was owned and operated by Cody, an American hipster barista, and it sat next to a grocer, the till manned by Hyacinth Bucket's sister. A saddle and tack shop was bookended by a store selling animal feed and medicine, and a potter shared space with a small art gallery.

Alistair released another, more brutal curse and rubbed the back of his neck. Eden dropped her legs and wandered over to squint at the screen. He was running code.

'Are you coding in Python?' she asked, intrigued.

'I'm bloody trying to,' Alistair growled. 'The sodding thing won't sodding work.'

'Can I help?' she asked, a little hesitant.

'You can code?'

Eden explained that she'd taken an advanced Python coding course at uni, but didn't bother telling him that, in her spare time, she played around with software development. It was, strangely, something she instinctively knew how to do. She could speak computer.

Alistair stood up and motioned for her to take his place. Eden slid into the warm seat and listened to his concise, logical explanation of what he was trying to achieve. Her eyes read the code while he talked, looking for discrepancies.

'Got it?' Alistair asked.

She did. Knowing what he needed, her fingers flew across his keyboard – there was nothing nicer than a superfast computer – quickly sliding into the rhythm of the code. Oh, yeah, she'd forgotten how much she enjoyed this.

When she sat back, she tested the programme and it worked. Satisfied, she sat back in the chair and pushed her hair out of her eyes. Then she noticed three pairs of eyes on her and frowned. 'What?'

'You rewrote my program in'—Alistair checked his fancy watch—'twenty minutes. You made it cleaner, faster and more efficient. It took me three hours just to get to this...'

She shrugged. 'I like coding.'

'You're damn good at it,' Alistair stated, shutting the lid to his laptop. He scooped it up and stalked out of the study.

'In case you didn't realise, that was Al thanking you for your help.' Justin walked over to the desk and held up his hand for a high-five. 'You impressed him, and Al is rarely impressed.'

'I'm glad I could help,' she replied, smiling. 'It was fun.'

Justin and Troyden exchanged conspiratorial grins. 'Being better at Al at anything doesn't happen often, so enjoy those three a.m. calls when he's stuck,' teased Justin.

'I— What? No!' She wasn't good at three in the morning. Her blood only started to circulate after 7am and two cups of coffee. Eden was about to ask Justin if he was serious when her phone beeped with a message from Mick, asking whether she could help her out for a couple of hours.

And if she could, could she come down to her cottage as soon as possible?

Tucking her phone into the back pocket of her denim shorts, Eden shoved her feet into her flip-flops and told Justin she'd hold him responsible if his husband called her at an obscene hour. Justin didn't, damn him, look even remotely scared.

Leaving the house, feeling happy and *useful* for the first time in a while, she wandered down to the cottages, enjoying the slight breeze rustling through the tall oaks, sweet chestnut and beech trees, enjoying the patterns the late afternoon sun created on the path through the small wood. Wildflowers, bluebells and daffodils added colour to the many shades of green, and Eden smiled at a robin's call. Or she thought it was a robin, but she wouldn't place any money on it.

Through the trees, she could see the polo field where Jed and his teammates normally practised, and sighed when she saw it was empty. She hadn't been able to stop thinking about him during the day and dreaming of him at night.

He was sex, sin and temptation all rolled up into one hearty, healthy, sexy package. If they hadn't fallen through the door like some slapstick duo from the silent movie era, she could easily imagine him taking her where she stood. She certainly hadn't considered stopping him.

Eden pushed her hands into her hair and tugged. Whenever she laid eyes on him, her body started to hum and she lost all the moisture in her mouth. All she wanted was to be back in his arms, her breasts pushed into his chest, his mouth covering hers, his fingers heading south…

Arrgh! Jeez, she was losing her mind. Maybe she needed to return to her flat, find her infrequently used vibrator and take the edge off. And maybe bring it back to Elmsleigh House with her. But Eden knew that some self-love wouldn't help; it was Jed she craved.

She was in *so* much trouble.

How stupid was she to fall for the son of Tara's good friend? She'd, carefully, mined Troyden, Diana and Mick for more information about the Bancrofts' relationship with the

Castle clan, and learned that the Bancrofts had met Troyden through Jed's mum. Jed had spent a lot of time with them after his mum died, and they'd offered to have him live with them. But Jed had chosen to live at Elmsleigh with Troyden, and he'd retained a close relationship with the Bancrofts ever since.

Jed, so she'd been told, was a guy whose loyalty was absolute. He would walk through fire for the people he loved and would fight dragons on their behalf. She instinctively knew that once Jed took you into his inner circle, you were there through everything life could throw at you. And God help anyone who tried to hurt you…

It wouldn't matter to Jed that she'd agonised over her decision to report them and had spent many sleepless nights weighing whether the good they did trumped embezzlement. He wouldn't care that turning them in was agonising, but it was the only decision she could live with.

Bottom line: if he learned she was the one who'd snitched, he would never forgive her. And if the police found out she'd told them about the investigation, they'd charge her, and prison orange wasn't her colour.

Rock, meet hard place.

And that was why one kiss was all they could ever share. They couldn't have more, not when a maelstrom of secrets churned beneath the surface. So the sooner she stopped thinking about him and lusting over him, the better.

God, she wished attraction was a simple switch she could flip to OFF.

Eden knocked on Mick's door, heard her harried call to come in, and stepped into a hectic, chaotic mess. Like Jed's place, the kitchen, lounge and dining were all open plan, with the bedrooms, she presumed, upstairs.

Mick carried a grumpy-looking Liam on her hip. She still wore her work outfit of black pants and white shirt, with a smudge of God knew what across her chest. Liam's face was streaked with tears. Behind her, Gemma looked mutinous. She held her kitten like a baby, and for a change, it was wide awake, eyes big in its shocking-orange face.

'Hi, Eden, thanks for coming over,' Mick said, looking on the edge of tears herself.

'What can I do to help?'

Mick rubbed her hand up and down Liam's back. 'I need to get Gemma to a party this afternoon, but she won't leave Bizzy on her own.'

Ah, so the kitten now had a name. Gemma lifted her deep brown eyes to meet Eden's. Her expression was part street thug, part heartbreak. 'He's just a baby, and he's in a new place.' She glared at her mother. 'How would you feel if someone made you leave your baby alone in a strange place?'

It was a fair question and Eden hoped Mick had an answer for her. But judging by the frustration on Mick's face, she didn't. 'She's a *cat*, Gemma, and we've closed every window, and we'll lock the door when we go. She can't *go* anywhere.'

It was obvious this was an argument she'd tried before, with little success. 'She's a *baby*, mum She'll be alone.'

Mick closed her eyes in frustration and looked at Eden. 'Could you please stay here for two hours max, to keep the cat company?' she asked. 'If I spend another minute arguing about this, I might lose it.'

She was being asked to babysit a cat? This she could do. 'I'll stay with Bizzy,' she told Mick. Her shoulders dropped and relief jumped into her eyes. Eden knew that this was probably the last straw at the tail end of a long day, and if she could make Mick's life easier for a short time doing nothing, then she would.

Eden placed her hand on Mick's arm and squeezed. 'Can you take ten minutes? I'll make you a cup of tea?'

Mick looked at her watch and nodded. 'Yeah, we can be ten minutes late, and I'd like that.'

She put Liam on his feet and told the kids to watch TV until she called them again. Eden followed Mick into the kitchen – bomb site! – and bumped her hip when Mick picked up the kettle. 'I'll make it, you sit.'

Mick slipped onto a bar stool, placed her arms on the island and rested her forehead on her fist. 'Tough day?' Eden asked, quickly making her a cuppa.

Mick's reply was muffled. 'Tough week, tough month.' She rubbed her hands up over her face. 'Sorry, I hate whining.'

'It's okay.' Eden set the mug down on the island counter. 'I have so much respect for single mums, Mick. My mum was one, and it's hard not having a backup.'

Mick sat and up reached for her tea. 'I appreciate you saying that, but I have more support than most, Eden. Troyden, my brothers, Justin. I feel like a fraud for complaining.'

No, it was still hard, because she carried all the responsibility. 'I remember reading somewhere that when you give birth, a vacuum is created, and guilt is sucked back in.'

Mick laughed, finally. 'That's it, exactly.' She sipped, closed her eyes and sipped again. 'I needed this. Do you want kids?'

Eden's eyes widened at the question. She'd never had anyone ask her that before. She nodded. 'I do. Not now, but sometime, I guess. I'd like to be the centre of someone's world.'

'Are you talking about a man or a kid?'

She wrinkled her nose. 'Both. I was never my mum's priority, her first choice, so I guess I'd like to be that to someone.'

Mick's sympathetic eyes met hers. 'Losing her to the Church was horrible, right?'

She nodded. 'When she became a novice nun, I was still her daughter; we could still communicate; I could visit her, call her my mum. But when she became cloistered, she made the conscious choice to choose the Church, or God, over me. To leave me behind, to renounce me. That was'—she touched the tip of her tongue to her top lip—'tough.'

'Tough as in soul-stripping and devastating?' Mick softly asked.

She dipped her head and blinked rapidly. 'Basically.'

She'd never told anyone, not even the Bancrofts, how much it hurt, about the tears she'd shed, the long nights she'd lain awake running through her life, trying to figure out if she could've done anything different that would've made her mum choose her, choose being a mum, choose a life with her. Judging by the way Mick reached for her hand and squeezed, she understood.

Man, talking to Mick was far better than talking to a psychologist.

Gemma strolling into the kitchen pulled Eden back to the present, and she was grateful. Mick stood and took a few hasty sips of her tea. 'Gem, give the cat to Eden and let's go.'

Gemma narrowed her eyes. 'The *cat's* name is Bizzy,' she stated, her tone as pointed as the tip of a dagger.

Alrighty then. Eden held her hands out for the kitten, Gemma reluctantly handed it over and placed tiny fists on her hips. 'You can't give Bizzy milk; she'll get a tummy ache. And you need to remind her where her litter tray is; it's in the mudroom. You need to give her lots of cuddles, and she likes Taylor's music.'

As did everyone. Eden tried not to smile.

'And you cannot let her out!' Gemma said, raising her voice to near shouty levels. Okay, got it, don't let the cat out. Keep her eyes on the cat. Do not lose the cat. She could do this. She had to, or else Gemma would ram a stake through her heart.

'For God's sake, Gemma, Eden knows how to look after a cat,' Mick said, picking up her bag and slinging it over her shoulder. 'Help yourself to coffee, or wine, or anything. The TV remote is somewhere. You'll need to hunt for it because Liam thinks it's funny to hide it.'

Mick opened the front door. 'Thanks, Eden, I appreciate this, really.'

Eden smiled when Gemma dropped a kiss on Bizzy's tiny head and rubbed its ear with her finger. Her eyes held all the fervour of a fundamentalist preacher, and her chin all the stubbornness of a millennia-old glacier. 'Do *not* lose my cat.'

Ten-four, ma'am!

Eden lost the friggin' cat.

She'd carried Bizzy around for twenty minutes, and when it wriggled, she'd put it down to let it explore. Instead of running off, it stayed next to her, weaving in and out her feet, and she had to take mincing steps to avoid accidentally stepping on it. Thinking that she needed some coffee, she took the magazine she'd found under a pile of medical journals to the equally chaotic kitchen, the kitten trotting behind her.

Eden winced at the pile of dishes in the sink. The kitchen was a mess, but she couldn't judge Mick; there weren't enough hours in the day to work, look after the kids, do laundry and clean. Finally, she'd found something she could do for Mick, a way to be useful.

She'd tidy her kitchen. Eden quickly filled the dishwasher, put the condiments away, added more cups and glasses to the dishwasher and swept the floor. The kitchen instantly looked bigger and brighter. She'd reward herself with that coffee after all. She found some instant granules in the cupboard above the kettle. After wiping down the surfaces, she boiled the kettle and opened the fridge to grab the milk, poured some into her mug, and waited for the kettle to boil. Returning the milk to the fridge, she kicked the door shut with the back of her heel.

She finished her coffee while reading a short story in the magazine, then remembered she was here to babysit a kitten. She looked down. Mm, no kitten.

Bugger, it had high-stepped away while she'd been

reading. But she wasn't too worried, Mick assured her she'd closed all the windows, and the kitten couldn't get out.

She flipped through the magazine for a few more minutes and wrinkled her nose, uncomfortable with not knowing where her temporary charge was. Getting up, she placed her cup in the dishwasher and checked the mudroom, peaking behind the washer and dryer to check that the kitten hadn't fallen asleep there. Nope.

'*Psssppsssppp*, Bizzy, Bizzy,' she crooned, walking into the lounge. Eden looked under the couch and chairs, behind the curtains, lifted the cushions on the couches and checked behind the TV console and under the coffee table. Starting to become mildly concerned, her '*pssssps*' became louder and more frantic. There was no way she could've lost the damn thing, it was here ... somewhere.

A half-hour later she had to admit that, dammit, she'd lost the kitten. In a house with closed windows.

How? And why was this happening to her? And God, she didn't want to die, not at the hand of a pissed off, desolate six-year-old.

Eden stood in the lounge and lifted her hands to her face, not sure where else she could look. What the hell was she going to do? Panic licked the back of her throat, but she forced herself to think. She had an hour before Mick and the kids were due home, sixty minutes to find the tiny cat...

It would be easier if she had some help.

Remembering the list of phone numbers she'd seen on Mick's fridge, she half-jogged back into the kitchen and saw Jed's number at the top of a list of emergency numbers. Right, if he was Mick's first port of call, he could be hers too. She rocked from foot to foot as she waited for him to answer.

'Eden? Everything okay?'

He'd recognised her number which meant that he had to have her number in his phone... Why? But that wasn't important now. 'Jed, I need your help.'

'Are you hurt?' he demanded, tension in his voice.

'No,' she quickly replied. Though she might be if she didn't find Bizzy before Gemma returned.

'Okay, what's the problem?' Jed calmly asked.

Eden explained, and Jed chuckled. 'It's not funny, Jed! I can't find her.'

'And are you sure the doors and windows are closed?' he asked.

'No, I never thought to check that,' Eden sarcastically replied. 'Of course they are!'

'Then she has to be somewhere.'

'I've been looking for her for the past hour and I can't find her!'

'I thought the kitten was a he,' Jed mused.

'Jed! Concentrate! The kitten is *missing*,' she reiterated. 'And I need you to come and help me find her.'

'You just don't want to explain to Gemma that the kitten is hiding from you,' he said, laughter in his voice. 'You're scared of a six-year-old.'

'She was channelling Chucky when she told me not to lose her,' Eden admitted. 'Are you going to come help me, or not?'

'I can be there in five minutes,' he told her. 'But I'm in my riding gear and have been working with horses all day, so I might trigger your allergy.'

She so didn't care. She'd lost a little girl's kitten. And that was far more important than her skin erupting and her throat closing. 'Just get here,' she told Jed, now feeling frantic.

She was the worst babysitter in the world. And if she lost Gemma's cat, then an allergy was the least she deserved.

But where the hell could it have gone?

'You've lost the cat,' Jed stated. He stood in the middle of Mick's lounge and placed his hands on his hips.

No shit, Sherlock. Eden glared at him and stomped into the kitchen. 'But how, Jed? It didn't just disappear!'

He rubbed the back of his head, looking genuinely confused. 'I have no bloody idea, Eden.'

Great. She had ten minutes, maybe even less, before she had to explain to a six-year-old, and her mother, that she'd lost the newest member of their family. After this, the extended Castle family, and everyone at Elmsleigh House, would excommunicate her. A public execution, if Gemma had her way.

How was she going to explain this? Was there an explanation? Did aliens beam it up?

'I think we need a drink,' Jed said, looking hot, flustered and confused. She nodded, brushed past him to head for the kitchen and sneezed. And sneezed again. And her eyes started to water.

Jed joined her in the kitchen, washed his hands in the

sink before reaching for her hand and turned her palm over to look at her wrist and her arm. 'No hives?'

She shook her head. 'No, nothing so far. You make me sneeze and my eyes water, but I think the antihistamines and exposing myself to horses, even if it's just watching them from a distance, are helping to desensitise me. But I'm still too scared to venture into a stable.'

'So, no hot sex in the straw then?' he asked.

Oh, damn, there was a visual she could get behind. Him bare-chested, shirt open, and the buttons on his jeans undone. Her legs locked around his hips, panties pushed to the side, perfectly positioned to…

Not the time. Or the place.

Jed pulled a whisky bottle from a cupboard and held up the bottle, silently asking if she wanted a belt. She was tempted, but she owed it to Gemma, and Mick, not to be tipsy when she told them she'd lost Bizzy. But she could have a slug of wine. She'd seen a half-full bottle in the fridge when she'd made coffee earlier.

Eden yanked open the fridge, felt something brush against her ankle and she leaped a foot in the air. As the sound of a car rumbled in the distance, she looked down and saw Bizzy snuggling up to her ankle looking a little sorry for himself. Herself?

'Holy shit!' she yelled, scooping the cat up and plastering it against her chest.

'What?' Jed looked up, his eyes widening as he saw the cat in her arms. 'Where the hell did he come from?'

Eden snapped her mouth closed, barely able to get the words out.

'He was in the bloody fridge!' she hissed, conscious of

the tiny, cold body purring against her chest. Jed was bigger and hotter and emitted far more heat than she did. In one fluid movement, she yanked up his shirt and shoved Bizzy against his chest.

'Warm her up, for God's sake!' she said, hearing Mick's car slide into her parking space behind the garage.

Jed's hand covered Bizzy, and he rubbed her briskly. 'Dammit, close call. How did he get in the fridge?' he hissed, as car doors slammed.

'He must've jumped in while I was making myself a coffee,' Eden whispered. 'I always leave the fridge door open; it's a bad habit of mine.'

Jed started to smile, then laugh. His body shook with it, and Eden joined in, hers born out of relief. 'Would he have frozen in there?' she whispered, hearing Gemma and Liam's voices as they ran up the path to the front door.

Jed shook his head. 'Nah, no chance, and he's fine. A bit cold, but fine.'

The door opened and Gemma raced into the kitchen, looking around for Bizzy. Her eyes locked on to Eden's face, and she placed her hands on her hips. 'Where's my kitten? Why aren't you cuddling her?'

Wow. Okay, then. Eden hauled in a deep breath and gestured to Jed. 'Jed is cuddling her,' she said, pointing to the bump beneath Jed's polo shirt. Please, please, she silently begged, let the cat be warm enough not to raise Gemma's suspicions. Seeing the fridge door was still open, Eden kicked it closed with her foot. Then she opened it again, just to make sure, ignoring Jed's snort.

Gemma stomped over to Jed, shoved her hand under his shirt and took the kitten from him. Eden held her breath and so, she noticed, did Jed. Gemma lifted the kitten to her face and kissed her nose. She frowned. 'Why is his nose cold?' she demanded.

Eden looked at Jed, who gripped the counter with his hands, his shoulders shaking with laughter. 'Ah, that's because he's the most chilled cat in the world,' he stated.

Haha, not funny. Eden glowered at him, and he grinned at her. They both watched Gemma cuddle her cat, and she asked him how he was, whether Eden had been a good babysitter and whether he was, God of all things, satisfied with her service. If cats could write online reviews, she would get negative five stars for shocking service.

Eden reached behind Jed, swiped the whisky bottle off the counter and took a big sip. She took another and turned as Mick came through the door, carrying Liam who looked a little flushed. She handed them a tired smile. 'Hey, all good?' she asked.

'All good,' Eden said, taking another hit of whisky. At some point, she'd have to explain to Mick why she'd turned her house upside down and pawed through her drawers and cupboards, and she hoped Mick would understand. She didn't have that many friends that she could afford to alienate the ones she had.

'Liar,' Jed muttered.

'Sounds like there's a story there,' Mick said, placing Liam on his feet.

She had no bloody idea.

Chapter Ten

After Mick had listened to her explanation – conducted outside, in a low whisper – and she'd stopped laughing, Eden accepted Jed's offer of a decent drink and walked the short distance from Mick's front door to his own. Empty of his family, his cottage felt a lot bigger this time, and chaos-free. She walked straight over to the bigger of his leather couches and flopped backwards onto it.

She closed her eyes, took in the quiet and waited for her heart to slow down to a gallop. That had been one hell of a close call. And when she felt up to it, she and that damn cat would have a chat about staying out of bloody fridges.

She opened her eyes when she felt the cool, smooth surface of glass against her arm. She saw the wine glass Jed held and took it. 'You have no idea how much I need this,' she said, immediately lifting it to her lips and allowing the Chardonnay to slide down her parched throat.

He sat down next to her and stretched out his long legs. Eden ignored her prickling eyes and tried to swallow down her sneeze. This was Jed's house, and she couldn't ask him to take a shower or to change his clothes, that would be rude.

She'd just sit here, and ... *atchoo!* Damn, that felt like she'd expelled a lung. Another sneeze built up in her nose, and she couldn't hold it back. Without saying anything, Jed rolled to his feet, beer bottle in his hand, and walked down the passage. A few minutes later, she heard the sound of a shower running. Eden tipped her head to the side, surprised by his thoughtfulness. He came across as being grumpy and reticent, someone who did what he wanted when he wanted, so she was a little confounded by his attempt to make her feel comfortable.

She sipped her wine and tried not to imagine water sluicing over his muscled body, her fingers in his wet hair, warm water sliding over their lips as they kissed. She wiggled deeper into the cushion, and squeezed her thighs together, unable to stop the images of long, muscled legs, his hair pushed off his face, his lips on her bare breast… The cold tiles behind her back, the hot water, the length and hardness as he pushed—

'Want pizza?'

His question caused her hand to jerk, and wine spilt over her hand and onto the boldly patterned carpet beneath her feet. She looked down and winced. 'Sorry.'

He shrugged. 'My fault, I didn't mean to scare you. And don't worry about the wine, Mick spills hers all the time.'

She started to smile but it died when she took him in. His wet hair was finger-combed back from his face, and his biceps strained at the sleeves of a faded blue t-shirt.

He wore chino shorts, and was, once again, barefoot. He looked chocolate-mousse-cake good.

'You showered,' she said, mentally wincing at her inane statement.

He lifted one big shoulder. 'I sat down next to you, and you started sneezing. I went to shower. No big deal.'

It was. She wasn't used to people going out of their way to make her feel more comfortable and she wasn't sure how to handle the rush of warmth. Oh, she understood physical attraction, knew what to do with lust, but this unfurling spark of like? No freaking idea.

Jed walked over to the fridge to pull out a bottle of water. He drained that and lifted his eyebrows. 'So, pizza?'

Should she stay? Here? With him? Alone? There were so many reasons not to.

'Do you get deliveries out here?' she asked, to delay having to answer.

Jed released a derisive '*pfft*'. 'I make my own from scratch. I semi-bake, then freeze them.'

Of course, he did. Who *was* this man?

'Are your pizzas as good as your lasagna?' she asked, genuinely curious.

His eyes, direct and filled with confidence, met hers. 'Sweetheart, I do *everything* well.'

She believed that. From riding to polo, to being a good son, to being a good brother, he was a man who believed in excellence. She had no doubt he brought the same level of skill to the bedroom. The thought made her feel hot. And flustered all over again.

'Pizza sounds good,' she said, just managing to construct a clear sentence.

'Plain Margherita or fully loaded?'

She'd enjoyed too many crappy vegetarian pizzas as a kid. Meat-free pizza was an abomination. 'Fully loaded,' she told him.

Jed nodded, disappeared into his pantry attached to the kitchen and emerged with two frozen pizzas in hand. He slung them into the oven set to low and grabbed another beer from the fridge. He leaned his butt against the counter and grinned. Then he started to chuckle. And Eden immediately knew why.

'In the fucking fridge,' he said, shaking his head. 'Damn, I'm never going to forget today.'

Eden rested her glass against her forehead and closed her eyes. 'Mick was pretty understanding,' she said.

'That's because she could easily imagine it happening to her.'

Eden stood up to look out of his open French doors to the private garden and released a sigh. She liked his sister, liked that she was fun, didn't sweat the small stuff – or the big stuff, like a cat in her fridge! – but she loved the fact that she was a great mum. Not having had one herself, she knew Mick had the mum thing nailed. 'She adores those kids,' she murmured.

'Does their dad see them often?' she asked, wondering if she was overstepping any boundaries.

Jed sipped and rested his beer bottle on his knee. 'Not really,' he replied. She looked at the wine in her glass, and down at her feet. The big kitchen seemed smaller than it did before, and Jed seemed bigger. The smell of his shower gel and shampoo mixed with the aroma of pepperoni and garlic, and her tastebuds watered.

For Jed or the pizza?

Both. But if she had to choose... who needed food?

Jed closed the distance between them and suddenly he was an inch from her, their mutual heat an almost tangible shimmer. Her pulse thudded in her ears, so loud she was sure he could hear it, and she reminded herself to breathe. Eden knew she should step back and look for a plausible excuse to let this moment fade away, but his copper-coloured eyes, fierce and determined, caught hers.

'It's a terrible idea,' she muttered, her whisper hitting his lips.

His mouth quirked, his maddening half-smile promising trouble. But there was a softness to his eyes, in the thumb that drifted over her jaw.

'Maybe,' he said, his voice low and unsteady as he invaded her personal space. He placed his hand on her lower back and yanked her into him, her stomach connecting with his groin. She immediately noticed he was happy to have her there. He lowered his head until his lips were an inch from hers. Neither of them moved, neither willing to break, to yield. To be the one to back down or away.

She felt herself cave, surrendering and softening, desperate to repeat their out-of-body kiss. She needed his mouth on hers, to be in his strong arms... It didn't matter who made the first move, someone had to and it might as well be her. *Be brave, Eden, reach out and take what you want.*

She lifted her heels to stand on her toes. Overwhelmed by the desire in his eyes, she averted her gaze, landing unfortunately on his fridge door. It took a second, maybe two, for the photo to come into focus. A dark-haired woman with Jed's smile beamed at her, her arm around Tara's waist.

Tara. Shit!

Eden felt Jed's lips hit hers and tensed. She slapped a hand on his chest, wrenched her mouth away and dropped back to her feet. Jesus, she couldn't do this. She wanted to, she did – more than she wanted her heart to keep beating – but there was a picture of Tara and his mum on his fridge! Tara, the woman who might end up in jail because of her.

'Whatever is going on in that pretty head of yours, push it away,' Jed told her, sounding a little desperate. She noticed that his lower lip was slightly chapped, that he had a scar on his chin and that his dark stubble held the odd fleck of grey.

'I haven't been able to stop thinking about our kiss last week. I want to kiss you again. *Everywhere.*'

She jumped, just a little, shocked by the heat in his fabulous eyes, the seriousness of his expression.

Oh, God, she needed to be strong, to step away from him. But she'd have to explain her Sudden Onset Hesitation.

He narrowed his eyes and pulled back. 'What's the problem?' he asked, his voice rough with frustration.

She hauled in a deep breath, hoping to push blood into her brain. 'Having sex with you is a complication,' she admitted.

He picked up a lock of her hair and allowed it to slide through his fingers, a tender action that was at odds with his unreadable face. 'Why?'

'I'm Troyden's niece. You're his stepson.'

'There aren't, thank God, any blood ties between us,' he

murmured, looking fascinated by her hair. 'It's perfectly okay for us to sleep together.'

'I'm leaving soon,' she told him, grasping at the thinnest of straws. 'I'm going travelling, to Croatia.'

'So? We can sleep together until you do,' he told her, his tone both confident and assured. His big hand lightly encircled her throat, his thumb on her jaw. 'It's not like I am asking you for a commitment. I was thinking more along the lines of a one- maybe two-night stand, or possibly a fling.'

No, she couldn't do this. She couldn't risk it. Because with Jed, it wasn't just attraction or a passing crush – it was more. Bigger, deeper, brighter. He felt dangerous.

She glanced at Tara's picture again. She knew what it was like to be left behind, to be the one who almost mattered. If she opened this door, she risked falling for him. And how would she cope when the truth was revealed and he decided she wasn't enough?

It was too much. Too scary, and too risky.

For a moment, just a millisecond, Jed leaned into her, as if were considering pulling her into him, but then his sigh brushed over her cheek, and he pulled back and dropped her hand. 'Okay, message received.'

A wave of regret rolled over her, both spiky and acidic. Why couldn't she, just once, take what she wanted without overthinking everything? Without projecting?

'I think you should go,' Jed told her, pushing a hand through his hair. Was it shaking, just a little, or was that her imagination? 'I know I offered you food, but if you stay, you're going to be on the menu.'

Man, that was so tempting, she couldn't think of

anything she wanted more than to be loved by him. Could she backtrack? What would he do if she put her hand on his chest, lifted her lips to his, and slid her tongue inside his wicked mouth? Shoved her hand between the band of his shorts, undid the button...

'Jesus, Eden, when you look at me like that...' he muttered, every word coated with a layer of frustration and desperation. 'I'm a man, not a goddamn saint!'

Lust retreated, just a little, enough to get the sparkplugs powering her brain working again. She couldn't keep changing her mind; she wasn't a kid.

Slipping her feet into her shoes, Eden picked up her phone and walked to his front door. Jed reached around her to open it, and Eden sighed. How she wished she could be spontaneous and live in the moment, to be brave. Not worry about the consequences.

She gestured to the kitchen, closed her eyes and pushed her fingers into her forehead. 'I'm sorry about...' *Jeez*. She swallowed. 'I'm sorry.'

He didn't pretend to misunderstand. 'Me too,' he said. 'I think we would've had some fun.'

His words were light, but his eyes held a load of regret and ... was that curiosity? He knew there was more to her no than she was saying. She swallowed and tried to find a breezy, hopefully cool, way to say goodbye. A bit difficult when she didn't want to leave him, when she was oh-so-tired of being on her own.

When all she wanted to do was feel his big arms around her, his mouth on hers, and have him sliding into her and making her whole?

But present pleasure wasn't worth future pain.

'Have you decided whether to get involved in organising the charity polo match?' he asked.

Her head whirled at his conversational one-eighty, as she'd been thinking about their hot-as-the-earth's-core kiss the last time she'd stood here.

'I am waiting for the first meeting and will decide after that,' she told him.

'I hope you do get involved because Mick will need the help, and you need something to do besides watching us practise.'

Jed made her sound like a K-pop fangirl. Not that there was anything wrong with fangirling, but she never thought she was the type to spend so much time watching a guy. On a horse. 'Is me watching you train a problem?'

His eyes narrowed. 'You're hell on my concentration,' he told her, his voice rough. He looked up at the sky, shoulders hunched around his ears. 'There's no fun in being tempted by something that's not on offer, Eden. So, please, for the love of God, find something to do.'

She wanted to protest and thought about arguing, but then realised she'd come across as being difficult and immature. She couldn't drool over him and then bat him away. She wasn't fifteen, for God's sake.

Eden was about to walk away when Jed flashed her a dimmer-than-normal, but still knee-dissolving smile. 'By the way, if you still want pizza, there's a couple in the freezer in Di's pantry. Defrost it slowly, then blast it on high.'

Later, when she was tucking into his pizza, she thought that if Jed made love as well as he made pizza, then she should say to hell with worrying about complications, confusion and the future, and jump him as soon as she possibly could.

What the hell was he doing at this meeting?

He had a polo team to captain and manage, ponies to train and gym sessions to attend. Yet here he was, sitting in an ex-church, now village hall, waiting for his sister to roll in so that they could finally start the inaugural meeting for the charity polo match.

Why did he think this was a good idea?

Jed shoved his hand into his hair and leaned back on the rickety chair, placing his ankle on his knee. He was tired, pissed off and sexually frustrated, and the reason for his constant state of horniness sat directly opposite him, a pen and fresh notepad on the long steel table in front of her. Until today, he'd never realised how sexy a white t-shirt and a denim skirt could be.

Why hadn't she just said yes when he'd offered to take her to bed? Their chemistry was off the charts, and they would've enjoyed a week's worth of good sex, had she agreed. Instead, he felt like a rabid beast was gnawing on his insides and his skin felt too tight for his body.

He couldn't figure out why she'd said no, and why she was avoiding him. Was it because he stated he didn't want a relationship, that he was only interested in a fling at most? She was in her late twenties, surely she didn't expect sex to equal a relationship? Was she turned off by his lack of commitment? Maybe.

And for the record, while he couldn't commit to a

woman, he was fully able to commit to everything else, his family, polo, his friendships, his carpentry projects. What was her problem?

Frustrated, he looked at his watch and decided he'd give Mick five more minutes and then he was done. Thankfully, the heavy wooden door opened ... *finally*. Jed gritted his teeth as his half-brother strolled in, all polished confidence in navy chinos and an untucked shirt, his expensive watch peeking from under a silver and leather bracelet. Jed, in contrast, knew he looked like hell, unshaven, dirt-streaked, his polo shirt sporting God knew what. So far, Eden had yet to sneeze, and he was covered in horse dander and dust. Was her horse allergy improving?

He hoped so. He plucked his dirty shirt off his sticky chest. He still felt like the grubby peasant their father refused to acknowledge.

And it royally pissed him off.

'The Duke of Dick,' he said, on a snarl. 'What are you doing here?'

Henry briefly closed his eyes, and then, straightening his shoulders, he walked into the room, eyes locked on his. 'Jed. Can we please stop with the bullshit and have a beer?'

'I'd rather be branded,' Jed whipped back.

Paul, the owner of the Goat, the village pub, stood up and held out his hand for Henry to shake. Paul invited Henry to take a seat at the trestle table opposite him, next to Eden, and Jed ground his teeth together. A few people sat at the table, the lady from the pharmacy, the owner of the bookstore and another grey-haired lady with hair so stiff a category-five tornado wouldn't dislodge it.

All their eyes bounced from his face to Henry's and back again.

'We're so happy to have you here,' Paul said, unaware of the undercurrents. 'The late Duke didn't show much interest in village affairs.'

'I intend to change that,' Henry replied smoothly, laying his arm across the back of Eden's chair. Jed swallowed his growl. He was going to break his bloody fingers! 'The village and the Hall have been intrinsically connected for centuries, and I want to foster that relationship.'

'Bullshit!' Jed muttered.

Henry pushed every one of his buttons at the same time. It didn't help that everyone else seemed to like the guy. Even Mick beamed at him when she finally arrived, dropping into a chair, filching Eden's notepad, and launching into full-throttle planning mode.

Thirty minutes in, the group looked shellshocked at her grasshopper ideas. Jed was about to call for a break when Henry – of all people – took charge. Within ten minutes, he had a clear vision and had assigned tasks, and annoyingly somehow everyone, including Mick, was letting him lead.

'I think we got a lot accomplished,' Henry said, looking around pleased.

And all of it within a short time. Jed didn't want to be impressed but was. Damn, he needed a beer. Or better still, a whisky.

Eden lifted her head and raised a hesitant hand. The smile Henry directed at her was too warm, far too flirty. Jed clenched his fist when Henry half-turned to face her, his expression suggesting she was about to explain the mysteries of the universe.

The man had skills. And if he used any more of them on Eden, he might lose his shit. 'Would you like to say something, Eden?' Henry asked.

'Um … just that you don't know what you're raising money for. People won't donate just for the hell of it.'

Mick propped her chin on her hand. 'We could split it between the RSPCA, the British Heart Foundation and the Bancroft Foundation,' she suggested.

Eden flinched. She clearly didn't like that suggestion … at all.

'Would you consider another option?' she carefully asked.

Everyone nodded.

'There's a collective of single mums in Southend who run a house for kids in emergency foster care. They've lost their funding. Without help, they'll have to shut down or drastically cut back. It's called Hope Harbour.'

Silence.

Jed's gaze locked on Eden, noting the way she gripped her pen, the tension in her shoulders. This was personal and he wanted to know more.

Everyone was silent for a moment, taking in the horror of kids who'd experienced too much, too young. Jed wanted to know how Eden knew of this collective. He opened his mouth to ask, but Henry jumped in first. 'I'm happy to consider them. I like the idea of helping kids.'

'I'd also like to know more about Hope Harbour,' Paul said, looking at Eden. 'Can you get us some more information on the organisation, Eden? And if it checks out, I'd like to propose that the funds we raise be donated to them.'

Eden released the smallest gasp and placed her hand on her heart. Were those tears in her eyes? Jed squinted, but then she blinked and they were gone. 'Of course, I'll do that as soon as I get home,' she said.

Home. She'd called Elmsleigh House home. He sat back, folded his arms and smiled. If Eden had a connection to the charity she would want to help make the polo fundraiser as success.

Eden Ennis wasn't going anywhere. Not for the time being.

It both pleased and terrified him.

This was it. This was the real deal.

The practice event a month ago had nothing on the high-stakes polo match unfolding at Cowdray today. It was another perfect spring-melting-into-summer day, filled with sunshine and a slight breeze that kept the day from being overly uncomfortable. After consulting Mick on what to wear and raiding her cupboard, Eden had finally settled on an off-the-shoulder, paisley-patterned maxi dress cinched in at the waist with a broad leather belt. She'd also borrowed a slouchy hat to keep her face out of the sun.

Eden, a glass of champagne in her hand, stood on the grassy bank, revelling in the late afternoon sunshine. It was the last chukka between the Castle Kings and a team whose name she couldn't remember, and tension and excitement permeated the air.

'The Kings got the last goal of the chukka because

Montoya was blocked by number two. That's what allowed Harris to get the run around to the goal.'

'Montoya is a *chatto*.'

Eden smiled. She'd been hanging around polo players long enough to know that *chatto* in Argentinian Spanish meant dick, but in polo terms, it was the commonly used term for saying someone was a crap player. Not that anyone at this level could be called crap; they were all at the top of their game. But Jed, scorer of most of the goals for the Castle Kings, was freakin' bloody fantastic.

Eden took in the spectators filling the grandstands, a vibrant sea of colour made up of summer hats, airy dresses and sharp, feminine suits. Their voices, weaving a luxurious tapestry of murmurs and laughter, were further punctuated by cheers of approval as the game resumed.

This was it, the end of her first proper, grown-up, high-stakes game. The field, a rectangle of emerald green, was meticulously manicured. With every breath, she inhaled the combination of freshly cut grass, leather from the saddles and bridles of the players' ponies, perfume, cologne and the delicious scents emanating from the food carts situated at the far end of the grounds. Her allergy was a lot better, and these days she was only plagued by a few sneezes here and there.

Jed sat in his saddle, his eyes sharp and gaze focused, radiating precision and power. His shirt clung to his torso, streaked with dust and sweat. He held his stick with an easy, almost casual grace as he waited for the chukka to start. His pony's glossy coat gleamed – he was riding Rey – and she quivered as she waited, taut with anticipation.

The opening whistle cut across the ground and the ponies exploded, surging forward as they thundered across the field. Dirt and grass flew up as the players steered their mounts to make quick changes in direction with a shift of their weight and barely discernible tugs on the reins.

The sharp *crack* of Jed's mallet smacking the ball sent a thrill through the spectators and down Eden's spine, and pushed heat into her core. This was such a sexy, sexy sport...

She followed the ball as it raced across the field, a small, swift blur against the vivid green. Jed, bent low over Rey's back, chased down his opposite number, and cheers erupted as he stole the ball and whipped Rey around to head in the opposite direction. The crowd surged to their feet as he leaned low, guiding Rey in a sprint toward the goal. Eden groaned when he was blocked by another player in what the people around her immediately, and vociferously, called a foul.

Eden barely breathed during those final few minutes of the game, as the score remained tied. In the last moments, Kit stole the ball from his opponent and passed it to Jed who was waiting on his outside. Using all the power in his broad shoulders, his mallet cut the air as he thwacked the ball in one last strike. It sailed through the posts, and Eden, along with the rest of the crowd, screamed her delight, jumping up and down on her spot.

She got it now, got why people were mad about this sport. It was exhilarating and heartbreaking, exciting and, yeah, as sexy as hell.

And damn, she needed a drink. And a cold shower.

Forty-five minutes later, Eden stood with Mick in the

main hospitality tent, a gin and tonic in her hand. The atmosphere was now relaxed and convivial, a marked contrast to the tension earlier. The players, still dusty from the field, chatted casually with spectators, took photos, and signed autographs.

Jed, looking fine in his dirty jodhpurs and grubby shirt, held a beer in his hand and was laughing with Troyden and a dapper man in a suit. He looked relaxed and happy, a satisfied smile on his face. She'd thought he was a good player before, but now she was aware of his skill.

Talking about excellence...

She looked around and internally grimaced. Cowdray was one of the premier venues for polo in the country and had a rich history of hosting amazing events. Eden hoped that the village's organising committee, and the sponsors, didn't expect the charity polo match to be as slick as this. There was no chance of that happening.

Somehow, and because they were now raising funds for Hope Harbour, Eden had become the charity committee's PA and was virtually organising the event single-handed. And that was okay; she was used to working behind the scenes, making other people shine. She had played that role for the Bancrofts for years and was a whizz at logistics. You couldn't funnel millions to charities and projects without having your ducks in a row.

Her ducks, admin-wise, were military-trained and never stepped a foot out of line. She might struggle with people – she *did* struggle with people! – but she could organise the shit out of anything. And because she was doing this for Hope Harbour, she wanted it to be a stunning success.

But the meetings were a nightmare, mostly thanks to Jed

and Henry being annoying, competitive bastards. If one said the sky was blue, the other said it was pink with purple spots. It was exhausting and counterproductive and she was on the verge of suggesting that one, or both, should resign.

But Jed was their polo consultant, and she needed his expertise about how to run the matches, the timings and the logistics around grooms and horses. Henry had a million contacts in the City and through him, she'd arranged sponsorship of the tents, stands and advertising. He'd also offered to host the charity match at Bythesea Hall and was spending money to transform an unused piece of land close to the Hall into a polo field.

They both had their strengths and uses, but they were doing her head in. Eden rested her cool glass against her cheek and watched Henry interacting with a girl in a barely-there dress. If he was a perfectly polished diamond, then Jed was Alexandrite, that amazing gemstone that changed colour depending on the light source.

Henry was every inch the young, handsome duke, but Jed exuded a don't-care, highwayman vibe.

She liked Henry – they'd met up for a few coffees and had a drink at the pub – but she didn't experience the same chemical reaction, shivers-down-her-spine, moisture-leaving-her-mouth, do-me-now reaction with him as she did whenever Jed walked into the room. Around Jed, she was in a constant state of hyper-awareness, conscious of every move he made, all the time.

She didn't want to think of Jed, and the way he'd kissed her, and the fact that she'd had more than a few X-rated dreams lately. Since their wild kiss, she'd woken up most mornings sweaty, wild-eyed and more than a little damp. She'd had one or two sex dreams in the past, and some fantastic orgasms in the process, but lately she always woke up before the crucial moment.

Which meant that she was in a state a constant horniness.

Get your mind out of the bedroom, Ennis. She switched thoughts and wondered why Jed and Henry hated each other. Or, to be fair, why did Jed constantly goad Henry? Henry had inherited a dukedom, not something he could control, and was down to earth, or as much as a guy who owned a fifty-something-room mega-mansion and most of the land surrounding the Bythesea village could be.

Sure, their acquaintance was brief, but she knew he wasn't a bad guy and sensed he was as lost and alone as she was. Someone standing outside the cool kid's gang, wanting to join in but not knowing how. She knew how he felt, she was a pro at standing on the outside looking in.

What was Jed's problem? That he hated him – and no, she wasn't exaggerating – was easy to see. But what on earth could Henry have done to elicit such a reaction in Jed who, from all accounts and what she'd seen, prized logic over emotion?

Maybe she'd broach the subject over dinner tonight. Henry had invited her out early in the week and he'd used the excuse of her working hard as a reason to treat her to a meal. But when he told her he'd make a reservation at an upmarket restaurant two villages over, she wondered if he was thinking *date*.

How could she go on a date when she spent her nights, and a good portion of her days, mentally beating herself up for walking away from Jed?

Jesus, she was screwed. And not in a good, set-her-panties-on-fire way.

Jed looked up and their eyes collided. Eden hauled in a deep breath as Jed's eyes dropped to her chest before slowly, too slowly, coming back to her face. He pushed his hand through his hair, his bicep bunching and straining the band of his shirt. Desire flickered then whooshed through his eyes, turning them a burnished gold. Underneath his scruff, a muscle in his tightly clenched jaw ticked and he widened his stance, folding his arms. She knew he wanted her to go to him, while she wanted him to come to her…

It was another battle of wills, one she was determined to win. The man was far too competitive and needed to be taken down a peg or two. Preferably naked in bed, his wrists latched to a bedpost, while she tortured him with chocolate body paint.

Hoo boy, it was hot in the tent.

A pair of feminine arms encircled her and Mick rocked her from side to side. 'There you are! I've been looking for you everywhere!'

Eden looked into Mick's glassy eyes and grinned. Her friend was dressed in tailored shorts and a boxy jacket that was held together with one button, with nothing, except for a pair of sticky boobs, underneath. She looked sensational and had been surrounded by male admirers all day.

She was also happily drunk. 'Do you need some black coffee, Mick?'

'I need another drink,' she told Eden, dropping her arms. 'What an amazing day! Have you had fun?'

Eden nodded, smiling. 'So much fun.'

'It's great, right?' Mick threaded her arm through Eden's elbow. 'The first polo match always feels like the start of summer to me.' She shifted from foot to foot and looked around. 'I need another drink.'

Mick needed food. Eden was about to head over to the canapé table to make a plate for them to share when she saw Jed there, his back to them. God, he had the best arse…

'Talking about polo—' They hadn't been, but okay… 'I'm looking around and thinking of how much hard work goes into making a day like this happen. Thank you for making our upcoming charity match a reality, E. You've been an absolute blessing.'

She still wasn't used to being called E, but she liked it. She smiled at Mick. 'Even though I nearly froze your cat?'

Mick grinned and waved her words away. 'Bizzy was, at most, a little chilled. And really, you'll laugh about it someday.'

No, she wouldn't, because she lived in constant fear that Gemma would discover how she'd lost her cat and would shave her head while she slept. She was as obsessed with the cat as Eden was with…

No, admitting that she was obsessed with Jed was a step too far. And sounded a bit too stalker-y.

'Hey.'

Talk of the sexy devil and he arrives. Eden resisted the urge to stroke a hand down her hair, to tuck it behind her ears, to rock on her heels. Even rumpled, he was cover-of-a-men's-health-magazine sexy. Eden was sure the lipstick she'd slicked on earlier was long gone, and that her mascara was smudged. She was sure that if she touched her fingertips to her forehead, she'd find micro-droplets of perspiration.

He was hot, while she was simply a hot mess.

He lifted his beer bottle, sipped and swallowed. 'Congratulations on your win,' Eden said, silently cursing her breathy voice.

'Yeah, you weren't half bad,' Mick blithely told him.

'I can't handle your effusiveness, Mick,' he drawled.

Mick, because she often reverted to being a teenager around her older brother, stuck out her tongue. He bumped her with his big shoulder and looked at Eden.

In the blink of an eye, everyone around them faded away and they were alone. They were all lovers in history: Jack and Rose on the Titanic, intrigued and fascinated. Or Jesse and Céline in the café, silently acknowledging their connection without saying a word. No, maybe they were Elio and Oliver with their smouldering looks expressing their growing desire and confusion about their feelings. And dammit, did her breath have to catch and her heart race? Why did she feel this ache deep within her, something pushing her toward him, desperate to be in his arms? The air between them crackled with electricity and anticipation.

How much longer could they stare at each other until Mick noticed?

Mick, thank God and all His cherubim and seraphim, didn't.

'Eden, one of my boobs has fallen off,' Mick whined, and she was hurtled back to reality. She held out the silicone, adhesive cup and, almost instinctively, Eden and Jed moved closer to her. Thankfully, because Jed was so big, between them they hid Mick's hand.

'What are you guys doing?'

Eden jumped at Kit's voice behind her and in doing so, created a gap for him to see what Mick was holding. 'Lost a boob, Mick?' he asked, laughing.

Mick threw it at his head, Kit ducked, and the cup went sailing past the nose of a man wearing a deerstalker. It landed, with a plop, on the grass outside the tent.

'Shit, I've lost my boob,' Mick moaned, looking forlorn. She tried to shove her glass into Eden's hand. 'Hold this, I'm just going to get it.'

Eden gripped Mick's hand, knowing that claiming the boob was a bad idea. The tent was already buzzing with laughter, trying to suss out who threw the insert; Mick didn't need to make a tit – bad pun – of herself by retrieving it.

'Just leave it, Mick,' Eden hissed.

Mick slapped her hand against her chest. 'But now my boobs are uneven!' she wailed.

'Your real boobs always look good to me,' Kit drawled.

Jed sent his teammate a death stare. 'Do you want me to end you?' he growled. Eden caught Kit's eye, shook her head and widened her eyes. There was teasing and then there was playing with fire. Messing with Mick's sister was a good way to get incinerated. Kit, insouciant as always, just grinned.

The man had the common sense God gave a pot plant.

'Eden...'

Ah, shit. *Henry*. Eden spun around and plastered a smile on to her face. While she was fine discussing Mick's sticky-boob malfunction with Jed and Kit, she didn't feel comfortable with the idea of Henry knowing Mick was currently minus one.

'Henry, hi. Enjoying the day?'

'Very much so,' Henry replied. His eyes landed on Mick's chest, and he frowned when he saw her clutching her jacket together. Because he was a nice guy, he was about to offer if he could help, something that would skyrocket Mick's embarrassment. She shook her head and saw Henry's quick frown and even quicker nod.

She sent him a grateful smile. 'I had a look at Velour's menu. I'm looking forward to trying their breaded pork cutlets.'

Henry flashed a smile. 'I'm also looking forward to our date.'

Crap, he used the D-word. Eden bit her lip, half-turned and looked at Jed, who was marble still. Was that a growl she'd heard? Her eyes skittered from his face down his body, her attention caught by his clenched fist at his side. His other hand wrapped so tightly around his beer bottle he might snap it in two.

That he didn't like the idea of her going on a date with Henry was six-foot-high, flashing-neon-sign obvious. Damn. It wasn't like she was deliberately trying to make him jealous; she wasn't that keen on this being a date either. It was pretty hard to spend hours in a fancy restaurant with a guy – no matter how nice and good-looking he was – when you desperately wanted another man to pin you up against a wall and kiss you stupid.

How had it come to this?

But she'd made her bed, and now she had to lie on its

scratchy sheets. Eden sent Henry a quick smile. 'I'll see you later, Henry,' she said, reaching for Mick's hand. 'Mick, come with me.'

She needed to put space between her and Jed, and if that meant her using Mick's boob situation, or lack of it, to get out of Dodge, then that's what she would do.

Chapter Eleven

Dinner was fine.

A little upmarket, lively enough conversation, damn good wine which she drank and Henry didn't. It was *nice*. But dinner dates with good-looking men should be more than nice; they should be…

Something. More.

Or was she expecting too much?

Eden watched Henry's tail lights drive away and tipped her head back to look up, and up, at the towering, too-dark manor house. There was a light on in what she knew was Diana's suite of rooms, but because Troyden was away, only the yellow spotlight outside the kitchen door pierced the darkness of the country night.

So, Henry…

After their 'date', Eden knew he didn't make her sexual radar blip.

Jed did though. Grumpy, annoying, bossy, rude, totally off limits…

She'd thought about him far too often tonight, which was both unfair to Henry and bloody annoying. She was both infuriated and wistful that he wasn't the one sitting opposite her, pulling out her chair, topping up her wine glass, asking her questions about her childhood and life, few of which, if any, she answered.

Henry wasn't the man she wanted to tell her secrets to.

And Jed wasn't interested in hearing them.

Arrgh. Eden stomped her foot, causing gravel to fly and sting her bare calves. It had been a long, long day; it was late, and she was tired. She'd sneak a whisky from Troyden's study and take it up to bed with her, drinking it in the decadent slipper bath with bubbles up to her neck. Then she'd climb into that too-big, lonely bed...

She looked toward the cottages, seeing the lights in the houses glinting through the trees. Al and Justin were back, and Mick's bedroom light was on, but Jed's cottage was in darkness. Had he gone to bed already – it was past eleven – or was he out? Oh, God, was he out on a date, in someone's bed, naked?

With that thought settling in her brain, she was going to need more than one whisky. Maybe even a bottle.

'Enjoy your date?'

His voice came from behind her and Eden slowly turned, her heart a wild drumbeat in her ears. She should have been surprised but wasn't. She was simply happy to take him in, shoulders hunched, hands in the pockets of his jeans, his expression nothing short of a glower. He looked pissed.

She lifted one shoulder and tucked her hair behind her

ears. 'It was … nice.' That word again. 'Good wine, good company…'

'I'm so fucking happy for you.'

He delivered the words in a monotone and even a toddler could pick up on his sarcasm. 'You left at six and got home five hours later. What else did you do?'

She thought about lying, about telling him that they went back to the Hall and had rollicking, dirty, bend-her-over-the-sofa sex but she couldn't. Something in his expression, a vulnerability she didn't expect, held her back. 'We ate. He drove me home,' she replied, keeping her voice level. She felt compelled to add, 'Not that it has anything to do with you.'

His '*really*' was a low, intense growl, and then his mouth was on hers, and his hands lifting her butt had her standing on her toes. His tongue invaded her mouth. She tasted need, desperation, jealousy and her old friend, frustration, in his kiss. This – *this* – was what she'd been thinking about for most of the night.

Being with Jed. Touching his skin, allowing his heat to warm her, his scent to envelop her. His hand snuck up under the hem of her dress and his fingers wrapped around her thigh, lifting her leg so that her mound pressed against his hard cock. Stuff being sensible, there was nothing she wanted more than to have him inside her, rocketing her up and into the orgasm she'd been dreaming about for weeks.

He lifted her again, her back against the house's cool stone wall. The fingers encircling her thigh tightened and she understood what it meant to be branded. Heat coursed through her, a raging wildfire, and the last silken threads of rational thought fled. It didn't matter that they were standing under a weak outside light, that they were out in the open: she needed her hands on him.

Eden didn't know if she said those words aloud or if he heard her silent plea, but Jed yanked his shirt up and over his head and dropped it to the ground. Entranced by his hot skin and hard muscles, she slid her hands over his chest and lightly bit down on the ball of his shoulder, the bulge of his bicep.

She traced the line of his collarbone with her tongue, her fingers dancing over his abs, teasing him by running her thumbnail over his long, delicious, denim-covered cock. It had been a while, and he would be big for her, but she couldn't wait to feel him inside her, stretching and pushing and sliding and...

Cool air hit her skin, and Eden looked down to see her dress in a puddle at her feet, lying on top of his shirt, her bra God knew where. His lips closed around her nipple, and he tugged it against the roof of his mouth, before rolling it between his teeth and swirling his tongue around her. There was so much pleasure here to be explored, so much to be felt, so much that could go wrong.

She took a mental step back, wanting to remind him that she wasn't staying, that they were playing with dynamite with lit fuses, that the complications weren't worth the pleasure. That she was taking too big a risk...

But tonight she didn't care about the future, not when his mouth was trailing over her ribs. He dropped to his knees, and his fingers pulled her panties to one side and then his mouth was there...

And ... *God*, that felt good. He knew exactly how to suck

her, how to tease and to make her tremble, when to increase pressure, the right time to pull back. Eden lightly banged her head against the wall behind her, and pushed her fingers into his hair, holding him to her, praying he wouldn't leave her hanging. She wanted this. She wanted *him*.

One long, thick finger slid into her, and she gasped at the intense intrusion but lifted her hips in a silent request for more. She whimpered when his hand retreated, and sighed when one finger became two and he licked her clit with perfect pressure and precision.

'I'm so close, Jed, you've got to give me this...' she panted, feeling like she was standing on the beach, arms stretched out wide, waiting for the tsunami to sweep her away.

In a blur of movement, too fast for her to comprehend, Jed was on his feet, his jeans around his knees, and he was ripping open a condom. He grabbed her hand and roughly ordered her to put it on. Eden swore... How could he expect her to do complex tasks when her entire brain was a gooey mess? Somehow she managed, and as soon as the latex hit the bottom of his shaft, he cupped her elbows and lifted her off her toes.

'Look at me, Eden.'

It was both a demand and a plea, and Eden lifted heavy eyes to meet his. His cock was at her entrance so why was he hesitating? 'Jed...'

'Do you want this?' his voice rougher and deeper than normal. 'Do you want *me*?'

She was panting, on fire, about to scream from undiluted frustration. How could he ask such an inane question when she needed him more than she needed the world to remain spinning on its axis?

'Eden? I *need* an answer.'

Then it dawned on her that he was checking that being with him was what she wanted, that he needed her reassurance that he wasn't the only one drowning in need. Lifting her hands, she held his face, her thumbs stroking his cheekbones, sliding through the soft stubble on his cheeks and jaw. 'I'm naked against the stone wall of a stately house, Jed,' she murmured, dropping a kiss on his lips, 'begging you to do me. Yes, I want you.'

He stiffened and horror flew over his face. Oh, God, what now? 'Shit, what am I thinking taking you here, like this?'

Oh, damn, she hadn't meant for him to start thinking, to start second-guessing where they were and what they were doing. She wiggled so that he just penetrated her, smiled when he sighed and closed his eyes. 'I don't do this. I rarely have sex,' she told him, her voice a little dreamy. 'And I never have it in such a wild, exposed place.'

'Yeah, I got carried away.'

Yet again, he was taking responsibility for something that wasn't his fault. Or not wholly his fault. 'That's not what I meant. I like it.' A little deeper, and she felt him harden. Damn, that felt so incredibly good.

'And if you do not take me now, up against this wall, I will stab a fork in your eye,' she told him, not joking.

The corner of his mouth pulled up in that, rare sexy smile. 'Are you seriously telling me that you, at five foot nothing, are tall enough to stab me? And where would you get a fork?'

Why was he still talking? Why wasn't he *doing*? She lifted her hips, shimmied, just enough to create some friction, and was rewarded with a little gasp, the smallest expulsion of air against her lips. His little loss of control was a balm. And a victory. 'Are you telling me you could walk away?'

His answer was to drive into her in a hot, wild slide that suspended her heartbeat and heated the air in her lungs. She stared into his bright, wild eyes, wanting to hold on to this moment, this first time – there was only *one* first time – but she also wanted more. She needed everything he could give her: his soft, infrequent smiles, a sense of safety, his intense loyalty, his heat and power and strength…

He scared her, but she needed him. In ways she'd never thought she could need a man.

He moved in her, strong and sure, lifting and filling her, making her feel more like herself than ever before. Then Eden stopped thinking and started feeling, and her world morphed into a vivid, technicolour light show. She felt his lips on her neck and inhaled the smell of his shampoo on his soft, messy hair. His fingertips pushed into the soft skin on the underside of her thighs. She'd probably have bruises in the morning, but they were marks of his possession, and she was, as archaic and anti-feminist as that sounded, okay with that.

She thought their passion would burn fast and fade quickly, but his rhythm was strong and sure and … prolonged. Eden sobbed, tightly coiled as she hit one level of intensity, thought that was it, and then realised she could go higher. He took her there, teased more, and hauled her up a notch. Tears rolled down her face, need and want coalescing in a tight explosive ball, utterly convinced she couldn't take anymore. And she was right, when she morphed into light and sound and swore that she heard the sound of angels singing, emotion and tension exploding from a place deep inside her as she became a million fragments of fairy and stardust. From a place in another galaxy, sometime in the future, from a place in the past, she felt his final surge, her back pinned against the wall. His shudder jumped from him to her and his lips latched onto her collarbone. He pulsed into her, and then Eden welcomed his slumped weight.

Because, really, what did breathing matter?

Eden wasn't sure how long it took for him to lift his body off hers, to pull back and out. He gently lowered her feet to the ground, lifted her hand and placed it on the wall next to her, making sure she was steady on her feet. Without embarrassment, he removed the condom, tied it off and hauled up his jeans. He did up his belt, slid the condom into the back pocket of his jeans and bent down to pick up her dress. After straightening her panties, he gently lowered her dress over her head and carefully folded her bra before pushing it into her hand.

'You okay?' he asked, stroking a strand of hair off her forehead.

She was still incapable of speech and nodded.

He wrapped his arm around her waist, pulled her into him and rested his lips against her temple. When he spoke, his voice held both a command and a plea. 'No more dates with Henry, okay?'

She rested her forehead on his chest, coming back to

reality with a hard thump. 'I don't know what we are doing, Jed,' she quietly murmured.

'Me neither, Eden,' he nodded, his hand sliding into her hair to hold her head to his chest. 'It's just sex. That's all this can be.'

Of course it was. There wasn't a possibility of more. Not when she was the catalyst to, at best, ruining his godmother's reputation, at worst, being the reason they landed in jail. At some point, not too long in the future, he'd hate her. But for now, she'd take what she could get.

For the first time, she was prepared to wing it. 'Just sex, Jed,' she said, sliding her hands around his waist to explore his hot skin and the muscles of his back.

She'd enjoy the experience and bank the memories.

'Let me rephrase that... I know I can't ask anything from you, but I'd appreciate it if you didn't go on any more dates with Henry,' he said, his voice deeper than before. She felt the tension in his back muscles and saw his jaw tighten.

Even if she wanted to, she wasn't experienced or sophisticated enough to juggle two men at once. 'Okay,' she quietly agreed.

He stroked a strand of hair off her cheek and pushed it behind her ear. He jerked his chin up. 'Can I come inside with you? Can I spend the rest of the night with you?'

Eden had no idea what tomorrow would bring, but she had zero objections to his plans for the rest of the night, so she followed him into the house and up the stairs.

After winning the Queen's Cup – held within the grounds of Windsor Castle, the poshest tournament in the country – the Castle Kings were on a bit of a winning streak. A few weeks later Eden was back at Cowdray for the start of the Cowdray Gold Cup, Europe's premier high-goal tournament held over three weeks. It attracted, as she'd learned, international polo stars, celebrities and fans from around the world. Today's event, the Midhurst Cup, was held on the opening Sunday of the tournament and she liked the idea that it was a free event, open to families and polo fans alike and kid-friendly with tractor rides, face painting and kids' games. The game was changing, with both players and organisers trying to make it more accessible and inclusive. Focusing less on the wealth and the luxury and more on the sport and its complexities could only be, in Eden's opinion, a good thing.

Eden cast her eye over the club's meticulously maintained polo fields, including the historic 'Lawns' where the championship games were held. Each field was encircled by grandstands and open grassy areas for picnics. With its gentle hills, lush greenery, and the views of Cowdray Castle ruins in the distance, it was a perfect advertisement for the English countryside.

A horn signalled the end of the game and Eden watched as the horses slowed to a trot. The backs of the riders' shirts, including Jed's were wet with sweat. He ripped off his helmet, revealing his messy, damp hair. He looked vital and powerful, and Eden smiled at the contentment on his face. Being on a horse was his happy place.

She adjusted her floppy hat and watched the riders clasp hands, before dismounting and handing their ponies and helmets over to their waiting grooms. En masse, eight fit, hot players, with Jed leading the way, walked over to the players' tent.

Should she wait for him here? They'd spent two nights together, one after the other, but they hadn't done a hell of a lot of talking. He'd made it clear she was only a fling, and she had no right to act like his girlfriend, to kiss his cheek and congratulate him on his team's win. But if she didn't, would he think she was uncaring or uninterested? And what did it matter if he did? They were sleeping together, that was *it*.

But once or twice, she'd caught him looking at her with an unnerving intensity. And instead of dropping his eyes, he'd kept looking, as if trying to figure out who she was, mentally drilling into her to see what made her tick. Having his concentrated attention on her was both unnerving and exhilarating.

And God, when one of those looks was followed by a kiss, their clothes started flying…

Sod it, she could walk over to the tent; it wasn't prohibited. Standing on the edge, she saw Jed clock her presence, the slight raise of his head, his mouth lifting slightly. He was deep in conversation with his teammates, arguing about an umpire's call. Kit, the hothead, thought it'd been unfair, with Mateo agreeing, but Jed's calm reply reminded them there was nothing they could do and that they needed to focus on winning the next game.

He was a natural leader: tough when he needed to be, supportive and positive in defeat.

A light hand on her back made Eden turn, and she smiled, surprised to see Henry. He looked stylish in grey trousers, a white shirt and a grey vest, with a gold tie pin under his perfectly knotted pink and red tie. He wore a peaked, flat cap and expensive aviator sunglasses. Behind him, a group of women had their eyes glued to his back. Or probably his bum. Henry was a great-looking guy and she'd seen more than a few women trying to catch his attention with sly smiles, flicking hair and lifted chests.

'Eden.' He greeted her with a kiss on both cheeks.

'Hi, Henry, how are you?' She wrinkled her nose. He'd sent her a few texts asking her out again, and she'd missed a couple of calls. Not because she was avoiding him... Okay, she'd been avoiding him. 'Henry, I'm sorry...'

His mouth lifted in a self-deprecating smile. 'I've been around the block once or twice. Or ten. I know when a woman isn't into me.'

She winced, but wasn't going to insult him with the 'it's not you, it's me' line. Actually, it was Jed; she couldn't think of being with anyone but him.

And, really, she barely had the time to juggle one man, let alone two. Jed's polo schedule was intense, and he was always heading off somewhere for a match or a tournament, and she had the charity polo match to organise. And because she was everyone's go-to person, the one every committee member turned to for help or advice, her to-do list was a mile long and kept getting longer.

But Henry, bless him, had not only offered to host the event at Bythesea Hall, but had also thrown some sponsorship money at the event, which allowed her a little breathing room. Her ever-changing budget said that they were still on track to a decent sum for Hope Harbour.

Right now, Mick, who seemed to know everyone in the

horse world, was in the clubhouse, talking up the event. Eden knew she should be doing the same, but she didn't know anyone, and felt awkward about walking up to random strangers and punting a charity event.

And that was why she was a behind-the-scenes, logistics and organisational cog in the wheel. The Bancrofts had always been the face of their foundation, but she was the one who got things done. Their calls over the last month had faded away and she wondered how they were doing, before reminding herself that their foundation was no longer her concern or problem.

But old habits died hard.

Eden felt the pressure building in her nose, her eyes watering and she sneezed, then sneezed again. Someone shoved a white handkerchief into her hand, and she took it gratefully. Through watering eyes, she clocked Troyden standing next to Henry. Dressed in a sharp suit and snazzy tie, he didn't look like he'd been anywhere near the stables, so it couldn't be him setting her off. She slowly turned and Jed was standing just behind her, feet apart, arms folded, his eyes on Henry.

His frosty eyes jumped from her face to Henry's and he lifted an eyebrow. Then he moved, just a little, putting his big body between her and Henry, silently staking his claim.

Jesus. *Men.*

Henry, fluent in grunt, lifted his hands. 'Message received. I didn't know you two were together.'

'It's new,' Eden said, blushing.

'Last time we checked, we're adults and don't owe anyone an explanation,' Jed spat. Right. Eden darted a glance at Jed, his eyes still locked on Henry's face. Their animosity was not only uncomfortable but annoying.

Troyden looked from Henry to Jed and shook his head. 'When are you two going to bury the hatchet?' he asked, echoing Eden's thoughts.

'I've been trying,' Henry hotly responded. 'He's the one who won't move an inch or have a bloody conversation!'

'There's nothing to talk about,' Jed replied. Eden looked up at the sky, waiting for the thunderbolt to refute that whopper of a lie. But Zeus had more pressing matters on his mind.

'That's bullshit and you know it!' Henry replied. When Jed didn't respond, he threw up his hands. 'You are the most stubborn person I've ever met in my life.' He narrowed his eyes. 'No guesses where you got that from, huh?'

'Shut the fuck up, Henry,' Jed said, his tone almost conversational, but Eden heard the menace underneath it. Right, she was now seriously uncomfortable. Moving to stand next to Troyden, she sneezed into the handkerchief. She immediately checked her arms and hands, and was relieved when she didn't see any welts erupting on her skin.

'Have you taken your antihistamines?' Jed demanded, his eyes not leaving Henry's annoyed face.

'Yes,' Eden replied. How could he talk to her and not look at her?

'Good. I'll catch up with you later. Dad?' Jed asked, still not dropping his gaze from Henry.

'Yes?'

'Will you take Eden to get something to drink?' he asked, sounding a little robotic. Eden scowled at Jed, hating that he made her sound like a dog who needed a bowl of water.

'Sure,' Troyden replied. 'Oh, Tara and Vincent are here. They asked me to tell you they'll be in the champagne tent for most of the afternoon, and they'd love to see you if you have some time.'

Eden tensed as something in Troyden's voice pulled Jed's attention off Henry and on to his stepdad with a frown. 'Is something wrong with them?'

Troyden grimaced. 'I'm not sure. They are saying all the right things, being the life and soul of the party, but something is off. They seem worried.'

Eden clenched her fist and bit the inside of her lip. Oh, she knew exactly what had her ex-bosses acting twitchy. When she'd spoken to the detective handling the case last week, he'd told her the police were planning to search their offices and seize their records. Eden had suggested where to look and what they would find. The Bancrofts had to be thoroughly rattled and scared. They'd siphoned, at least, half a million from the foundation, and if convicted, they faced serious jailtime.

She felt guilty about that, she really did – she couldn't imagine how either of them would cope in prison – but she was also incandescently angry. While she believed they were entitled to a salary for the work they did, they'd used, and might still be using, donor money to fund luxury holidays, designer clothes and cars. They'd defrauded the donors and cheated the charities, and that was despicable. Would she be as mad if Hope Harbour hadn't been affected? That was a question that had kept her up at night in those earlier weeks. Had they not stolen from Hope

Harbour, would she have been tempted to let their actions slide?

Eden bit down on her lip. She wished she could answer with a silent 'hell, yes'. The best she could come up with was a 'maybe'. And she despised herself for that.

But at the end of the day, they'd hurt Hope Harbour, raised the mums' hopes, made them believe they were secure and encouraged them to use their emergency savings fund, assuring them that money would flow in. It hadn't – the Bancrofts had nicked it – and Hope Harbour was now in a worse position than they'd been before.

Eden remembered the countless nights her mum had spent trying to juggle too little income with too many expenses, looking for food and clothing bargains, and worrying about the gas bill.

The Bancrofts stealing from Hope Harbour was deeply damn personal. It felt like they'd stolen from her, from her mum. And she'd never forgive them for that.

Jed looked at his watch. 'I have another match in an hour. I'll find them after.'

'Ask what's bugging them,' Troyden replied. 'They were there for you and your mum, and we need to be there for them if they need help.'

To be honest, this was the perfect time to jump into the conversation, to chime in to say that she knew the Bancrofts, that she'd worked for them for years. She could also casually mention she was at odds with them.

She opened her mouth to speak, but she couldn't form any words. She was terrified of their reaction, especially since she wasn't able to explain why she'd resigned. They'd assume she was in the wrong and that she'd done something to make them fire her.

If she confessed to knowing the Bancrofts, it would, she was certain, change the dynamic between her and Jed. They were having fun, enjoying each other, keeping things light and surface-based, but that would evaporate like water on a sizzling hot iron if she spoke up. He would be angry and upset, and he'd choose his relationship with the Bancrofts over her.

And she'd be left behind.

Jed's long, low 'hmmm' pulled her attention back to the present. 'I'll chat with them,' he agreed. His eyes swivelling back to Henry. 'Where do you think you are going? We need to talk.'

Henry, who'd been edging away from them, stopped suddenly, and Eden caught hope flaring in his eyes. Why? God, she didn't understand the dynamic between these two. At all. 'Okay.' Henry nodded, sliding his hands into his pockets. 'Good.'

Jed turned to look at her, and she hauled in her breath at the bolt of lust she saw in his eyes, wanting to melt at the passion in his eyes. 'Be careful in the sun, you'll burn. And take some more antihistamines if you need to. This isn't the ideal environment for you.'

No, it wasn't, but Jed was here, and because she was – temporarily, she hoped – addicted to him, she wanted to be wherever he was. That meant being around horses. Oh, well. She'd either develop some antibodies or she'd be popping pills for as long as she was at Elmsleigh.

Troyden briefly touched Eden's back. 'Let's head over to

the refreshments tent. I can introduce you to Tara and Vincent. You'd like them, I think.'

Just a few months ago she'd loved and respected them; they'd been her favourite people. Now she couldn't think beyond loathing what they did. And there was no way she could exchange small talk with them.

'Eden?' Troyden asked. 'Are you okay?'

She pulled herself back to the present and touched her fingertips to her cheek. 'Actually, I have a cracking headache.'

'You're probably dehydrated,' Jed snapped. He did that when he felt out of control. 'You need to get in the shade, and I'll text Mick to bring you a rehydration sachet.'

He was a fine-looking man, but he could also be a bossy arse on occasion. And she didn't have a headache because she was a redhead and too stupid to stay out of the sun.

'I'm perfectly capable of sorting myself out, Jed.' She stepped away from the group and dredged up a smile for Troyden. She adored her uncle and loved spending time with him. He seemed to enjoy her just as much and they'd settled in to an easy friendship.

But she didn't want to be around Troyden today. Today she needed to be alone.

'I'm going to the ladies' room,' she told her uncle. 'I'll find you when I am done.'

She didn't like lying but this time it was necessary. She wasn't going to the ladies' room; she was heading straight for the parking lot and driving home. She'd text Troyden with an excuse after she left.

Troyden nodded. 'Okay.'

Jed folded his arms, his expression hard and unhappy. 'You need to rehydra—'

'Will you stop fussing, Harris?' Eden replied, irritated. She needed to leave, to get away from the people from her past, and she wanted to do it now. She couldn't risk meeting the Bancrofts because she'd face a million questions from them and the extended Castle clan. They were in a legal fight for their lives, and she knew them well enough to know they wouldn't hesitate to bad-mouth her to Troyden and his family.

And because the bond between them was strong and decades long, Troyden and Jed, and everyone connected to Elmsleigh House, would believe them. At the risk of sounding pathetic, she'd yet to experience someone taking her side, standing with her in a crisis. She'd always stood alone, and this time the situation wouldn't prove any different.

Eden walked away from the players' tent. There was no chance of avoiding the Bancrofts forever. At some point, sometime soon, she'd be outed, and she'd lose this family, which, despite the short time they'd spent together, she'd come to love. She'd be labelled, at best, a bitch, at worst, a thief, an embezzler and a troublemaker, disloyal and deceitful. Jed, Troyden and the rest of the family would believe them. She was the outsider, and the Bancrofts were part of the inner circle.

They had a history together; she had a few weeks. She was fighting a lifetime spent together, loyalty forged by walking through the halls of death, stumbling through the thick mists of grief. She couldn't compete, and losing them all, Jed, Troyden and Mick, was guaranteed.

Chapter Twelve

Late the next morning, on a rare polo-free day, and in his workshop, Jed stroked sandpaper over the leg of a coffee table, then cursed when he saw the scratches the sandpaper left in the soft olive wood.

He was in a mood and thought it safer for the world to hide out in his shop. Yesterday had been a shitty day. His team had lost their matches, and it'd been mostly his fault. It was only the second round of the tournament – they'd won the first – but he'd made their path to the finals much harder than it needed to be. The reason for his lack of concentration? Shit, it was embarrassing to admit it, but Henry's interaction with Eden, him acting with familiarity and affection, had put him off his game. He'd never experienced that weird, toxic mixture of jealousy and fury before and didn't know how to handle it.

'Eden is off limits, and if you so much as look at her, I'll end you.'

For a reasonably evolved guy, he'd acted like a

Neanderthal. Henry, the cool bastard, just smiled at his threat. Because he felt like a fool, or a jealous kid – he wasn't sure which one was worse – he'd changed the subject.

'I heard you're thinking about selling the Duke's polo ponies.' Like Troyden, the Duke had been a polo nut, and while his team wasn't as skilled or ranked as the Castle Kings, today's poor performance notwithstanding, Henry had inherited a decent stable.

'Not thinking about it. I'm selling them.'

'Why?' Was he mad? Why would he want to do that?

'I need the money, Jed. And the stable is an expense I can't afford.'

Jed thought it was more likely it was money he didn't want to spend. The man wore a Rolex, for God's sake, and his designer wardrobe must cost thousands. 'If you sell them now, it'll take years to build up a stable again. Don't you want to carry on the legacy of being a polo patron?' Jed reached for a water bottle and cracked open its lid.

'If I could divorce myself from my name, the Hall and the last five hundred years, I would. In a fucking heartbeat.'

Wow. Jed winced at the vitriol in Henry's voice. He'd always imagined he and the Duke riding their lands together, playing cricket on the long stretch of lawn in front of the Hall and the FD leading his legitimate son around the Hall, stopping at the portraits of each ancestor and passing on their family history.

'Our father was a perfect prick.'

Shocked at the bitterness he heard in Henry's voice, he'd wanted to walk away, to leave the past where it belonged. But another part of him needed to know. 'Explain.'

Henry shook his head. 'Jesus, you're a bossy asshole,' he muttered.

'It's probably inherited,' Jed conceded. He didn't like wasting time with superfluous words or explaining himself.

'You might be interested to know that he kept pretty close tabs on you.' Henry explained. 'He kept a log of everything he heard about you. I found it in a secret drawer when I cleared out his desk. You can look at it if you want.'

He didn't want to. 'I have no interest in the Duke or anything he thought or did.' He cursed himself for engaging. If you didn't, if you kept yourself apart, you couldn't be vulnerable. Or be hurt. His next sentence to Henry had been, shockingly, more difficult to say than he'd expected. 'I have no interest in you, either.'

Henry hadn't looked surprised by his harsh comment. 'Can I ask you one thing, just to satisfy my curiosity?' He didn't wait for Jed's permission. 'How can you accept Al and Mick so easily? They aren't related, or have any genetic ties, to you. I know I bullied you, but you gave back as good as you got. But you won't even consider acknowledging me. I guess that old Bible saying about sins of the fathers is right, huh?'

Jed couldn't answer the question, didn't want to. Gripping the bridge of his nose, Jed had needed to change the subject, immediately. 'I'll take a look at the ponies you are selling. Tomorrow works.'

One side of Henry's mouth lifted. 'There's been a lot of interest in them, and they'll move quickly.'

Jed didn't like his smug expression. 'I said I'll look at them tomorrow.'

Henry grinned. 'If you want the chance to buy my horses, you're going to have to have that beer with me, Jed.'

And with that sally and minor blackmail threat, Henry walked away. The bastard – metaphorically, as Jed was the real bastard – was persistence personified. But his question about accepting his non-blood siblings reverberated around Jed's mind, and he kept returning to it, like an itchy mosquito bite needing to be scratched.

The past, and its memories, were never far away. He'd never met Al's mum and he got along okay with Mick's mum, but Kael's mum had been Satan's Bride. She'd resented him and Mick, loathed their connection to Troyden, and had done everything she could – snide comments, blaming them for anything and everything – to make their lives miserable. But after the divorce, Jed didn't cut Kael out of his life. It just made him want to protect him more, to be the big brother and tuck him under his wing.

Kael, being the free spirit he was, hated having three bossy older siblings and took off overseas to assert his independence. But the point was, he never blamed Kael for having a witch for a mother. And, if Jed was being fair, Henry shouldn't have to pay the price for his father's sins either. Yeah, Henry had been a precocious, annoying, entitled shit as a kid, but Jed had also been an arsehole.

Mick and Al would say he still was.

He was judging Henry on the kid he'd been, and on the father he'd been lumbered with, and that wasn't fair. So what was holding him back from Henry? The Duke was dead, and nobody cared that he'd got a stable girl pregnant so long ago. Nobody gave a damn.

Was he resentful of Henry's wealth and status? Was he

angry because Jed should be the Duke and not Henry? Fuck, no, that wasn't it. The core of it was that he didn't know the role Henry wanted him to play. They were the same age, so it wasn't like Henry needed a big brother, nor did he need a protector. If you gave credence to that bullshit, and he didn't, Henry was also higher up the social pole than he.

His half-brother didn't *need* him, so what did he want with him? And if he didn't need him, how could they have a relationship? What could Jed bring to the table?

The door to his workshop opened. Balancing on the balls of his feet, he turned and watched Eden move into the middle of the room, trailing her hands over a piece of wood on his far worktable. He wasn't sure how he would use it yet, but thought it resembled the curve of a woman's back as it dipped in to meet her hips, the swell that followed.

'Hey,' he said, standing up, tossing the piece of sandpaper to the side.

'I knocked, but you didn't answer. Is it okay for me to be in here?'

His workshop was his bolthole, his private space, but he was surprised to find he didn't mind her presence. He also appreciated her asking. 'It's fine.' He glanced at his watch. It was after twelve and later than he thought. 'I thought you would be busy with the charity match stuff.'

'I was, but I needed a break and decided to walk.'

She was working more closely with Henry than he liked. But there wasn't a damn thing he could say about it. And he had to give it to them, the two of them were producing results. What had started as a vague idea was now a highly publicised event. 'You're doing a fantastic job, by the way. Everyone is impressed.'

She waved his words away. 'It's mostly Henry.'

'It's mostly *you*, Eden. He might be the face of the project, but you're its body and soul.'

Her smile hit her eyes, and her cheeks flushed at his compliment. Unlike the women he usually dated, she had no idea how to deal with praise. 'Anyway, I saw the door open and peeked inside.'

He always headed into his shop when he needed to decompress. He stretched, arching his back before resting his butt against the table. He'd returned late from Cowdray Park yesterday, and after showering, he'd crawled into bed and slept for ten hours. But he'd missed her, missed waking up to strands of her hair tangled in his stubble, her soft body pressed against his.

'You disappeared yesterday afternoon,' he commented. He'd wanted to introduce her to Tara and Vincent but couldn't find her. Neither did she answer his calls or text messages.

He'd been annoyed at the time, but maybe he was jumping the gun introducing her to the Bancrofts. Firstly, he and Eden were just sleeping together, their fling having an expiration date, and introducing her to old, important friends was such a couple-y thing to do. The thought made the back of his neck itch.

Secondly, Troyden was right: Tara and Vince had seemed out of whack yesterday. They'd both been overly bright, a little spacy and pretty shattered. He'd asked if they were okay, and they'd assured him that they were.

He didn't believe them.

He'd call them later to check up on them. Looking across at Eden, he still wanted to know why she'd vanished yesterday. 'So why did you leave?'

She looked away, trying to find the answer in his bandsaw. 'Ah, I was peopled out and needed some peace. Also, I couldn't stop sneezing.

'And you guys were losing,' she added, her eyes sparkling with mischief.

'Yeah, it wasn't our best day,' he admitted. 'I was unfocused and missed a couple of shots at goal. That's not something I normally do.'

Eden walked around his bandsaw to boost herself up onto his worktable. 'It was a strange afternoon.'

He knew what was bugging him – Henry, the Bancrofts and his addiction to her – but he had no idea why worry dulled her normally bright eyes. He wished he was better at expressing himself, communicating, at cajoling people to talk. Maybe then he could get Eden to talk to him, but throttling his emotions and words was an old habit – he sorted out other people's issues and kept fears and worries to himself – and it was the one habit he didn't know how to break.

What he'd realised recently about Eden was that she didn't take. From the moment she'd arrived at Elmsleigh House, she'd never asked for anything – not from Troyden, not from Mick, not from *him*.

In fact, she was the one doing the giving. Yes, Troyden had provided her with a room, but Eden often came home from the village with bags loaded with fresh produce, wine and chocolates to put into Di's overflowing pantry. She often turned down invitations from him and his siblings –

she was currently Al and Justin's favourite person – to eat with Troyden, to keep him company in the big house. She was the reason none of them had to deal with any Sugar Babies lately. Troyden hooking up with younger women wasn't, he now knew, about his ego or sex, but about keeping loneliness at bay.

They were so much alike in strange ways. Like him, Eden was fiercely independent, and determined to never be demanding or a burden. Unlike him, she was happy and preferred to let others shine. Eden's feet swung back and forth, and her hands held the edges of the bench in a tight grip. She looked around, taking in his lathes, tools and enormous stack of wood piled in the corner. She stroked the curved wood next to her, with the same reverence she touched him, taking in the angles and curves, feeling her way, enjoying the process. It was sinuous and sexy and … *yeah*.

He was now sporting a woody in his workshop.

'Your work is incredible, Jed. When did you start making stuff?'

That, at least, was easy enough to answer. 'Shortly after I came to live with Troyden.' She lifted an eyebrow, silently asking for more.

'A couple of months after my mum died, I was bored and wandered into a workshop where Troyden's now-retired farm manager was making a bench. He handed me a piece of sandpaper, showed me how to work with the grain, and in the quiet, in the repetitive motion of stroking that paper across the wood, I found … a measure of peace.'

'So it was a form of meditation?'

'I suppose it was,' he admitted. 'I always left his shed

feeling better. Over the years, I started learning more, doing more, and trying different things.'

'You're damn talented,' Eden murmured. Then she tipped her head and pointed her finger at him. 'And when you feel out of sorts, you hide out in here.'

Hide was a strong word. But, yeah ... whenever he felt overwhelmed or upset, he slipped into this cool building and eased his tension by transforming raw wood into something usable and beautiful.

Her smile was as soft as a chambray cloth. 'Just so you know, I'm a huge fan of anything that helps a person get through the day, or situation, or conversation.'

It was deeply reassuring to know that, in Eden's eyes, it was fine to admit that not everything was okay all the time.

And as that thought faded, desire rolled through him. He wanted her exactly in that position, sitting right there, but naked. She could lean back on her elbows, and he'd drop to his knees to tongue her. He didn't think he'd take the time to undress properly; he'd just shove his pants down and slide into her, but her being naked was something he wouldn't compromise on. Long after her departure, he wanted to remember taking this amazing woman while she sat on the table where he expressed himself through his creations.

It wasn't sex; it was making a memory.

'So what's the beef between you and Henry?' she asked, running her finger through a layer of sawdust on the table.

Her question obliterated his thoughts as irritation strolled in and parked its arse down. He wanted to snap at her, to tell her that it wasn't any of her business, but couldn't. He wanted, for some reason, to confide in her, and that scared him shitless.

But could he trust her? Nobody but Troyden – and Henry, obviously – not even his siblings, knew he and Henry were half-brothers.

Henry pulled all his deepest insecurities to the surface, and he hated him for that. *Why can you accept them and not me?* He still didn't know what was behind Henry's push to acknowledge him as his brother. What was he getting out of it? What did he want from him? What price would Jed have to pay?

And how would his siblings feel when they heard that he'd been keeping his connection to the Duke and Henry a secret? Would they look at him differently when they found out his father couldn't acknowledge him? Would they see him differently and question whether their love was misplaced? How much damage control would he need to do? Would they still want him? Would they trust him enough to continue to let him be Troyden's, and their, protector and shield? And if they took that away, where would he go? What would he do?

'Jed?'

He fought his way back to the present, his eyes slowly focusing on her lovely face. 'Mm?'

'You're miles away. Are you okay?'

Yes. No. Shit, he didn't know. What he did know was that he was tired of being in his head, sick of running scenarios, and second-guessing himself. He needed to lose himself, to step out of his head and feel rather than think. And he knew of a perfect way to do just that.

Eden jumped off the bench and dusted the sawdust off

her very nice arse. The arse he wanted to hold as he slid inside her…

'Sorry, I was miles away. I was thinking about my family and then taking you here, in my workshop.' He winced as his words landed. 'Jesus, the two thoughts weren't linked. I mean … fuck, that came out wrong. You're Troyden's niece. You're not related to me or anything like that.'

He didn't recognise the stuttering fool talking right now. Generally, he was a lot smoother than this. Her eyes lightened with amusement. 'Thank God, because some of the things you've done would be illegal in certain countries,' she told him, her eyes made bluer by laughter.

Okay, he enjoyed a little bondage, nothing that would even rate on the Shades of Grey scale, and was a fan of different positions, but geez, they'd done nothing extreme. She'd either had a very tame, missionary-style sex life or was uncomfortable with him being dominant in bed. 'Am I too bossy?' he asked, wondering if he was now overthinking everything.

'Yes,' she promptly answered.

'In *bed*, Eden,' he said, trying to hold on to his patience. 'Have I made you feel uncomfortable?' Please say no. Just a quick, solid no.

She punched him on the bicep, her small fist holding all the power of a toddler's. 'I was joking, Jed! And if I didn't like anything, I would sure as hell tell you.'

Of course she would, because she was an adult who didn't play games. He released the air he'd been hanging on to in a long whoosh. 'Okay, good.' He glanced at the bench and shrugged. Since they were being honest… 'So, as I was saying, I was thinking about you sitting on my bench, naked, legs spread wide while I went down on you.'

She stood on her tiptoes and brushed her sexy mouth across his. He went from a semi to hard-as-steel in a heartbeat. 'I know. I saw it all play out in your eyes, Number Three.'

He fed her a deep, intense kiss while tugging her shirt up and over her head. The next moment both her bra and shirt were draped over his bandsaw and his mouth was on her nipple. He sucked her deep, then pulled back to look down at her jeans, reaching for the button and the zip. His burnished gold eyes met hers and her mouth curved into a sexy grin as she ran her thumb along the length of his shaft. 'Let me play with some wood, Harris.'

It was a terrible joke, but he couldn't help his quick laughter. He pressed his hand against hers, heat from her palm branding him. 'Go for it, sweetheart. I'm all yours.'

And for the first time in, well, forever, he didn't follow up his statement with a silent 'for now'.

In the kitchen, Eden, still reeling from one of the most intense orgasms in the history of the world – not hyperbole, her legs were still shaking, and her heart had yet to leave its temporary location between her legs – ran a hand over her messy hair and tried to make sense of where she was and what she was doing.

Right. Big house. Kitchen. Via group text, Diana had summoned for lunch everyone who was around, as she'd made her world-famous chicken pot pie. Obviously, Diana's chicken pie was the stuff of legend because the Castle clan were all seated around the big, battered kitchen table, and Alistair had yet to look away from the eye-level oven where two huge pies were slowly turning a golden brown. Jed ruffled the kids' hair and sniffed the garlic- and rosemary-scented air. 'Smells amazing, Di. Where's Dad?'

Di tossed a dishcloth over her shoulder. 'He's with the Bancrofts in the study.'

Eden was instantly rocketed back to the present, and she just managed to catch her shocked gasp. Shit! They were *here*? Tara and Vince? In the house? What the *hell*? Meeting them when her head was still reeling from good – no, fabulous sex – and feeling upside down and inside out, was not an option. If, or when, she spoke to them again, hopefully never, she needed to be calm and collected, mentally alert.

'Are they staying for lunch?' Jed asked breezily.

'I asked, but they said they have to get back to the city, but Troyden will persuade them,' Diana said, sounding certain.

Jed smiled. 'He always does.'

Shit. She *had* to avoid them. And that meant missing out on Diana's famous chicken pie. A pity, because she was starving.

Eden edged away from Jed, her hand in his. She tugged, but he refused to let go. She tugged harder and finally got him to look at her, and she widened her eyes, silently asking him to release her.

'Where are you going?'

His grip on her hand tightened. Dear God, the man had no idea how to take a hint. Stepping closer to him, she stood on her toes so that her lips were an inch from his ear. 'Jed, I need to go to the bathroom, and … clean up,' she whispered. It was, she thought, a decent excuse, and one he couldn't argue with.

It worked as a hint of a blush appeared on the ridges of his ears. 'Ah … right.' He squeezed her hand and touched his lips to her temple.

'Hurry back, Alistair might eat your portion if you're not here.'

What excuse could she come up with if the Bancrofts joined them for lunch? Could she manufacture an emergency around the charity polo match? But Jed and Mick were on the committee and could easily fact-check her. Maybe she could say that a pipe in her flat had burst?

God, she hated lying, but what choice did she have? She had to avoid the Bancrofts, and not only because she wanted to. She'd been instructed to keep her involvement in the case quiet, to not discuss it with anyone and she did not want to get on the wrong side of the Metropolitan Police. She could live without an obstruction of justice or impeding an investigation charge levied against her.

She would figure out an excuse later, crossing that bridge when she came to it. Right now, she needed to slip up to her room, use the bathroom – she had the opportunity so she might as well clean up, brush her hair and splash water on her face – and then she'd tiptoe down the stairs, and wait in the corridor. There was a massive, convenient suit of armour she could hide behind, just a few yards from the study door. She'd hang out with the seventeenth-century equivalent of Iron Man until she could establish whether the Bancrofts would be joining the family for lunch or not.

How much longer could she keep juggling these emotional balls? She pushed her hands into her eye sockets, feeling the burn of tears. She was physically tired and emotionally whipped.

Hopefully, not for that much longer. But whether it was five days or five weeks, what choice did she have? Walk away from Jed and the family now, or stay for as long as she could, banking a few more memories? It was a simple choice to make. She'd been alone before and would be alone again, but not today. Not tonight.

Hopefully not tomorrow, or the next day. The best scenario was to keep the situation under wraps until the charity polo match was over. The Castle clan might hate her, but at least Hope Harbour would be saved. And by helping to organise the event, she would've been a force for good, not destruction.

That had to count for something, right?

Chapter Thirteen

The suit of armour topped out at more than six and a half feet. It was wide and broad – the dude who used it back in the seventeenth century must've been a giant – and a perfect place to hide. Eden rested her back against the wall, her shoulder touching the arm plate. Her hiding place wasn't that far from the kitchen, and she could still hear Mick fretting about returning to her patients. The kids were both home because of a head lice outbreak at the school and Justin was looking after them for the afternoon. Justin had asked Mick, twice in ten minutes, whether they were bug-free.

Down the passage, she could see Troyden standing in the entry hall with the Bancrofts, still entreating them to stay. As they talked, Eden wondered how the investigation was going. With her phone on silent, she sent a message to the detective in charge, asking for an update, then jumped when her phone vibrated with his almost instant reply.

> Still reviewing the evidence. Interviewed the Bancroft bookkeeper, she confirmed some dodgy transactions but didn't want to rock the boat. They are coming in for an interview later this afternoon.

Right, that was why they couldn't stay for lunch. Since he was being chatty, she risked asking another question. Well, two.

> Has the search warrant been served? And when will you press charges or not?

She stared at the phone, but nothing appeared on her screen. Dammit. She considered running up the stairs and trying to call him but knew he probably wouldn't answer. *Ugh*, she hated feeling small and insignificant and unimportant.

'We really must go,' Vince said, and Eden heard the hint of impatience in his voice. 'We have a meeting back in the city.'

A meeting? That was a hell of a euphemism for an interview with the police.

'It's been lovely seeing you,' Troyden said, opening the front door and ushering them out. Thank God. 'Jed will be sorry to have missed you.'

Please stay in the kitchen, Jed. Please assume Troyden is talking them into staying for lunch, don't come out.

Annoyed, Eden shifted, and her arm clanked against the suit of armour, and it released a loud squeak. Eden immediately plastered herself against the wall and held her breath. Shit, shit, shit. Why did this house have to have such amazing acoustics?

'What on earth was that?' Tara demanded from outside the front door.

'That's Elspeth, our resident ghost,' Troyden replied, without missing a beat.

Tara's oh-so-familiar laugh sounded a little strained. 'Oh, really, what nonsense. You know I don't believe in ghosts.'

'You should,' Troyden told her. 'As you know, I've seen Elspeth many times, and she sometimes moves things. That suit of armour is her favourite thing to play with.'

Through the open door, she watched the trio disappear from view. Car doors slammed and an engine purred. They were on their way, thank God.

Her phone vibrated against her hand and she looked down to see the number of the Metropolitan Police on her screen. What? They never called her unless it was an emergency.

She swiped, lifted the phone to her ear and whispered a hello. Detective Gosling's voice boomed in her ear. 'Gosling here. Battery on my cell died. Working on the warrant.'

He never spoke in full sentences and Eden blinked. 'Okay. Do you know when this will be over? When they will ... you know?'

'Be arrested or acquitted? Not sure. Keep your head down.'

'Okay, but—' Eden heard the phone beep and knew she was talking to dead air. Dammit. Would it hurt him to give her a little more information? An end date? Something more to keep her from climbing the walls?

Desperate to scratch an itch on her ankle, she placed her hand on the suit's shoulder to keep her balance, smiling as Jed stepped into the hallway from the kitchen, at the same time as Troyden walked back into the hall. She felt herself beginning to teeter. She recovered only to watch, horrified, as the suit of armour toppled sideways and crashed against the hardwood floor, the sound bouncing off the walls. The various plates fell apart and skittered away.

Oh, shit. Why did these things keep happening to her?

The door to the kitchen widened, with Mick, Alistair and Justin standing on the other side, looking astonished. Gemma and Liam pushed past the adults, expressions of horror on their faces.

'*Oh, oh*,' Gemma said, slapping her hands on her cheeks.

That didn't sound good.

'Was it Elspeth?' Mick asked, jamming her hands into the pockets of her doctor's coat.

The ghost? Was she taking the piss? Eden pushed her shoulders back and shook her head. 'No, it was me. I bumped it.'

'Why were you hiding?' Mick asked. 'Why didn't you come back into the kitchen?'

Now there was a question she didn't want to answer. Ignoring Mick, she forced herself to look at Troyden. 'I am so sorry,' she quietly stated. 'I wasn't thinking. I'll pay for it to be fixed or put together, or whatever they need to do.'

And how much would that cost? A thousand pounds? Two? Ten? How would she raise that much cash?

Troyden looked at the pieces and pushed a breast plate to the side with his foot. 'If I had a dollar for every time this thing fell apart... I really should move it.'

'You really should, Grandpa,' Gemma told him, looking serious. 'Besides, Elspeth doesn't like this one either. She says you should put it in the attic. And that the man who wore the other one wasn't nice at all.'

Instead of telling Gemma not to talk nonsense, Troyden tipped his head to the side. 'Really? Did she tell you who he was?'

'Someone from a long time ago,' Gemma replied. 'Elspeth says he speaks with a funny voice. But Elspeth isn't good at talking either, because she called the man a "night". She's confusing sometimes.'

Troyden smiled. 'He speaks with a funny accent because the man who wore it came from Germany. And he was a knight, someone who protected the king, and they wore this to save themselves from being stabbed by long spears. And by all accounts, no, he wasn't a nice man.'

Nobody but Eden seemed surprised to hear that Gemma spoke to a ghost and that her information seemed startlingly accurate. Come on, this had to be a set-up, right? They were pulling a prank on her. Because, hell, everyone knew that there wasn't any scientific, definitive proof that ghosts existed.

'I didn't know you still talked to Elspeth, Gemma,' Mick said, sounding a little too nonchalant for someone whose career was based on science.

'Not that much anymore,' she said, shrugging. 'She's been busy.'

With what, Eden wanted to scream. What the hell did ghosts do that took up time? Mick put her hand on Gemma's shoulder. 'Go get some lunch, guys.' she said.

Eden watched the kids scamper away, trying to make

sense of the last five minutes. Her uncle didn't seem to be mad about the armour toppling over, and nobody was fazed that the second youngest member of their family had the occasional conversation with a spirit.

She looked at the dismembered suit of armour and bit down hard on her lip. 'I'm so sorry, Troyden. I'll pay to have it fixed.' It was armour. Surely it could be fixed, right? It was, after all, built to take knocks.

Mick wrinkled her nose. 'Sixteen something, E. That's four hundred years of history scattered on the floor.'

Oh, Jesus. She felt awful. Eden dropped to her haunches and picked up a piece of the breastplate, surprised it wasn't heavier. She reached for another piece and looked up when Justin cleared his throat. She caught his grimace. 'The restorer said that if anything happened to it again, he wouldn't put it back together again. He wasn't going to condone such ill treatment of a museum-quality piece.'

Ah, come on! Seriously?

'You guys are such pricks,' Jed said, moving to stand next to her.

Justin shot him a grin. 'Sure. But teasing her is fun.'

She was being teased? Jed reached down, curled his arm around her bicep and gently lifted her to her feet. He sent her a small smile as he stroked her from shoulder to her hand. He linked his fingers with hers and squeezed.

'It's a copy, Eden. Troyden had it commissioned about thirty years ago and moved the original suit of armour into storage.' He nudged a piece with his foot. 'This dude has been shot with paper-pea guns, had cricket balls tossed at his head, has been knocked down more times than we can count. He can be put back together in ten minutes.'

So she hadn't destroyed a vital piece of the country's cultural heritage? 'So you were all in on the joke?' she asked, unsure.

'Oh, E, teasing is our love language,' Mick told her.

'Yeah, they are jerks,' Jed muttered, glowering at his siblings. 'A lot of what you see in the house, the treasures, are fakes—'

'Copies of the original, to be accurate,' Troyden interjected. 'I only make copies when I own the real thing.'

Right, she was having difficulty following their conversation. The suit of armour was a fake? The house was full of copies? 'But *why*? Why wouldn't you want to look at the originals?'

'Oh, I regularly do,' Troyden assured her, 'but in the safety of my undisclosed, super safe warehouse-museum.' He looked around and smiled. 'But this is a family home, and I had a choice between allowing my kids, and grandkids, to run free without worrying about breaking anything or making them tiptoe around the house. A good thing I did, because Alistair broke a copy of a Ming vase because he wasn't looking where he was going, and Jedson smacked a cricket ball through the window and split the canvas of the Monet copy in the library.'

He owned a Monet? Holy shit! Jed snorted. 'You made me pay for the restoration of the fake painting,' he muttered, still sounding annoyed.

'Because I told you, at least twenty times, to play away from the house, and you insisted on playing outside my study window,' Troyden retorted. He looked at his daughter. 'And I don't know why you are smirking,

Michaela. If I recall, you carved your initials into the leg of the fake Chippendale desk in your bedroom.'

Mick's smile quickly faded and she sighed. 'If it makes you feel any better, Liam fingerpainted his bedroom walls the day before yesterday, and Gemma broke the clasp of my Elsa Schiaparelli necklace while playing dress up.'

'I'm so glad you are raising yourself,' Troyden told her, chuckling.

Al checked his watch. 'Can we have lunch now, please? I've got a riveting report to read.'

Jed shook his head. 'Dude, no report can ever be called riveting,' he insisted. He looked at Justin. 'He was the best you could do? Seriously?'

Justin shrugged. 'He's super sexy,' he said, a tad dreamy. 'When he's naked, wearing just his black-rimmed specs, when he looks at me like I'm—'

Jed rubbed a hand over his face. 'Jesus, *enough*.' He placed his hand on her back, and Eden sighed as the heat of his palm radiated through her. She understood what Justin meant. When Jed looked at her in a certain way, when every atom of his being was focused on her, she would do anything he asked. She would move mountains and corral lightning if he asked her to...

She looked up at him and saw his eyes locked on her face. She'd never understood the term 'smouldered' before, but right now she felt singed as tiny flames danced over her skin. It took everything she had not to slap her hand on his chest, push him back to the opposite wall and climb him like a ladder.

But there was a small pile of worked iron they'd have to negotiate, shoulder plates and arm braces they'd have to step over. With her luck, they'd both end up on the floor, beaten up by a fake suit of armour.

She needed some perspective, something else to think about, to pull herself back to normal. She was behaving like a hormonal teenager who squealed when her crush so much as noticed her. Pathetic. She needed to be sensible and rational, for God's sake.

So she pulled in a deep breath and stepped away from temptation and returned to what they'd been talking about before. The very sensible and rational topic of sharing their house with a ghost. 'You guys don't believe in ghosts, do you? You were joking when you said you saw Elspeth, right?' she asked.

Jed's smile slowly grew, and his expression turned to amusement. Yay, he was about to tell her that he'd been joking earlier, that Elspeth was Gemma's imaginary friend, that he'd been taking the piss.

'It's been a while since I've seen her, three or four years, but yeah, she's around doing whatever ghosts that haunt old houses do,' he easily replied.

Oh…

Right. That wasn't the answer she expected.

'I saw Henry on my coffee run this morning, Jed,' Mick said, making her way through her second helping of chicken pie. 'He said to remind you about that beer. Why does he keep asking you, and why do you keep refusing him? You two are like an estranged couple trying to decide whether to get back together or not.'

She wasn't far off. Jed placed his fork on his plate and rubbed his forehead. He was so very tired of lying to them. Troyden sat at the head of the table, concern on his face.

Mick being Mick wouldn't leave the subject alone. 'What does he want from you?'

'Everything.'

He felt the tension rise, and cursed when he realised he'd said that word out loud. 'Jed … what does that mean?' Justin asked. He looked at their confused faces, all waiting for him to explain the secret growing heavier with every passing day.

'Just put it down, Jed,' Troyden quietly said. How did his father always know what he was thinking? 'It's time to put it down.'

Jed shifted uncomfortably, before meeting their eyes one by one. Here goes nothing. His stomach tightened, and he wondered if his just-swallowed lunch would make its way back up. Then he felt Eden's hand on his knee, and his heart rate settled down to a wild gallop.

'I should've told you this years ago,' he began, his voice low but steady. 'But I didn't. I kept it from you, and for that, I'm sorry.'

Mick frowned. 'Kept what from us, Jed?' she asked, her voice sharp with the unmistakable trace of hurt.

He exhaled, clenching his jaw. 'Henry is my half-brother. We're both the Duke's sons. He's legitimate; I'm not.'

The words were out, and Jed couldn't take them back. The silence that followed felt like an eternity. His siblings looked at him, their faces a mixture of shock, confusion and disbelief.

Al shook his head, knife clattering onto the table as Mick

quietly told her children to go and watch TV. 'Wait. You're saying Henry, *the Duke*'s son, is your brother?' Al let out a short laugh, but there was no humour in it. 'That's a hell of a thing to keep to yourself.'

'I know,' Jed said, his voice rough. 'I should've told you a long time ago. But every time I thought about it, I convinced myself it wasn't the right time.'

Mick crossed her arms, tears in her eyes. Mick *never* cried. 'Why are you telling us this now? Would you have told us if he hadn't come back?'

No, probably not. He winced at the bite in her tone. Her anger was justified. They all had a right to know. 'Why did you keep a secret, Jed? Who were you trying to protect?' Justin asked.

Shit, that was a hell of a question. Not Henry, or the Duke. When nobody moved, when their eyes didn't drop from his face, he knew he'd have to answer. He owed them that. 'I was trying to protect *me*.' He pushed his hand through his hair and released a ragged sigh.

'From whom?' Mick demanded.

'I've spent my whole life wondering if I was even worth being part of this family. I didn't want you to look at me differently. I didn't want you to see me as … as some kind of mistake.'

Troyden, who had been unusually quiet up until now, finally spoke, his voice soft but firm. 'Jed, you're not a mistake. Never that.'

Jed looked at him, his throat tightening. He could feel the emotions bubbling up inside him, raw and unfiltered. God, this was hard. And awful. 'You've always treated me like one of your own, but it never felt real. Not all the way.

I felt – feel – like I constantly had to bring something to the party to belong to this family. Even as a little kid, I needed to be needed. Sometimes I still feel like that.'

'We do need you, Jed! You're our brother. End of!' Mick yelled, properly upset.

'Of course, we need you. You're the family rock.' Al added. 'But did you really think we wouldn't accept you because the Duke didn't? That we'd see you as something less?'

He couldn't talk anymore, explain. He was done. He'd said more than he'd expected to, more than he'd wanted to. It was too much.

Mick softened slightly, uncrossing her arms. 'Jed, family, especially this family, isn't about titles or bloodlines. It's about who's there for you, who's got your back when it matters. You've always had our back. But I think you've forgotten, or never knew, that it's a two-way street. You need us to need you, but we need *you* to need *us* too.'

Al leaned forward, his voice gentle, but his eyes still sharp. 'And let me be very clear, Jed, I don't give a flying fuck who your real father is or isn't. You're my brother, a part of this family. Always have been. Always will be.'

Jed felt a lump form in his throat as he took a shaky breath. 'Okay.'

Troyden stood up, moved toward Jed, and placed a hand on his shoulder. 'Our love isn't conditional, Jedson. It never has been.'

Jed nodded, patted his hand and pushed back his chair. He needed to leave. His emotions were too big, the relief too great. He couldn't fall apart. He was the protector, the strong one, the one who stood between them and the world.

He couldn't break down. He couldn't let them see him crumble. Habits, after all, couldn't be broken by one conversation. 'I need to get going. I—'

Mick stood up, leaned across the table and punched his arm. Because he'd taught her how to punch, it held a reasonable force. 'You're a moron. And for what it's worth, a huge pain in the arse. You always have been, so nothing's changed.'

Jed let out a low chuckle, his shoulders dropping fractionally.

Alistair stood up and Jed moved back, in case he punched him too. His brother was a lot bigger than him and might put him on his arse. 'For once, I agree with Mick. You are a moron. But you're our moron.'

'Yeah, got it,' Jed said. Look, it would take time until he felt like he was, *intrinsically*, a part of the Castle clan. But a weight had been lifted, some of his decades-old fears calmed.

It had only taken twenty-five years. But better than never, he supposed. Now he just needed to decide what to do about Henry.

Eden knew enough about Jed to know that he needed time to himself, but not too much time, because then he would start overthinking and brooding. There were only two places he'd go when he was upset, his workshop or the stables. His workshop was on the way to the stables, so she poked her head inside the long building – images of how well he'd loved her earlier on that bench flashing behind her eyes and heating her core – but the place was empty, the machines asleep.

So that meant the stables. Eden hesitated and wondered whether she'd have an allergic reaction. She pushed back her shoulders and forced steel into her spine. Well, she was about to find out because there was no way she was going to leave Jed to deal with his thoughts and emotions by himself. She'd seen the pain in his eyes earlier and heard the fear in his voice. Nobody, not even stoic Jed, should be alone after dropping a conversational hand grenade.

And if that meant her morphing into a hive-covered beast, then so be it. She wouldn't die.

She slipped through the huge stable doors, easy to open despite their size, and walked into the cool interior, trying to take shallow breaths. There wasn't any reason to inhale more dander than she needed to. She loved the stillness of the mostly empty stables, the soft sounds of a sick or pregnant horse shuffling, the occasional nicker, and the smell of hay and horseflesh. With its high, wooden-arched ceiling it looked a little like a cathedral, and it held the same peace. She understood why this was where Jed needed to be. There was peace here.

She was barely three steps into the stable when a muscled arm encircled her waist and lifted her off her feet, her back to his chest. She squealed and held on to Jed's arm as he walked her out of the stables and back into the bright sunshine. 'Are you mad?' he roared. 'What the hell do you think you are doing?'

Her feet hit the ground, and she gripped his arm to keep her balance. 'Uh—'

'You have a severe allergy to horses, you idiot!'

Jed yelled, his eyes sparking. 'The last time you were in a stable you fainted and scared the shit out of me.'

She could feel a sneeze coming on and prayed it would go away. She held her breath, not wanting to give his words credence. But because her body was a bitch, the sneeze hit the back of her throat, and she cupped her hands around her nose and released the inevitable.

Three sneezes later, she lifted her head to look at a scowling Jed. 'Happy, now?' he asked, his mouth thin with displeasure. Before she could answer, he lifted her arms and gently twisted them, checking for any incoming welts. 'Tight throat? Difficulty breathing?'

'No, I'm fine.' She hadn't, thank goodness, had a hive since that first time. He dropped to his haunches, balancing on his toes to inspect her legs. Thank God, she'd shaved them this morning.

'Nothing on your legs yet.' He stood up and gripped her shoulders in a tight grip. He was a strong guy, but conscious of his strength. He shook her, just a little. 'What the hell were you thinking, Eden?'

She held his wrists and looked up into his angry-at-her and angry-for-her face. 'I was thinking that you just dropped a bombshell. And that you might be having trouble processing it.'

He dropped his head, and his grip loosened. 'I'm okay,' he gruffly stated. When he looked back at her, his eyes were blazing with intensity and a healthy dose of irritation. 'Nothing is so important ... *nobody* is so important, that you need to go into a stable, Eden.'

Ah, she could push the point but decided that was an argument for later. Right now, he looked shattered.

Eden suspected another emotional blow would cause him to become a human version of the suit of armour hitting the floor.

Eden knew he wanted to hold it together and that he wasn't used to feeling vulnerable. He was the glue that held the Castle family together, but sometimes glue became brittle and hard, and started to crack.

She took his hand, interlinked her much smaller fingers in his and tugged him toward a small knoll of grass, under the stately oak tree. It was where she'd lain after collapsing the first time she'd visited Elmsleigh over two months ago. She sat, leaned her back against the tree, and patted the grass beside her. When he turned his head away and looked at the horses in the paddock, she shook her head at his stubbornness.

'Jed, sit down,' she firmly stated. Imitating her mum's taking-no-shit tone worked, even on thirty-five-year-old alpha males.

Good to know.

Jed bent his long legs and rested his arms on his knees. 'I don't want to talk about it, Eden,' he stated, his voice rough.

Of course, he didn't, because Jed was a doer and a solver, not a talker. But her aim wasn't to get him to talk, but to let him know he wasn't alone. 'I get what you said earlier, about needing to do something, or be someone for your family, to feel like you have worth,' she said, trying to keep her tone casual.

He didn't look at her, but Eden sensed his interest, so she continued. 'My mum was a foster mum, I told you that, right?' When he nodded, she continued. 'There were so many kids, and I was just another one. She couldn't give anyone too much attention; she didn't have the time or the emotional resources. Kids came in; kids went out. I was the one that stayed. I only got as much from her – brush your teeth, make your bed, fix your hair – as they others did. Food, a roof over my head, a bed. Not much else.'

Eden looked for the right words to explain her unique situation. 'My mum wasn't … warm, is the right word. She did a lot of good, but…'

'But you were a long-term foster kid. Someone she didn't connect with on an emotional level. Now I understand why raising funds for Hope Harbour is so important to you.'

God, he got her. On levels no one else had ever before. It was like he could peel her apart and look directly into the heart of who she was. It scared her on levels she didn't think were possible.

But this wasn't about her; it was about him. And the fact that he'd been dealing with the death of his biological father – that had to raise some unwelcome feelings – and his brother's sudden reappearance in his life, demanding a relationship. Maybe demanding was too harsh a word, but Henry could be persistent. He clearly wanted the relationship with his brother that their father had denied them, and Henry appeared to be determined to make it happen, no matter what. Eden sighed, remembering the flinty stare in Jed's eyes as he'd told his family the truth. How worried he'd been that Henry's arrival would affect his relationship with his siblings and his stepfather.

'I remember spending a couple of nights at a foster home like your mum's,' Jed said, his voice lower than normal. Holy hell, really? She whipped her head around and took in his profile. 'Really?' she asked. 'How did that happen?'

'My mum went through a rough patch a couple of years before she met Troyden. She came to London. I presume she thought she could find work here and look after me. But childcare, even back then, was so damn expensive, and she fell out with the Bancrofts for a few months. We ended up moving, often, eventually into a shelter for a week or so.' Jed's voice trembled a little. 'I was young, and I still don't know why they took me away. I only spent a night in care, and the Bancrofts picked me up the next day. It was something that embarrassed her, so I didn't push for the hows and whys it had happened.'

He took a shaky breath, then quirked a half-smile. 'It would've been cool if we'd briefly met as kids, though, huh?'

She never pegged him for a romantic. Shifting closer she curled her hand around his big bicep, and kissed his shoulder, feeling the heat of his skin beneath his cotton t-shirt. 'Very cool,' she sighed in response. But she knew London was a big city; there were so many shelters, so many foster homes, so much need.

'Was your mum always religious?' Jed asked, his hand playing with her fingers holding his arm, as they settled into this pocket of vulnerability.

Was he done talking about his father? It seemed so. But maybe by talking about herself, she'd ease him into opening up. Eden shrugged. 'Yes, although I didn't realise how religious until I was an adult. But she was very … how do I put this? … private. She didn't talk to me, Jed. Or to anyone.' Her mum had no friends. Eden had been just like her up until a few weeks back: lonely, isolated, friendless. Now she had Mick and Troyden, Al and Justin and, to an extent, Jed.

She rested her temple on his bicep. 'I didn't even know who my dad was until I met Troyden.'

Could she say the words she thought often but had never expressed? Yeah, she thought she could. 'My mum joined the Church when I was eighteen, and I didn't understand why. When she went into the cloister, I finally understood: I'm her sin, Jed, her biggest mistake. Every day for eighteen years, whenever she looked at me, she was confronted with the fact that she'd gone against God's will and had sex and a baby out of wedlock.'

He started to protest, but she shook her head. 'It doesn't matter if we think it's archaic or whether we believe in it or not; she did, *profoundly*. She felt that she had disappointed God, and I was the living proof.'

He was silent for a long time. 'You couldn't possibly be a disappointment, Eden.'

That was the nicest thing anyone had said to her, in a long, long time. 'I now get why she joined the convent, sort of, why she retreated. She could concentrate on her relationship with God and on repairing it. I think it was the only relationship that ever mattered to her.'

He turned his head to lay his lips on her forehead and she closed her eyes when he kept them there, murmuring against her skin, 'I'm so sorry, sweetheart.'

She pulled back and handed him a shaky smile. 'I'm okay.' Well, apart from the fact that she was hiding her relationship with the Bancrofts from him, that she didn't know how she was going to walk away from him and this place, that she might, possibly, be falling in love with him…

Apart from all that, she was just dandy. Jed didn't look convinced and so she squeezed his arm. 'I've had a long time to get used to my reality, Jed.' It was time for him to talk now. 'Just as you have. But I can see that Henry pushing to acknowledge you as his brother has floored you.'

He pushed his other hand through his messy, thick hair. 'That's the understatement of the century.'

She waited him out, not knowing whether he'd open up and let her in. She'd learned that Jed never did anything he didn't want to do.

'He says that his life wasn't as great as it looked.'

She heard doubt in his voice. 'And you don't believe him?'

He half-turned to face her, his expression stubborn. 'As a kid, he was entitled, rich, superior, and annoying as hell.'

'You are the stepson of a billionaire, Jed,' Eden gently pointed out. 'With respect, you were probably just as entitled and just as much of an arse. All teenage boys are. Rich teenage boys are the worst.'

He sighed, twisted his sexy mouth and looked away. 'Stop being sensible, Eden,' he grumbled.

She smiled at his surly tone. 'People change, Jed, you know that. Henry isn't the teenager he used to be.'

She lifted their joined hands and kissed the back of his hand. 'So, here comes a hard question…'

He groaned. 'Oh, shit.'

She lowered their hands to rest them on his thigh and rubbed her thumb along the side of his palm. 'Are you trying to punish Henry because you can't punish your biological father?'

He was silent for so long that Eden knew she'd hit on a seam of truth. But she had to tread carefully because if she pushed too hard, he'd shut down. Possibly forever. 'Give Henry a chance to explain. Judge him on what he says, not on your assumptions. Judge him on the person he is now, not who he was back then. Also...' His lips tightened and she knew he was, mentally and emotionally, slipping away.

'Don't do anything you're not ready to do, Jed. Give yourself the gift of time. If you aren't ready now, he's just going to have to wait until you are.'

'But what if he announces our connection?' Jed demanded. 'He can tell the truth, and he will be believed.'

Henry wasn't going to do that, Eden assured him.

'How can you be so sure?' Jed asked, a little petulantly.

She smiled. Despite Jed wanting to believe he was a dick, Henry was, fundamentally, a nice guy. Effortlessly charming, sure, a little superficial to those who didn't know him, but Eden suspected that his surface urbanity and charisma were skin deep. The man had more depth than most imagined. 'I think he's a good guy, Jed.'

He snorted. 'You just like his car and the way he looks in a suit.'

Henry did look great in a suit, and she did like his car, but she wasn't that shallow. 'I think I like him because I see in him what I see in you.'

'We are *nothing* alike, Eden,' he protested, scowling.

'You're both hard-working, persistent, talented and determined,' she replied, and then waved her hand airily. 'He's better-looking than you, but four out of five isn't bad.'

Jed glared at her, but she now knew him well enough to see the glint of amusement in his eyes. 'But he didn't make you scream earlier, did he?'

'No,' she solemnly replied. 'And he never will. Besides, I think he has a thing for your sister.'

'Bullshit.'

'Between Kit and Henry, Mick's got her hands full.' To be fair, she couldn't be certain she was right, but something about the way Henry tensed when Mick was around, how he became ten times more intense, suggested he'd caught feelings of some kind. It was highly possible, because he was a man and not very emotionally evolved, that he'd yet to recognise them for what they were. It certainly explained why he hadn't been that disappointed when she'd fobbed him off.

Jed pulled back to place the back of his hand against her forehead. 'Are you feeling alright?'

She swatted it away. 'God, men can be so dense. Kit teases Mick because he doesn't know how else to capture her attention, and Henry's eyes follow her everywhere.'

Jed jumped up, bunched his fists and lowered his thick eyebrows. 'I will kill both of them if they make a move on my sister.'

Eden suppressed her grin. Mick was strong and capable, confident enough to juggle both men, but if Henry's quiet crush on her was a way to get the half-brothers communicating – even if they had to fight to do it – she was all for it. 'You should tell Henry that. Tell him your sister is off limits, but I bet he tells you to get stuffed,' she cheerfully stated.

'I can scare him off,' Jed assured her. 'I'm a pretty scary guy.'

But Henry wasn't the pushover Jed thought he was. 'Henry's a lot like you, Jed. If there was someone you wanted and you were told to back off, what would you do?'

'Try harder,' he admitted.

She pointed her finger at him and mimicked pulling the trigger. 'Exactly.'

Jed reached down to hold out his hand for her to take. He effortlessly pulled her to her feet and she bounced off his chest, but he snaked a hand down her back and pulled her into him. 'You're bloody annoying, Eden,' he murmured, sliding his lips across hers.

Her lips curved upwards. 'I know, my mother has told me that often enough.'

He tunnelled his hand into her hair, his broad hand covering most of her head. 'I didn't mean it that way,' she heard the remorse in his voice and sighed.

'I know you didn't, Jed.' She nuzzled her lips in the scruff on his jaw and kissed the outside of his mouth. She moved her mouth to his ear. 'I liked what we did earlier, by the way.'

'Me too. Let's do it again,' he suggested. 'I'd suggest the stable, but I'd prefer for you to still be breathing at the end of it. Let's go back to my place?'

Why did he even bother to ask? Didn't he know, by now, that she would follow him pretty much anywhere?

Chapter Fourteen

A garden party at the Hall, Henry had decided, was a good way to promote the charity polo match and had invited *Tatler* and *Hello!* to cover the event. Eden, in her excitement, had got ready with hours to spare and, instead of waiting for Jed to pick her up at the big house, had ambled down to his place to wait for him there.

With the charity polo match happening next weekend, a day event squeezed in between the more serious matches, she was jittery from too much caffeine and too little sleep. Everyone in the village, in big ways and small, had pitched in to help with organising the event, keeping her stress levels manageable. Jed's teammates and colleagues were playing in exhibition matches, and they'd sold a lot of tickets. It had to go well because Hope Harbour needed the funds, and the Bythesea villagers had put their trust in her. She didn't want to— No, she *couldn't* let them down.

Another layer of worry had nudged its way into her current list of things that could go wrong: would Tara and

Vince attend Henry's cocktail party? Their names weren't on the updated RSVP list, thank God. But A-list celebrities, football players and movie and West End stars were.

The Bancrofts' absence meant she could relax and enjoy being dressed up for a day. Her hair and make-up had taken ages, but she was happy with her 'natural' look. She wore her prettiest dress, a wraparound sky blue with a slit that showed a good portion of her thigh when she walked or sat, and her kick-ass, albeit second-hand, silver vintage too-high shoes. She couldn't think of a better way to spend an English summer afternoon than sipping champagne, eating tiny cucumber sandwiches and ogling James MacAvoy and Benedict Cumberbatch out of the corner of her eye.

Bliss.

Flip-flops on her feet, sexy shoes dangling from her hand, she lifted her face to the sun and smiled. She'd spent her nights in Jed's bed, with him loving her in every way imaginable. How the man functioned on so little sleep, she didn't know. He was up at dawn, put in a jam-packed day training and exercising, and then a full night with her. A natural, unforced affection existed between her and Troyden, and she adored spending time with Mick. Justin was completely wonderful, calm and supportive, and she'd even managed to bond with Alistair over code.

She felt at home here, on the estate, and couldn't imagine returning to London with the day-to-day slog of trains and buses, crowds and anonymity. And loneliness. God, she'd never realised how lonely she was until she'd come to Elmsleigh House.

And notably, she hadn't watched a single K-drama since arriving in Gloucestershire, and considering she was an addict, or at the very least, mildly obsessed, that was saying something. But then again, she had the English version of Hyun Bin in her bed and her life.

The phone in her bag buzzed and she pulled it out, her eyebrows lifting when she saw Detective Gosling's name flash up.

'We raided the foundation's offices. Seized computers and documentation. We are expecting to arrest the Bancrofts soon.'

Soon? What sort of time frame was that? 'Can you be more specific?' she asked, frazzled.

'CPS is reviewing the case. I'll try to remember to let you know when charges are filed, or arrests have been made.'

He'd *try* to remember? That was all she got? Then Eden remembered his desk, the stacks of folders on it, the blue shadows under his eyes and him mainlining black-tar coffee. Their resources were stretched and the Bancrofts weren't his only case. She sighed, thanked him and disconnected.

Almost instantly, a headache appeared behind her eyes, the sun suddenly too bright. There was no avoiding the fact she was living in a bubble of sunshine and sex, and it was going to burst, soon. Turning off onto the drive to take the path through the trees to the cottages, she blinked back tears. She was happy here, content, was enjoying helping to arrange the charity polo match, and had somehow slid into village life. She'd joined Pilates classes at the village hall, had volunteered to pick up litter on a community drive, and the barman at the pub now knew her favourite wine and poured her a glass without asking.

She was starting to recognise the rhythm of the village

and felt a part of it. She'd finally raised a smile from the taciturn lady with the steel hair at the grocer's, and Cody, the barista, saw her coming and prepared her double shot frappé without asking. She was now part of Mick's team for the Goat's quiz night, where they consistently came in last. In London she either felt ignored or dispensable. Elmsleigh and the village could become, with very little effort, her place.

But that was impossible. She and Jed were living on fresh air and hormones, caught up in the moment. He didn't know she was a bitch-monster on every third or fourth period, and she'd yet to see him drunk. They were still showing each other the best versions of themselves, and Eden knew it wasn't real life. Nobody could keep up the pretence forever, and she didn't want to. She wanted raw and real, dark and light and all the shades in between. If she was going to love someone, she wanted to love all of them, not just the bits she liked.

Stopping outside Jed's door, she slipped off one flip-flop, slid on her shoe pushed the back strap over her heel. She'd found them at a vintage shop in Camden Market years ago and this was their first outing. She repeated the action on the other side, and then held her foot out, smiling at the elegant line of the shoe, loving its slight shimmer in the sunlight. Her life might be an out-of-control spinning top, but her shoes were *ama-zing*.

'Sexy shoes, sweetheart.'

She looked over her shoulder to see Jed striding down the path to her, sweaty and hot, still dressed in grubby jodhpurs and a sweat-stained t-shirt. He looked wild and wired, his gold eyes sparking with adrenalin and appreciation. He looked at his watch. 'I know, I know, I'm late. Give me five minutes to shower.'

Yeah, but first she needed to kiss him, kiss this hot, handsome man with his wild cowboy vibe. She stepped up to him, wrapped her hand around the back of his neck and slapped her lips on his. Keeping his lips on her, he arched his spine back, arms akimbo to keep his shirt and pants away from her dress.

She growled, annoyed. 'Come back here, Number Three.'

He shook his head. 'I'm sweaty and horsey, and I don't want to make you dirty or sneezy, Sneezy.'

She glared at him. 'What if I'm perfectly happy to get dirty and sneezy?' she demanded, placing her hands on her hips. Okay, truthfully, it would be a pain in the arse because it had taken ages to curl her hair and finagle it into its messy, just-rolled-out-of-bed knot, and she'd spent much longer than her usual five minutes on her make-up. She wore base, and concealer, and had contoured her cheekbones, for God's sake. *And* she'd applied a setting spray. She'd worked damn hard to look this good. Which he hadn't noticed or commented on yet.

As if reading her mind, he stepped back and looked at her. 'You look stunning.'

He put so much emphasis on the last word that she blushed. He stroked his thumb over her pink-rose-stained lips. 'I want to kiss you and take you to bed, but we're already late and you're too pretty to mess up.'

She pouted, feeling the heat between her legs and the familiar ache in her breasts. 'I can redo my make-up, and so what if we are late?'

He smiled at her, his expression turning tender. 'I love that you want me as much as I want you.' He stretched out his arms and gestured to his body. 'How could you *not* want this?'

She knew he was teasing, as Jed didn't put much stock in his looks. Talent and hard work were important to him. Genes? Not so much.

'Well, strip down and let me see what you've got, cowboy,' she drawled.

He grinned at her poor American accent. 'Don't give up your day job to become an actor, sweetheart.'

She chuckled, loving the fact that their banter could range from sexy to ridiculous in the blink of an eye. And back to sexy, as he took in her dress with its deep cleavage, showing the smallest sliver of a lacy bra the same colour as her dress.

'But'—man, she hated that word—'there's no way I'm going to risk you sneezing and welting because of me. I've been on a horse or around horses since this morning.'

She was vain enough not to want to arrive at the garden party not only late, but sneezing, red-eyed and spotty too. She wrinkled her nose. *Pooh.* Jed opened his front door and gestured for her to precede him. 'I can take a shower and then get you off,' he casually offered, tossing his phone onto the hall table. The hall table he'd made. Because the man had amazing hands and an even more talented mouth.

And yeah, she wanted an orgasm. Like right damn now. 'What about you?' she asked, her voice scratchier than she liked. God, she sounded horny. Okay, she was, but she really needed to up her cool game.

He tapped her nose. 'I can wait. Unlike you, I have a modicum of control.'

Bastard for teasing her. She stepped closer to him and placed her hand on his bulge, and he hardened beneath her, strong and sure. Yeah, that was more like it. 'Control, huh?'

He closed his eyes and pressed her hand against his shaft. 'Five minutes to shower and then I'm going to take you fast, Eden. You up for that?'

She felt a sneeze building and nodded. 'Hurry,' she told him.

He swiped her lips, his tongue doing a too-brief slide against hers. 'Dress up, panties down,' he ordered and turned to run up the stairs.

'You touched me so don't forget to wash your hands,' he yelled. 'Your eye make-up is too pretty to sport allergy red eyes.'

Fair point.

Bythesea Hall and gardens was everything a ducal country house should be: huge, imposing and bloody impressive. Eden, standing in the rose garden – behind her was a maze and a knot garden – looked up at the Hall looming over them and shook her head. 'I'm glad I'm not the one who has to clean those windows,' she murmured. 'How many are there, Henry?'

Henry, dapper in a grey suit, patterned vest and an open-neck white shirt, slid his hands into his pockets. 'Far too bloody many,' he morosely replied.

'How many bedrooms?' she asked.

'Twenty-six,' he reluctantly admitted. 'Most of which are closed up.'

'You have twenty-six beds in that house?'

'That's about twenty-three too many,' Henry said, and Eden saw frustration flicker across his face.

'Only a duke with a massive house on a huge farm could say that,' she said, thinking that she'd grown up in a two-bedroom flat and never once had had the room to herself. She'd always been expected to share her room with a child, or two, who needed a bed.

'It's not as wonderful as you think it is,' Henry told her, raking his hand through his hair. 'It's a bloody burden, to be honest.'

Yeah, because how hard could it be to have that much room? She patted his arm and grinned. 'You poor thing, being an actual duke with an actual title and an actual bloody great mansion to your name.'

Henry forced a smile and Eden frowned. Come on, surely he knew she was teasing? 'Did I say the wrong thing—'

He shook his head, took her hand and squeezed. 'No, it's okay,' he replied, raking his hand through his hair. 'Sorry, it's just been a long week.'

Eden's eyes drifted over the hundred or so guests who stood around, sat on sofas, lounged in deck chairs or on garden benches. Waiters circulated with trays of nibbles – sushi and teeny-tiny sandwiches, one-bite sausage rolls and quiches – and endless trays of champagne. Soft drinks and hard liquor were available from the bar set up under the white, exquisite nomad tent. Staging this party had to have cost a fortune, Eden mused, but it was great publicity for next weekend's polo match.

Inevitably, it would take a hefty chunk out of Henry's bank account, but the publicity value was through the roof. She was so grateful, so she stood on her heels, took his hand and kissed his cheek. She squeezed his fingers. 'Thank you for doing this, Henry. You're pretty amazing.'

He sent her an uncomplicated, friendly grin. 'I think you're pretty amazing too.'

How could she feel absolutely zero for such a good-looking guy, when Jed just had to look at her and she melted into a puddle at his feet? Like earlier… After his shower, and super quick, freakin' mind-blowing sex, he'd dressed swiftly. When she took in his outfit, her jaw had dropped a little. Okay, maybe a lot.

Jed in jodhpurs and jeans was sexy, but clean-shaven, and wearing beige trousers, an open-collared white shirt under a milk-chocolate linen jacket and trendy trainers, he looked like he'd stepped out of a photoshoot. A blue-and-brown patterned handkerchief peeked out of his jacket pocket, and she was reminded that, while he loved being in the saddle and his workshop, he'd grown up with wealth and was stylish to his core.

Talking of Jed, where was he? Her eyes scanned the crowds. He was tall, so he wasn't hard to find. Footballer, footballer, footballer's wife, fashion designer, Vince and Tara.

She gripped Henry's hand so hard he gasped.

Henry tugged his hand from hers and shook out his fingers. 'Jeez, Eden, you nearly broke my fingers.'

To hell with his fingers, he'd recover. The Bancrofts were

here. This party wasn't big enough for her to hide from them, so she needed to leave *now*, before they saw her. And because Henry was the Duke and a drawcard, she needed to get away from him as soon as possible. Putting her back to where they stood, she looked up at Henry. 'I've got to go,' she told him. 'I need to leave. *Right now.*'

He threw up his hands. 'But why? What's wrong?'

'I can't be—' She pulled back her words and shook her head. She touched her temple with the tips of her fingers. 'I have a headache and need to go.'

'A headache? It came on so quickly?' Henry asked, sounding sceptical.

Eden thought fast. 'I think it might be the start of an allergic reaction,' she lied. She hated lying but it was the only valid excuse she had for leaving the party so abruptly. 'I'm going to have to take an allergy pill, but I didn't bring any with me.'

'I'm sure I have some—'

She shook her head, quite violently. 'No, Mick told me I have to be quite careful about what I take.' Now she was dragging Mick into her subterfuge. She laid a hand on Henry's arm. 'Do me a favour, please?' When he nodded, still looking unconvinced, she continued, her words coming fast. 'Please tell Jed that I've taken his car home and ask him to hitch a lift with one of his sibs or Troyden.'

Henry grimaced. 'Even *I* know that Jed hates anyone driving his E-type.'

Right, that. Eden winced. She'd been surprised when, instead of leading her to his Land Rover, Jed steered her toward a garage behind his workshop and lifted the door to reveal a stunning cream, vintage Jaguar.

It was a sexy car, perfect for a guy wearing designer threads to drive a post-orgasmic woman to a fancy garden party. And she'd noticed the way his hand drifted over the bonnet, it was the same way he touched her.

'I don't think that's a good idea, Eden,' Henry told her, heart attack serious.

Well, running into the Bancrofts would be worse and she was out of options. She stood on her tiptoes to kiss his cheek. 'It'll be fine, Henry,' she assured him. 'And if he kills me, say nice things at my funeral, 'kay?'

Not giving him a chance to respond, she spun around and sped off toward the car park to put herself behind the wheel of Jed's treasured car. She hadn't driven in four years, and it had been a decade since she'd last driven manual.

She could either stay and have a confrontation with Tara and Vince, after the police raid, or take her chances with Jed's car. The choice was really easy to make.

Jed made it to the car park just in time to see his beloved car – and the woman he was beginning to realise he was crazy about – passing through the ornate gates of Bythesea Hall. She took the corner too fast, the car had a lot of power, and even from a distance, he knew she was in the wrong gear.

Fuck. *Fu-uck.*

He pulled his phone from his pocket and dialled, his temper heating rapidly. He loved his car, but Eden's safety was his priority. If anything happened to her, if she so much as broke as nail…

Her phone rang and rang, and eventually went to voicemail. He had enough sanity left to be happy that she had both hands on the wheel and wasn't trying to handle the car and answer her phone. 'You'd better have a damn good explanation for this, Eden,' he said, when her bog-standard 'leave a message' voicemail ended.

'And you'd bloody well better text or call me when you get home. I want to know that you are in one piece.'

He rammed his phone into the inside pocket of his jacket and linked his hands behind his head, staring at the long driveway leading to the road. Should he call a taxi? Ask one of his sibs to run him home? But that would raise their curiosity, and he'd have to answer questions about what was wrong with Eden and why she'd bolted.

What *was* wrong with Eden, and why *did* she bolt?

He'd been on his way to join her and Henry, unhappy at their hand-holding. But because he'd been caught in a conversation with a wealthy team owner who'd just pledged a significant amount to Hope Harbour, he couldn't immediately disengage and plant his fist in Henry's face.

Metaphorically.

Maybe.

It had taken him ten minutes to cross the garden and when he did, he hadn't bought Henry's explanation of Eden's sudden disappearance due to an allergy attack. He'd been sleeping with her for a few weeks now, and brief contact and a kiss with his horse-dander-covered self wasn't enough to bring on an allergic reaction.

She was a lot better than she'd been initially, and he knew she took a daily dose of antihistamines and that her allergy was under control. No, whatever had sent her bolting wasn't an allergic reaction. But what?

Henry came to stand next to him and Jed whirled around, happy they were alone and that he had a target for his anger. 'What the fuck did you say to upset her?'

Henry lifted his hands, palms up. 'Nothing, I swear. She was happy, then she said she had a headache, then an allergic reaction. Then she bolted.' He looked genuinely confused and Jed remembered that he'd had his hands on his woman. And wasn't that a stupid word for whatever Eden had come to mean to him? It was too weak, too pale, too bland. Too everything.

'Last warning,' he said, wrapping his hands around the lapel of Henry's jacket. 'I'll rearrange your face if you put your hands on her again.'

Henry broke his hold with more ease than he expected. 'Oh, get over yourself, you prick. Everybody can see that she doesn't have eyes for anyone but you.'

Was that true? A little deflated, Jed stepped back and dropped his hands into his pockets. If he kept them there, he might not strangle Henry. Keeping control was a pain in the arse. He wanted to do *something* to *someone*. He scowled at the road, trying to decide whether his pride would let him ask Henry if he could borrow a car. He simply needed to be with Eden. Partly because he was curious… Why had she fled from a party she'd been looking forward to? But mostly because whatever upset her, upset him.

Shit, this caring-for-a-woman was complicated. He remembered now why he'd always steered clear. But he had two choices: to go back to the party or follow Eden. It wasn't much of a choice.

'Can I borrow a car?' he asked, gesturing to the now-empty driveway. 'I need to … check up on her.'

Henry tipped his head to the side and handed Jed a strange smile. 'Let's walk around the house, that way we won't get waylaid by guests.'

Since he didn't want to speak to anyone but Eden, Jed quickly agreed. They headed away from the party and toward the back of the enormous house. As they moved away from the expertly manicured front of the property into what Jed called the business end, he noticed the broken fences, farm implements that had been left to stand in the rain too long, and the missing gutters from what was once a grand stable block. The open garage had space for ten, maybe fifteen cars, but only two were used. One held Henry's Land Rover, the other, a beat-up, a breath away from disintegrating into a heap of rusty parts.

Henry gestured to his top-of-the-range Land Rover. 'Keys are in the ignition.'

Jed took a step toward the car and stopped, frowning. He looked at Henry and noted the tension in his face, the frustration and humiliation in his eyes. 'What's wrong?'

'Why do you care?' Henry whipped back.

'Henry? There's something you want to tell me so spit it the fuck out,' Jed said. Yes, Eden needed him – or he needed to know what was up with her – but Henry looked … lost? Yeah, lost. And out of options.

Henry rubbed the back of his neck and tipped his head up to look up at the sky. And Jed watched frustration chase anxiety across his face. Henry was going through something. He opened his mouth to ask what, then abruptly snapped it close.

He needed to get to Eden; he didn't have any time to spare. And why did he want to? Henry meant nothing to him.

He's your brother...

Henry's eyes met his, his expression now flat. He nodded at his Range Rover. 'Try to get the car back to me as soon as you can,' he asked, his voice flat. 'I need to be in London tomorrow.'

Jed, off balance and confused, watched him walk away. He looked so damn alone, the same way Eden occasionally did. Growing up, he'd had Troyden and his sibs, while Henry, like Eden, seemed to have had no one.

'You can easily accept people who aren't your blood, but not me.'

Maybe it was time to change this status quo, to open his mind up to the possibility of connecting with his half-brother. Maybe find some common ground. Maybe Henry was the wanker he believed him to be, but maybe he was just a guy trying to play the best hand with the cards he'd been dealt. Jed believed in fair play, that all men needed a chance, but he hadn't been prepared to give his brother one, choosing instead to punish him because of what the Fucking Duke did.

'Henry...'

Henry stopped but didn't turn around.

Jed rubbed the back of his neck. 'Thanks for lending me your car, I'll get it back to you as soon as I can...' How to say this? What words could he use that would not box him into a corner, that wouldn't raise his expectations? He didn't want to give the guy false hope, but neither could he leave him like this. 'Maybe we could get that beer sometime, talk some more.'

Henry whipped around and his glower burned a hole straight through him. 'Why don't you take your fucking pity and fucking patronising attitude and just fuck off?' he asked, but Jed heard the heat, his banked frustration.

Jed liked that he'd chosen anger, that he hadn't lost his pride, and that he wasn't prepared to take any shit.

'You've been bugging me to get one, and now you're being pissy,' Jed said, pushing him. He opened the door to the car, climbed up and settled in. He rested his hands on the steering wheel and lifted his eyebrows at the high-tech dashboard. Nice.

'Fuck you.'

Jed's smile broadened and he shook his head as he pulled the seatbelt across his chest. Stubborn too. They definitely shared some of the same personality traits. Turning on the ignition Jed hit the button to lower the window, remembering how they used to work off their anger as kids.

'Then how about we climb into a ring and punch it out?'

He regretted the words as soon as he said them. It had been a hundred years since he'd boxed. With his luck, Henry had probably kept it up and would annihilate him. Ah, well.

Henry rested his tight fists on his hips. 'Works for me. Text me a time and place.' He pointed his finger at Jed. 'Do not scratch my car, it's the only asset I have that's worth anything and I need to sell it soon.'

Huh. He hadn't thought Henry was being serious about not being financially liquid. They'd talk about that and a hundred other things. 'We'll pummel the shit out of each other, then we'll grab a beer,' Jed told him, looking in the mirrors as he reversed the car. Needing to mess with him, he dramatically gasped and then winced. 'Shit, I think I hit something.'

'Jesus Christ, are you being serious right now?' Henry shouted, two strips of red appearing on his cheekbones.

Jed grinned at his brother. 'No.'

'You fucker…'

Jed accelerated away, smiling. If he and Henry were to have any type of relationship, he'd have to learn how to take some shit. He was looking forward to imparting that particular brotherly lesson.

After he had the shit knocked out of him in the boxing ring.

Chapter Fifteen

Eden sat on the edge of her double bed in Troyden's house, her eyes on her pretty, just-painted-today toes. Earlier, she'd needed to choose between fight or flight, and she'd rocketed away. There was no avoiding the obvious: at some point, sometime soon, she was going to have to come clean to the family that she'd worked for the Bancrofts and that she was responsible for the abrupt changes to their lives and lifestyle.

They'd hate her. And she'd lose them. The Bancrofts were a part of their history, family friends, and the last living link to Troyden's wife and Jed's mother. Who was she? Just a girl who had a tenuous blood relation to Troyden though her father, a half-brother her uncle never much liked. She was, in the grand scheme of things, nobody.

And maybe that was why she felt a connection – totally platonic – to Henry. She sensed that, despite his wealth and title, he was lonely. People, she'd recently learned, needed people; they needed the connection and the trials and joys that came with loving, laughing and talking to others. Humans were social animals and weren't designed to be on their own.

Well, except for people like her mother, people for whom a relationship with God was enough.

But when faced with conflict, people always chose the familiar over the new, the devil they'd met before. They liked the comfort of familiarity and made decisions based on personal history. If she told the Castle gang the Bancrofts were thieves, it would be natural for them to push back, to accuse her of lying. Their experience of them, the need for familiarity, would make her out to be a liar and a troublemaker.

And if they were forced to choose between them, Eden knew who would win the vote. Her father had chosen to run away; her mum had chosen God over her. If her mother couldn't choose her, then what hope did she have of Jed and the family believing and accepting her? None. And God, it broke her heart.

Eden flopped back on her bed and wished the police would bloody arrest Tara and Vince and drop the axe. Living in this state of suspended animation, waiting for the world to shift, was driving her mad. And to make matters infinitely worse, she'd fallen in love with Tara's best friend's son. The one thing she'd absolutely, unequivocally forbidden herself to do.

Eden crossed her arms over her face, completely overwhelmed. Maybe she should just throw her clothes in a suitcase and leave. But running away from their kindness without an explanation, not that she could give one, given her police gag order, was a slap in the face. And there was the polo tournament next weekend, and if she left now, she would place the event in jeopardy and would throw the day into chaos. No, she owed it to Hope Harbour. If nothing happened by the end of the weekend, she would call Detective Gosling and ask how much she could disclose. If he said nothing, she'd figure something out.

It was just a week. She could hang on for seven days. Right?

Eden heard footsteps pounding up the stairs and winced. Even Jed's footsteps sounded angry. She'd run away, taken his precious car without permission and was acting like a lunatic. Why did he keep coming back for more?

Jed knocked once, more an alert than seeking a permission to enter, and stepped into the room. It took an incredible amount of effort to sit up, straighten and look at him. She sucked in a breath as she clocked the worry on his face.

'Are you okay?' he demanded, dropping to his knees and balancing on his toes in front of her. 'Did you have an attack? Why didn't you come find me? I could've driven you home...' He turned her hands over, looked at her arms, and then her neck. Fury replaced anger in his eyes, and he was white under his tan.

'You didn't have a reaction,' he calmly stated. He pushed up to his feet and slipped out of his jacket, bunching it in a ball before throwing it onto the bed. Needing to do something with her hands, Eden stood, picked up his jacket and smoothed it out. It was gorgeous, definitely designer, and deserved to be treated with care.

She walked into the all-but-empty walk-in closet – her

own clothes didn't take up much room – reached for a hanger and slipped the suit jacket onto it. Jed appeared in the doorway. 'Stop playing housewife and give me an explanation. Why did you run from an important party you were looking forward to, a party for the charity you are helping?'

What if the police hadn't made any moves yet? What if she said something and he told the Bancrofts and they left the country? What if... No, she couldn't. Not just yet. 'Your car is okay, I didn't scratch it or anything.'

'I don't care about the car,' Jed shouted, his loud words bouncing off the walls. 'I care about you!'

But experience told her that he didn't, not yet and not enough to choose her when the time came to pick sides. Because, as childish as that sounded, that was what was going to happen. Eden pushed her hand into her hair, felt resistance and started angrily yanking pins out. She wanted to get out of this stupid dress and wash her face, pull her hair up into a messy ponytail and lose herself in *Hospital Playlist* or *Descendants of the Sun*. Reality *sucked*.

Jed batted her hands away and looked around her head, his big fingers finding bobby pins and pulling them out of her hair. He dropped them onto the closet's credenza. She couldn't look at him and kept her eyes firmly on the open vee of tanned skin at his neck.

'What aren't you telling me, Eden?' he softly asked.

Anger had left his voice, but curiosity remained. 'What do you mean?' she asked, then wished she hadn't. There was no point in discussing any of this, her past, where she worked and her crazy flight from the party, because she couldn't explain. Not yet.

'I've always felt like you're hiding something,' Jed said, picking up a strand of hair and wrapping it around his index finger, his eyes not leaving her face. 'You don't talk about yourself much, and if you do, you talk about your distant past or your current present.'

She hated having to lie to him, but she didn't have a choice. 'There's nothing to tell, Jed.' She forced out a laugh that sounded like it belonged in a bad slasher movie.

'Don't insult my intelligence, Eden. I'd far prefer it if you just told me to mind my own business.'

'Mind your own business,' she replied, trying to keep her tone light.

His intense gaze didn't waver. His body posture didn't change. And she was, damn her, unable to move her feet. 'But you have become *my* business, Eden. I want to know what you're dealing with, what keeps you up at night. I'd like to protect you.'

She wanted to scoff, to tell him that she was a modern woman who didn't need a man's protection, but she couldn't form the words. Yes, he might want to do that. Protecting the people he cared for was baked into his DNA, but if he had to choose, he'd protect the Bancrofts first. Jed was a loyal guy – it was his defining trait – and his loyalty did not lie with her. How could a couple of months stack up against decades? And no amount of wishing could make it so.

God, it hurt.

He saw something on her face – yearning or need? – because he gently pulled her into him, his strong arm wrapping around her waist and his other hand cupping the back of her head. He rested his lips on her temple and his breath tingled across her skin as he spoke. 'Can't you trust me, Eden? Just a little?'

She rested her forehead on his collarbone, explanations on her tongue, ready to spill. She bit the inside of her cheek too hard and tasted blood. 'I want to,' she admitted.

'Then do it.' He rubbed circles on her back with his big hand. 'I won't let you down, sweetheart, I promise.'

But she believed in her heart of hearts, deep down in her soul, that he would. Because he'd have to choose and she wouldn't be his first choice. And it would eviscerate her.

'Jed,' she pleaded. What she most needed from him was time. 'I *can't*. Not yet. Please don't push me on this.'

'How can I not?' he demanded, his fingers on her jaw lifting his head. 'How can I, as a man crazy for a woman, not want to offer her help, or at the very least, understanding? How can I be me if I don't offer to stand between you and whatever is hurting you? I can *help* you, Eden.'

Sure, because that's how the world worked. Disappointment and anger sliced through her. She slapped his hand away and stepped back. 'You think you can, but it doesn't work like that! You can't change a situation. You can't undo the choices others made, the choices I had to make.'

He frowned. 'No, but I can try and understand them. Help you work through them.'

'God, you make me sound like such a loser,' she snapped, angry at the situation, angry at him for being so completely wonderful, everything she wanted in a man. Furious because the police had boxed her into a corner and silenced her, robbing her of her chance to explain. But if and when she did, the radioactive shit would hit the fan. 'It's not like you are Mr Chatty about what you are feeling either, Jed!'

He folded his arms and widened his feet. 'Are you talking about Henry?' he asked. 'Because we are going to try and come to an understanding next week.'

That was a little bit of good news. But sadly, it changed nothing between them.

'I think we are making progress,' his expression darkened. 'But I can't say the same for you.'

Her heart thumped, banging against her ribs hard enough to bruise. 'We're only having an affair, Jed.' She pointed out. Oh, it was way past an affair for her, but she'd use anything and everything in her arsenal to get him to back off.

'That's not only hurtful, Eden; it's also untrue,' Jed told her, his expression grim. 'I call bullshit.'

Of course, he did.

She pressed her fingers to her forehead. 'Can we not go back to how we were before the party?' she pleaded.

'No! We can't just sweep your distrust of me, your inability to talk to me under the bed, like it's an inconvenient detail. It's a major stumbling block to us moving forward.'

What? 'You want us to move forward?' What did that mean?

He looked up at the ceiling and hauled in a deep breath, obviously agitated. 'Jesus Christ, I feel like I am talking to myself or that you've lost your ability to listen.' He bent his knees so that their eyes were level, and the heat and frustration in his seared her skin. 'I like you. More than I've liked any woman, ever. I could fall for you, but that's not going to happen unless you can trust me, unless we can be honest with each other. And you're not being honest with me, are you?'

She shook her head. They were long past the point of her denying it.

'Are you married? In a relationship?' he asked.

She shook her head again.

'In trouble with the law?'

She took a moment to think about that. They'd investigated and cleared her. 'No.'

'You took a long time to answer a simple question.' He linked his hands behind his head and moved to stand by the window, his expression distant. 'I don't like this, Eden.'

Neither did she.

Her phone buzzed, and they both turned to look at the screen. Tara's name flashed up and Eden released a frustrated gasp. She lunged for the phone, but Jed, possessing longer arms, got to it first. He picked it up. 'Why is Tara Bancroft calling you?' he asked, his frown deepening.

She didn't know how to answer him, couldn't form any words to explain. Every synapse she possessed was on the verge of shorting out. The phone mercifully stopped its strident jangling, but the walls of the room had moved six feet in.

There was only one reason why Tara was calling her now after weeks of silence. She'd definitively linked her to the police investigation and had to suspect she was the police's informant. There was no one else who could give them so much information about the foundation.

'How do you know Tara, Eden?' Jed asked, his question a sharp snap.

The moment she'd been dreading had arrived, and it was time to deal with the revelations and then the fallout. Was there an exit ramp she'd missed? Could she still try to bluff her way out of this?

Her shoulders slumped. No, the police had interviewed the Bancrofts; they had to know they were suspects. That ship had sailed. She'd just be delaying the inevitable. And she was so tired of the pretence that she was running short of the mental energy she needed to watch her words. And of sneaking around. Tara's call was, frankly, a relief. Now all she needed were the right words and the courage to tell Jed the truth.

Her phone rang again, and Eden knew it was Tara calling again. She watched, resigned, as Jed's thumb swiped her screen and answered. He hit the speaker phone button and Tara's screech filled the room. 'Eden, did I see you running away from Bythesea Hall? Of course I did, because you don't have the guts to look us in the eye after the hell you've put us through!'

There was panic in her voice, fear and outrage. But given what Tara was facing, Eden thought she was holding it together rather well. 'You ungrateful, manipulative, disloyal bitch!'

Tara certainly hadn't lost her ability to come out swinging. Eden slid down the wall to sit on her haunches. She placed her forehead on her knees. So this is what it felt like when the sky fell in.

'Tara, this is Jed. What are you talking about?' Eden

couldn't look at him. She couldn't face his disgust and disappointment.

'That bloody woman has ruined us!' Tara's scream rose a pitch. 'It's because of her that we're being investigated, but she's the one who siphoned the money. And she's trying to pin it on us!'

'Explain!' Jed's one-word command was an armour-piercing bullet straight through her heart.

'We've had the police searching our offices and we might be arrested!'

'Not you, Tara,' Jed interjected. 'Eden, what's going on?'

Eden lifted her concrete-heavy head and rested the back of the head on the wall. She shrugged. 'Where should I start?'

'At the beginning and make it quick.'

Tara started to squawk, and Jed told her to be quiet.

Eden continued. 'Years ago, I did a DNA test and discovered that Troyden was my uncle. I applied for a job with the Bancrofts because I read that Troyden is their biggest donor and I wanted to find out more about him before I met him. I worked for the Bancrofts for five, nearly six, years.'

'Why not just meet him directly?' Jed asked.

That would've been the reasonable thing to do. But she'd wanted to see what he was like before she put herself at risk of being disappointed and disillusioned again. She'd been trying to protect herself. Was that so wrong?

'I was busy at work. I loved my job and my employers, and I kept putting off the decision to meet Troyden. Then a few months ago, my mum married God, and I discovered what the Bancrofts were up to. I resigned and I was completely alone. It was … tough. Then I started thinking about Troyden. That first weekend at Elmsleigh, I was still deciding whether to meet him or not,' she told Jed. Damn, why couldn't he give her a hint of a smile, a show of warmth, a smidgeon of support? The man she'd slept with, laughed with, and loved, was Greek-god remote, as cold and unresponsive as the statues in Athens' National Archaeological Museum.

'Rubbish, she just wants his money!'

'Unhelpful, Tara,' Jed shot back.

'Where does the missing money come into it?' Jed asked, his laser gaze slicing through skin, muscle and bone.

'She stole money and blamed it on us!' Tara screamed. Eden rubbed her forehead. God, she hoped Tara was somewhere private and wasn't making a scene at Henry's garden party, yelling in front of his guests. No, Tara was too aware of her image to risk her reputation by airing her grubby laundry in public.

'Our bank accounts have been seized. We can't operate,' Tara explained, her words machine-gun fast. 'She reported us to the police, and they are investigating us for fraud. *Us?* Can you believe it?'

Judging by Jed's shocked face, no, he couldn't. His reaction didn't surprise her: the situation was unfolding exactly as she'd expected. Jed's shock. Tara's denial. And, of course, she was the bad guy. Frankly, Tara ramming a rusty icepick through her ribs would've been less painful.

He'd been tossed into a leaky life raft on a stormy North Atlantic sea and the waves were twenty feet high. He had one woman screaming at him through the phone, another sitting in total shock on the floor, her eyes glassy and her face bloodless. Eden looked so frail that he was scared that if he so much as tapped her she'd shatter into a million pieces.

Jed hauled in a deep breath, desperately searching for a measure of calm. Look, he knew Eden was secretive and kept parts of herself and her life hidden, but this was bigger than he'd imagined. He gripped the bridge of his nose and squeezed. He needed to push his emotions aside and think. Okay, step by step…

He found it hard to believe that the Bancrofts had embezzled money from their foundation. Yes, they could be persistent, but he'd never doubted their commitment to the foundation and charities they supported.

'You've got to believe me, Jed,' Tara demanded, her too-high voice drilling into his skull. 'Eden was our right-hand person. We trusted her implicitly and we gave her too much freedom and access. It would've been easy for her to set us up, to make it look like we are the ones guilty of re-directing funds.'

He shook his head, equally sure that Eden, the woman he couldn't contemplate letting go, hadn't stolen money from the Bancrofts and set them up to take the fall. This was a perfect shitstorm! He didn't have enough facts. There were too many secrets, and too much emotion. He needed time and space to think, and a hell of a lot more information.

He felt the phone leave his hand and watched Eden

punch the red button to end the call. She tossed the phone onto the bed and when her eyes met his, the lack of emotion in them scared him. They were the blue-green of ice chips, diamond hard. 'So much for not letting me down, huh?

'It looks like you've already made up your mind who you believe,' she continued. Her tiny smile was brittle and hard. 'Don't worry, it's not a surprise.'

No, hold on, he hadn't! He was still trying to make sense of the last minutes. He pushed his hair back from his forehead and watched as she stomped into the closet and reached for her rather battered suitcase. 'What the fuck are you doing?' he asked. Okay, he could see that she was packing, but...

She ignored him and kept ramming her clothes, bundling them into scrunched piles, into her suitcase. Her shoulders were pushed back, and her back and neck tight with tension. 'Jesus, Eden, just *talk* to me.'

She sent him a scorching look. 'About what?' she demanded, in high-pitched, cold voice. 'You heard the gist of it. I sicced the police on them.'

He linked his hands behind his neck and tipped his head up to look at the ceiling. Before he could formulate his next question, she spoke again. 'I understand they are likely to be arrested. They're going to need a very good lawyer. Maybe Troyden or Alistair can recommend someone.'

He couldn't believe what she was saying. 'There *must* be some mistake, Eden.'

'Money, lots of it,' she said, her voice flat and emotionless, 'is missing from the foundation. There's no mistake about that, Jed. There are only two options...

Either they took it, or I did, setting them up to take the blame. And you're leaning toward option number two.'

She slammed her suitcase shut, clothes poking out from the sides.

'I didn't say that!' he yelled, an out-of-control car skidding wildly on her layer of ice. 'I'm just trying to understand, Eden.'

'No, you're trying to make the facts fit to make you feel more comfortable,' she retorted. She released a sound that was a cross between a snort and a sob. 'But you've yet to tell me that you believe me. What's missing is your emphatic show of support, even a vague statement that you're sure I haven't done anything wrong and that we can find our way through this.'

Hadn't he? He winced. But in fairness, *she'd* kept this from him. 'You're the one who didn't tell me any of this, Eden!'

'And why do you think I did that, Jed? What would you have said if I'd blurted this out when I first met you?' she asked, her voice rising. 'If I came to you and said, "Hey, your mum's best friend is a thief and she's nicked a load of donor money", how would you have reacted? You and Troyden would've kicked me out!'

Okay, that was a fair point. They would've reacted swiftly, and probably without bothering to hear her out. But they'd been sleeping together for a while now and they had … *something*. 'But you've had ample time to tell me, so why didn't you?'

'I couldn't tell you, Jed. I was instructed not to by a pretty intimidating detective at the Metropolitan Police.' She threw up her hands. 'Besides, I knew you wouldn't believe me, and this conversation proves my point. You don't *want* to believe me, Jed. Because your loyalty is to them, to the people who knew you when you were a kid, who were connected to your mother, who *loved* your mother. They are Troyden's friends. I didn't want to hurt you with this.' She rubbed her hand across her forehead. 'I was waiting for the news of their arrest to come out, for the police to make a statement. At least then I would've had a chance of someone believing me.'

She disappeared into the bathroom and almost immediately returned holding a toiletry bag. In quick, sure movements, she unplugged her phone charger and laptop and tossed both into a large tote bag. The toiletry bag followed, and she looked around the room, scooping up a tube of lip gloss, a five-pound crumpled note and the keys to her car. Her sexy shoes went into the tote bag, and she slid her flip-flops on.

Tears smudged her mascara and eye make-up, but he couldn't go to her, not when he was so churned up and off balance. If he did, he might confess his love and beg her to stay. He couldn't do that, not until he had all the facts. As he'd recently learned from his interactions with Henry, there were always three sides to a story, and the truth wasn't something that could be determined from one heated conversation.

And his deep, innate sense of loyalty was screaming its disgust for even considering the idea that the Bancrofts were guilty of theft. As Eden pointed out, they'd been good to him, good to his mum, part of the fabric of his life.

But believing them meant disbelieving Eden, and he couldn't do that either. She'd slipped into his heart and was what he never thought he needed. She'd, somehow, with her red-gold hair and sea-glass eyes, her softness and grit, become the glue that stitched his life together. She was his future, his way forward. He knew he was fucking this up, but he didn't know what to do or say, or had any idea how to walk this tightrope stretched over a fathoms-deep, soul-sucking cavern.

Eden sniffed and pushed her hair off her forehead. 'Nothing else to say?' she asked, her words pointy-spear sharp.

'Don't go, Eden,' he implored, his voice gritty. 'Let's work this out.'

'That's your way of asking me to spend the next few hours begging you to believe me,' she snapped. 'Thanks, but I'll skip.'

'C'mon, that's not fair! I'm just trying to understand!'

She grabbed the handle of her suitcase, pulled out the extension and rolled it to the bedroom door. Hoisting her heavy tote bag over her shoulder, his instinct was to take it from her, lighten her load, but he knew he would probably lose his head if he tried.

'This is what I understand, Jed,' she said, her words low and so very sad. 'You didn't take my side. Your instinct wasn't to support me, but to defend them. Yet again, I wasn't someone's first choice. I really should be used to it by now.'

And with those heartbreakingly, pierce-his-heart words, she walked out of the room. And probably his life.

Chapter Sixteen

Eden slipped out of the B&B as the first streaks of dawn lit the sky, last night's tears still burning her eyes. Fresh air, some exercise. She'd feel better after both. She hoped.

But what she needed was to wake up in Jed's arms and to realise last night had been nothing more than a vicious dream. But nightmares required sleep, and she'd stared at the ceiling all night.

Yanking her cap down low over unbrushed hair, Eden jammed her hands into her sweatshirt pockets and walked toward the village. She'd pick up a coffee from Cody at his shop, if she could stop crying long enough to order it.

She sniffed, wiped her face, swallowed the sob clawing its way up her throat. Enough, dammit.

'Eden.'

Her stomach lurched. She couldn't deal with him now. Not while she was barely holding herself together. Jed stood in front of her, his face painted with pain. His hair was damp, his t-shirt sweat-stained, his jeans dirt-streaked, his low-heeled riding boots caked with mud.

'Don't come closer, I've been riding and at the stables,' he said. Did he think she was going to fling herself into his arms? That wasn't going to happen anytime soon. His hands curled into fists in the front pockets of his jeans, his broad shoulders halfway to his ears. 'Did you sleep?'

Sleep? When every emotional scar she possessed had been ripped open? She should've been used to it by now. Her mum had chosen faith over family, and the Bancrofts, people she'd trusted and loved, half-friends, half-family, had plummeted off the pedestal she'd put them on, after she'd discovered their crimes. Although she'd always expected them to pass the buck, to try to pin their embezzlement on her, Tara's accusation had hit harder than she'd expected, another mortal blow that buckled her knees. She'd been close to them, more of a daughter or a younger sister than an employee, and they'd filled the gap left by her mum when she'd joined the Church. While she had them in her life, she hadn't felt the need to connect with Troyden. She had what passed for family, by choice and not blood, and had been content. Happy.

Not for a minute had she imagined they could be capable of embezzlement. Or that they'd try to frame her for their crimes. She'd trusted them, and it was a bone-deep ache, betrayal wrapped in barbed wire.

And Jed? Well, he hadn't hesitated, automatically believing them over her.

'No.' She scuffed the toe of her trainer over a tuft of grass. 'Why are you here, Jed?'

He exhaled, rubbing a hand over his face. 'I came to tell

you that I'm going to see the Bancrofts. I need to talk to them.'

She barked out a hollow laugh. 'Because you can't just trust me.'

His jaw tightened. 'That's not fair, Eden.'

Fair? Fair would've been him choosing her. Fair would've been him proving her wrong, that maybe – just maybe – he was different. Showing her that somebody could put her first.

He raked his fingers through his hair, frustration in every tense line of his body. 'I've known them forever. I need to understand—'

Her heart cracked wide open, but she forced herself to meet his gaze. 'Do whatever you want, Jed. We were just having fun, right? It was never going to last.' She shrugged, feigning indifference, going in for the kill. 'And let's not forget, your first instinct has always been to think the worst of me.'

He flinched at the reminder of him thinking she was a gold-digger. It was a hit. A solid one, an emotional punch to the throat.

'I just need time to process this,' he said, his voice rough. 'Can't you give me that?'

'You can't give me what I need so…' She was being childish and petty. She knew she sounded churlish and resentful, but she couldn't help it. She was bleeding here. Dragging her hands over her face, she sighed. 'I don't need this, Jed.'

And because she was drowning in pain, because she wanted him to hurt like she did, she went for the knockout punch. Said the one thing she knew would make him back off, too.

'I don't need *you*.'

Her lie was a throat punch, and she saw the blow land when shock flared in his eyes. His eyes darkened, his breath caught, and his sun-kissed skin paled. She'd gone too far, she knew it, but she couldn't take back the words burning through his soul.

He nodded, once. It was a full stop at the end of the sentence that was their relationship.

Without saying anything, he turned and walked away.

Eden watched him go, the ache in her chest threatening to rip her apart.

'Why couldn't you believe me?' she whispered, her words wrenched from the deepest part of her. 'Why couldn't you put me first?' He didn't look back, and Eden watched him until he disappeared from view, tears streaming down her face, dripping off her jaw and chin. She wasn't a crier. But Jed, damn him, had made her one. Not even her mother had pulled this amount of emotion to the surface. Oh, God, what was it about this man that could dismantle her with so little effort?

She needed to run, to disappear from Elmsleigh House and leave the Castle clan behind. Individually and collectively, they could eviscerate her. She needed to start somewhere new, to fade into a different background, to make herself small again, to survive.

To protect herself. Because, as she kept being reminded, no one else ever would.

After twenty-four hours in hiding, Eden walked into the courtyard behind Elmsleigh House, exhausted. She sank onto the kitchen steps, powered on her phone and braced herself. Missed calls. Messages. Troyden. Mick. Henry. More from Mick.

Nothing from Jed.

So, this was what a broken heart felt like. A sharp, jagged rip, a relentless, aching thud. Breathing felt impossible, the thick tension in her lungs making it difficult to inhale. The early morning air tasted like regret. The summer sun, having turned its back on her, held no warmth. Her heart ached with the weight of what could've been, the endless possibilities never to be realised. Eden wrapped her arms around her knees, waiting for something, anything: a sign, a nudge, the strength to move on.

The door creaked open. Troyden wore cargo shorts, a flannel shirt with sleeves rolled up and carried two mugs in his hands. His assessing gaze told her everything. He knew that her world, and maybe Jed's, had split open and fallen apart.

'Walk or sit?' he asked.

'I'll walk if you want to—'

'We're sitting,' he decided, dropping beside her and handing her coffee. She clutched the warm mug, thankful for something solid to hold on to.

'What did Jed tell you?' she asked, her voice raspy.

'You two fought, and you might or might not tell me why.' Troyden frowned. 'I'm presuming it's serious.'

She inhaled, steeling herself, then laid it out. The truth. The evidence she'd gathered and taken to the police.

Her reasons for turning his good friends in. She offered to show him the detective's messages, to give him the number so that he could call and verify her claims. When she finally stopped talking, her stomach twisted at his silence and her heart dropped at his sober expression.

'I'm sorry,' she said, voice small. 'I didn't want to hurt your friends.'

Troyden took a long sip, watching her. 'So, after seeing them at the cocktail party at Bythesea Hall, you bolted.'

'Yes. I didn't want a scene, and the police wanted me to keep my distance.'

'Then, after you and Jed fought, you packed up and left Elmsleigh.' He tilted his head. 'Why did you run, Eden?'

She frowned. 'It was partly instinctive, a need to get away. And partly because I thought I wouldn't be welcome here anymore.'

He exhaled sharply. 'Let me get this straight. They stole money, ripped off charities and me, and you thought I'd kick *you* out of my home and life for reporting them?'

Well, yes. 'They're your friends. Tara is Jed's mum's best friend.'

'So?' His jaw locked. 'What does that have to do with them stealing?'

Her breath hitched. 'Are you saying … you believe me?'

His eyes softened. 'I think if you were lying, you wouldn't be offering up evidence. The police wouldn't be investigating, searching offices and issuing warrants if there wasn't something to your claims.'

Tears burned. God, having him believe her was such a relief. Air, a thin stream, lightened the grip on her agonised lungs. 'Thank you.'

Troyden tapped her knee. 'You still owe me an apology.'

Eden's heart plummeted to her toes. 'I don't understand?'

'You owe me an apology for not coming to me, for not asking for help. You're part of this family, Eden. You don't go through things alone when I am willing to stand next to you.'

His words landed deep. A sob rose, part relief, part hope. There was a light in the distance, and it was tangible, real. Their relationship was salvageable. They could get through this. Her and Jed's relationship was on life support, and it would take a long time for those wounds to heal, but she might not lose Troyden. There was the possibility of something new, better and deeper, between them, and Eden sucked in her first proper breath that day.

'Are we ... okay?' She needed to check, desperate for reassurance.

'I'm angry,' he admitted, his voice still tight. 'Not at you. Okay, a little at you for making me worry. But I'm furious at your mum and at my brother, at everyone who made you believe you couldn't count on family. But I'll get over it.'

Then he stood, pressing a quick kiss to her hair. 'Check out of the B&B. Move back into your room. *Today*.'

Eden nodded, tears slipping down her cheeks. She wasn't alone. She still had her uncle. But Jed? That was another story.

Their fight had been ugly, and she regretted how it'd ended. Oh, she was still furious he hadn't instinctively taken her side, but maybe – just maybe – she should've given him space instead of storming out. She definitely shouldn't have told him she didn't need him. Her lashing out had stopped them talking and blown up their chances to work their way back to each other. Saying she didn't need him had been a lie, cruel and unnecessary. Shame, fierce and suffocating washed over her, robbing her of the air she'd found when talking to Troyden.

She'd been in the wrong, caught up with wanting – *needing* – him to choose her without hesitation. But he wasn't that guy. Measured. Thoughtful. Slow to leap. She'd asked for too much, too soon.

But as Troyden had just shown her, people weren't black and white. They were made up of a million shades ranging from off-white to pewter grey to hell black. She'd assumed Troyden would be like her father and mother and would bail, but he'd proved her wrong.

Maybe this was the wake-up call she needed to move on, to come to terms with her past. People blithely said that you couldn't lug the baggage from your past behind you forever, and that, at some point, you had to discard what weighed you down. So much easier said than done though. For most of her life, her core belief had been that she was destined to come in second, that she wasn't worthy of being someone's first choice. Tara and Vince had let her down and disappointed her, but she couldn't use their actions to reinforce her belief that she was less than, not worthy of being a priority.

The people who were supposed to love her the most had disappointed her the most. Her father had been weak and vain, feckless and irresponsible. Sleeping with a much younger girl, a teenager, had been a crappy thing to do, and she wondered whether he'd regarded her mum, religious and hesitant, as a challenge. She suspected that after he'd got what he wanted from her, his interest in her had waned.

Her mum had let her down in big ways and small. But for the first time, she considered how hard it must've been for her mum to find herself pregnant and alone at eighteen. Was becoming a foster mum, giving her time to kids who needed her help, her way to atone for what she'd done, for going against the will of her god? Maybe? She couldn't know for sure, but it sounded right. And when she'd felt that Eden was old enough and strong enough, she'd decided she could finally devote her life, as she'd probably always wanted to do, to the god she'd disappointed.

Her mum hadn't been able to love her, but that was her mum's failing, not hers.

And in a crisis, Jed hadn't been able to put her first. They'd probably never be able to recapture what they had, but she didn't need to forgo her relationship with Troyden, her wonderful friendship with Mick and Justin, and Alistair's rare smiles, because she and Jed hadn't worked out.

She needed this family, these people. She was not going to keep running, keep chasing affirmation and acceptance from other people. It was time to plant her feet, to stick and stay. Sure, seeing Jed was going to be hell, but all pain eventually faded. Love couldn't be forced, and it meant nothing when it was demanded. Love wasn't a bargaining chip or a source of affirmation. It was something you offered.

Sometimes you were lucky enough to get it back, but it didn't stop existing, or meant less, just because it wasn't reciprocated.

She lifted her head when she felt tiny paws kneading her shoulder and smiled at Bizzy's cute orange face. Gemma, eyes wise beyond her years, sat beside her on the step.

'You're crying,' she observed.

Eden swiped at her face. 'I guess I am.'

Gemma considered this, an old soul in a six-year-old's body. 'I think you need my mum.'

Eden shook her head. 'Your mum's busy, sweetheart.'

Gemma wasn't buying it. She stood, held out her hand, and Eden took it, following the little girl to Mick's cottage.

The moment she stepped into the kitchen and Mick saw her face, she tipped her head, smiling softly. 'Oh, honey. What do you need? Food, coffee or a hug?' She paused. 'A day of K-dramas?'

Warmth flooded Eden's chest. This was love. And acceptance.

She managed a watery smile. 'I'll take the first three, and since I have a charity polo match to arrange, a rain check on number four?' And as Mick hugged her, Eden finally understood the old saying that having one loyal friend was better than ten thousand crappy relatives.

'Ow, shit, *ow!*'

Jed touched his nose, spotted blood on his orange glove and glared at Henry sporting an arrogant smirk. He was enjoying this a bit too much, the *dick*.

'I thought we said we were going to avoid head punches,' he growled, dabbing his nose and smearing blood across his glove. Damn, was it broken? That would just top another shitty day in a shitty week. Feeling like he was about to burst out of his skin, he'd needed to work off his frustration, so he'd called Henry and asked him whether he was up for some sparring. Henry had quickly agreed. They'd exchanged minimal conversation while they wrapped their hands and pulled on their gloves, and were soon exchanging body blows that were both painful and pressure-releasing.

Cleansing.

'You dropped your guard, and I couldn't resist,' Henry replied, dancing on his toes. 'And yours is such a punchable face.'

'Prick,' he muttered.

'Wanker,' Henry replied with no heat. Jed gripped the edge of the Velcro strap on his glove, ripped it and pulled. He'd taken more than enough body blows from Henry's far-too-quick fists and now his nose was on fire.

He was exhausted, and after a few hard days in the saddle – somehow the Castle Kings were still in the mix for the British Polo Championships – he should be sitting in a sauna, having a massage, catching up on sleep. Sleep? Hah, funny, he'd had so little of that lately.

Eden's lovely face appeared on his mental big screen and he swallowed at the memory of her hurt eyes and pale skin, her freckles and bright splotches on her white face. She was back at Elmsleigh House, but he hadn't seen her since they'd met in the village, and he felt like he'd lost a limb. He would roll over in the morning, eager to open his eyes to see her hair on his pillow, her face buried into his neck, but was met with emptiness. He continuously checked his phone to see if she'd called, consistently disappointed when he didn't see her name on the screen.

He missed her. Every inch of him, inside and out, longed for her. Love had to be deserved, and what could he give her? By not calling him, she was reinforcing her statement that she didn't need him. And if she didn't need him, how could she love him?

He flung his gloves onto the floor of the ring and took the water bottle Henry offered him. He'd pulled on a shirt, but Jed was still bare-chested. He dropped to the padded floor, feeling utterly wiped, and lay back, his knees bent as he tipped water down his throat. Scared that Henry might see too much in his eyes, he placed his forearm over his head, hiding the top half of his face from his newest, but also oldest, brother.

'The arrangements for the charity match all seem to be going well,' Henry said from somewhere next to him. He moved his arm and glanced at Henry out of the corner of his eye. He sat a little way from Jed, arms resting casually on bent knees, his water bottle dangling from his hand. 'Eden is doing a fabulous job. She managed to secure Neon Alibi to play at the after-party next weekend. For free.'

Even he, someone who didn't follow pop culture, had heard of the up-and-coming band. The demand for tickets had skyrocketed and they were on track to triple the profit they'd originally aimed for. She was, simply, so damn good at her job. Simply amazing.

'I heard that the Bancrofts are being investigated,' Henry said.

Shit, yeah. Jed released a low groan, thinking about his and Troyden's very awkward conversation with Tara and

Vince. *It was a misunderstanding; Eden got it wrong; they would never steal money. The police would come to that conclusion.*

Neither he nor Troyden were convinced but had agreed to give them the benefit of the doubt – they owed them that much – until the police investigation was concluded. Tara especially had been viciously scathing about Eden and ignored both his and Troyden's request not to bad-mouth her. Their meeting left him with a sour taste in his mouth and the knowledge that, no matter what happened in the future, their relationship would never be the same.

'Do you believe Eden's or the Bancrofts' version?' Henry asked. *Eden*'s. His reaction was quick and instinctive, and Jed wished he'd been as quick to respond the night of their fight. Shit, he was so screwed.

Needing to talk and think about anything but Eden, he changed the subject. 'When I borrowed your car, you said it was the only asset worth anything,' he said. 'What did you mean? How much financial trouble are you in?'

'I'm drowning.' Henry raised his hand, his thumb and index finger an inch apart. 'I'm this close to losing it.'

Jed frowned at him. 'Seriously?'

'The Duke borrowed money from banks, loans I am now responsible for. I never fucking wanted the title or assets, but I'm the one left to deal with it.'

'You sound … pissed off.'

Henry nodded. 'I am. Because … what did you call him? … the Fucking Duke died, and now I'm the one who'll lose four hundred years of history.' Henry rubbed his face. 'You have no idea how lucky you are, Jed.'

'How so?' he asked, disconcerted by Henry's expression.

'He didn't acknowledge you, but you have no idea what

a blessing it was not to have that prick in your life.' Henry started to tick points off his fingers. 'You have a family, a father and siblings, people standing in your corner. I have millions in debt, a house I hate and a mother who's more worried about money than about me.'

'If you are so broke, then why did you spend so much sponsoring the charity polo match?' Jed asked, confused.

Henry released a low laugh that held no amusement. 'Because I want the Bythesea name to be associated with something good before we become another aristocratic family to lose everything and before this place gets turned into a hotel, or a hospice or a country club. Because I wanted a way to spend time with you.'

Jed shuffled on the mat, unexpectedly moved. Henry was anything but the entitled wanker he'd believed him to be. And maybe he'd turned out to be a decent guy despite having a tosser for a father.

'Is there anything you can do to save the Hall?' He knew better than to offer money. He knew Henry wouldn't take any.

'My last-ditch effort is to convert the stables into accommodation units. There's a shortage of affordable, long-term housing in the area,' Henry said. Jed sat up and raised his eyebrows. That was true, houses and flats were hens'-teeth scarce around here. 'Actually, Eden gave me the idea when she popped around for dinner last night. She's thinking about staying in the area, but wants to get her own place. She adores Troyden, but she's too independent to live off her uncle. We chatted about her renting a suite of rooms at Bythesea Hall.'

Jed stared at him, not sure what part of his statement to

focus on. The fact that she was staying, that she'd had dinner with his brother last night, or that she was looking to permanently move off the estate?

'What the hell was she doing having dinner with you? And there's no way in hell she's going to move into your place!'

Henry had the gall to smile at him. 'And how do you plan on stopping her, Jed? Aren't you two done?'

He didn't know what they were. 'She said that?'

Henry raised an eyebrow and Jed groaned. 'We had a fight and haven't spoken since,' he admitted.

'Yeah, *that's* a good way of finding a solution,' Henry sarcastically stated. 'Well done.'

'God, you're annoying,' Jed informed him. He picked the label off his water bottle and stared at the laces on his trainer. A bead of sweat rolled down his side, another down his neck. 'Did she say anything else?'

Henry lifted the bottle to his lips, but Jed suspected he was only drinking to give him some time to work out how to answer. 'No.'

A door slammed somewhere behind them, and they heard the grunts of a guy lifting weights in the far corner, earphones in, sweat rolling down his face. He felt his brother's – he still couldn't bring himself to say the word aloud – eyes on his face and met them. Henry's expression was softer than he expected. 'Talking like this is weird, right?'

It was.

'So, was pummelling each other a once-off thing?'

He knew what he was asking. This was a do-or-die moment, to trust or not, to accept Henry into his life and world, or to lose him forever. Because Henry wouldn't beg for a second chance. He knew that because neither would he.

Jed, feeling horribly off guard, shifted on the mat, his fingers pushing into the vinyl as he tried to ground himself. He wasn't used to this, bonding with someone who'd been little more than a name and an uncomfortable, just-out-of-reach shadow until recently. It felt unnatural, like wearing someone else's trainers. But at the same time, there was an odd comfort in it and a strange sense of relief that Henry, his parentage and his connection to the Bythesea family, was something he could stop worrying about. Things that were left to grow in the dark became mouldy and disfigured. He was glad they had brought their relationship into the light.

Henry let out a low chuckle, and his next words suggested he was on the same wavelength. It was a strange sensation, this tentative connection. Like walking on thin ice but feeling, for the first time, that it might just hold. 'It's odd, isn't it? Us sitting here, trying to talk. I spent my whole life thinking of you as … I don't know, some abstract idea. And now…' He shook his head.

'Now we're real, and we don't know how the fuck to handle it.'

'Succinctly said.' His brother scratched his cheek, the flicker of a smile on his lips. 'God, you look as awkward as I feel. So … where do we go from here?'

Jed pulled in a deep breath and took a leap of faith. 'Let's take a shower and have that beer.'

Chapter Seventeen

Jed leaned his arms over Rey's stable door and smiled at the sleepy expression on her face. She'd been brilliant today as they'd chased down the British Polo Championship title, but the Castle Kings only scraped in third.

It wasn't bloody good enough. Troyden didn't pay him a huge salary to be satisfied with third place. It was just another in a series of fuck-ups lately. *Jesus.*

'Brooding, Jedson?'

He turned his head to look at Troyden, hands in the pockets of his grey-and-black checked pants. His white shirt had a frayed cuff, but his cufflinks were, he thought, turn of the century and by Fabergé.

'Dad,' he murmured, dropping his arms and rubbing his jaw. 'Sorry about today.'

Rey stuck her nose over her stable door and nuzzled Troyden's shoulder. He instinctively hooked his arm around her neck, leaning into her. His eyes didn't leave

Jed's face. 'You only call me Dad when you want to make appoint or when you are feeling particularly sorry for yourself.'

He shrugged, not able to deny the charge. Sorry for himself, flat, lost, at sea. Any of the above worked. But bottom line… 'You pay me to win. I didn't do that.'

Troyden jerked his head, and Jed followed him to the bench outside the tack room door. Troyden sat down, crossed his legs and Jed sat down next to him, his arms on his thighs. 'Do you think your only value to me is that you win?'

Jed rubbed the back of his neck. He didn't want to say yes, but couldn't say no. As much as he wanted to think otherwise, he still believed love was conditional and tied to what he could offer. But he couldn't tell Troyden that.

'You pay me a huge salary. You deserve to have your team win.'

'And it does, more often than not,' Troyden replied. 'God, you worry me, Jed.'

Jed jerked. 'How?'

'When are you going to stop believing that you have to earn your right to be a part of this family?' Troyden demanded, obviously frustrated.

'I—' How was he supposed to answer that?

Troyden linked his hands around his knee and leaned back. 'Of all my children, you were the most challenging, Jed. I made bigger mistakes with you, and they caused deeper wounds. I regret that so much.'

What was he talking about? 'I don't understand.'

'I don't think I realised, until recently, how much you were affected by your mum telling you that you had to make yourself indispensable if you wanted to be accepted … or something like that.'

Jed frowned at him. 'You knew about that?'

Troyden's jaw hardened. 'I did, and your mum and I had such a fight about it. Man, I lost it.'

He did? 'Why?'

'Why?' Troyden shouted. 'Because you were a kid, and no one, especially not your mum, should've put that much pressure on you. And here's an answer: because it was fucking bullshit!'

Jed's eyes widened at Troyden dropping an f-bomb. He was properly upset. 'My love for you was never dependent on what you did or how you acted, and I'm gutted to think that you still believe that you have to prove your worth.'

He could deny it, but that would be yet another lie. 'I don't *want* to believe it, Dad. It's just … there.' He sighed, every atom of air leaving his body. 'Do we have to talk about this?'

'Yes, I think we do. Explain it to me, Jedson.'

Did he have to? And how? But because this was Troyden, he'd try. 'I believe love comes with expectations and risks, and I'm terrified of not making the grade, of failing. Of being rejected and being left behind.'

He stared at the stable floor, his vision a little wavy. He felt Troyden's hand on his back and it steadied him. 'Love is conditional.'

'Not in this family, Jedson.' It was a relief to hear the determination in his voice, the power. The *'I've got this so you can relax'*. Troyden kept his hand on his back, the slow circles reassuring. 'I failed you, Jed.'

Jed frowned at him, shocked. 'Don't be absurd!'

Troyden shook his head. 'You were always so adult, so damn responsible. And as you grew into adulthood, I let go of the reins and let you take over, mostly because I'm a lazy, selfish git. I pick up young women and let them use me because I knew that you wouldn't let it go too far. I knew that you'd put your foot down, so I didn't need to. You are the family backstop, the one everyone turns to … when it should've been me. I abdicated responsibility and you picked it up out of some misplaced sense of emotional debt.'

Well …

'Well, it stops. Right here, right now.' Jed raised his eyebrows at the determination coating his words. 'Let me make it very clear … you are not responsible for us, Jed. We … *I* love you, no matter what you do or do not do, or achieve. My love for you is *not* conditional.'

Until he heard the words, he hadn't realised how much he needed them, how he ached to believe them. Shards of hard cement and bits of steel dropped off his heart and crashed to the ground, splintering. He felt raw, but free.

Loved.

He might be the captain of his country's polo team, an ace carpenter, his siblings' protector, but he was also a son, a brother … someone who sometimes needed to lean, finally safe in the knowledge that everything he'd worked for and valued wouldn't be taken away because he wasn't enough.

Yet, according to Troyden, he was. Enough. More than, as it turned out.

He pushed his index finger and thumb into the corner of his eyes and sniffed. He wasn't crying, but, shit, it was close. Troyden patted his back. 'Now that we've got that sorted, what are you going to do about Eden?'

He sighed. 'I have no bloody idea,' he admitted. He clasped his hands together and bit down on his bottom lip. 'I didn't believe her, stand up for her, and that's on me.'

'Yet you still haven't apologised. It's not like you to avoid a problem,' Troyden commented. 'So why are you ignoring her?'

Ah, shit, this was hard to admit. 'Because if I don't do anything, if I leave it, then, in my head, we are still together. By talking to her I risk losing her.'

Troyden shook his head, but his face was full of love. 'You, my boy, are a bloody basket case.'

Well, he wasn't wrong. 'She doesn't need me, Dad,' he whispered.

'Jed, that's the most foolish thing I've ever heard you say.'

He huffed out a laugh, but it was hollow. 'It's true. She's brilliant and strong, and—' He swallowed, his chest aching. 'She was fine before me. She'll be fine after me.'

His father's eyes softened. 'Yes, maybe she will be. Maybe you'll both be okay. But has it occurred to you that fine isn't the same as happy?'

Eden skidded into the kitchen and winced when she saw the family *sans* Jed (he was still avoiding her) gathered around the table in the kitchen. They could afford to have a leisurely breakfast, but it was the day of the charity polo match, and she had a million things to do. Breakfast was not on the list.

'Sit down, Eden,' Diana told her, her stocky frame enveloped in an apron embroidered with I'M GORGEOUS AND I CAN COOK across her ample chest.

Eden shook her head. 'No time, Di. I'll just take a cup of coffee in a travel mug.'

Diana pointed her spatula at the open chair next to Mick. 'Sit. Stay.'

Damn, she wasn't a goldendoodle. 'Okay, but only for five minutes.'

Diana dumped a hefty amount of bacon onto a slice of home-made white bread as big as a doorstop and slid the plate in front of her. She slapped another slice on top and expertly cut it in half. 'Eat.'

'Not exactly a gourmet breakfast, Di,' Mick said.

'Do you want food?' Diana retorted. When Mick nodded, chastised, she turned back to the stove. 'Eden has a long day ahead of her and needs the energy. Eden, you said you were in a hurry, the sooner you eat, the sooner you can go.'

Right. Okay, then. Eden lifted the sandwich to her lips and took a huge bite. God, it was good. A bacon butty was the food of the gods.

While she chewed, she took in the family sitting around the table. Mick was dressed in tailored shorts, a pink camisole under a thigh-length jacket, and stiletto ankle boots, Justin in a gorgeous white linen shirt and Alistair in a grey suit. Troyden rocked the eccentric billionaire look by wearing old brown cords, an untucked white, collared shirt, a bright red silk scarf and a pink baseball cap. Eden's gaze hopped from face to face. They were so different, but they looked like a family.

They were *her* family. Obsessed with his spreadsheets, constantly-on-his-phone Alistair, fun-but-astute Justin, her soul-sister Mick, and Troyden, the closest to a father figure she'd ever have in her life. But the picture was missing its centre: it had a big Jed-sized hole. She didn't know if it would be filled or not…

Her roiling emotions, her anger at being disappointed by him, had faded to more manageable levels, but she knew they needed to have a conversation in order to move forward. Since she was the one who'd shut down their lines of communication – so stupid! – she had to approach him and hash it out. Whether moving forward meant walking side-by-side, she still wasn't sure. Trust was imperative, and if Jed couldn't give her that much, they were doomed from the start. They'd needed a little time, some distance, so she'd put off walking down to his cottage to talk to him for a couple of days, then a couple more. The urge to find him and beg him to give her a chance to redo their last conversation had been overwhelming at times, but that was quickly swamped by the thought that if she confronted him, there was an excellent chance he'd call it quits and dump her. She was terrified she'd blown her chances and preferred to keep them in a state of suspended animation rather than risk him breaking up with her.

Cowardly? Absolutely.

But there *had* to be a way they could get past this or, at the very least, talk about it. They couldn't keep avoiding each other for ever. That would be ridiculous. She'd regret it if she didn't tell him she loved him. Her love for him was rare and infinitely precious and needed to be fought for. She couldn't treat it lightly or brush it away because it was inconvenient or scary. She had to be brave and face it. She had to try and make the picture complete.

But she had a decent excuse not to talk to Jed today. She was in charge of making sure the charity polo match was a success. If she dropped the ball now, at the last moment, the pledges they'd been promised wouldn't materialise and Hope Harbour would be in dire straits. Strangely, she felt like she needed to get the charity on its financial feet so that she could move on too.

Her phone rang and Eden snatched it up, expecting to see a call from Henry or one of the committee members. The bread stuck in her throat when she saw Detective Gosling's name. She answered and met Troyden's eyes. He frowned, held up his hand, and the table fell silent.

'I'm calling to inform you that we arrested Tara and Vincent Bancroft half an hour ago at their residence,' Detective Gosling told her.

She nodded, realised he couldn't see her and cleared her throat. 'Are they... Are they okay?' she asked, then shook her head. How okay could they be when the police arrived at their door holding an arrest warrant?

'Being arrested is never fun. They'll go before a judge and will probably be granted bail in a couple of days.' He cleared his throat. 'It was a quiet arrest, no drama.'

'And the foundation?' Eden asked.

'All their bank accounts have been frozen, including the foundation's.'

Eden grimaced. So many charities and people wouldn't be getting the help they needed anytime soon.

'We'll be in touch, Ms Ennis.'

Eden thanked him, cut the call and looked down at her sandwich. There was no chance of her eating anymore. She bit her lip and closed her eyes, hearing nothing but the sound of the clock ticking behind her and the sizzle of bacon in the pan.

'I'm sorry to tell you … but the Bancrofts are in custody,' she stated quietly. 'The foundation isn't operational either.'

Alistair looked up from his tablet. 'I expected that. It will take a while to untangle the funds, get the money distributed. And by a while, I mean it will take many months, possibly years.'

Eden bit down on her bottom lip, feeling a little sick. 'So many charities will be scrambling now, desperately worried because the money they thought they could rely on isn't forthcoming.'

Mick pushed her chair back and shot around the table, hugging her from behind, her cheek against hers. 'It's not your fault,' she murmured. 'I promise, it's not.'

She squeezed Mick's wrist and nodded. 'I know, Mick,' she softly said. And she did. It was their choice, their consequence, but the charities were suffering because of the Bancrofts' greed. But she still felt awful for them. She patted Mick's arm. 'I'm okay, Mick. I promise.'

Troyden's gaze held hers, steady and sure, his slight smile reassuring. *It's okay. I've got you.*

Eden hauled in a deep breath, took a sip of her coffee, and tried to unjumble her conflicting emotions. Concern for the people she'd once loved and relief that the sword had dropped juggled for dominance. Did that mean she could move on? And what did moving on mean? Was she able to hate what they did, but still retain affection for the people who'd nurtured and supported her? Could she keep the good memories of working for the Bancrofts and discard the bad? Could she hate what they'd done and still like them?

She didn't know and couldn't take the time to figure it out. Right now, she could only do what she could do: making sure the polo event was a success to keep Hope House afloat. One step, on one charity, at a time. Eden pushed her plate away and lifted her mug again, desperate for a caffeine rush. Was there something more than coffee, but less than cocaine?

She stood, pushing back her chair. 'I need to go,' she said, bending to pick up her bulging tote bag.

Troyden lifted his cheek for a kiss. 'Good luck, darling, we'll find you later to see how you are doing.'

Eden squeezed his shoulder and smiled at Justin, who held up his hand for a high-five. Mick, because she was Mick, pulled her in for another hug. She rocked her from side to side, before pulling back to grin at her. 'My best idea, ever, was to ask you to join the committee. I'm totes brilliant.'

'Nobody says totes anymore, and you're truly incredible at getting someone else to do the work, Michaela,' Justin countered.

Mick, because she was a mature adult, lifted her middle finger.

Alistair looked up from his phone and sent Eden a sweet, rare smile. 'I'll send you the employment contract on Monday,' he said, before returning his attention to his phone.

Uh ... what employment contract?

'Initial each page, get two witnesses. Got to make it official.'

Justin sighed and rolled his eyes. 'Alistair, we agreed that we would talk to Eden after the polo day was over,' he said.

'She's here. We're here. We can talk,' Alistair responded.

Talk about what? She had no idea what they were going on about, but she didn't have time to play guessing games. She needed to get to Bythesea Hall and start running through her million and one checks.

'Guys, I've got work to do,' she warned. 'If you have something to say, it's got to be now.'

Mick and Justin both looked at Troyden. Mick hopped from foot to foot, the same way Liam did when he was excited. Or needed to pee. 'I want you to run my foundation,' Troyden calmly stated.

Eden narrowed her eyes. 'You don't have a foundation.' She knew this because his donations were funnelled through the Bancrofts' foundation. And that couldn't happen anymore.

'Alistair is setting one up,' he replied. 'But we need someone to run it and grow it. Someone we trust. You've done a marvellous job setting up today's event, but that isn't why you are getting the job.'

Confusion trickled through her. 'It isn't?'

Troyden's phone beeped and he picked it up to read the text message, before typing a reply.

'I'll explain...' Alistair leaned back and folded his huge arms, and Eden knew what it felt like to be a bug on a researcher's slide. 'I did some digging into you, and I discovered that the Bancroft Foundation really took off once you came on board. You brought order, stability and consistency to the foundation. You worked behind the scenes, but you made a massive impact.'

Eden blinked at him, trying to make sense of his words. He sounded impressed. Was she imagining it? 'I'm seriously impressed with your work, Eden.'

Not imagining it then. Wow. Okay. Eden placed her bent fingers against her cheek, feeling the heat. To get a compliment like this from Alistair, so quiet, so broody, so difficult to impress, was … *everything*.

'I want you to run the Castle Foundation,' Alistair said.

'I think that's my line,' Troyden said, smiling, putting his phone into the inside pocket of his jacket.

'Say yes, say yes,' Mick muttered, her hands in a prayer position, her fingers resting on her lips.

Oh, it was one hell of an offer, but she couldn't accept it, not yet. She couldn't discuss working for Troyden's foundation until she'd had a conversation with Jed. While she wouldn't stay or go on his say-so – this wasn't the 1950s – she wanted to hear what he thought and where they stood before she made any decisions about her career.

There was more at stake than just her career. Jed hadn't been up to the big house for the past week, and she didn't know how he felt about Troyden's offer to run the foundation. If he knew of their plan to offer her the job and objected, would her working with Troyden and Alistair cause a rift between Jed and his family? His family was everything to him, and she didn't want to be an obstacle between them. He was just starting to reframe his relationship with them into something healthier, and she didn't want that to be jeopardised because he was avoiding her.

All she wanted was for Jed to be happy. He only had one family.

It's your family too…

Eden tensed, as the words rolled around her mind. Historically, everyone who was supposed to love her, including, sadly, Jed, had never put her first, and by putting Jed's needs before hers, she was doing the same thing. To herself.

Jed's needs weren't more important than hers. Even if Jed told her they were done, that didn't mean she had to fade away. It was Jed's choice to love her or not, just like it was hers to accept or reject a job offer. She didn't have to sacrifice an opportunity, *her* family, because having her around would be uncomfortable for him. She owed it to herself to do what made her happy, to put herself first.

Oh, a life spent with Jed would be more fun, but if that wasn't what he wanted, they'd have to find a way to negotiate sharing the Castle clan. That was non-negotiable.

'What do you think, Eden?'

Troyden's question pulled her back to the kitchen, and she took in their expectant faces. 'Can we talk about this later?' she asked, biting the inside of her lip. As exciting as this offer was, she had work to do, people to check on, and a giant event to oversee.

'Noooo!' Mick wailed. 'Just say yes, Eden, you know you want to. We can do more events like this—'

We? Since handing over the files, Mick's role had been bringing her tea and introducing her to the villagers, and millions of her horsey, country and school connections. Important, but not the beating heart of the event.

Eden placed her hand on Mick's shoulder. 'Mick, I need to have a proper chat with Troyden and Alistair. Preferably around a table, and not in the kitchen while I'm rushing out the door.'

Mick pulled a face. 'I know we can't discuss your salary here, or your perks. But I – *we* – just need an idea of whether it's something you'd consider. I know it's not London, but maybe you could be happy here, with us?'

There was something vulnerable in her expression, and Eden knew this was how Gemma would look on Christmas morning as her biggest wish was granted. She'd thought that, of the two of them, she, Eden, was the more 'needy', and that Mick, with her contact list of millions, considered her simply another of her many friends. It was touching to realise how much Mick valued her, and it was obvious she wanted her to stick around.

She wouldn't give them up. Not now. Not ever. Not even for Jed.

She gave Mick a quick hug, wondering if she knew it was the first time she'd hugged a girlfriend. 'I need to go,' she said. 'I'll catch you later.'

'If you do take the job, I promise to buy and pay for BTS tickets whenever they next come to London,' Mick told her as she was halfway out of the kitchen door.

Eden couldn't help messing with her. It was what best friends, and sisters, did. She braked, turned and raised her eyebrows at Mick. 'I'll think hard about it if you make them VIP tickets. And you need to buy me *all* the merch.'

As she expected her to, Mick gulped, turning a little

pale, obviously thinking about how much she'd have to shell out. Then she narrowed her eyes at her. 'Do you think you are worth VIP tickets?' she asked, lifting her nose. The affection in Mick's eyes was in direct contrast to her snotty tone.

'Yes, actually, I do.'

Mick pulled a face. 'Dammit, of course you are. VIP BTS tickets...' She pushed her hand into her thick hair, and grimaced. '*Shit*. I'm going to need a loan.'

Eden shot her a wide grin as she headed out of the room, the warmth in her chest spreading. This was what family felt like: banter wrapped up in unconditional love. And damn it, she liked it.

And she loved them. Best of all, they seemed to love her too.

Eden glanced at her watch, saw that it was just past five and took a long sip from her oversized travel mug filled to the brim with ice and a high-caffeine energy drink. Given how many she'd slammed back today, she was pretty sure her liver was in shock. But as she was operating on only a few hours of sleep and sheer willpower, with barely any food, at this point caffeine was the only thing between her and collapsing.

Standing next to the main tent, she looked down at her iPad, the words a blur on the screen, and rubbed her eyes before hauling in a deep breath and trying again. Right, the last match of the day, between the Castle Kings and a team Henry had pulled together, was happening on the field.

Surprisingly, judging from the earlier roars of the crowd, it was turning out to be a cracker. Given how much she had to do today, she hadn't had a moment to spare to watch any polo.

No, that was a lie. She'd deliberately kept her eyes away from any players, horses or the field in case she laid eyes on Jed. Eden looked at the electronic scoreboard and saw that the last chukka was about to start. In seven odd minutes, the day's matches would be over and soon the prize-giving would begin. Henry would do a welcome speech, present a rather substantial cheque to Hope Harbour, and then hand out the day's prizes. She was expecting many people in the crowd to stay for the after-party, as Neon Alibi had proven a huge drawcard. Free music and booze? The place would be packed until the alcohol ran out.

The day was a roaring success and she was proud of how she'd taken Mick's half-arsed idea and turned it into this buzzy, vibey, *fun* day. Working for the Bancrofts had given her the skills to organise something like this, but from today, she could step out of their shadows and claim her place in the sun.

It was safe to be seen.

Admittedly, the new Duke of Bythesea had been a godsend this past week, calm and controlled and quietly supportive. Good-looking and quietly charming, confident and self-assured, Henry was – if you ignored the fact that his house was falling down in places and that he was, as he'd confessed to her over dinner last week, living on his last credit card – a catch. If she hadn't met Jed, she might've made herself fancy him.

With Jed, she didn't have to try. From the moment she'd

met him, he'd filled her heart and mind, and there had been no room left for anyone else. If she couldn't work things out with him, would she ever be able to look at another guy or be with anyone else? Not, she thought, for a long time.

A long, long time.

'Eden!'

Eden stopped pretending to consult her iPad and waved at Mick, looking movie-star famous in her oversized sunglasses. Eden closed her tablet and walked over to where Mick stood with Troyden. Justin and Alistair were making their way over to them as well, Justin's hand around Alistair's massive bicep. Al had a beer in one hand and scrolled through his phone with the other. Troyden sent her his sweet smile, the one she knew he kept for the special people in his life, and she surprised him by kissing his left cheek, then his right. Troyden placed his hands on her shoulders and cocked his head. 'Now what was that for, my darling?'

She ducked her head, embarrassed. Unable to explain, she lifted her shoulder and looked at the field. Harris, Number Three, was swapping horses, once again not bothering to dismount.

'Pull your eyes off my brother's arse,' Mick commanded her, shaking her arm. 'It's gross.'

Only a sister could look at Jed on a horse and shudder with distaste. Eden, reluctantly, turned her attention back to the Castle crew. Mick clutched her arm. 'Oooh ... is that Tom Holland at the bar?'

Since he was accompanied by a curly-haired, exquisite woman who looked exactly like Zendaya, Eden thought it just might be.

Holy hell, Spider-Man was in the house. *Score!*

Eden took a moment to look around. Behind them stood Bythesea Hall, a benevolent beacon of old-money splendour. Food and drinks tents and trucks were lined up like little ants, feeding and watering the crowds. Guests, some in oversized hats or bouncing fascinators, wore designer threads and off-the-rack, mingled in big and small groups, or watched the match from their blankets laid out on the thick grass. Throughout the day their laughter, commentary and chatter had accompanied the rhythmic thud of polo mallets meeting the ball. She resisted the urge to dance on the spot. Her hard work had put smiles on faces, raised money for a deserving charity, and was giving people a lovely day's respite from a frequently harsh, mentally taxing world.

Good job, Ennis. Her eyes returned to the field where Jed sat astride Rey, the pony's muscles coiled beneath him like a loaded spring, ready to launch as soon as the chukka started. He adjusted his helmet, scanning the field as though it were a chessboard and he the grandmaster. Across the way, Henry, an adept polo player, flashed his signature grin – a little too wide, a little too smug – and saluted him with his mallet.

'Ready to lose, brother?' Henry's voice carried across the field, his tone breezy. Most people would think it just a fun nickname, but the group around her let out a collective sigh. They all smiled, their eyes a little wet, immediately understanding the meaning beneath the banter. Jed and Henry had come a long way over the last few months.

They all had.

Eden sensed rather than saw Jed's smirk. 'Hope you

brought tissues,' he shouted. 'It's going to hurt when you lose.'

Since Henry's team had some eight and nine handicap players, Eden thought Jed was being a little over-confident. The horn blew, and suddenly, everyone's focus was back on the game, their world narrowed to the gallop of hooves and the blur of movement. Jed, as usual, was fast, reckless and infuriatingly good, zigzagging through the defenders with the kind of flair that made women swoon and sponsors salivate.

The game swung wildly, with Jed's team surging ahead, only to be yanked back. Both teams scored again, and the tension inched up a notch. It was a hard-fought game, entertaining and fast, and everyone's eyes were on the field. In the last minute, Jed surged forward, leaning low, his mallet slicing the air with surgical precision as he sent the ball rocketing toward the goal. The crowd screamed and Jed looked satisfied at their win.

'Textbook, Jed!' Kit shouted. The final horn blew. Jed trotted back to the sideline and Henry rode up beside him, mockingly slow clapping.

'You're not terrible,' he called, and the crowd broke into laughter.

Behind Eden, the champagne tent buzzed with excitement, bets were settled, and someone cranked up the music. She reluctantly pulled her eyes from the field, to see that everyone belonging to the Castle clan was watching her. 'What?'

Mick took her hand and squeezed. 'You did this,' she muttered, her voice thick.

She glanced back at the field to where Henry, Kit and Jed

were dismounting, laughing as they handed their horses over to the grooms. 'I think Jed and Henry worked it out themselves.'

Mick smacked her arm. 'I'm not talking about them, you numpty!' She widened her arms, trying to gather the day into them. 'You did *all this*! It's bigger and brighter and more fun and more professional than anything we could've pulled off.'

Eden looked around, and the earlier pride rushed back in, hot and bright. 'I did good, right?'

Surprisingly, it was Alistair who answered. He lifted his head, and his dark, fiercely intelligent eyes met hers. 'You did *very* good,' he rumbled the words.

Eden nodded and her throat closed. Getting two compliments in one day from Al, who rarely bothered to engage, was *everything*. She placed her hand on his forearm and squeezed. 'Thank you.'

'Sign the contract,' Alistair ordered, his voice gruff. 'We need a family member running the foundation. Someone we can trust, someone who can read a bloody spreadsheet, decipher the simplest code.'

'Blah blah,' Mick muttered.

Tears welled at Al's gruff endorsement. She might not have Jed, but she was part of this family. And that was everything. Well, nearly everything. Her eyes watered, but Eden knew she couldn't lose it now; she needed to be *Hello!* and *Tatler* photo-ready.

'Dammit,' she muttered, fanning her hands in front of her face, trying to dry her tears. She blinked and sniffed, her knees a little weak at the idea of having her people, her place and a soft place to land.

Troyden touched her shoulder. 'Sweetheart, you can't cry. You have things to do, an event to close out.'

Dammit, she did. She had a million – okay, an exaggeration – items to tick off her list before she could throw back a tequila and chase it with a beer. But the sooner she started, the quicker she'd be done...

But as soon as she stepped into the tent, she started to sneeze. Right, too many sexy polo players in too confined a space. Well, at least she could blame her horse allergy for her red-with-emotion eyes.

Chapter Eighteen

The late afternoon air hummed with booze-tinged enthusiasm, courtesy of the crowd gathered around the small stage in front of a massive square banner boasting the names of the day's sponsors.

The polo players stood in a loose formation, their uniforms stained with the dirt and grit of the match, their hair sweat-streaked and their grins wide, their expressions a combination of exhaustion and adrenaline. Jed stood in the middle of the group, his jaw hard and sporting a restrained smile. His shirt was partially untucked, his hair was all over the place and dark stubble covered his lower face, yet he exuded confidence, certain of the world and his place in it.

She thought she'd missed him, but on seeing him, she knew it was a small word for a huge emotion. Smart, reticent, alpha … achingly tender in the quietest of ways, he was everything she never knew she needed. He saw straight through her, steadied her, the only man who encouraged her to be authentically herself. Being without him had left her hollow, like she wasn't taking in enough air. Living without him wasn't living at all.

The announcer's voice rang out, smooth and commanding, drawing everyone's attention to the stage. Glass trophies gleamed and names were announced. Polite applause followed, growing louder when the Castle King team were declared the victors. Jed accepted his nominal prize with a nod and a handshake, his movements unhurried, smooth and self-assured. He was every inch the superstar of the polo world. The smile he offered the cheering crowd was polite, camera-ready, a little distant, until his eyes slammed into hers. For a fleeting moment, his mask slipped, revealing something raw, something she didn't understand, an emotion she didn't recognise. Was it longing? Need? Or was she, desperate for a reconciliation, seeing what she wanted to see? It was highly possible, likely even, he was done with her. Maybe he'd already called it quits and just needed to tell her.

Their eyes met again and Eden's heart sputtered, restarted, sputtered again. Their shared moment was electric, charged with an undercurrent of something that seemed bigger than both of them, something she couldn't name or describe. It just ... *was*.

The announcer invited Henry, as the day's host, to step up to the podium, and he took the microphone, voice as smooth as a vintage cognac. His speech was both funny and heartfelt, as he thanked everyone, from the volunteers to the supporters, for throwing their enthusiasm behind the day.

'Our fabulous event coordinator, Eden, without whom this day would've never happened, has just handed me the latest figures raised for the shelter and I'm happy to report that we raised an incredible amount for Hope Harbour...'

Eden, wanting to get out of the limelight, tried to slip back into the crowd, but Jed reached out and gripped her wrist, tugging her to his side. His fingers moved from her wrist to her hand, fingers sliding between hers and holding on tight.

He dropped his head to kiss her temple. 'Stay,' he murmured.

Did he mean for the rest of the presentation? For the summer? God, for *ever*? What? Heat radiated off him, and he felt so solid. She fought the urge to slump against him, needing to lean, to soak up some of his strength. She was physically whipped and mentally drained and she wanted to sleep for a week. Tears, from stress and a touch of heartbreak, burned her eyes, and she pinched the skin on the inside of her wrist. If she fell apart now, she didn't think she had the strength to gather her pieces and stitch herself together again.

It took everything she had to tug her hand from Jed's, but he didn't loosen his grip. 'No, we're not running again, Eden,' he murmured, just loud enough for her to hear.

We. He'd said we. It gave her enough hope to take a chance. She gathered her courage. 'Jed, I *need* you. Only you,' she whispered and watched as, somehow, her quiet words reached him. 'I should never have said that I didn't. It was such a lie.'

Their eyes caught, held, and Eden bit her lip, unable to decode the emotion in his eyes, the expression on his face. What was he thinking?

'We're getting out of here,' he muttered, wrapping his

arm around her waist, and lifting her off her feet. His barked 'move' caused the wall of polo players to break and shift. Kit immediately stepped into the space they'd vacated, shielding their escape from the crowd in the tent.

After he'd placed her on her feet, Eden followed where Jed led, too numb to protest. Instead of climbing the stone steps to Henry's huge house, Jed veered left and took the path to the rose garden. He looked around, saw a bench and steered her over to it.

'Did you mean what you said back there?' he demanded.

She nodded. 'With all my heart. I was trying to hurt you back then, and I'm so, so sorry.'

He nodded at the bench. 'Sit,' he commanded. 'I have things to say.'

Oh, God, that didn't sound good. She clasped her hands between her legs, dread coursing through her. What if he said there wasn't any hope for them, that sharing a family would be torturous? What if she'd misread him?

'Let's deal with the Bancroft issue first,' Jed said, standing in front of her. She wished he'd sit down; he looked so tall, hard, and remote.

'I'm sorry I snitched on them, Jed.'

'Eden, *Jesus*.'

No, he *needed* to understand. 'It wasn't a quick decision, Jed. I *agonised* about what to do. There was no one to talk to, so I had to go by what my heart told me, what I thought was right. I'm *so, so* sorry my actions hurt you.'

Could he understand? Would he ever be able to forgive her? She heard his sigh as he sat, and felt his big arms encircle her, pulling her into him. 'Sweetheart, why are you apologising? *You* didn't do anything wrong.'

He stroked her hair off her forehead, his gaze tender. 'They did, when they stole money, Eden. It was their decision, their choice, and getting charged for theft is their consequence.'

'But it was me who shopped them. And they are *your* people.'

'I can be grateful for what they did for me and my mum, for the role they, especially Tara, have played in my life. But that doesn't excuse them for stealing from their foundation, from people who needed it. I can be thankful, but I can also hate what they did and who they became.'

He placed one hand on her back and the other on her thigh. 'They have lawyers, money and they got themselves into this mess. At some point, I might reconnect with them, I might not. I'm also furious Tara tried to shift the blame on you.'

Did that mean— Could it mean he was choosing her? Was that possible? The possibility made her feel a little dizzy, and, dammit, weak-kneed.

Her eyes met his, and she saw his banked anger and frustration. Not at her, but at the Bancrofts, at himself. He touched her jaw with the tips of his fingers. 'I should've planted my feet, Eden. Last week, I should've told you that you were a priority and told you that I believed you.' He paused.

'I fucked up.'

It was a simple, but heartfelt statement, she heard the disappointment in his voice and it was all directed at himself. He was so used to doing everything well, accustomed to knowing how all the moving parts of his life fitted together, who did what and where and how. But here, with her, he looked as confused as she often felt. She tipped her head, a silent entreaty for him to continue.

'I'm used to thinking about the world in terms of how it affects me, how it affects my family,' Jed explained, linking his hands behind his head. 'But this last week has taught me a fling with you isn't enough.'

Her heart bounced off her ribcage. 'It isn't?'

'Is it enough for you?' he demanded, his eyes bright in his tanned face.

'No, but we were talking about you and your feelings,' she gently pointed out.

'And I'm not having any fun,' he muttered.

She smiled at his sullen tone. 'Tell me what you want, Jed. From me, and us.'

He sighed, pushed both his hands into his hair and gave her a wild-eyed, I-don't-know-what-I-am-doing look. 'I'm not good at love, Eden. I'm still learning. I've always believed that it had to be earned, and I can't help thinking that I've done nothing to deserve you.'

'Jed...'

'I hurt you. I didn't stand up for you. I didn't instinctively believe you.'

'I don't know how to be a partner or a lover or'—he swallowed, panic in his eyes—'more. It's not something I'm good at.'

Excellence was bred into his DNA, and she had no doubt he'd be an incredible partner or ... more.

He pushed an agitated hand into his hair. 'But I want to try. I want to love you, hell, I *do* love you,' he corrected, his words as fast as bullets from a machine gun. 'But I also want you to *feel* loved, I want you to know what it means to be at the front and centre of someone's world.

'Because you are the centre of mine,' he added. He rested his forehead against hers and closed his eyes. 'Be mine, Eden. Let me love you. Love me back. Be the heart of my family.'

Tension seeped from her muscles, loosened her shoulders and the pressure in her head. She gripped his shirt and twisted the fabric around her fingers. She was not going to let horse dander spoil this moment! Happiness, soft and sweet, filled her. 'Okay,' she murmured.

He lowered her head to kiss her temple, her cheek, the side of her mouth. 'I swear I'll make you happy, sweetheart. I'll put you first. I'll make you a priority.'

So, when Jed Harris committed, he went all in. She tipped her head back to gaze into the gorgeous eyes she would look at for the rest of her life. 'Thank you. Thank you for giving me a family, for saying that.' She lifted her hands to hold his face, his stubble rough under her palms. She tasted the unfamiliar words on her tongue, a sentence she'd never spoken before, one that was as unfamiliar as Farsi. 'I love you.'

He seemed to understand the importance of this first time, the full impact of her words because his eyes glistened with emotion. She couldn't say he was tearing up, but it was close. 'I love you, too. So much. I'll love your more tomorrow, and the day after.'

When their lips met, she tasted his banked passion, all the words they'd yet to speak, the stories they'd yet to tell. Trust and faith, laughter and magic, it was a dizzying combination of flavours. This was the essence of who they were, what they meant to each other, a taste and scent profile that would form the basis of their life together. Pure, intense and, for now, uncomplicated.

Oh, there were going to be times when they'd lose the intensity, when anger and misunderstandings would cloud their feelings, when sadness or stress would taint their relationship, and when they would think they'd lost the magic. But she'd remind him, and herself, of this moment when time stood still and everything seemed possible.

Instead of deepening their kiss and letting passion sweep them away, Jed pulled back and gathered her to him, his big arms around her, enveloping her in his strength and solidness. Nothing could touch her when Jed held her like this.

She looked at his long legs. His boots were dusty and scuffed, his white jodhpurs stretched over muscled thighs. She couldn't wait to go home, she wanted him naked again, to be at the mercy of his clever hands and wicked tongue.

Jed sat up straight and pulled a face. 'Don't look at me like that, Eden. We still have to go back to the tent,' he complained.

'Do we have to?' she whined. 'We could just sneak away and spend the rest of the night in bed.'

'Oh, we're going to do that, but not for a few hours yet,' Jed confidently stated. He picked up a strand of her hair and wound it around her fingers. 'Once I get you to my place, I'm not letting you go. Thank God my cottage is an easy commute to the big house where, I hear, Troyden is turning the music room into a study for you.'

The music room was a smallish reception room, with

bright light and an awesome view of the polo field where Jed routinely practised. She'd have to put her back to the window or else she would never get any work done when Jed was training.

'So you know about Troyden's offer for me to run his foundation?' she asked, crossing one leg over the other. She placed her elbow on her knee and rested her chin in the palm of her hand. 'Are you okay with that?'

'Very. You'll consult with Troyden, but you'll report to Al via Justin. I know it will work out just fine.'

She appreciated his confidence in her, more than he'd ever know.

'But it's up to you. If you want to do it, do it. If you don't, I'll support you.'

'Alistair won't let me say no,' Eden explained, smiling. 'Mick will whine until I agree. Troyden will give me his puppy dog expression—'

'So maybe you should just cave in now and agree?' he asked, laughing. Then he placed his forearms on his knees and turned his head to look at her. 'Can I get super serious, just for a minute?'

She didn't want to. She didn't want them tainting the moment, after they had declared their love for the first time. She wrinkled her nose and sighed.

He took her hand and wove his fingers through hers. 'I meant what I said about loving you more in the future than I do right now. I know I hurt you when I didn't believe you, but I promise you Eden, that'll never happen again.'

'And I hurt you when I said I didn't need you. I do, Jed. So much.'

He nodded, looking fierce. 'Going forward, our

relationship will top my priority list. I will fiercely guard our love, Eden, because it's been hard-won and infinitely precious. I will not allow anything or anyone to threaten what we have, this love we have found.'

It was time to put down all their baggage, to start a new journey. She couldn't wait. Jed waited for her eyes to meet his and her breath caught at the love she could see in his. 'Deal?'

She nodded, relief and happiness causing her eyes to mist over and a couple of tears to fall. 'Yes, absolutely. You will always be my priority too, Jed.'

He squeezed her hand, and the corner of his mouth kicked up. 'Good to hear,' he replied. He stroked her cheek and brushed his lips across hers, then he deepened their kiss and Eden sighed. She was home. Finally.

After a few minutes, he pulled back and put a little distance between them but kept a possessive hand on her thigh. 'We'll move your stuff to my place tomorrow. I plan on keeping you naked for the next twenty-four hours, so you won't need clothes for a while yet.'

She loved how confident he was, how decisive. Mick would call him bossy, and she was right. She loved him intensely, and his personality was jet-fighter forceful, but she wouldn't allow him to steamroll her. Not without a pushback at the very least.

'Maybe we should take some time to reset our relationship, to ease our way into it,' she suggested, suddenly scared that this was too good, too soon. 'Neither of us have been in a committed relationship, and I'm not sure if living together should be our next first step. Maybe we should take some time to digest everything and to allow the family and anyone else who cares, to get used to the idea of us being a couple.'

Jed stood up and looked down at her, his eyes narrowed. Without speaking he reached for her hands. Instead of pulling her to her feet, he boosted her up and over his shoulder in a fireman's hold. One moment she was on her feet, the next her head was looking at the streaks of dirt on his very fine bum.

'Jed, what the hell?' she spluttered.

'By the way, why aren't you sneezing?' he asked, as he started to walk. 'I'm covered in horse dander, but you've yet to react.'

She hadn't sneezed much all day, hadn't had the time to. Maybe she was building up a tolerance to equine dander. She slapped his shoulder. 'Maybe if you put me down, we could discuss my allergy and other subjects, like reasonable people.'

'Mm ... *no*. But when we get back to the tent, you need to take an antihistamine,' he told her, patting her bum.

Forthright, alpha, single-minded, more than a little arrogant. But, God, *hers*. Eden bounced along as his long stride ate up the grass beneath his feet. They were on the path and the sounds coming from the main tent got louder. She turned her head and saw the slightly shocked and amused faces of spectators bored with the speeches in the tent.

She slapped Jed's back. 'Put me down, dammit!'

He ignored her and walked into the tent. Using her core muscles – *ouch!* – she lifted her torso to orientate herself; Jed had stopped in front of the stage. His family, including a gorgeous, green-eyed stranger with a buzz cut and heavy stubble, stood in a half-circle in front of him.

Eden reached back to make sure her dress covered her in-the-air bum. Bloody Jed! She heard the whirr of cameras clicking and the flashes seared her eyeballs. She had no doubt many people were recording this moment on their phones.

Brilliant. She was going to *kill* him.

'You done being the Duke?' Jed asked Henry, allowing her to slide to the ground.

Eden's feet hit the ground and she swayed, but Jed's arm around her waist steadied her.

'I've got you,' he told her, and a warm glow burned away her irritation at being handled like a sack of flour. She'd found her someone...

Jed looked back up at Henry who glanced at the microphone in his hand and nodded. 'Yep. I'm done.'

Henry joined their family group, his eyes bright with curiosity. Eden looked at them, her heart sighing. For once Al wasn't on his phone. Mick had both her arms wrapped around the blond guy's waist, who Eden recognised as Kael, the elusive, and very hot, photojournalist brother. Troyden simply looked amused.

'Eden and I are together and it's serious,' Jed stated, his deep voice carrying across the tent. 'I love her, she loves me. I want her to move in with me, but she thinks we need time because you lot need to get used to the idea of us. I call bullshit, but in case she's right, get over yourselves.'

Right, well. That was one way to make friends and influence people.

Jed, acting as if he hadn't just lobbed a conversational

hand grenade at his family's feet, looked at his younger brother. 'And it's about bloody time you got your arse home, Kael,' he stated. 'I'd hug you, but I'm keeping a tight grip on Eden here.'

Kael lifted a blond eyebrow, green eyes mischievous. 'I'd rethink that, Eden' he murmured, grinning. 'He's a grumpy, bossy bastard.'

He was flirting and Jed was not amused. She laughed. 'I know, but the heart wants what the heart wants.'

'I thought you were going to move in with me for a while, Eden,' Henry asked. Eden shook her head. He was making it sound like they'd come to a firm arrangement, when they'd only floated the idea in the most general of terms. Yeah, he was messing with Jed.

Jed glared at Henry, who held his do-it-and-die stare. After thirty seconds, Henry threw up his hands and looked at Eden, his expression amused. 'Sorry, Mary, but there are no longer any rooms at the inn.'

She rolled her eyes. 'Wuss,' she muttered, sending him a mock-glare.

Henry laughed and walked up to her to kiss her right cheek, then her left. Because Jed didn't let her go, she, Henry and Jed shared a *lot* of personal space. 'I'm happy for you, Eden. If you get sick of him, you know where I am.'

Crank, crank... More winding up.

Judging by the fact that Jed was bristling again, it worked. *Men.*

Mick pushed her way between Jed and Henry to pull her into a tight, hard hug. 'Welcome to the family officially, E. I'm so glad to have you here to balance out the testosterone, especially now we have another pesky brother back home.'

Over her shoulder, Eden eyed Kael. And what a fine brother he was. He was a few years younger than Jed, fit and blond, beautiful in a rough and ready way. Nothing to see here, just another bold and beautiful Troyden Castle stepchild.

'Weren't you the one who begged me, sometimes multiple times a week, to come home?' Kael asked Mick after she'd released Eden from her tight hug.

Justin tipped his head to Kael. 'He's younger than both Jed and Henry,' he said, not bothering to be subtle. 'Better-looking too.'

She couldn't help her giggle and slapped her hand over her mouth. Her eyes met Jed's and although he looked grumpy, there was laughter, and love, in his eyes. Teasing, she'd remembered, was their love language.

'I'll keep that in mind,' she told Justin, and smiled at Kael. 'When he can't keep up with me, I'll give you a shout.'

'Funny girl,' Jed murmured, his eyes heating. 'We'll see who's begging for sleep later.'

Eden blushed, and his siblings, even Al, laughed. Eden looked at Troyden, who'd yet to say anything. She held out her hand to him and when he took it, she sent him a wobbly smile. 'Thank you for creating this awesome family, Troyden.'

Troyden hugged her tight and rested his cheek against her hair. In her uncle's arms, she turned her head to look at Jed, eyes on her, his face saturated with love. Over her head, Troyden cleared his throat.

'It hasn't been perfect, but it's been fun. We've argued

and screamed at each other, hurt each other and there were days when I would've given everything I had for a quiet, calm house.

'But family', Troyden said, his arms around Eden's back, holding her to his chest, 'is a choice of the heart. Parenting you lot has been the joy of my life.'

'Great speech, Dad,' Jed replied. 'Now, will you please give me back the love of my life?'

Troyden let her go and Eden walked over to Jed, to step into her spot within the Castle family, next to his side. She stood on her toes to kiss his sexy mouth, smiling when he fed her a soft, intense 'you belong with me' kiss. She'd found her place. And her person. Life didn't get much better than this.

She was, she decided, the dictionary definition of riding high.

Acknowledgments

Thank you so much for reading *Riding High*, and I hope you love Eden and Jed and the extended Castle clan as much as I do. This book was so much fun to write. On a side note: I've had an allergic reaction like Eden's, and the kitten found in a fridge story? It happened to me, and my daughter still – fourteen years later – has not forgiven me for unknowingly trapping her beloved cat in the fridge.

It takes a village to raise a book, and I am so grateful to Charlotte, Helen, Kara and the rest of the One More Chapter crew for helping me whip *Riding High* into shape, it's such a delight working with you all.

Thank you to my amazing husband Vaughan, who listens to me whine about characters going rogue and that I – again! – forgot a brilliant idea because I didn't write it down. He also constantly reminds me that no, this isn't the book that will kill me.

As I write this, Rourke and Tess, my two children, are spreading their own wings to fly off to discover the world. I'm so excited for them and can't wait to see where they land and what they do. They carry my heart with them. Being their mom is the biggest privilege of my life.

Please follow me on my socials, everywhere @josswoodbooks.

Happy reading!

The author and One More Chapter would like to thank everyone who contributed to the publication of this story...

Analytics
James Brackin
Abigail Fryer

Audio
Fionnuala Barrett
Ciara Briggs

Contracts
Laura Amos
Laura Evans

Design
Lucy Bennett
Fiona Greenway
Liane Payne
Dean Russell

Digital Sales
Laura Daley
Lydia Grainge
Hannah Lismore

eCommerce
Laura Carpenter
Madeline ODonovan
Charlotte Stevens
Christina Storey
Jo Surman
Rachel Ward

Editorial
Janet Marie Adkins
Kara Daniel
Charlotte Ledger
Federica Leonardis
Jennie Rothwell
Sofia Salazar Studer
Helen Williams

Harper360
Jennifer Dee
Emily Gerbner
Ariana Juarez
Jean Marie Kelly
emma sullivan
Sophia Wilhelm

International Sales
Peter Borcsok
Ruth Burrow
Colleen Simpson
Ben Wright

Inventory
Sarah Callaghan
Kirsty Norman

Marketing & Publicity
Chloe Cummings
Grace Edwards

Operations
Melissa Okusanya
Hannah Stamp

Production
Denis Manson
Simon Moore
Francesca Tuzzeo

Rights
Helena Font Brillas
Ashton Mucha
Zoe Shine
Aisling Smyth
Lucy Vanderbilt

Trade Marketing
Ben Hurd
Eleanor Slater

The HarperCollins Distribution Team

The HarperCollins Finance & Royalties Team

The HarperCollins Legal Team

The HarperCollins Technology Team

UK Sales
Isabel Coburn
Jay Cochrane
Sabina Lewis
Holly Martin
Harriet Williams
Leah Woods

And every other essential link in the chain from delivery drivers to booksellers to librarians and beyond!

**Read on for an extract from *One Bed*
The hottest forced proximity romance for 2025
set in Santorini!**

Rising star author Bea Williams needs a vacation.

And her godmother's snug Greek island retreat is the perfect place to use as an escape from her writer's block.

Until she finds she's going to have to share her idyllic one bed cottage with him – Gibson Caddell, one time childhood friend and a great big, drop-dead-gorgeous red flag.

As the sun sets on Santorini, Bea's thoughts soon turn to something much more pressing – there's two of them. And only one bed…

Available in paperback and ebook now!

Extract from One Bed

Chapter One

Driving her rental car away from the airport, Bea Williams wished she wasn't in a rush to get to Golly's Santorini villa near Oia. It was midday, and the sun was high in the dense blue sky, coating everything in a luminous glow. Despite summer being over, the bougainvillaea, jasmine, and potted geraniums still pulsated with colour, while the lake-smooth turquoise sea shimmered. The Greek sun created sharp contrasts between light and shadow and accentuated the contours of the cliffs and rocky outcrops of the caldera.

Mid-October, when many of the accommodation establishments closed their doors and the owners wiped the sweat from their foreheads and checked their bulging bank accounts, was her favourite time to be on the island.

The sunsets were as vibrant, the sea still warm, but the island, especially the famous, blue-roofed town of Oia, wasn't a portly man's vest bursting its buttons. In October, Oia returned to being part of a community, a place where people lived year-round, where you didn't need to fight your way through the streets because the selfie crowd needed to pose in front of the iconic views of the caldera, or because they *had* to capture the always amazing sunset.

Thank God the island was, for Santorini, relatively empty. Bea didn't know if she could contend with hoards of pushy tourists. The next two weeks were going to be busy. She was organising Golly's joint retirement and seventieth birthday bash while wrestling with a combination of writer's block, imposter syndrome and characters who wouldn't bloody talk to her.

She'd visited Santorini in every season, sometimes several times a year, sometimes to write, sometimes to relax. This island was her second home, the place where she'd banged out the first book in her *Urban Explorers* series, where she'd gathered her courage to show Golly her work, praying her acerbic godmother wouldn't strip ten layers of her skin while she critiqued her work before telling her it was unsaleable.

It *had* been unsaleable, back then, but Golly had made a series of suggestions and Bea had rewritten the book three times. A year later, her super-agent godmother sold the first three books in the series. Bea'd submitted book nine of the series a few weeks back and was currently plotting book ten. Lately, she was as insecure as she'd been as a debut author five years ago, jumpy and jittery and second-guessing herself at every turn.

She couldn't remember when she'd last lost time in front of the keyboard, stumbling out of the story bleary-eyed with cramping fingers, knowing the letters she tossed onto the screen were pure gold. The voices in her head – snatches of conversation between her characters, some in whispers, some shouted – were silent. She no longer saw short video clips of what they were doing or how they were reacting.

Writing, her solace, her joy and her escape felt like dragging stone-heavy feet through peanut butter…

Blup…

Bea cocked her head and hit the volume button to turn down Shaboozey's 'A Bar Song' blasting from the rental car's small speakers. She usually caught the bus from the airport to Oia, with just a rucksack on her back, but this trip to Golly's Folly required a large suitcase and dresses in bags. What *was* that strange noise? Not recognising it, she shrugged, lifted the volume, tapped her fingers against the steering wheel and wished for her own double shot of whisky.

As Bea's professional crisis was ratcheting up, Golly had announced her retirement and told the publishing world she was closing her literary agency. That meant Bea (and the agency's other clients) needed to find alternative representation. She'd been tossing back antacids like chocolate-covered peanuts since first hearing her godma's news.

'I've got more money than God, Bea-darling, and I want to spend it! I want to spend some time at the Hidden Beach Resort, party at Tomorrowland, and drink Ayahuasca in the Orinoco basin. I want to read for pleasure, *Bea-darling; if I find the time between learning Spanish and my Pilates and Bikram yoga classes. I also intend to find a lover.'*

The fact that Bea needed to look up the Hidden Beach Resort – it was a luxurious nudist colony on the Mexican Riviera – and refresh her mind about Ayahuasca – the Amazon version of psychedelic 'shrooms – was a little embarrassing. Golly was extremely eccentric, vivacious and super cool. Everything she was…

Not.

Her godmother – actually Golly was her mum's godmother but, thanks to Bea being dropped on her doorstep every holiday since she was six because her mum couldn't be arsed to have her during the summer as per her parents' custodial agreement – lived life at a thousand miles per hour.

While Bea was still trying to take in the soul-sinking news about her retirement, Golly went on to say that she wanted her seventieth birthday and retirement bash to be on the Greek island of Santorini, at her villa on the outskirts of Oia.

Golly was a stalwart of the London and New York literary and art scenes and had a vast network of contacts all over the world. She wanted everyone she worked with: editors and authors – *friends* and *foes, Bea-darling!* – to attend. It took Bea a week to whittle the thousand-plus guest list down to two fifty, with Golly kicking, shouting and pouting while they argued about whether a lover she'd had in her forties warranted an invitation. Or her beauty therapist or her new hairdresser.

Golly didn't see the point of holding a small party. She wanted a crowd, dammit, so she could be the belle of the ball and be painted with adulation, buoyed by blandishments. Bea thought she was being a tad optimistic believing everyone thought she was wonderful. Golly'd had numerous lovers, had broken up a marriage or two – *I didn't cheat, Bea-darling, they did*! – and was once a powerful editor in publishing before establishing the G&T Literary Agency, a play on her initials and her favourite drink. It started out small and exclusive, and stayed *very* exclusive. The agents she employed looked after the interests of many well-known and mid-list authors, but Golly repped a couple of New York Times bestsellers, a Booker Prize winner, and the publicity-shy Parker Kane, an author *Library Journal* had called 'an exceptional, exciting talent'.

Bea tuned back into her music and hit the button to drop the window open and allow the fresh, herb-scented air to stroke her cheeks and mess up her hair. It wasn't a bad way to spend a Sunday.

Golly was her anchor, her true north. She was the font of irreverent wisdom, the kick up her butt, the Doric columns holding up her world. The only person she trusted to be there for her. Bea had friends, but she kept them at arm's length, never allowing them to get too close; and thanks to her mum and her ex hooking up, Bea rarely dated. What was the point when she was terrified of being hurt and being disappointed again? But she'd allowed Golly behind her mile-high wall. Her life would be paint-dryingly boring without that tiny, cigarillo-smoking, alcohol-swilling, filter-lacking loudmouth, the person who invented the concept of giving no fucks, in her life.

Golly's house had always been where Bea escaped to when life with her dad became too overwhelming, the only place she could be a kid. Golly had scooped her up after her father died when she was sixteen, becoming her mentor, aunt, grandmother and best friend all rolled into one. And as her literary agent, Golly was the only person (apart from Reena, Golly's oldest friend) who knew that Bea was Parker Kane, the author of the surprisingly successful *Urban Explorers* series for pre-teens. Golly – confident, loud, gregarious and generous – was whom Bea strived, with little success, to be.

When she'd dropped the news of her retirement – without the gravity it deserved – Golly had asked Bea to help with two things: one easy, one bitterly hard.

'I'm combining my seventieth birthday with my retirement, and I need you to organise everything, Bea-darling. I'm saying goodbye to my old life as a literary doyenne, so I want a blowout, raise-the-roof, fuck-with-everyone's-head party. Can you organise that for me?'

With the help of an event planner, that part was easy peasy.

Her second request was more difficult.

'You also need to think about how my retirement affects you, Bea. Currently, I'm the shield between you and the world, and you need to figure out what you are going to do. I'd like you to step out from behind your pseudonym. I can't force you to do that, but, if you still want to hide, then you need a new agent. How do we get you one without revealing who you are?'

It was a conundrum and one that made Bea's head ache. She was no closer to an answer than she was when she'd first heard Golly's news. What nobody, not even Golly, understood was that she and Parker Kane were two different entities. The Parker Kane who replied to reader's letters and bantered with her fans on social media was hip and switched-on; a little glam, a lot confident; someone cosmopolitan and creative, who knew how to use words like 'yeet' and 'sus' and 'flex' and didn't have to look them up on Urban Dictionary. Parker was on the ball, confident, funny, and smart.

Parker Kane was the protective barrier between Bea and the world, a way to shield herself from the criticisms of reviewers and readers, and the fluctuations of an industry that could, on some occasions, be brutal. Bea, the person she was away from her computer, was plagued by self-doubt, someone who found it difficult to trust herself, someone who occasionally, despite some success, often felt lost, and overwhelmed. She could blame her useless parents for her F'd-up mindset.

And she did.

Her parents couldn't have been more different, and despite racking her brain, Bea failed to comprehend how polar opposites had come together to produce a child. Lou, her mum, was loud, vain, narcissistic, selfish and ambitious. Her dad had been, up until his death fifteen years ago, spineless, ineffectual, a classic victim who believed the world was against him.

They'd never married, nor lived together, and Bea only saw Lou a few times a year. Her father, a twig on some aristocratic branch, had lived off a family trust and royalties and was, on paper, her primary parent.

Like Bea, he'd been a children's author, but also an illustrator. He'd had little time for children, though, and hated being bothered by them. It was lucky for her – was it luck or a means of survival? – that she'd been the adult-iest child ever. Bea couldn't remember a time when she didn't feel like he was the child and she the person holding it all together. She always felt grown up, loved being praised for being a mature and responsible child and she withered under criticism.

At ten, she'd cooked their meals, at twelve she'd paid the household bills and kept an eye on her dad's finances. And the more she did for him, the more he relied on her. She'd been addicted to his infrequent validation, and all her wheels fell off when he criticised her. To avoid any censure, Bea did everything in her power to avoid making a mistake. Two decades later, she still never went anywhere without doing a week's worth of research, and never argued a point unless she had salient facts to back her up.

In her early twenties, Bea had met Gerry, and within weeks she was living with the aspiring musician and immediately became his caregiver and solver of his problems. It took her five years, numerous infidelities on his part, and the threat of physical violence for her to realise she was reliving her childhood, prepared to move mountains because he'd occasionally, usually when he wanted something, told her he loved her.

When Golly sold her *Urban Explorers* series, Bea's constant second-guessing of herself – oh, and her mum's public hook-up with Gerry, but that was another story – led her to publish under a pseudonym, hiding her true identity and avoiding the vulnerability of public criticism and scrutiny.

And yes, she knew she'd recreated her missed childhood through her books, she'd figured that much out! And yes, Parker Kane was her alter-ego, but she was someone who lived outside of her, *apart* from her. Parker was someone that Bea – who spent far too many hours on her arse mainlining coffee, and the bulk of her time alone, who constantly second-guessed herself – wasn't.

Bea rolled her shoulders, frustrated by what she was – scared, uncertain, a little lonely – and what she wasn't – brave, outspoken, confident.

She turned up the volume to maximum, hoping to drown out her thoughts. She'd start thinking about herself and her future when her two-week working holiday was over.

But she'd probs find another excuse not to confront the PK question – revisions, deadlines, plotting her next series – when she got back to London. It wasn't something she could put off forever.

Next week. She'd think about her future as Parker Kane, a future without Golly steering her, next week. Or maybe the week after.

Blup, blup, blup…

The steering wheel started to vibrate under her hands and Bea noticed the flashing light on the dashboard. She steered the car off the road into a lay-by and switched off the engine, placing her forehead on the steering wheel as spiteful trolls excavated her brain with pickaxes. Since hearing Golly's retirement news four weeks ago, her headache was her most faithful companion, the result of far too much stress and way too little sleep.

She'd asked Golly if she'd continue to represent just her, selling it as a way for Golly to keep her hand in, to stay connected to the world of publishing. Golly'd immediately seen through her ruse, told her she was a manipulative baggage, and refused. Golly wanted to be free, to not have to worry about anyone or anything book-related, and that *'includes, Bea-darling, you!'*.

Golly'd made up her mind and there was no changing it. She was determined to enjoy the golden years of her life, vowing to fly into old age with a huge smile on her face, yelling like a banshee.

Nuts. She was nuts. Batshit crazy.

But, God, Bea loved her.

There'll be lots of drinking and lots of dancing at my party, Bea-darling! We can let our hair down and have some fun, in bed and out.

She'd rather not think about Golly's bed-based antics, and Bea wasn't a one-night-stand type of girl. Truthfully, she was more of a got-my-heart-smashed-and-now-I'm-done type of girl. She'd only had two lovers before she met Gerry, and, unfortunately, sex with her ex wasn't anything like romance novels described – it had been messy, quick and a little boring. Genuinely, she did not understand why sex sold. But it did, and many authors made gang cash by writing dark, sexy romances and erotica.

She pushed her sunglasses up into her thick, dark brown hair—Golly called it walnut brown, Bea called it boring – and opened the door to step out onto the gravel area of the lay-by. To her left was Oia, with its distinct blue-domed churches and blindingly white buildings. She had a one-eighty view of the entire caldera, the lava islands at its centre, the island of Thirasia in the distance and the sea a shade of blue she called Santorini Stunning. On the other side of the island were the famous beaches, Red Beach and Kamari, as well as her favourite, Baxedes Beach, popular amongst locals because of its seclusion, white sand and shallow waters. She hoped to have time to visit them this trip, but she had the next book to plot and a spin-off series to plan. She wanted to get that down before the revisions came in for book nine, but she was expecting, hoping, they would be light.

She also had to make sure Golly's party would be a classy success.

She'd learnt the hard way that if she didn't keep an eye

on her godmother, there was every possibility this coming weekend would turn into a bacchanalian feast.

Bea placed her hands on her hips and scowled at her car. She couldn't see any steam or smoke drifting out from underneath the bonnet, so that was a plus. Maybe. She walked around the car, the hem of her brown-and-white patterned dress swirling around her calves. She kicked the back left tyre with the toe of her flat sandal, it looked fine. But the front left tyre was not. It sagged into the gravel, looking sad and sorry for itself. Damn, she'd picked up a puncture...

And changing a tyre wasn't a life skill Bea possessed. She was a writer, someone who used words, and her arms were day-old noodles strong. Now Pip, the enterprising and practical twelve-year-old ringleader of the motley bunch of underprivileged miscreants who were the stars of Bea's books, would whip out tools and would know where to find the spare wheel.

It's in the boot, dummy...

It was the first time she'd heard his voice in a while, and she smiled. Was he back for good? God, she hoped so. 'Pipe down, squirt.'

So what was she going to do? There was nobody at the villa who could help her, so she'd have to call the rental company or get a mechanic out from Fira. Bea was about to reach for her phone, when she heard the low-pitched rumble of a deep-throated engine. Over the roof of her car, she watched a roof-and-doorless Jeep pull up to a stop behind her. A big man with aviator glasses and windblown hair sat behind the wheel. A bright blue canoe rested on the passenger seat behind him.

She watched as he climbed out of the Jeep and her eyebrows shot up when the unfamiliar hum of attraction vibrated up and down her spine.

So … *wow*.

Want to find out what happens next?
Available in paperback and ebook now!

ONE MORE CHAPTER

One More Chapter is an award-winning global division of HarperCollins.

Subscribe to our newsletter to get our latest eBook deals and stay up to date with all our new releases!

signup.harpercollins.co.uk/join/signup-omc

Meet the team at
www.onemorechapter.com

Follow us!
- @OneMoreChapter_
- @onemorechapterhc
- @onemorechapterhc
- @onemorechapterhc

Do you write unputdownable fiction?
We love to hear from new voices.
Find out how to submit your novel at
www.onemorechapter.com/submissions